CU00822151

BLOOD OF THE KAMI

OF THE KAMI

BAPTISTE PINSON WU

Ebook ASIN: B0DLB8JJGM

Paperback ISBN: 9798306169767

Hardcover ISBN: 9784991276880

Copy editing and Proofreading by L.Simpson Editing

Cover Art by Voyager (Christian Benavides)

Map by Diana Kolomiiets

Bestiary by Rrhamananda

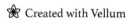 Created with Vellum

To dad, for being my why.

To mom, for being my why not.

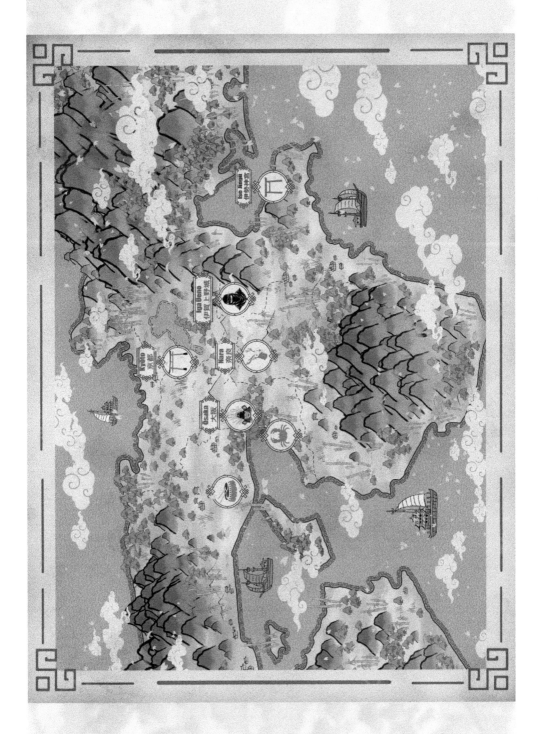

YASEKI'S ARCHIVES

YOKAI BESTIARY

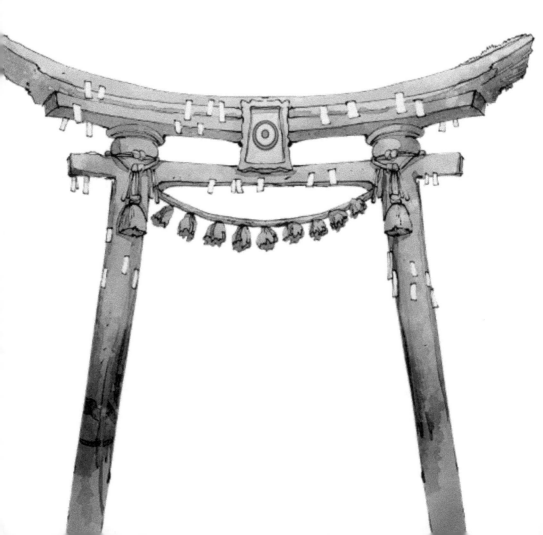

河童

KAPPA

CATEGORY: SAVAGE/FEARFUL

STRENGTHS: CLAWS, SWIMMING

WEAKNESS: DRYNESS

DANGER LEVER: MENACING

POPULATION: COMMON

ADVICE:

-LURE WITH FRESH CUCUMBERS

-GROWN MALE KAPPA ARE KNOWN TO ACCEPT WRESTLING CHALLENGES

-PRETEND TO DROWN IN A RIVER TO ATTRACT

濡女

NURE-ONNA

CATEGORY: CLEVER/AGGRESSIVE

STRENGTHS: CUNNING, SPEED, VENOM, SHAPE SHIFTING

WEAKNESSES: THE HUMAN PART OF HER BODY

DANGER LEVER: LETHAL

POPULATION: UNCOMMON

ADVICE:

-AIM FOR THE HEAD, THE NECK, OR THE CHEST

-BLUNT WEAPONS ARE UNLIKELY TO CAUSE DAMAGE

-SHINSHI CAN SEE THROUGH THEIR DISGUISE

木の葉天狗

KONOHA TENGU

CATEGORY: CLEVER/FEARFUL

STRENGTHS: FLIGHT, SHADOW-LURKING

WEAKNESSES: CLUMSY ON LAND

DANGER LEVER: MENACING

POPULATION: UNCOMMON

ADVICE:

-TRACK IN GROUP TO AVOID BLIND SPOTS

-WILL AVOID FIGHTS UNLESS CORNERED

-FEEDS ON WEAK PREYS UNTIL EVOLVING

蟹坊主

KANIBOZU

CATEGORY: CLEVER/AGGRESSIVE

STRENGTHS: CLEVER, BRUTE STRENGTH, RESISTANT, PATIENT, SELF-HEALING CAPACITIES

WEAKNESSES: TALKATIVE, PRIDE

DANGER LEVER: LETHAL

POPULATION: RARE

ADVICE:

-STALL WITH A CONVERSATION IF NEEDED. LOVES TO DEBATE

-MOST WEAPONS WILL NOT HARM A KANIBOZU

-ITS SIGHT WEAKENS WITH THE SUNLIGHT

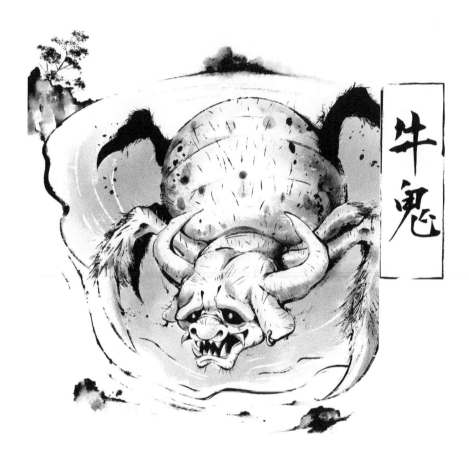

牛鬼

USHI-ONI

CATEGORY: SAVAGE/FEARFUL

STRENGTHS: BRUTE STRENGTH, VENOM, SWIMMING

WEAKNESS: AGILITY

DANGER LEVER: LETHAL

POPULATION: UNCOMMON

ADVICE:

-USHI-ONI ATTACK WITH THE TIDE, BUT ONLY IF ITS PREY IS ALONE

-NO SPACIAL AWARNESS, ATTRACT TO A NARROW LOCATION

-AIM FOR THE NECK

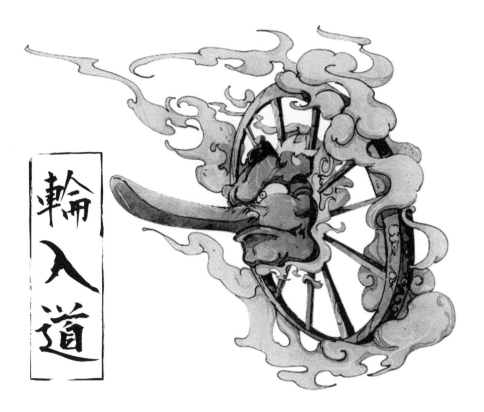

輪入道

WANYUDO

CATEGORY: SAVAGE/AGGRESSIVE

STRENGTHS: SPEED, FIRE

WEAKNESSES: IMMOBILITY, TALISMAN

DANGER LEVER: LETHAL

POPULATION: UNCOMMON

ADVICE:

-USE A "KONOTOKORONOBASHO" TALISMAN TO IMMOBILIZE

-RUNNING AWAY WILL ATTRACT THEM

烏天狗

KARASU TENGU

CATEGORY: CLEVER/AGGRESSIVE

STRENGTHS: FLIGHT, WEAPONS, HYPNOSIS

WEAKNESS: UNKNOWN

DANGER LEVER: LETHAL

POPULATION: RARE

ADVICE:

-FLEE ON SIGHT

-AT LEAST THREE BLOOD HUNTERS OR FIGHTING HANDS TO ENGAGE

NUE

CATEGORY: SAVAGE/AGGRESSIVE

STRENGTHS: CLAWS, VENOM, BRUTE STRENGTH, FANGS, HEARING, SMELL

WEAKNESSES: HAMAYA ARROWS

DANGER LEVER: LETHAL

POPULATION: UNCOMMON

ADVICE:

-NO SMARTER THAN A WILD BEAST, IT IS EASILY TRICKED

-CUT THE SNAKE TAIL BEFORE IT SPITS VENOM OR BITES

-HAND THE REMAINS TO THE CLOSEST RIVER

HANATAKA TENGU

CATEGORY: UNKNOWN

STRENGTHS: UNKNOWN

WEAKNESS: UNKNOWN

DANGER LEVER: CATACLYSMIC

POPULATION: EXTREMLY RARE

ADVICE: FLEE

Over the wintry
forest, winds howl in rage
with no leaves to blow.

Natsume Sōseki

PROLOGUE

The White Tengu

From the moment the sun rose, the boy had been shivering with an ever-increasing fever. It should have been the most special of days, the first of his twelfth year. The next would mark the official beginning of his apprenticeship in his father's tannery. And since his mother knew how little he cared for the family's craft, she had promised a day of sumptuous food and a set of freshly sewn clothing to her man-turning boy.

Twelve years, a cycle.

From the kitchen, she shook her head with an air of wonder, telling her son, still lying on his futon, that not so long ago she held him in one arm, and now he was about to outgrow her. Ren loved when she said so. He was short, even compared to boys his age, but his mother kept telling him every so often that she found him taller.

She made a face upon cutting thick layers of meat. It had been more than a decade since flesh had passed her lips, and even when last it did, it was to recover from his birth, and only after the local abbot allowed her. Yet she had promised her husband that as long as the boy grew, he would receive meat from time to time, and since he loved rib meat so much, he would receive a double share in his bowl of noodles.

"I'll give you the fattest piece," she said, winking at her son. He smiled back, then rolled over, his head splitting with another wave of migraine. His mother crossed the small room and dropped the back of her hand on his forehead. Her tongue clicked. She told him she would add some spices to cure this mean-spirited fever.

His father walked into the house, releasing a hard scent of tannin and smoke from the moment the door slid open. He stepped toward his son on bare feet, though the boy could not see him because of the sudden light. The familiar sensation of rugged fingers combing through his hair preceded a chuckle.

"Look who's enjoying a lazy birthday morning," his father said in his dry yet loving voice. Ren did not like the idea of smelling like his father after a day of work, but it suited the man.

"I'll get up as soon as the bowl is on the table," Ren said, earning another chuckle.

"That's my boy," his father replied before walking away.

The bowls clunked on the table, and Ren tried to lean on his elbow, but his head barely left the pillow before it started spinning. He felt himself fainting, called for his mother, and crashed back. The last thing he heard as his consciousness departed was his mother shouting at her husband to get the abbot.

Ren drifted from dream to half-consciousness for the rest of the afternoon.

It was getting dark by the time the abbot came in. He chanted some sutra while striking a metallic bowl, but Ren recognized none of the words. The incense kept him awake for a time, and he heard the man tell his parents that it was as if his blood were boiling in his veins. They needed to keep the blood clean while the body fought the fever. He promised to return on the morrow with more to offer than incense and basic tea. Ren did not even notice when he drank it.

His mother's scream startled him from a fever-mad dream. It was night, yet the candles and lamps had been blown out. The house was shaking, and the wind howled while his mother whimpered somewhere nearby. No, not the wind, Ren realized. Animals were howling. He heard them creep against the walls, their fangs scratching the house from outside, and the low murmur of moans and whispers they exchanged. Was he dreaming still?

He guessed the silhouette of his mother crawling toward the kitchen, hand covering her mouth to prevent her panic from attracting them in, for that is what they intended to do. Why the swarm remained outside was a mystery. The house was no fortress. The lock on their side of the door required little effort to subdue, and those creatures seemed intelligent enough to communicate in their horrendous way. The drawer of knives opened, and his mother rummaged through it. She prayed to Kannon when the clink of metal accompanied the fall of the drawer. Silence suddenly fell.

Ren could no longer breathe, or think, or move. In the dark, he found his mother's eyes across the room, checking him with utter panic. She lifted the knife toward the door, and, as if answering her challenge, it blew inward in a myriad of wooden chips.

Ren screamed as the night wind flooded their house, and through the frame of the broken door appeared a creature of nightmare. It first gripped the edge of the door frame with human-like fingers, though its hands were wide and covered in angry, pulsating veins. A heavy foot set in a *geta* sandal mounted on one tooth thumped into the house, and the beast dragged its other foot across the dusty floor without haste. It twisted to let its massive body through.

Once in, white wings stretched open from its back. Its face was white too, so impossibly white, the lack of color made more impressive by the blood-red of its flame-shaped eyebrows and mustache. Its nose stretched straight out, a hand's length from the rest of the face. Ren had seen tengu masks before, but this was no such childish item. The face shifted from a scowl to an angry grin that reminded the boy of some of those *Myō-ō* statues flanking a Buddha or another in the temples. But the most frightening part of the creature was his eyes. They seemed to burn and crave violence.

The tengu scanned the room. He sneered at the sight of Ren's mother and ignored her, then frowned when he spotted the boy looking up at him from his piss-soaked futon.

Ren whimpered and mumbled for his mother to come, though it came out in a pitiful series of squeaking sounds.

The White Tengu raised his left hand, which held a short sword the likes of which Ren had never seen, straight and single-edged, with a flame-shaped guard and a beast head pommel. The moonlight gleamed on the blade's sharp surface. It appeared huge and unforgiving in Ren's mind, even if the beast still stood a few steps from him.

Why did it seem so eager to slice him open? the boy wondered in his terror. What had he done to deserve such punishment?

The *yōkai* smirked and lowered his left hand, only to raise the right, the one holding a gourd-shaped war fan. Ren's mother screamed and ran from the kitchen. Her voice pierced the silence of the room that had so far only been disturbed by the thumping of Ren's burning blood in his ears and the furnace-like breathing of the beast.

She rushed toward her boy as the fan descended. The air seemed to coil around the fan for a second, then the beast unleashed a gust of dark purple wind that came raging in the boy's direction. Ren gasped, but his mother's hand covered his mouth.

She had reached as far as her arm would let her, but nothing protected her, and Ren heard her inhale the foul purple wind.

Ren screamed, and the tengu screamed, and all those creatures outside screamed, but not his mother.

Then his world turned dark, and he lost consciousness.

CHAPTER I
REN

Five years later

A shriek pierced the night sky and froze every animal in the forest. A fearful black shrew kept to the ground, its snout pointing at the moon and its heart beating faster than ever in expectation of a winged beast. It flattened itself and waited, head swinging left and right to catch a glimpse of the shadow preceding death. But instead of flapping wings, the shrew heard stomping feet, dead leaves creaking, and a string of curses.

"Shit, shit, shit!" the young man said as he burst through a thicket, scaring the shrew back to the dead root it called home.

Ren ran for his life, waving thorny stems from his path and ducking thicker branches every other step. He dared a look over his shoulder and regretted it when a leafy twig slapped his face with the speed of his run. Looking had not even allowed him to spot the creature, yet it was after him; this he knew. He came to this forest, to this very mountain, because of what he'd been told he would find. But it found him first, and now Ren ran from his prey without a single trap in place and no idea where to go.

"Shit!" he shouted when the tip of his sandal caught a root and threatened his footing. It was getting darker as he dashed toward the center of the forest, a necessary problem, for if there was a shrine nearby, it had to be deeper. So Ren traded the moonlight for the prospect of sacred ground. Leaves showered him, and the young man forbade himself a much-needed few seconds of breathing and sprung forward.

The beast landed on the spot where he had been standing a second before and shrieked a shriek to freeze the blood, even that of an experienced Soul Hunter like Ren. A timid light bounced on thick, white fangs extending from a screaming red face, the same kind he had seen on the monkeys inhabiting the snowy mountains. But this one showed none of those animals' mischievousness, only pure rage. The head rested on a striped yellow and black feline body, as big as the tigers drawn on those paintings of old, but with long curved claws. It spotted Ren and darted after him.

"A *bakeneko*, my ass!" Ren spat. "I told them they don't live in forests."

Ren spoke to no one but his own regret for accepting to check the yōkai inhabiting the forest. The beast swung from tree to tree, gripping the lowest branches as a monkey would or leaping against the trunks. The hunted hunter felt claws scratch the back of his *shitagi* shirt, and his pace increased a notch. He veered left, using the closest tree to shield himself from a wide swing of the beast.

"It had to be a *nue*! Why did it have to be—"

The ferocious yōkai landed with a loud thump in front of Ren, forcing him to a stop. It growled like a bear, throat trembling and eyes shining ferally. It had trapped its prey and was going for the kill. Ren's hand went to the pocket inside his shirt, and he tossed its content at the beast's face. The nue moaned when the sacred salt got in its eyes. It shook its head vigorously once, just enough time for Ren to vanish between the closest trees.

"Oh, Yahata-no-kami, I humbly call your name in prayer."

Ren's voice sounded steady despite the effort of running, looking backward, and remembering the next words. Without looking, he shuffled through the bag of linen hanging from his shoulder and jumped over the stump of a fallen redwood. Five steps later, he heard the nue doing as much. The creature gibbered with each step gained on the young man as if mocking him.

"I speak from an honest heart, oh great kami, and beseech you to help me find that stupid arrow!"

The nue screamed in response to Ren's shout. His fear was feeding it. The young man exhaled, remembering what he'd learned about self-control, and finally found the shaft. He tossed his bag over his shoulder again, keeping only the arrow in his left hand. With the right, he grabbed the hilt of the sword tucked on his lower back, which he drew an inch from its scabbard, just enough to pass his thumb over the razor-sharp blade. Ren winced with the familiar pain, then clicked the blade back home.

"I beg for your forgiveness, Yahata-no-kami, for what I'm about to do with your arrow."

The beast's breathing came louder. Each of its hands landed with urgency on the uneven ground of the forest. Ren heard the claws' sharpness on the stones and roots they sliced effortlessly. He pushed the thought of his imminent death from his mind and focused back on the power of his words. His bleeding thumb caressed the flat of the arrowhead, leaving a red trail. Then, for good measure, he painted the shaft in one swift motion, leaving only the straight feathers of paper white.

"While I lack a bow, make my aim true and strike our enemy!"

On those words, Ren twisted on his heel and threw the arrow

with all the energy he still possessed after this mad rush through the forest.

The arrow twirled with speed, though time seemed to slow in Ren's mind. His aim was true, which wasn't hard since the yōkai stood less than ten steps from him. The beast leaped, arms and fangs stretched forward, eyes red from the purifying salt. If it noticed the arrow, it did not show. Ren's eyes followed the sacred weapon as it split the air toward its target and struck right between the dilated nostrils of the beast, where it bounced off harmlessly.

The nue stopped in his tracks, apparently confused, and shook its head before planting its bestial eyes on Ren again.

"Figures," Ren said. He lowered his stance, grabbed the hilt of his sword again, and waited.

Nue were weak to arrows, a point this one seemed unaware of, so Ren prayed his sword would work better. And at least he knew how to use this weapon.

"Well, come on, you ugly turd. I don't have all—"

The nue did not let the young man finish and pounced, twisting its head so that it would catch its prey by the neck. Ren waited until the last moment before he let himself fall and slashed the blade upward. The tip pierced the skin, scraped a rib, and if the beast's knee had not smashed into Ren's cheek, the hunter would have pushed deeper. They both fell; the boy, dazed by the strike and the beast against a mighty tree, moaning pitifully for a few heartbeats before it became still.

Ren rolled on his belly when he found the sky from the ground, dead leaves sticking to his bruised face. It took a few seconds for his sight to stop spinning, but when it did, the young hunter was pleased to see the yōkai unmoving. The nue's chest heaved frantically a few times, then seemed to empty itself and remained flat. The short sword jutted from the lower abdomen, halfway through the blade. Ren had aimed higher, closer to the heart, but the creature's speed did not let him act as planned. Nothing that night went as planned.

"I hate nue," Ren spat as he stood, using his knee for support.

The forest seemed to breathe now that the beast had been slain. Its kami would feel at peace again. If nothing else, Ren had done that, though, on a personal level, this wasn't the point of the whole journey.

"Now, let's see what you were made of," he said in the tone of a merchant about to inspect a horse. The creature was somewhat even more impressive lying still. Almost as long as a pony, with powerful shoulders, a chest like that of a bear, and claws that could split a tree in half with one swing. How could the folks mistake it for a bakeneko? Ren wondered. Unless it had grown recently. It wouldn't be the first of late. Its soul would fetch a good price, he thought with greed, maybe even a couple of months' worth.

He was about to grab the hilt of his sword to finish his task when a hiss stopped his hand a few inches from the blade's hilt. The hiss whistled from the rear end of the creature, and suddenly Ren remembered why he so hated nue. Those yōkai were the results of different animals mangled in a grotesque being. They often had the head of a monkey, the body of a predator, some different parts from birds or dogs, and they always, *always*, ended with a snake for a tail.

The reptile-tail rose from the back of the nue, its dead little eyes shining black. Ren refused to move, wondering if immobility would keep him hidden. But when the snake hissed with rage while looking at him, he knew acting was safer. He went for the sword, but the snake darted faster and almost bit his wrist. Ren jumped back, swordless.

The snake coiled around the hilt and plucked it with strength, sending it flying into the dark forest, where Ren heard it smack into a tree. He swallowed hard, knowing what was going to happen before it did. The snake could not separate from the rest of the creature, but this was only a brief respite. The gash where the sword had hit healed in front of Ren's eyes, and when the skin closed completely, the nue returned to the living with a powerful shriek of pain, ire, and hunger. It thrashed the ground with its claws as it recovered the use of its limbs, but Ren left before it happened.

The snake had tossed the sword the other way, and Ren cursed, for he would have to get it back later. For now, his only chance was to find this damn shrine. The nue howled like an ape. It was coming again.

The young man was about to curse, for this forest, contrary to what he'd been told, seemed empty of shrines, but he was suddenly bathed in moonlight. He'd reached a path, and at the end of it, there must be sacred ground. Or so he prayed. His side hurt from the run, and his head buzzed from the beast's knee, but when the creature burst through the trees and reached the path a few seconds behind, Ren seemed to regain some energy and ran faster.

An empty bell called for him with a gentle breeze, but so did the beast on his back. Stone lanterns covered in moss lined the path, unsurprisingly unlit, and, as a cloud unveiled the moonlight once more, Ren spotted the *torii* gate at the end of the sacred *sandō* path. It was a small, once-red painted, now partially rotten gate, with the upper of the two top beams gnawed halfway through by time, but Ren's heart leaped with hope. He ran under the arch a mere second before the beast swung a clawed hand at him. Ren entered the shrine's ground, mostly unharmed, but the nue slammed into the open space of the torii's frame and was denied entrance. This was sacred ground; no corrupted soul was allowed in.

Ren's hands dropped to his knees as he tried to regain his breath, finding solace in his safety. Nue were not strong enough to force a passage through a torii, not even one as old and shabby as this one, and not even if the ground in question belonged to an abandoned shrine covered in weed and moss. The single building of the shrine still stood, barely bigger than a shed, but much of the *jinja* had toppled long ago. When the attacks began near the forest, the folks had called for a priest to consecrate the shrine anew, thinking that the forest's kami would protect them if it was worshipped properly again. But the priest had not been from the Yaseki, and his life ended in the beast's stomach. Ren only understood the latter part as he rushed from the nue.

The beast raged against the invisible barrier, head-butting the sacred protection and clawing at the poles of the torii. Ren needed to take care of it, or it would kill again, and then, who knows how much stronger it could get or which soul it might corrupt. His options were limited, though, but there had to be something here he could use.

The *goshintai* treasure where the kami resided might be a sword, but seeing the state of the shrine, Ren assumed it would be rusted beyond use. The bell hanging above the single step of the *honden* hall might repel the beast but would not hurt it, and he didn't see himself strangling such a fierce creature with the bell's rope. There was only one thing he could use, but Ren would rather not, for it would call old Osamu's fury, and the hunter feared the head priest's anger even more than the nue's.

There was a crack, accompanied by a screech, then the long, plaintive sound of solid wood splitting. Ren could not believe it, but through sheer violence, the yōkai had planted its claws inside the right pole of the torii and was cleaving it in half.

"Shit," Ren whispered. Nue should not be that powerful. The choice was made for him, and screw Osamu, he thought.

"I humbly pray to the guardian of this shrine and call for you with a sincere heart," Ren recited as he stepped back on the central path leading to the small building. *"In this time of need, I beseech you to*

honor our pact." On those words, Ren knelt in front of a pedestal of rock, showing his back to the yōkai.

The guardian lion-dog statue resting on it was looking toward the torii being savaged, its mouth open as a promise of vengeance for any who defiled the sacred ground under its protection. Its body was more green than gray after so many years without proper care, and Ren hoped he could still call the guardian through this conduit.

"*I offer you my prayer and this blood.*" He bit his thumb, enlarging the previous cut to draw more blood, and started tracing the eight strokes of the character carved into the pedestal. The torii suddenly collapsed in a loud crash of wood and dust, and the beast growled with pleasure as it stepped into the shrine. Ren then spoke with more urgency. "*Protect me, guardian spirit, and help me cleanse the corruption from these woods!*"

The character flickered red twice as the stone drank the blood, and the bell of the honden chimed. The growl of the nue, now halfway up the path, turned more aggressive, and it lowered itself. It looked at Ren, then at the statue, hesitating. Ren put his back against the pedestal and felt it vibrate, and then the whole ground did.

The monkey face snarled as the stone of the statue started cracking and peeling. When Ren looked up, the guardian burst, sending pieces of rock flying in all directions and engulfing the young man in a cloud of dust.

A bark cut through the night, the nue got quiet, and the guardian darted from the cloud. Big as a horse, the lion-dog landed between Ren and the yōkai, shaming it with its size and ensuing roar. Its coat was the color of sand, though its curly mane and tail shone bright orange like a golden, rising sun, even in the middle of the night. Ren could not see it, but he knew the guardian was snarling curved fangs at its enemy. Not to scare it away, no, for the nue had defiled a shrine, and there would be no forgiveness. It did so because it was pissed.

For a few seconds, none of the beasts moved, contenting themselves in snarling and growling. Then the nue made the mistake of looking over its shoulder. The guardian was on it in the next second, and the shrine became a battleground of fangs, claws, and bestial fury. They rolled and slapped in turn, but the nue's claws could not break the guardian's skin, while the lion-dog claimed brown blood with each strike. The yōkai tried to run away, but the guardian stepped on its back and pinned it to the ground.

"Watch out for its—" Ren shouted a heartbeat before the maws of the lion-dog closed on the snake-tail, which it ripped from the body with a twist of its neck. "Never mind."

The guardian spat the snake at Ren's feet, where it rolled a few times, dead. The nue screeched. It sounded like a plea, but the guardian did not listen, even when the yōkai rolled on its back in submission. The lion-dog swung its huge paw and cleaved the creature's face in half, then severed the nue's throat with its fangs. The limbs of the yōkai fell to the side. Ren had nothing to fear, not from the nue, at least.

The lion-dog turned around, blood dripping from its fangs, growling and snarling. It found Ren still sitting against the now useless pedestal. The young man raised his hand in a peace offering, but the lion-dog took the first step.

"Wait," Ren said. "Don't you dare!"

But the lion-dog did not listen to *this* plea either and charged the young man.

Ren closed his eyes, knowing what would happen, powerless to prevent it. "Damn it," he still muttered when the guardian reached him. His eyes shut tighter, his mouth too, and he stopped breathing. A raspy yet slick sensation passed over his face, smearing it in stinky yōkai blood. The tongue licked Ren's face again, leaving a thick trail of drool. Ren then had to breathe.

"Stop, Maki, stop!" Ren said.

The lion-dog only heard the laughter in the young man's voice and took it for a sign to continue, so she did. He tried to push her head away, but she rubbed it against his chest, then let herself fall on his legs, forgetting that she weighed ten times as much as he did. She looked at her friend with loving eyes, tongue lolling, and tail brushing the sacred ground. Ren patted the guardian between the eyes, which increased the speed of the tail, then moved his other hand under her chin for another scratch.

"You knew I was in danger, and you came," Ren said. "Who's a good girl? Who's a good girl?" Maki barked in reply, and the sound was so loud it startled Ren. "By the kami, your breath stinks," he went on.

An unspoken signal passed between them, and the lion-dog stood, allowing her friend to do as much. She still prevented him from moving by dropping her massive head on his shoulder and whimpering.

"I'm all right, Maki," Ren said, rubbing her bright orange ear in his left hand. "I'm all right. You came right on time, and you saved me. I'm all right. You're a good girl. But I need to finish the job now."

The lion-dog let the man pass but remained at his side, never farther than a step from him. Ren knelt by the carcass of the nue and slowly passed a hand over its striped belly. He felt a slow, vanishing hum under the sternum and some heat. Using the closest piece of broken rock, the hunter stabbed the carcass and tore the skin a few inches. He then shoved his left hand into the gash, gagging at the sudden stench and squishy substance squirming between his fingers.

"I hate this part," Ren said to no one.

Then he felt what he was looking for. Hard, smooth, and curved, as big as his palm, the soul shell. He yanked it out and sighed with relief, for it still contained the yōkai's soul. The *maga-*

tama shell shone with a dark, faint, purple light. Its essence was almost gone; it was now or never.

"By the blood of the kami, I hereby seal you."

A pearl of blood bloomed from his right thumb, and Ren smeared the back curve of the shell with it. The magatama stopped humming and shining. He'd done his part; another member of the Yaseki would do the rest. The hunter let himself fall on his ass and held the shell in the air, using the light of the moon to get a better look at it. There was apprehension in his eyes. The light revealed a gray surface with silvery glints, and Ren sighed with disgust.

"A stone magatama? All of this for a stupid, worthless stone magatama? For Inari's sake, how can such a beast be only a stone soul? Damn it."

The lion-dog barked in agreement, getting agitated as he spoke. Ren tightened his grip on the shell, tempted to break it, but eventually relented and stood up. "I'd be lucky to get five days out of this one," he told Maki, who twisted her head in confusion. "Just this useless arrow cost me three. I can't believe it."

Once done venting, Ren dropped the magatama inside his shoulder bag, where it clinked against a good dozen others. He then rubbed his last pinch of salt against his thumb, wishing he could wash the blood from his hands before he realized that most of his clothing was just as drenched. It would take more than a stream to clean himself from all this filth. At least the people of the region had nothing to fear anymore.

He walked to the shrine, bowed twice, clapped his hands twice, then closed his eyes and asked the kami to forgive him for ruining the *jinja* even more than it already was.

"I will have a priest sent here and tell the folks to take better care of your home," he told the kami before bowing one last time. It was as long as Maki could wait, and she barked for his attention. "What is it, Maki?"

The lion-dog whimpered and moved her head from her friend to the carcass of the yōkai, licking her lips.

"What? You want to eat it?" he asked in a tone showing his disgust. She did not care about it and woofed. "You know I'm supposed to give the body to a river." Maki whimpered again and dropped her head in a pitiful gesture she knew would get Ren.

"Fine," he said, prompting her head to come back up with a beaming smile. "You deserve it; go ahead. I'm already going to get scolded for yet another broken statue, anyway." Maki did not wait for him to finish and hurried to gulp long chunks of yōkai flesh. "But after that you help me find my sword, all right?"

The hunter sat on the step of the temple while his guardian ravaged the body to bits and pieces. Dawn was approaching, and a fresh, pinkish light appeared over the forest. Soon, Amaterasu's light would bathe the land.

"And make it fast," Ren told the lion-dog, who didn't need much of a push. "I want to get back to Ise before noon."

CHAPTER 2
ISE JINGU

Despite his best efforts, Ren didn't spot the first torii gate of the great shrine before the middle of the afternoon. Finding the sword, cleaning the untouched remains of the nue, and, more difficult than those two tasks, convincing Maki to return home pushed his departure from the forest by nearly three hours. The fresh spring sun was already well on its way down when he caught his first glimpse of the most sacred shrine of Japan, yet a never-ending stream of people still traveled toward Ise.

People spent a fortune on lodging if they intended to stay nearby for the night and then some more for any service from the temple. Yet, they kept coming from the four corners of the nation. Dozens of kami had been enshrined in Ise. They bore names too long to remember and answered so many types of prayer that whatever a person could ask in Ise Jingū, a kami was bound to listen.

Women came to pray for a safe birth and then protection for their children. Men flocked to ask such and such spirits to bless their shops, their blades, their crops, or even their horses. They traveled all the way to Ise to pray for a safe journey, a point Ren found ironic to no end. They begged for a good season of fishing or for their sons to come back from the war alive.

But most of all, they prayed for misfortune to avoid them. They came when the land was at war with itself, as it so often was, and they came during the few, short, and fragile moments of peace, such as it was now, though many said this peace must last, for it followed the longest civil war of the nation's history.

Even if this plethora of kami came to disappear from Ise, the shrine would remain the most blessed land of Japan, for it is where Amaterasu, goddess of the sun and ancestor of the imperial family, was enshrined. Amaterasu-Ōmikami, the light of the nation, shone over Japan from Ise, and no life could be considered full without a pilgrimage to this sacred shrine. For centuries, believers from all over Japan had donated enough money to turn Ise into an earthly version of heaven.

Stone lamps lined the roads one *ri* before the first torii, no matter the direction the traveler came from, though most came from the west or the north if they approached Shima Province by boat. The roads themselves were well-maintained, not only by the numerous workforce of the shrine but also by the people using them.

If a horse defecated on the road, the owner had to scoop it and carry the feces to a distance of one *chō* on either side before dropping it. If a man spat on the road, he would need to fetch water from the nearest river in the palm of his hands to clean his mistake. And if anyone, be they men, women, or children, bled on the road while in view of the shrine, they had to return home and restart the pilgrimage. None of those rules came with punishment; the threat of displeasing a kami was enough in itself.

Except for Ren, who had long decided the kami couldn't care less about a few balls of fuming dung or a few drops of blood. And since he often bled on his way back to Ise, and since the shrine was the closest thing he had to a home, it made this whole rule system rather irrelevant. Neither did he care about the travelers' glares, whispers, and horrified faces as they stepped away from his path.

A child gazed at him in awe when his mother pulled his arm and removed the finger from his nose to point it at the down-trodden Soul Hunter. She slapped the finger down and told the boy to look away.

If only they knew, Ren thought with a sigh. If only they knew the truth about Ise. If only they knew that without him and a few others, Japan was doomed to slowly fall into darkness, they would forgive his blood-smeared sleeves, his shredded shirt, and the stench.

The first torii grew with each step, less ostentatious than most with its natural light-gray color but obvious nonetheless against the lush background of the sanctuary forest. Like most important shrines, the entrance was marked by two torii gates built on both ends of a bridge crossing the Isuzu River, thus making those bridges neutral zones between the secular world and the sacred shrine. Yet it was already part of Ise Jingū, and just like the road before, people were supposed to avoid the center and walk on the sides. The center of the road was for the kami. Another fact Ren vividly and regularly ignored.

The sound of the flowing river under his feet usually soothed Ren, but not this time. His mind had yet to let go of his last hunt. This nue had been too powerful, too big, and more savage than any other he had met. Even more worrisome, it haunted a forest a few hours' walk from Ise, and no one had sensed it. Maybe, the young man thought bitterly, Old Osamu was right, and things were indeed getting worse.

And, just as he thought about the head priest, Ren heard his voice, as did every soul on that bridge. "Ren!"

Osamu sounded pissed. Had the young man seen the old priest stomping his way, he would have walked back. But he was too late, and all he saw of the priest when his head shot up was the blur of a rapidly descending arm.

The flat scepter of authority smacked on top of Ren's forehead with so much strength that the hunter dropped to one knee. He meant to spring right back up, but a second, weaker blow slapped his skull. "You do not walk the central path! How many times did I tell you?" Another series of blows rained on Ren's shoulders and head, and the hunter shielded himself with his left arm. "And how dare you step on sacred ground all bloody and filthy as you are?"

"Enough, you old goat," Ren shouted, standing up with the support of the priest's robes, which he grabbed with grubby fingers. The passersby gasped at the blasphemy, and Ren swore internally.

Osamu Shirakawa, Saishu of Ise Jingū and the greatest spiritual authority of Japan, was dressed in his pristine white ritualistic robes, worn over white *hakama* baggy pants. As the leader of the shrine, Osamu was always expected to perform one ritual or another, which meant he wore a new hat every day, his clogs were polished every morning, and he fasted and purified himself on a regular basis.

His oiled, black and gray beard framed a pair of thin lips, currently shut tight into a scowl, and his hawkish eyes reminded Ren of those fearful Buddhist statues flanking those of peaceful looking *nyorai* and *bosatsu*. He was barely a man in the eyes of the pilgrims, more kami than human, and grabbing his garments with dirty hands was a serious offense.

"Listen, I didn't mean to—" Ren said apologetically.

"Let go of me," Osamu said.

To anyone else around them, it sounded like an order, barely more than a request, but to Ren, it felt as if his brain was stabbed with needles. His hand prickled and numbed, and despite his best efforts, the words penetrated his mind and forced his fingers to open.

"Not fair," he said through his teeth. When the fabric slipped from his grasp, the buzz quieted, and Ren regained control of his hand. "You didn't need to use *kotodama* on me. A simple *please* would have sufficed."

"That will be the day," Osamu replied, stretching the pangs of his robes and sighing at the stain of Ren's fingers on the white fabric. "Do you know how long it takes me to perform the purification rituals?"

"Just go change your robes," Ren replied. "No one will know."

"The kami will know."

Ren scoffed and waved the comment down. "The kami have greater things to worry about than some stain on a priest's robes."

"But not about a homeless-looking ruffian walking at the center of the sandō. So go wash yourself, enter the shrine from the proper path, and then we'll talk." Osamu stood a good head taller than Ren. Since the hunter had just reached seventeen years of age, it was doubtful he would grow any taller, but the priest breathed of authority, and even if they'd been of the same height, Ren would have felt dwarfed by the old man.

"Just let me get inside. We have proper baths there, and we have much to discuss."

"In the river, by yourself," Osamu replied, pointing at the Isuzu below. "And don't make me command you, or I'll make you jump from the bridge buck naked." He was serious and capable of it, so Ren grumbled in acceptance.

"What about the blood?" Ren asked, nodding toward the red drops forming a wider circle between his feet.

"You're bleeding on my bridge?" Osamu asked with renewed anger.

"Because you smacked me on the head! Don't put this on me, you crazy old goat. And I'm pretty sure you're not supposed to use your scepter this way."

"Neither am I supposed to teach one of my hunters how to

enter the shrine, but here I am!" Osamu replied. "You! Come here," he then said, snapping his fingers.

Ren had not noticed the young girl standing behind the priest. She was a *miko*, a shrine maiden, wearing the traditional white kimono tucked inside a bright orange, pleated hakama, and like all the other miko, she had gathered her long, black hair in a tail bound with a colorful *mizuhiki* cord made of several lengths of paper.

She kept her head down, but Ren guessed she was pretty and no more than fifteen. Even younger and even prettier than the usual miko serving Osamu. Ren had never seen this one, and from the way she avoided his gaze, he thought she might have arrived at Ise recently. She carried a package of neatly wrapped garments, which she presented to her master with a bow. Her steps were heavy; she wasn't used to footwear.

"I am sorry to ask you this, but please wash this blood while I make sure this animal cleanses himself properly."

"Yes, Osamu-sama," she said. Her voice rose barely over a whisper.

"Come," Osamu said, moving past the hunter without a second look and carrying the clean clothes like a glorified servant.

Though she had yet to look him in the eyes, the girl nodded at Ren, and he left her wondering who she might be and why she looked so out of place.

The Saishu of Ise Jingū was not supposed to leave the shrine's ground except on rare occasions, and those did not involve accompanying a feral-looking teenager to take a bath in the river. Ren, despite their day's encounter, smiled at the old man's pretense. From the moment he had entered the Yaseki five years ago, Osamu had been a father as much as a tutor to the young man, while many would have given up on him.

"How did you know I was coming?" Ren asked as they walked under the first torii.

"You had the wind on your back," the head priest replied before turning back and bowing reverently. Ren copied him and realized he had not done it on the way in.

"Hilarious," Ren said. "Some kami whispered it in your ears, I assume."

"Obviously," Osamu replied. They followed the river for a hundred steps, for too many people used the water for purification near the bridge. When no one stood at earshot, Osamu pointed at the river and invited Ren to peel the ruined shirt from his back with a snap of his fingers.

"What else did they whisper?"

"I'll tell you later," Osamu replied. He winced at the sight of Ren's bare chest. Some scars hadn't been there the last time he saw the hunter undressed, and Ren made a show of turning around to display the others. "What got you like this, anyway?"

"A nue."

"A nue?" Osamu scoffed. "A nue got you so bad? Should I send my grandmother to protect you next time?"

"Please," Ren replied as he untied his belt, "as if you still have a grandmother. And when was the last time you went on a hunt or just got your hands dirty, for that matter? Yes, a nue gave me trouble, but it wasn't a typical nue. It was big and fast, and it destroyed a torii."

"It did?" Osamu asked, serious at last.

"It did. An old, abandoned shrine, but it still held power, and yet the nue broke the barrier. If not for Maki, I might be dissolving in its stomach right now." Ren shook the pants from his ankles and stood in nothing more than a red *fundoshi* loincloth.

A group of women walking on the road above the river banks giggled and blushed when Ren stared at them. The hunter might have been on the short side, but he was athletic and proud of his muscular body shaped by years of hunting corrupted spirits. And, from what he'd heard recently, the fundoshi stuck between his butt cheeks made his ass look fantastic. Of course, the woman who said so had been a yōkai trying to trick him, but he took the compliment for an honest one.

"Why don't you puff down, you peacock?" Osamu said. "Remove that and get in the river."

"Even the fundoshi?"

"Especially the fundoshi."

Ren grunted, removed his last piece of clothing, and entered the Isuzu River, cursing as soon as his feet penetrated the icy water. He looked at the bridge, where the young miko from before stood watching him. She saw him noticing her and scurried away toward the shrine.

The river had swelled with the melting snow, but not enough to reach higher than his waist, so Ren sat when he got to the center. Nothing but his head stood above the water. The dry blood and dirt vanished from his skin with the force of the river, and Ren scrubbed the most stubborn parts from his arms.

"How long?" he asked the priest.

"I'll tell you," Osamu replied. They had to speak louder, for the river drowned the sound of their voice. "Where did you fight the nue?"

"Four hours from here. Not too far from Watarai."

Osamu's lips moved, but he had been speaking to himself, so Ren did not hear. He guessed the priest had mumbled something like, "So close." Osamu shook his head and looked back at Ren, whose feet were quickly losing their feeling because of the cold.

"What else did you encounter on your journey?" he asked.

"A fox-lady," Ren answered with an impish smile.

"I don't want to know about that one," Osamu replied, frowning. "What else?"

Ren thought about it. It had been four months since his last visit. Snow covered the shrine then, and he had traveled hundreds, maybe thousands of ri since. Many yōkai had fallen to his blade and more still to Maki's fangs, but none stood out more than the nue.

"A few *kappa*, one hungry *onibaba*, and a particularly ugly *dorotabo*," Ren said. He stood up, but the priest waved him down. His teeth were chattering, and his face was turning blue. "The usual, really."

Osamu adopted a thoughtful pose, so Ren coughed in his hand for attention.

"Under the water for a few seconds, then you can come out."

Ren closed his eyes and leaned backward. His short hair waved in the river. Now that he was getting used to the cold, he actually enjoyed the bathing. It was quiet, peaceful, and soothing. When he resurfaced and walked back to the bank, Osamu had his eyes closed, and held his scepter in front of his face. The priest was reciting a prayer of purification for the hunter's benefit. His voice came in a murmur, but it was a good voice, rhythmical and warm. It lasted longer than usual, and Ren felt the bitterness of the wind on his naked body. Then he noticed the smirk on the priest's lips and understood he was being tricked.

"All right," the hunter said as he bent to pick up the heap of fresh garments while Osamu chuckled.

"Did you deliver the nue to the river?" the priest asked, just as Ren put on a black cotton shirt. "You didn't, did you?"

"I... buried what Maki didn't eat."

Osamu grumbled and started massaging his right temple. Someone would have to clean up the remains of the yōkai. "And how many guardian statues this time?"

"Three," Ren answered right away. He had destroyed nine during the winter, but three sounded better and still realistic.

"Ren, how many?" Osamu asked. The prickling sensation of the kotodama fired inside Ren's skull, and his lips moved by themselves.

"Nine," he answered unwillingly. "Damn it, don't do that."

"Don't lie, and I won't have to."

Ren put on his black hakama pants, tied his *obi* belt, and moved to the pair of white, two-toed *tabi* socks and their accompanying straw sandals. "Why the long face?" he asked when he finished tying the sandals.

Osamu let a long hum pass his throat. "You're not the only one who had odd encounters this winter. And kappa, fox-ladies, and dorotabo might seem fine to you, but in my youth, we hardly encountered them. I'm telling you, Ren—"

"Something dark is coming," Ren said before Osamu could, imitating not only the old man's voice but also his pose by stroking a nonexistent beard. "Ease off, old man. The world hasn't changed in thousands of years and will remain more or less the same for thousands more. That's why the Yaseki exists, after all. For all we know, this nue got more powerful because it ate a priest."

Osamu shrugged as if to say it was a possibility, and Ren congratulated himself for marking a point.

He tossed his rags into the river, then they rejoined the road and the bridge. Any trace of the blood had been cleaned off, but the girl was nowhere in sight. Ren wanted to ask about her, but somewhere farther the plaintive sound of a *shō* called the beginning of a procession. Osamu dropped his hand on Ren's shoulder and squeezed gently.

"I have to go," the head priest of Ise said. "Go see the Clerk and your mother, then come find me at the pond. I have something to tell you."

He did not wait for a reply and walked with more urgency than before, though it barely showed. Ren bowed at the old man's back and waited for him to be on the other side of the bridge before he straightened up. He longed to see his mother, but since Osamu had not mentioned her before, Ren assumed nothing had changed with her. Maybe the Clerk would have good news Ren could share with her, which is why he always visited the old woman first.

The people on the bridge walked faster behind the head priest, thinking they would get a chance to see him officiate, though they would not know in which shrine he would lead them. It left Ren strangely alone, which suited him just fine.

The bridge ended with the second torii, and though Ren felt no different, he breathed better knowing he now stood within the most sacred part of Japan. Ise Jingū was nested inside a crook of the Isuzu, making the river a barrier separating the shrine from the outer world. From afar, it looked like nothing more than a forest, but the sacredness of the place became obvious once one stepped into it.

The trees grew high, most of them straight, but their disposition was not random and left the pilgrim unbothered by the oppressive feeling of a regular forest. Hundreds of novices, miko, and priests kept the path clean, changed the lights within the stone lanterns, gathered the leaves, fed the hens freely roaming in Ise as the messengers of Amaterasu, and altogether maintained the purity and serenity of the shrine so that one felt as heavenly kami must feel in their realm.

Following the believers, Ren passed by the *temizuya* pavilion, where people purified themselves with a ladder of water, then the *kaguraden* stage, which a miko swept clean in preparation for the next dance she or one of her sisters would perform. The flow of travelers weakened, and Ren assumed the ongoing ceremony keeping Osamu busy was taking place in the closest shrine, though he forgot which spirit inhabited it.

The hunter kept going. One could walk for hours in Ise without encountering the same building twice. Some said Ise covered a larger area than most cities, but few ever discovered the hidden nature of the shrine.

The hunter passed under two more torii before he bowed at the bottom of the stairs leading to the main building of Ise, the palace of Amaterasu-Ōmikami, from where the Holy Mirror of the

Sun Kami blessed the nation. The main hall stood at the center of a structure made of four wooden fences, and most visitors would not even set their eyes on it from anywhere closer than the third barrier, at best. If they did, they would gaze upon a stilted structure of light-colored wood, smaller than one would expect of such a sacred hall but bigger than most honden of the country.

The roof was the most particular part of the building, with its golden, crossed finial and the *katsuogi* decorative logs running perpendicular to the roof's ridgeline. Just like any other structure of the shrine, the hall was made anew every twenty years, and this one had been completed two years ago and thus had kept the freshness of its construction. The previous one, Ren recalled, had turned dark and mossy despite the best efforts of the priests in charge of its maintenance.

Ren crossed the first two barriers and, just like any worshipper, was denied the path by the third gate. There, he bowed twice, clapped twice, and, after making sure no one stood nearby, clapped three times more. The doors opened upon the signal, revealing the main hall to the hunter.

Two priests stood on either side of the fence's door and welcomed Ren by showering him with a handful of salt. He had expected it but still closed his eyes and proceeded toward the building. Yata no Kagami, the Holy Bronze Mirror, passed down from Amaterasu to her grandson, then from her grandson to his great-grandson, Jinmu, the first emperor, could be found in this very hall, but Ren ignored both and walked around the building. His business stood farther.

No one challenged him when he opened the door in the fence at the back of the hall, nor when he stepped through the eight straight torii gates separating the visitable part of Ise Jingū from the Yaseki, the secret behind the mirror.

Few ever heard of the Yaseki, and if they did, it was in the form of whispers and half-formed theories. Some believed it was the name of a secret organization leading the nation from the shadows, using the emperor as their puppet the way some shōgun had. Others murmured it was, in fact, a group of corrupt officials using the funds donated to shrines and temples to finance their lascivious lifestyle.

It was all ridiculous, but those rumors never failed to draw a smile to Ren's lips. Yet again, in his journeys, he had heard from a couple people that the Yaseki was the name of a spiritual body spread all over Japan, in which trained members worked to fight the darkness threatening to engulf the human world. Those people were right and made Ren's life a little more complicated, for they had to be invited in or silenced. He chose the former more often than not.

Of course, the truth was more complicated, and even after years as a member, Ren would not be able to define the Yaseki in a few words, not that he knew everything about it, anyway.

The headquarters of the Yaseki stood at the center of Ise Jingū, deep inside the sanctuary forest. A wooden wall surrounded it, and only one entrance allowed people in, though most who set foot within never left. The kami's power kept the lost and the curious from approaching the wall, and if any yōkai somehow managed to enter the shrine's ground, they would be repelled by trained members of the organization or the multitude of guardians protecting it.

If Ise Jingū was a haven of quietness, the citadel, as the members of the Yaseki called it, hummed like a beehive. Seven hundred people lived there, with more room for the rare visitors and external agents, such as Ren. There were no enshrined kami per se in the citadel, for it was considered a kami itself, but enough buildings stood in a neatly crisscrossing fashion that one thought himself lost in an ancient city.

Most served as barracks, but anything necessary could be found: fields, farms, schools, a hospital, offices, three armories, twelve wells, and a few worshipping halls. There was even a meditation hall for the vast group of Buddhist monks living here, for the Yaseki cared little about whom one prayed to as long as they fought to preserve the light of Amaterasu over Japan.

Ren had heard as a joke that the only establishments missing in the citadel were a brothel and a couple *izakaya*. Now that he had visited both kinds of establishments, Ren was inclined to agree.

The citadel had been Ren's life for his first year within the Yaseki, but he would not trade his current situation for anything in the world. Living here was, by all accounts, boring and way too clean for his comfort.

He walked all the way to the Clerk's office, a short building tucked between two much larger offices, with a single room divided in two. The first part, which Ren entered after removing his sandals, was a square of nine straw-smelling tatami facing a fence-like counter. The Clerk stood on the other side.

Ren had never seen the old woman anywhere other than in her office. Her side of the room was floored with wood, with a few tables on which awaited a few hot cups of tea—and many more that had long stopped fuming—a set of weighing instruments and a stack of records for bookkeeping.

"How are we doing today?" Ren asked as he slid the door back behind him.

"*Ara, ara,* if it isn't my little Lotus Root," the Clerk said, beaming at the sight of him. Well, not the sight, for she was blind as a mole, but her hearing was sharp, and she most likely recognized him by the sound of the sliding door.

She stepped down from her high chair, so short that she almost vanished from his sight, and pattered to the closest group of cups. She touched five with the back of her hand before deciding which suited her best and returned to the window of the counter, on which she dropped the cup. Ren did not need to check. It was roasted-smelling *sencha*, neither too hot nor too cold, just as he liked it. She never forgot.

"We missed you here," she said as Ren sighed with pleasure upon the first sip. "I got sick soon after you left. It was bad; I didn't think I'd see you again." The Clerk's hair had thinned even more, revealing brown spots on an already spotted skull. No one knew how old she was, but she was the only person who dared rebuke Osamu, so Ren assumed she was a good twenty years older than the head priest.

"A young flower like you?" Ren scoffed. "I'm sure you recovered in no time. You'll cremate us all."

"Ren," she called, grabbing his wrist with thin, bony fingers full of strength. "You're not supposed to joke about death here. Don't make me tell Osamu-kun."

"Apologies, *obā-san*," Ren gently replied. "I will be more careful."

"It's all right," she said, waving it off. "Now, why don't you show me what you got? I'm sure you'd rather see your mama than sip tea with an old bat?"

"And miss the best tea in the citadel, served by its most beautiful lady?" Ren asked, thinking she looked more like a mole than a bat. She giggled like a young girl and blushed, or so Ren assumed.

"Oh, you mischievous charmer," she said. "I won't give you a better rate because of your flattery."

"Too bad," Ren said honestly. "To business then."

He emptied the cup in one sip and lifted the shoulder bag to the counter, where it clinked as if full of marbles. Now that his old clothes and most of his items had been used and thrown away, all that remained were the magatama with their sealed, corrupted souls.

The Clerk expertly grabbed the bag, loosened its mouth, and emptied the contents on the table on her side of the window. Her fingers swiftly rearranged them as she made a quick tally, then she picked up a brush, licked its tip, and inscribed a number on a piece of egg-white paper.

"Thirteen," she said, "plus the one in your pocket."

"I have no idea how you do this," Ren replied with heartfelt pleasure as he fished the magatama he had kept from her. He dropped it across the counter, earning himself a grumble from the old woman who did not like people reaching farther than the window.

She picked the first shell and brought it a couple of inches from her tired, graying eyes, then wrinkled her nose with the effort of inspecting the brown magatama, increasing her resemblance to a mole, and sighed. "Can't see farther than the tip of my nose," she said.

She then picked up a small, metallic bar, no longer and no thicker than her little finger, and lifted the magatama all the way to her left ear. The bar struck the shell, and Ren held his breath while the Clerk listened to the vibration of the ringing. It seemed to last an eternity to Ren.

"Three days," she said in the most neutral tone before dropping the shell as far as possible on her left.

"Three days?" Ren blurted. "That was from a kappa, you know? It took me a week to find it and a day of swimming through icy water to kill it."

"You dressed as a child and pretended to drown in the river for five minutes before it attacked you," the Clerk replied, making Ren swallow nervously. "You killed it in one move. Besides, your struggles don't change the rate. A magatama is a magatama, and I don't decide."

There was no more friendly old woman when it was time for the Clerk to do her thing, and Ren should have known better than to whine or lie. He still muttered a curse, which she pretended not to hear, and then her attention shifted to the gray shell containing the nue's soul. She repeated the process of knocking it but frowned. She let the ringing end and knocked it again.

"What is it?" Ren asked. This was the first time he'd seen the Clerk check a shell twice.

"I'm not sure," she said, sounding surprised. "You're the third hunter to bring me such an odd soul in the last month."

"So, how much?" he asked, his hope soaring. Odd was good. Odd meant rarity, and rarity meant a better price.

"I've been told to tell hunters to wait until they get purified before giving a rate. But, between you and me," she whispered, leaning forward, "the last one got twelve weeks out of it."

"Twelve weeks!"

The Clerk shushed him, waving her hand to keep him quiet. But there was no settling his heart. Twelve weeks was worth as much as all the rest put together and then some more.

"Don't get your hopes up too soon, though. And you didn't hear from me," she went on, looking over her shoulder. Ren answered with a gesture signifying his lips would remain closed, but he could not wait to tell his mother.

The old woman proceeded with all the other shells and concluded that besides the nue, he would get ten weeks and three days. She added another two days when he told her about the arrow, though he omitted to inform her that he had cursed during the prayer and thus rendered the sacred missile useless. The Clerk had little sympathy for those of the armory and granted those two days back after some negotiation. Then came the moment Ren always worried about.

"Go ahead," he said, straightening up. "Tell me."

The Clerk stretched to her right, dragged a pile of paper bound together in six or seven books, then dropped the top two. She leafed through the third, licked her finger when she got close to the part she was searching for, and went down a list of names. The black characters on the white paper allowed her to see, more or less, but she still squinted with the effort and bent over until the page remained a few inches from her face.

"Ren Fudō, here we go. I assume you want those credits on your mom's debt? In that case, you're still up for a five-year debt, or one thousand eight hundred and fifty days." Ren sighed. This was not news, but it always hurt. "As for your mother, I remove ten weeks, five days from her total, which gives us…" She bent the fingers of her left hand one by one, then up again, except one. "Eleven years, two months, and twenty days." Ren's head fell in his hands.

"How did it go over ten years?" he asked, frustration shaking his voice. "When I left, it was under."

"My boy, I'm so sorry," the Clerk said, patting his hand above the counter. She did sound sorry. "It's not fair, I know. But she needs three Hearts by her side at all times. It's not your fault, and you're doing so well. We're all rooting for you, you know?"

Ren wanted to thank her for her kind words, but it got stuck in his throat. He would never reimburse both their debts, even if Japan was suddenly teeming with those twelve weeks' worth souls. He didn't mind being trapped in the Yaseki for years, even possibly for the rest of his life; hunting souls beat his father's tanning activity. But he would be damned if he let his mother slave her days for the organization.

It was his fault if she was stuck here, at the doors of death, and he would make sure she left a free woman. But for all his ambition, Ren could not figure out a way to reimburse her debt, and those were untransferable. If a person contracted a debt with the Yaseki, it meant they had been chosen by the kami, and no human being could overrule a kami.

"Have faith," the old woman said, patting his hand again. "She might wake up any day now, or maybe you'll seal a truly unique soul and set you both free."

皿

Ren hated the hospital. Most of the agents working there were kind and selfless, and all the rooms were clean beyond reproach, but the unmistakable smell of illness coupled with the forever-hanging cloud of incense made it a difficult place for him to appreciate. Because she had spent the last five years in it, his mother had been moved to the back of the one-story building, which forced Rend to cross it to reach her. He inhaled a deep breath before opening the door and made himself brave.

Whenever he saw her lying unconscious on her futon, Ren felt like a child about to cry. One of the monks in the room tapped the side of his singing bowl, creating a soothing, low-ringing sound that would vibrate for a long time, and Ren stepped in.

None of the three Buddhist monks surrounding his mother reacted when he entered. They remained in their seated meditative pose, eyes almost shut, two of them pushing the beads on their strings with their thumb while the other held the singing bowl, and all three recited a mantra in unison. It was entrancing. The two monks with the beads sat with their backs to him, so he went to the other side, next to the third one, who hit the bowl as Ren sat down.

His mother had not changed since he last saw her. She was still a beautiful woman in her prime, tucked under a thick blanket of cotton and silk, lying on a thin futon. They took good care of her here; Ren could see it. The tatami floor was impeccable, the room fresh, and she'd been washed by the gentle hands of some nurse. Yet Ren would love nothing more than to see her sweat over the cooking pot of their shabby old home, though he doubted she would ever accept to cook for him after what happened.

"Mom," Ren said when he lifted her hand from under the

37

blanket. "I am back." He never knew what to tell her and always found himself stupid for speaking to a sleeping body. "I was gone all winter. I went as far as Aomori. Can you imagine, Mom? Aomori in winter? It was so cold. I didn't know it could get so cold. But the blanket of snow was so perfect, you wouldn't believe how thick it always is there."

The monk next to him struck the bowl again, lighter than before, Ren thought.

"I spoke to the Clerk. She said I might have found a unique magatama. Maybe precious enough to decrease our debt by several months." He didn't like lying to her, but either she couldn't hear him and it didn't matter, or she could hear him and it would make her feel better. Then came the weird moment when Ren did not know what else to say. He could not let her know of the dangers he faced when hunting for the Yaseki.

"Osamu-san wants to see me," he said as he gently placed her hand back under the blanket. "I guess he has another urgent task for me, so I'd better go. But I'll come back before I leave." Ren wanted to say more, much more, but the presence of the three monks kept the words in his heart.

He longed for a moment with her alone, yet knew it wasn't meant to be. Just a minute or even a few seconds without them caring for her would be her death. She hadn't spent a moment by herself since her arrival at the citadel, and every second increased her debt to the Yaseki. The mantra went another round, and Ren kowtowed to his mother before leaving the room.

皿

The sun was close to the forest canopy when Ren reached the pond. There was only one such place in the citadel, right at its northern tip. A quiet, man-made pond fit for meditation and prayer where a dozen colorful koi lazily swam. It wasn't reserved for the leaders of the Yaseki in the citadel, but when Osamu Shirakawa walked along its edge to feed the fish, no one dared bother him.

This was how Ren found him, lost at the sight of the fish cramming the edge of the pond and fighting for his attention. By his side stood the same young miko as before. She was carrying an unlidded box from where the head priest scooped small balls cut from apples. The water got more agitated when the balls fell.

"If only they waited in turn," Ren said as he stepped next to the head priest. Osamu behaved as if he knew the young man had been there all along, which was most likely the case. "They'd all get their share."

"It's not about getting their share," Osamu replied. The golden light accentuated the old man's wrinkles and made him appear more genial but also more tired. "It's about getting more than their neighbor. All they want is to be the one that gets the most."

"Well, they're just dumb fish," Ren replied, observing their long tube of a mouth as they gaped in expectation for the next morsel.

"Are we that different?" Osamu asked rhetorically. There was sadness in his voice, and Ren found nothing to reply. "Your mother is well?"

"As well as ever," Ren said. "The monks are good to her, and she doesn't get worse."

"That's good," Osamu replied, though none of this was new to him. The old man knew everything happening in Ise and much of what happened out of it. The Yaseki had grown to cover most of Japan, and its network, while thin and hidden, branched to every region and city.

"Did you receive any word concerning the White Tengu?" the hunter asked.

"None," the priest answered bluntly. "No one has ever seen a white tengu besides you, and who knows if that's really what you saw."

"I know what I saw," Ren replied through his teeth.

"You were just a child."

"But I was not confused, and I will never forget what happened that day. No one would." Ren released the tension in his fists when he realized he had closed them. "And *you* said that whatever had infected my mother still held power over her and that if it got killed, she would recover."

"I said *maybe*," the priest replied as he looked back over the pond. "And I should never have told you that. You were not ready then, and you are not ready now. Tengu are not to be messed with. They are dangerous, even for a Soul Hunter like you."

"So you said."

"Ren," Osamu called, turning his fatherly eyes on the young man, "promise me you won't fight any tengu, white or otherwise, without first informing us." The priest had not used his power this time, nor would he if he wanted a sincere promise, but the worry in his voice was enough to convince the young man.

"I promise," Ren said with a smirk. Behind the old man, the girl smiled too. "What did you want to tell me?"

"Walk with me." Osamu did not wait for Ren to acknowledge the request in any way and took the first step of what would be a brief stroll around the pond. Ren walked to his side and heard the girl's feet behind them. "I won't beat around the bush; I need to send you out again."

"Already? I just got here," Ren replied, doing his best to sound surprised.

"I wish it were otherwise, but this is not my decision."

"An oracle?" Ren asked. This time, the surprise was genuine.

"From Amaterasu," Osamu replied.

Ren gasped involuntarily. The sun goddess rarely bothered sending oracles and usually let lesser spirits contact her human

40

servants. As far as the young man knew, this was the first oracle from Amaterasu ever sent to Osamu. No wonder he had been waiting at the bridge.

"What did she say?" Ren asked.

"You are to go to Fushimi Inari. Immediately," Osamu answered.

"And?" the hunter asked expectantly.

"And that's it."

"That's it? Are you sure you washed your ears before she spoke? A destination, that's all I have?" The pond was curving, and the sun went from the side of their faces to their backs as they followed its contour.

"It's not like they ever give us specific instructions," the priest said.

"I know, but that's a bit light, don't you think? Wait," Ren said. "She named *me* specifically?"

"She said to send a Blood Hunter," Osamu replied, which got him a scoff. "And I don't see another one here."

"Send Tiger," Ren spat. "About time he does anything."

"Tiger can't leave the shrine."

"Can't or won't?"

"Both," Osamu said. "Though mostly can't. In any case, I have an intuition that it should be you." This got Ren quiet. Osamu's intuitions were closer to predictions than simple hunches, and the young man trusted them. "I have faith in you, Ren Fudō, and would send no one else to answer a request of the great kami."

"Don't force it, old man. You got no one else to send; you said so."

"Actually," Osamu replied, and the hint of pleasure in the priest's voice sent a shiver up Ren's spine. This did not bode well. "I am not sending you alone."

"No," Ren replied right away. "Uh-uh, no way, not a chance. I work alone, with my guardian at most, and that's the end of this conversation."

"I am *not* sending you alone," Osamu repeated, this time through gritted teeth. "And I don't recall asking for your opinion."

"Six months," Ren said, stopping in his tracks and dropping his arms. The swarm of koi caught up then and fought at the surface like the bubbles of boiling water.

"I'm sorry, what?" Osamu asked. Ren wondered if the old man had not heard or did not believe what had just been asked.

"It's a mission, so I get to negotiate my fee," Ren said, quoting the rules he'd been taught when he became a hunter.

"Six months is ridiculous," Osamu said, waving the offer down. "I give you three."

Now, that was amazing in itself. Ren had never been offered more than one, and even that had to be negotiated. He pretended not to be impressed and sighed exaggeratedly.

"Fine, ask Tiger," he said, then turned around as if about to go.

"Wait," Osamu said. Ren winked at the girl before he faced the priest again, which made her giggle. "Five months, and—" he went on, adding the last word with a raised finger to stop Ren from complaining, "whatever you want from the armory."

"Whoa," Ren said.

"Whoa, indeed. Do we have a deal?"

"Can I get your beads?" Ren asked mischievously.

"Of course, you can't get my beads!" Osamu barked.

"No deal then."

"Fine!" the priest spat, throwing his hands in the air. "Joke's on you," he said when he lifted the prayer beads from his neck and handed them to the hunter. "It's a new one, and only twelve beads are full."

"Twelve will do," Ren said with delight. Those beads were much bigger than those used by the monks in his mother's room, and since they had passed between the head priest's fingers, they were infused with his prayers and thus more potent than anything else he'd find in the citadel. "You must be desperate."

"I am now," Osamu replied. "Do we have a deal then?"

"We have a deal," Ren said. He had gotten much more than expected, and for nothing, as far as he was concerned, since the mission's nature hadn't been mentioned.

Fushimi Inari, the great shrine dedicated to the spirit of agriculture and fertility, was to be found south of Kyōto, an easy journey from Ise. Even better, the *kannushi* in charge of the shrine was a fellow hunter and, as far as Ren thought, a friend. He was glad at the prospect of meeting Kiyoshi again.

Ren took Osamu's right hand in both his and bowed, thus sealing the contract. His heart beat faster, thinking he had just decreased his mother's debt by five months for a week's journey. "Who is coming with me then?"

Osamu smiled, and it wasn't a pleasant smile. Ren cursed and guessed the words before they came out of the priest's mouth. "A Hand."

"No," Ren said again, shaking his head. "There is no chance on earth I take another Hand with me."

"You bowed," Osamu replied. He sounded happy with himself, and Ren understood that *he* had been made. "We have a deal. You should have asked about that before."

"Listen to me, you old goat. I am not taking a Hand with me. They always die. They die brutally, they die bloody," Ren went on, only stopping a second because the girl gasped in horror, "and they die in my arms. And I'm the one who has to carry their bloody remains all the way to Ise, so no thank you, take your beads back, and see you next time."

"Ren," Osamu called. "You bowed. You know the rules. If you back out now, you forfeit yourself in the eyes of the kami and reject their fortune for the rest of what promises to be a short life. Do you really want that?"

A low hum passed through Ren's throat, then through his mouth, and then he could take it no longer. "Damn it! Damn it, damn it, damn it!" Each curse was punctuated by a kick that sent pebbles flying into the pond and scared the fish from its edge. "Damn it!" Ren shouted, wasting the last of his frustration.

When he turned around, the girl was looking at him with eyes as round as eggs, her lips pinched tight. Osamu, he thought, was chuckling into his beard, which threatened to get another bout from the hunter. He breathed out, defeated. "Who am I to take on their last journey, then?" he asked.

"Ren Fudō," Osamu called. "Let me introduce you to Suzume from Sugimoto. The newest Hand of the Yaseki and your companion for the next few days."

Ren followed the direction of the hand Osamu had opened and met the eyes of the young miko, who gathered her hands in front of her stomach.

"I am Suzume," she said in a sweet voice full of youth. "Let's do our best together." On those words, she bowed. It was a terrible bow. Her bound hair fell over her shoulder as she waited for an answer.

"Damn it," was all she received, though this time he had just whispered the curse.

CHAPTER 3
SUZUME

No Soul Hunter in their right mind would deny the warmth of a bed in Ise for the dangers of the wild night or the costly room of an inn. The Yaseki had several affiliated lodgings across Japan, but obviously none so close to the citadel. So Ren and his travel companion left the next morning, two hours after sunrise.

The young man first paid a visit to the armory, where he acquired an amulet for safe travel, three bags of salt, one sacred arrow—which he promised himself to use properly—a pair of deer antlers taken from a young buck, and enough *ofuda* talismans to earn himself a disgruntled glare from the armorer.

Then he proudly paraded in the citadel, flashing the rosary previously adorning Osamu Shirakawa's chest. Of the twenty-four brown beads, only the twelve at the bottom had been infused with his power, but everyone here knew who used to own it, and it pleased Ren to see the astonishment on their faces.

He then visited the hospital, and for once, the words came easily. He told his mother about the five months, the destination, and, with less enthusiasm, about the company.

Suzume from Sugimoto waited for him at the end of the bridge where they had met the day before. Ren had never heard of her village before but assumed from her accent that it must be somewhere on Shikoku. The girl still wore her miko uniform and carried a bag of hemp across her back, but the most remarkable part of her attire hung in her left hand.

A spear, taller than she was, ending in a *jūmonji-yari* cross-shaped head currently hidden inside a similarly shaped sheath. Those blades were wicked polearms, but this one was much more than a tool, though the girl held it as if it were a shabby, old hoe.

"You will have to teach her on the road," Osamu had told Ren the previous evening, after he sent the girl to prepare his dinner. "She has been with us for less than a fortnight. The kami inhabiting the spear is strong, so is their connection, but she has barely begun to open to the spirit. She'll need your guidance."

"Osamu-san," Ren had replied. "She should be trained here, by another Hand, before going out there. You know I'm right."

"I know," the priest had said, his voice and his face low. "But I think she came here when she did for a reason, and she cannot stay here."

"Why not?"

"Ren, she cannot stay here as a shrine maiden." This was all Osamu said on the topic, and all Ren needed to know.

It was unfair, but only virgins could officiate in a shrine. Once they found out the truth about Suzume, her new sisters might become cruel to her, no matter if she had lost her purity to a lover or, as suggested her youth, to more unfortunate events. This, however, persuaded Ren to give the girl an honest chance. And the idea of mentoring a student amused him.

"Ren-san," she called, waving as if he had not seen her. Even so early in the day, the bridge teemed with visitors, but Suzume was hard to miss in her bright orange hakama. She seemed full of energy and beamed a warm smile to his benefit despite the harsh words he had uttered the day before.

"You can drop the san," Ren said. "We're bound to spend a long time on the road together, so let's make it easier for both of us, shall we?"

"Understood, Ren," she stiffly replied, making a bow containing too much energy for his taste.

It was bound to be harder than he'd expected. He sighed, walked by her, and meant to pat her shoulder in a brotherly fashion, but she gasped and got startled. Ren could have cursed himself for his lack of foresight.

"I'm sorry," Suzume said, blushing.

"It's fine," Ren replied apologetically. "I shouldn't have."

She refused to meet his eyes. Ren swallowed hard. Nothing had prepared him for his situation. Suzume's face had the natural glow of young people who live under the sun, and a few freckles embellished her gentle nose. Ren's skin was marked by some freckles, too, though his rested under the eyes. She stood an inch or two taller than him but appeared so pure compared to his natural gruffness that one would assume he was ten years older.

"Let's go, then," he said, unable to find the words to defuse the tension.

This was going to be a long journey, Ren thought.

They both forgot to bow after the last torii and stepped on the northwestern road, the one that would lead them to Kyōto, in accordance with Amaterasu's wish.

血

"Listen," Ren awkwardly said in the middle of the afternoon after an interminable silent few hours. "I'm sorry for what I said yesterday. You're not going to die; I'll make sure of it. And no one will have to carry your remains back to Ise. All right?"

"It's fine," she replied, trying her best to smile. "And I'm sorry for being a burden to you. I didn't mean to impose, but Shirakawa-sama didn't really leave me a choice."

"Oh, I can guess he didn't. That old goat." The last remark was spoken for himself, but the girl giggled in the way she seemed to favor, and somehow it made Ren feel better. It was as if everything had been forgiven or forgotten, maybe.

He suddenly realized the weather was more than fair; it was beautiful. The sun shined strong, only bothered by a few fluffy clouds moving with a gentle wind. Birds were singing their sweet songs of melodies pure and true, and optimistic buds burgeoned on the branches of the closest cherry trees.

"May I ask..." Suzume said, cutting her words short when Ren looked up at her.

"Yes?"

"Why did you say Hands always die? And, now that I think about it, what is a Hand?"

Ren scoffed at the question, not in arrogance, but because he thought she was pulling his leg. Then he understood she was seriously asking. "Well," he said, looking at her sideways, "*you* are a Hand. No one told you that?"

"Shirakawa-sama called me a Hand, but no one explained to me what it was," she answered, looking sorry for her lack of knowledge.

"Did they at least tell you what the Yaseki is? What we do? What yōkai are? What makes the spear in your hand so special?" To each question, Suzume replied with a head shake that left Ren sighing inside. "Do you at least know what kami are?"

"Yes!" she happily said. "They're spirits!"

A very, very long road, Ren thought. "They are indeed spirits," Ren patiently replied. "But they're a bit more than that. Kami are energy that acquired individuality, a personality, you could say. They are pure, simple, almost like children, but some are thousands of years old and can destroy cities according to their moods.

They are everywhere. They live in rivers, on their mountains, they protect their forests, and guard the people worshipping them from harm. They inhabit huge rocks—"

"And trees, too, right?" Suzume asked excitedly.

"Yes, venerable trees, tall trees, trees growing inside dead trees, too. Was it the case where you grew up?" The name of her village, Sugimoto, suggested the presence of redwood trees, and Ren guessed one of them was venerated since the first people called the place home.

"Yes," she answered with less enthusiasm. "There was a wide, tall redwood tree in Sugimoto."

The sudden sadness in Suzume's voice disturbed Ren. The story that had brought her to Ise Jingū would still be fresh and painful. Most people who found themselves passing through the eight gates of the citadel had suffered one way or another, but his new companion, he felt, was still suffering.

"All living things have a kami in them, actually," he said, changing the subject.

"Even humans?"

"Yes, even us," Ren replied. "Though very few people ever awaken their inner kami. It takes decades of dedication for a person to reach their kami. Buddhists call it enlightenment, but there are other ways to awaken our kami than meditation and abstinence. Some animals, too, can reach a new level of consciousness simply by living long enough. And, of course, each family has a kami watching over it, and this kami is made from all our ancestors' souls gathering upon our deaths."

Suzume stiffened when Ren said so, but when the hunter frowned, she faked a smile inviting him to go on.

"Kami with names, the ones we worship in many shrines, like Amaterasu, Inari, or Tsukuyomi, live in the high plane of heaven, and they are so powerful that they and their ancestors created everything around you."

A flock of white cranes floated down to the river when Ren said so and landed gracefully on the quiet Kushida River, giving a layer of spirituality to his words.

"Through our worship, we hope to receive their blessings and avoid their tempers when they have bad days, which they do have, or even bad years. Each of them has power over one or several aspects of the world's energy. That's why we pray to Inari for a good harvest, Okuninoshi for a good wife, or the Sumiyoshi sanjin for safety at sea. They have animal messengers on earth, *matsuri* festivals at dedicated times, and specific rituals and shrines. It's all a bit bothersome if you ask me, but we need their fortune to shine on us, or the world will turn to chaos."

Ren had stopped looking at Suzume while he spoke of the kami, but when he did, he found the girl staring at him with big eyes shining in admiration. Unwillingly, he blushed.

"You know so much, Ren-san," she said. "And you sound so much like Shirakawa-sama."

"Uh, you wound me," he said, pretending to be hit in the heart by an arrow. "And drop the san."

A couple of hours ahead, the two of them would reach their first stop, the merchant city of Matsusaka. It would be dark by then, but the city was so close to Ise Jingū that they had little to fear on this part of the journey. At least this is what Ren used to think before the nue.

"And then there are the Hasontama," Ren said somberly, "the corrupted spirits." A blade of wind combed through the rice fields along the road. It brushed Ren's hair and made Suzume's hakama wave.

"The Hasontama," she repeated as if committing the name to memory. She looked serious. "What are they?" A thicker cloud passed over the sun, weakening its light and turning the country gray.

"They are the greatest threat to our world and the reason for the Yaseki to exist," Ren answered. He had exaggerated the ominousness of his tone on purpose. "Hasontama are spirits born of negativity or regular ones damaged by it. Loss, war, extreme frustration," or abuse, Ren thought but chose not to say, "can corrupt the soul and change its nature. A corrupted soul will seek chaos and live to extinguish the light from our world."

"Are they the yōkai?" Suzume asked.

"Yōkai are the largest group of Hasontama, but they are not the only ones, though, as far as you and I are concerned, they are the ones we deal with almost exclusively," Ren explained. "Just like kami, yōkai are the individual form of a spirit, but a negative one, and they are vicious. Well, most of them." Ren smiled when he said so, thinking about the fox-lady from Nagano.

"There are two other kinds of Hasontama: the Yūrei, ghosts of dead people seeking revenge for whoever or whatever killed them, and the Dark Kami, regular kami corrupted irreversibly. The first, you and I can't do much about them, and the second... Let's say I've never met one and pray I never will."

"So we take care of yōkai," Suzume said. The nonchalance in her tone as she casually mentioned one of the most dangerous parts of the Yaseki world was refreshing. Ren might have behaved as such on his first hunt had he not encountered the White Tengu before.

"We do," he replied with a nod, "but not the same way."

"What do you mean?" she asked.

"What do you know of the Yaseki?" Ren then asked.

Suzume seemed confused for a second during which she switched her spear from her left hand to her right. The tip was covered with a scabbard made with the cotton grown from the citadel's soil, but even if it had just been a staff, it would have been heavy for such a young girl.

"I know it's a big organization, and the citadel is its center," she replied hesitantly. "Oh, and Shirakawa-sama is its supreme leader."

"That's how he introduced himself, isn't it?" Ren asked, receiving a nod in answer. "As the Saishu of Ise Jingū, he is the leader of the Yaseki, but there are other shrines and temples harboring great power, such as Fushimi Inari, where we are going. We have members all over Japan, though I don't know how many. We are a secret, even among the clergy. Besides the imperial family and a few chosen elite, very few are aware of our existence."

"Why?" Suzume asked. Ren had not understood the first time either.

"To keep corruption at bay," he answered, using Osamu's reply. "We don't meddle with human matters, and we don't let them meddle with ours. If they don't know about us, or more specifically about our powers, they don't try to bribe us, and we remain pure. It also means we can't intervene when a conflict arises between people; this is Osamu's number one rule."

"But," Suzume said, resting her chin on her finger in a thoughtful pose that made Ren chuckle inside. "If negativity creates Hasontama, shouldn't we intervene before conflicts happen?"

"Ah!" Ren scoffed. "Try telling that to that pig-head of Osamu. Well, don't try, actually, I have, but it's like telling the water to be less wet. He won't budge, and I guess it's part of our creed since the creation of the Yaseki."

Ren realized that through this conversation, he had repeatedly referred to the organization as *we*. When, he wondered, had he started thinking of himself as one of them with such certainty?

"We're stuck dealing with the aftermath of human stupidity. And, to answer your original question, we do it by using our gates. You haven't heard about that either, have you?" Ren asked when he noticed the confused look on Suzume's face.

Matsusaka was drawing on the horizon as soon as they

reached the tip of a gentle hill, and Ren wondered if he should keep the explanation about the gates for later. Suzume was obediently listening, but it was already a lot to take in, especially for a young person whose life had changed entirely a few days before, something he knew personally. Yet she looked eager to know more, and he only had a few days to get her ready for whatever Amaterasu expected of them and whatever had triggered Osamu's intuition.

"Yaseki means *eight gates*," Ren went on, picking the largest of the beads and rolling it between two fingers pensively. "And each gate represents a power we use to protect the light and fight the corruption. First, there are the Four Teachings, powers that can be taught to anyone, more or less."

Suzume was drinking his words. So much so that she forgot to watch the road and nearly tripped on a pothole. "Sorry," she said, blushing.

Ren answered with a smile. He truly hoped to be wrong about her future. The previous Hands traveling with him were not nearly as nice or pure, and while they didn't deserve their fate, Ren didn't mourn them much either. Suzume's death, he thought, would be harder to take.

"Let's stop here for a minute," he said, nodding toward the road's bank. His explanation could not be uttered where other people could hear them. It was better to remain off the road for a little while.

They stepped over the bank and climbed down to the closest rice paddy. In a few days, folks would plant the seeds that would feed a nation, but for now, the paddies were little more than water and mud. Ren picked up a stick lying around and traced the first kanji. The mud was so soft that it would reshape over the character in seconds.

"First," he said after tracing a squared shape, "there's *kuchigami*, the power of the mouth. Some call it kotodama, too. It's the power of prayer. It sounds dumb, but after years of practice, it can develop to an extreme level and grant one the ability to force their will on someone else. Osamu is the self-proclaimed grand master of kuchigami, and he might be right."

"That's amazing," Suzume said, observing the character as if it contained the said power.

"Not really," Ren replied. "Everyone has this power. That's a gift given to humans by the kami upon their creation. But the words need to be pure, sincere, and frank, which is harder than it sounds. Mouths are by far the most numerous within the Yaseki, and their prayers are used in different ways, for example, by filling amulets and talismans with power or simply calling the kami for help. Then there are *hogami*, the Ears," Ren said, tracing the character in the mud.

"They hear the kami's voices?" Suzume guessed.

"Pretty straightforward, isn't it?" Ren replied with a wink. "They are oracles of the kami. I don't have this power, but Osamu says it took him twenty years to hear the voices. To become a head priest of a shrine, one needs to have mastered it, and the more powerful the kami, the harder it is to distinguish their voices, or so I heard. The third one is *megami*."

"The power of the eyes," Suzume read. "They can see the kami?"

"Not so simple this time, no," Ren answered. He had been about to gently strike the top of her head with the edge of his hand but remembered her reaction to his previous attempted contact and stopped himself. "The Eyes have premonitions, or intuition is maybe a better term. Osamu is the only person I've met with this power, and even *he* says he's far from mastering it."

"Shirakawa-sama is truly remarkable," the girl said.

Ren refused to comment on it, though he had to agree. "The last of the teachings is *kokorogami*, the power of the Heart. This one's a bit tricky because it *can* be taught, but some people are more predisposed to it than others. Hearts are our healers, among other things. They use compassion, forgiveness, and selflessness to heal and purify, so, as you can imagine, a bunch of them are followers of the Buddha. Neither Osamu nor I have a single shot at becoming Hearts, believe me. I guess you'd make a good one, though."

Suzume blushed, and Ren traced the next characters.

"The next four are called the Four Blessings, because they cannot be taught, only given. Even then, one needs to train hard to master those powers. As far as I'm concerned, they could just as well be called the Four Curses, but I guess it doesn't sound as appealing. The first is called *tegami*."

"The Hands!" Suzume said.

"Yes, your power. Osamu had to tell you something about it, right?"

"He said it was the original power of the priests, even before the Yaseki," Suzume said, looking up as she searched through her memory. "But I don't really know what he meant by that."

"It means the Hands are mediums, shaman if you prefer," Ren explained, though he could see it meant little to her. "Hands are chosen by a kami, and your body becomes their receptacle. Their spirit fills you, and through you, they act on our plane of existence. But you need a conduit first. A shintai treasure, like a magatama, or a weapon, a spear, for example," the hunter said, nodding toward the cross-spear. He wondered what kind of kami inhabited it and when the time came, how it would use the girl.

"There are two types of Hands. The Right Hands are people who birthed their own kami, for lack of a better word, by treating an object with so much respect that it developed its own soul. It could be the hammer of a smith, the katana of a samurai, or the kettle of tea ceremony master. Their relationship is symbiotic; they need each other. We have a few within the Yaseki, and their task is to craft weapons and shrines, among other things."

"What about the Left Hands?" Suzume asked apprehensively.

"The Left Hands, like you, are chosen," Ren said, stopping himself from using the word *forced*. "Some kami decide you are worthy of being their vessel and possess you at their will. At first, the kami in your spear will have complete control over you, but with time, you will develop a relationship with it, and things will smoothen between you." Ren had spoken lightly, forcing an optimism in his voice that hardly belonged there, but Suzume was not fooled by it.

"If I live long enough," she said, looking at the ground.

Ren sighed. Speaking of death within a shrine, Osamu said, always comes back at you, and it just did.

"I'm sorry for what I said," he told her as the mud melted around the hand character, "but I won't lie to you either. Hands die young. The kami are not mortal like us and usually don't take good care of their vessels. Not out of wickedness, simply because they don't know our limits. Just hosting a kami is energy-consuming, and if the trance lasts too long, your body will be spent. That's why it's important for you and it to learn each other, but once you do, you will be unstoppable. I've seen it, trust me." This time, his words struck true, and Suzume gratified Ren with a heartfelt yet discreet smile.

"What about you then?" she asked.

"Me," Ren said, pointing a thumb at his chest. "I'm a *chigami*, a Blood of the kami."

"Oh?" Suzume asked. "I thought you were a hunter?"

"Hunter is my job, and so is yours. But among the eight gates, I'm a Blood."

The character for blood quickly followed the others, but Ren had traced it deeper, each stroke applied with pain. Being a Blood had destroyed his life and his family, and while he had learned to appreciate his power, Ren would have done without.

"We're a bit special," he proclaimed, "because there are only twelve of us, and there are always twelve of us. When one of us dies, the next baby born in Japan receives the blessing, though it takes twelve years for our power to wake." He chased the image of the White Tengu from his mind with a head shake; this was no time to remember the day his spirit bloomed. "Just to keep things simple, the twelve Bloods are associated with one of the sacred animals of the zodiac. Want to guess which one I am?"

"The—" Suzume said, elongating the syllable as she searched for an appropriate answer. "—Monkey?"

"Monkey? Why on earth would you think I'm the Monkey?"

"Because of your ears?" she replied, pulling herself back for fear of retaliation.

"What's wrong with my ears?" he asked, touching them as if they had started growing fur.

"Nothing's wrong with them," Suzume replied defensively. "Girls love big ears."

"Big—you know what, never mind," Ren said, promising himself to take a good look in a mirror next time he found one. Now, he had one more reason to hate his colleague, the Monkey. "I'm Rooster, by the way."

"Oh, I love birds," Suzume said, clasping her hands.

"Sure you do. Anyway, Bloods are rare, and yet we are the pillars of the Yaseki's mission. Without us, the world is doomed." He enjoyed the look of wonder on his companion's face. That he hated his blessing didn't mean Ren could not enjoy his statue either. Life will take you down, Boar used to say, unless you're the best at it.

"Our power is in our blood, as you might have guessed," Ren went on. "With it, we can seal souls in their shells, which will then be purified by a Heart or some master Mouths. That's the only way to save a Hasontama. They can't exactly be killed, you see."

"They can't?" Suzume asked.

"Well, their bodies can be destroyed. Hands are really good at this, but all it does is release their soul. According to the creature, the corrupted souls can take years or even centuries before they reform and are born again, but it will happen. Killing a Hason-tama without sealing it is the equivalent of breaking the ice of a frozen lake in winter. It works, but eventually, the lake will freeze again. You need the warm light of spring to keep the ice away. That's why Bloods seal corrupted souls to be purified before they are released. Don't get me wrong, destroying their bodies is also a solution, especially in times of crisis, and it's not like I *always* manage to seal a soul."

"You're so amazing," Suzume said. "You're basically saving Japan by yourself."

Ren blushed again; he had not expected that reaction. People usually scoffed at his arrogance, but not Suzume and it was unsettling.

"We're struggling, though," he said. "At the moment, only ten of us are active, and one of those ten was traumatized to the point that he will not leave Ise Jingū. So, really, it's the nine of us against an army of Hasontama, and they seem to grow in number, courtesy of the last hundred years of civil war. That's why the Yaseki prefer Bloods to travel with other members, to keep us safe. But it doesn't always work that way." Ren's thoughts drifted to his previous companions. He'd never been safer than by himself.

"I will keep you safe!" Suzume said. She looked strong, determined, and beautiful, but she also looked too fresh to boast this kind of claim.

"I'm sure you will," Ren replied sarcastically, though she did not seem to hear it. A stronger gush of wind passed between them, making Ren shiver with the sudden cold. The sun was getting low already. "It's about time to go."

"What about the last two?" she asked.

Ren traced their names in the mud hurriedly, *kigami* and *himitsugami*.

"That's going to be a bit disappointing," he said, "but I don't know much about them. The Ki are masters of Energy, but besides enshrining kami, I don't really know what they do. Their power is supposedly so precious that they wear a mask at all times, even within the citadel.

"As for the Secrets, as you might guess, no one speaks of them or what they can do. But I wouldn't waste time thinking about them. I think the founders of the Yaseki just wanted to get to eight and made something up." He shivered again and wondered how she could handle the cold better than him. "Now, if you have more questions, I suggest you keep them until we sit in front of something hot, preferably with noodles in it."

"I think I've learned enough for the day," she replied as Ren climbed over the bank again.

"You'll have much more to learn before we get to Kyōto," Ren said when they reached the road. "But don't you worry, most learning will be done by doing. And it starts tomorrow morning with your first yōkai hunt."

CHAPTER 4
FIRST HUNT

Ren yawned with the rising sun peeking through the hills as the girl hummed a folk song from her village. She would still be singing it if he had allowed it, but it was far too early for this. He had guessed his new companion was an early bird, but even robins don't wake so early or so perky, a point the owner of the inn seemed to agree with as she prepared their breakfast. They went out the door as the first rays of the sun filtered through it, and thirty minutes later, Ren had yet to emerge from his dreams.

He, like most hunters, belonged to the night, and the morning was not his friend, nor were those so intent on ruining it. He passed a heavy hand over his face as Suzume resumed a new chorus, skipping more than walking. She would soon lose her glee, Ren thought.

They had entered the inn early in the evening and ordered two bowls of roasted-pork ramen as soon as Ren's ass touched a stool in the dining room. Matsusaka was a city of respectable size, with a few thousand inhabitants, a trading port, and situated far enough from the main roads of Japan that few conflicts ever reached it. A little haven for the people of Mie Province.

Whenever Ren graced Matsusaka with his presence, he would go to Yoshimoto's Inn for three reasons. First, it was the only inn serving ramen, and this in itself made his choice easy. Second, it was among the cheapest. As Ren explained to Suzume, the Yaseki was far from poor, but money attracted the worst people and some vicious yōkai, so they used it with parsimony. The rest of the trip to Kyōto, he then said, would be spent within temples and shrines or simply in the wild. And third, Old Yoshimoto knew everything happening in Matsusaka and its neighborhood and was willing to respond to Ren's curiosity without wondering why he cared.

But this time, the rumors were poor. As she stirred the broth of pig bones, Old Yoshimoto told them about her neighbor who cheated on his wife with the daughter of his business partner, of the boat that sank in the port the previous week, and of some army marching through the western end of the Tōkaidō Road, but none of this mattered to Ren.

The civil war might have ended, but *daimyo* still liked to show their strength, like monkeys puffing their chests. These were human affairs and did not concern them, anyway. Ren had hoped the boat sinking might be connected to a yōkai, but Old Yoshimoto said the fisherman was a drunk idiot sailing a piece of junk. In the end, the cheating husband was the most interesting story, and Ren went back to his original plan of organizing the hunt the next day on the road.

The next day, he thought, not six hours later.

"Are you always so bubbly?" he asked Suzume when she landed from a jump, marking the end of her song.

"What do you mean?" she asked.

"Never mind, you just answered the question."

"I'm just excited to hunt some yōkai," she said, making a fist and punching the air. It was a terrible punch.

Ren was about to tell her they had to leave the road, but a yawn took him, almost unhinging his lower jaw, so he just pointed at the woods on their left and climbed down the bank toward the path cutting through a bare rice field. There were a few houses scattered between the square fields and a water mill, which turned out to be their destination.

"Do you remember everything I told you yesterday about the gates?" Ren asked as the sound of the paddles hitting the water and the creaking wood became noticeable.

"Most of it, I guess," Suzume replied. Ren invited her to recite her lesson with an open hand, and she adopted a thoughtful pose. "The Mouths pray, the Ears hear the kami, the Eyes see the future—"

"More or less," Ren interrupted.

"The Hearts heal; those are the Four Teachings. Then the Four Blessings are the Hands, like me, give their bodies for kami to use; the Bloods, like you, seal the souls; the Ki, you don't know much about them; and the Secrets, no one talks about them, and they might not even exist."

"Very good," Ren replied, honestly impressed. "And what do we, Hunters, do?"

"We chase corrupted souls, the Hasontama, to either seal their souls for purification or destroy them to prevent them from harming anyone if there is no other choice."

"Well put," Ren said.

The door of the closest shabby house flung open under the push of a toddler, who then stepped outside buck naked. Suzume waved at him, but the boy remained dumbfounded, even as he waved back and a second later stormed back inside to warn his sleeping parents that two strangers were walking through their fields.

"And how do we hunt yōkai?" he asked.

Suzume pondered the question but came up with no answer.

"Just like any other creature, we track them."

They reached the mill just then, and the noise forced him to speak up. The river was shallow and narrow, barely more than a stream, and just enough for the mill to keep on wheeling. Ren removed his sandals and his socks, rolled up his hakama, and invited Suzume to do the same. Then both jumped in the water, and Ren bent over, so close to the paddles that one almost hit him.

"You see this?" he asked, almost shouting, pointing a finger toward the base of a stilt in the water supporting the mill.

"No?" she replied. "What am I supposed to see?"

Ren shoved his hand under the water at the bottom of the stilt. The water was clear and cold. He found what he was looking for in a few seconds and straightened up, proudly showing a green and brown fluffy ball the size of a sparrow's egg.

"Is that a *marimo*?" Suzume asked.

"Not exactly," Ren replied, tossing the ball at the girl. "Smell it."

Suzume obediently lifted the green ball to her nose. "Heaven," she spat as her nose wrinkled and her arm stretched as far as possible. "It smells like—"

"Shit," Ren said. "Kappa shit, to be more specific."

"There are kappa in that river?" Suzume asked.

"Farther up, probably. That's a fresh one. You can drop it, by the way."

The ball plopped into the water and was taken by the stream. Suzume proceeded to wash her hands but would find out that the smell from the excrement of the yōkai was resilient.

"Kappa are mean little buggers," Ren went on as he climbed out of the river and held his hand for Suzume to take. She grabbed it, and Ren pulled her out of the water. They did not put their sandals back on and followed the river barefoot.

"They live in larger rivers, ponds, lakes, creeks, and swamps, never too far from human beings, but never too close either. Their young ones live in groups of five to ten individuals, and their adults mostly live alone."

"Are they dangerous?" Suzume asked. She didn't sound worried, but her grip on the spear tightened. The river was about to enter a thicket, and so were they.

"Every yōkai can be dangerous," Ren answered. "There are basically two types of yōkai. Those who live in cities or close to some human settlements tend to be more cunning than the others and enjoy tricking us more than hunting us. The more you go into the wild, the more savage the yōkai become. Don't misunderstand me, though; the city ones will rip you apart and eat your insides for breakfast. They'll just be a little more methodical about it."

"Which group are the kappa in?"

"A bit of both," Ren replied as he ducked under the first branches of the thicket.

It immediately turned darker, but the sounds of living animals and the stream of the river lightened the mood. The kappa would be farther.

"They can speak and trick us into the water, but they can also be wild in their attacks. If you let them, they will carve your bowels out with their claws, and their beaks are sharp enough to snap fingers from your hands." Suzume gulped, and Ren chuckled. "They can also be friendly from time to time, but don't let it fool you. Eventually, they need meat, and their favorite is that of human children."

"That's awful," the girl commented. "We have to stop them."

"We will," Ren replied.

Already, they had reached the end of the thicket just as the river widened. Farther ahead, it met with a pond, not big enough to be considered a lake, but almost. A perfect ground for young kappa to grow in peace.

"But first," the hunter said, "we need to get you ready." They stopped at the tree line, keeping to the shadows. "Can you call your kami?"

"Call my kami?"

"Can you summon her in your body at will?" Ren asked.

"No," Suzume answered in an obvious manner. "How do I do that?"

"I don't know," Ren replied, shrugging. "All the Hands I met seemed to do it at will. Did it ever take control of you?"

"She did," Suzume replied. There it was again, this sadness that seemed to suddenly cower her gaze away. Ren read guilt in it this time.

"She?" he asked.

"Her name is Sugi," Suzume said. "I call her Sugi-chan."

"Sugi, the spirit of the Sugi tree?" Ren asked, frowning and smiling at the same time. "Did you happen to name her as a child?"

"I did! How did you know?"

"Well, it's... never mind," Ren answered, thinking it was quite obvious. "Wait, did you receive her blessing when you were in danger?" Suzume nodded. "I see. It seems Sugi is acting as your guardian spirit. She will take over your body if you're in danger. We just have to put you in a dangerous situation then."

Ren's grin was far from reassuring, and Suzume did not seem to appreciate the nature of his amusement. He pulled the rosary from his neck and unknotted the bottom part where the string ended in a red tassel. One of the beads slid from the string to his palm, and Ren worked on the knot again, thus reforming the rosary.

"I'm not sure I like this plan," she said.

"Don't worry," Ren said as he pulled his sheathed sword from his belt. "I'll be with you, and I won't be alone." Suzume frowned in confusion, and Ren smirked in response. "You're going to love this."

The hunter dropped his bag on the thicket floor and took a couple of steps out of the shadows. He drew his blade just enough to pass his right thumb over the edge. Suzume gasped when she noticed the pearl of blood. Ren barely felt it anymore.

"*I offer you my prayer and this blood,*" the hunter said, eyes closed, before pressing his thumb on the bead. He then knelt and reverently pushed the red-marked bead into the ground. With a sudden movement, Ren stood and hurried to Suzume's side.

"What—"

"Just wait," Ren said excitedly. "It's going to be awesome."

The earth suddenly shook, prompting the girl to wave her arms for balance. Ren had expected it and lowered his waist just enough to keep his footing. It didn't just shake; it rumbled. Cracks formed by their feet and met where Ren had planted the bead. Then, it all got quiet. Ren did not look away, and his smile did not vanish. The ground by the bead exploded; dirt flew upward, raising a cloud of brown dust.

"Ren?" Suzume asked. He had not even seen her fall on her ass.

"Suzume," Ren said as he helped her back to her feet. "Let me introduce you to *my* guardian and friend, Maki."

A bark echoed throughout the plain, prompting birds to fly away from the closest trees, and as the dust settled, Maki spotted her friend and rushed to his side. Her massive legs could not run fast enough for her taste, even if the hunter stood but a couple of steps away. Ren opened his arms wide and, though he had been ready, puffed when Maki's head bumped into his chest. She knocked him against a tree, and his laughter fed her will to keep rubbing herself against him.

"Maki," he called between two bouts of laughter. "Maki, stop. We were together just two days ago." But Maki would not listen. "Come on, girl, sit."

The lion-dog obeyed, and the ground shook one more time as she sat, tongue lolling and mouth stretched into a smile. She then noticed the girl with the spear, and her smile vanished, soon replaced by a growl that turned Suzume's astonishment into distress.

"Easy, girl," Ren said, putting himself between the guardian spirit and his new companion. "She's a friend, see?" He put his hand over his chest, then moved it toward Suzume's shoulder, who forced a smile back on her face and waved her hand in a friendly manner. Maki seemed to resist the claim and snarled for a few more seconds, going as far as taking a prowling pose.

"Ren?" Suzume asked through her teeth. "If you wanted me to feel in danger, you're succeeding."

"Maki," Ren said in a scolding tone. "Enough."

The lion-dog barked once, and her whole face untensed back to a smile. The hunter held his hand flat to the ground, and Maki lay down with it, putting her face at the same level as his. "Good girl," he said, slowly advancing his hand to her muzzle. She closed her eyes when he started scratching the top of her snout, and Suzume breathed at last.

"Come closer," he whispered above his shoulder.

Suzume took a shy step, then another, careful to keep her spear behind her back. "Should I pet her too?"

"Not if you want to keep your hand," Ren replied. "She's pure energy. You'd burn yourself. Only those with the Blood can touch her."

"What is she?" Suzume asked when she reached Ren's level. Maki had yet to open her brilliant golden eyes again.

"She's a *komainu*, a lion-dog. Easy, Maki, easy," Ren told his friend when she stiffened at the sight of the girl. "Suzume is with us. We like her, all right? You protect her, too. Suzume, come a little closer if you want. Just don't touch her fur. It's all right; if she wanted to bite you, she would have by now."

"That's reassuring," Suzume said as she slid another step forward. "Is she a kami?"

"She's a *shinshi*," Ren said. "A messenger of the kami and a guardian of their shrines. You've probably seen their statues in front of halls."

"Amazing," Suzume said.

Everything was amazing to Suzume, Ren thought, something he found refreshing. After a few years within the Yaseki, the world had turned unsurprising, almost dull. It was good to see it through the eyes of an unspoiled hunter.

"Yesterday, I told you Bloods can seal souls, but we can also invoke shinshi with our blood. Usually, I need a stone guardian from a shrine to call them, but thanks to Osamu's beads, I can do the same from anywhere, at least with Maki and her siblings, with whom I have shared an oath."

"She's going to stay with us?" Suzume asked, finally relaxing in the presence of the lion-dog. Maki sat back up when Ren removed his hand, now seemingly unbothered by the girl's presence.

"Unfortunately, no," Ren answered. "She'll return home as soon as I sleep. I'll need to use another bead to call her again. Maki? Ready to hunt some kappa?" The guardian barked, standing at once. "Maki will find the kappa and sniff them out. All you have to do is follow me and stay behind. You might be scared, but you *have to* stay with me, understood?"

"Yes," Suzume replied hesitantly.

"And unsheathe your spear. You might need it. Ready, Maki?"

Suzume left the soft cover of her spear by their bags. She came to Ren's side, and the hunter could see the mixture of emotions drawing on her young face. He had been the same not so long ago.

"Just follow my lead and try to feel Sugi's presence."

She nodded but did not shine with confidence.

They walked closer to the pond, then around it. Ren counted two more streams flowing in or out of the pond, but none was bigger than the first one. "Maki, you start from here," he said before leaving the lion-dog where he had pointed and returning toward the original stream.

Suzume never walked farther than a step from Ren, her spear held with two hands close to her chest. They walked a little away from the pond, then Ren raised his fist. On the other side of the water, Maki lowered her stance and gathered her tongue in her mouth.

"Ready?" he asked Suzume.

"No?" she said.

Ren smiled and dropped his arm.

The lion-dog leaped from a dead start. Her huge yet graceful body seemed to hang in the air before she ultimately descended and splashed right in the center of the pond. A wall of water rose around her. Steam immediately started fuming. Maki then thrashed around like a dog searching for her toy, except that her face had turned feral. Thick ripples formed and hit the outline of the pond like waves crashing against the cliff.

"Any second now," Ren said to himself. He lowered his stance to a crouch. Suzume followed his lead, and both stood no higher than the tall grass of the plain.

The lion-dog suddenly straightened up and froze, her muzzle pointed toward the edge of the pond. She barked and ran after whatever caught her attention. A shriek pierced the sky as if a crow and a toad had screamed at the same time. Then, a bunch of similar calls answered it, and the pond came to life.

The kappa, six of them, jumped out in as many directions. The girl gasped. One of them had jumped in the river and was coming their way. It was fast, so fast that it seemed to run on the water. So fast that all the girl would see was a green-blue shape, the size of a regular dog, with a turtle shell on its back.

"Now!" Ren shouted as he left the cover of the grass and leaped toward the moving shape.

The beast shrieked in surprise and meant to alter its course, but this only slowed it down, and Ren smacked his scabbard in the kappa's face, sending it reeling backward in a jet of blood. The hunter did not let it go. The kappa was on its feet faster than Ren had expected and, this time, met the attack, jumping at him with its claws and beak wide open.

The claws caught nothing, and the beak closed on the scabbard as Ren slammed it in the yōkai's mouth. In the same movement, he pushed the kappa against the bank of the river and stabbed it through the shoulder, pinning the creature to the earth on its back. It shrieked and moaned, and its hands moved to the sword. Blood poured on the blade as the kappa tried to remove it, but Ren was stronger, and the creature soon gave up with a last moan of despair.

The hunter then remembered the girl. Panic hit him for a heartbeat before he saw her right behind him, drenched up to the waist, still clutching the spear against her chest. She looked petrified at the sight of the kappa.

"Good," Ren said between two heavy breaths. The chase had been short but energetic. "You followed. Now," he went on but stopped to catch his breath again. "Now I will let it go, and it will probably attack you. Just open yourself to your kami and kill it."

"No," the girl said in a panic. "No, I can't."

"Yes, you can," Ren replied patiently. "It's a young one, it's wounded, and I'm right here."

"No," she repeated. "I can't kill it. I can't—it's just a child."

Ren followed her gaze and observed the kappa. Like any of its kind, it looked like the mixed breed of a frog and a turtle, shorter than both of them and afraid. Its face was crisped with fear and pain, and its eyes were full of terror. It could not speak yet, but it would beg if it could. Of course, Ren understood the girl would take pity on it. Even he felt sorry for the creature. Its chest rose frantically, and it kept looking from him to her with a glint of hope for not being dead yet. There was not even a trace of hatred on this face, just fear.

"Suzume," Ren said, "this is a yōkai. We have to kill it."

"I can't," the girl said right away, shaking her head.

"Suzume!" Ren barked, taking her attention away from the child kappa. "Don't look at it like this. It's a monster. It will grow. Another year and it will start hunting, and what do you think it will hunt? Do you remember the boy we saw earlier? This," he said, pointing his scabbard at the beast, "will tear that boy apart. And it will be your fault."

Tears swelled at the corners of her eyes and soon fell in two lines, reaching the sides of her chin. They did not stop Ren. He had to push her to do it.

"You have to kill it," he went on. "And you know what, you're not even killing it. You're just liberating its soul so that we can purify it. You're doing this thing a favor."

"I know," she said, sobbing. "I know, but I can't. Ren, it's just a child."

"Fine!" Ren barked. "If you don't want to reimburse your debt, it's up to you."

He pulled the sword from the kappa, who slid into the water and covered its wound with its webbed hand. It looked shocked to be alive and observed the two humans with apprehension. Ren knew it would either try to flee or attack one of them, and since *he* had hurt it, the kappa would most likely come after the girl. He counted on it, and the sword in his hand was ready to draw more blood.

The young yōkai observed the young man, then the girl standing a step behind him, and stopped on her. Its face wrinkled in a snarl, and its beak seemed to clench as if the creature readied itself for action. Fear and confusion gave way to hatred, and the kappa tensed, about to pounce on the girl.

Ren had been ready, and his grip on the sword tightened. But before he could move, the kappa rocked brutally against the riverbank, where it gasped in pain. The hunter had not even seen the spear strike, but there it was, jutting from the beast's stomach, held from the girl's outstretched arm. The kappa died on it. Its head lolled, drooling brown blood over the pole.

"I didn't think you had it in—" Ren started saying as the cross-blade sucked out of the yōkai's body, leaving a bloody gap as big as a hand. "—you." Ren spoke the last word slowly, and whatever else he might have said got stuck in his throat.

The girl facing him was no longer Suzume. It was the same body, the same clothes, the same freckles, but everything else belonged to another being, starting with the violence in her eyes. They shone with a green glint, and her smile, usually so light-hearted, turned into a vicious smirk at the sight of the kappa slowly sliding into the ground.

The girl seemed to stand straighter and taller, and her grip on the spear was both lighter and more assured. She shook the blood from the blade in one expert strike, unbothered that most of it landed on Ren's shirt. In fact, she looked as if she had not noticed him. Ren had met enough spiritual beings to develop a sense of their nature, and this one, he felt, was strong. Strong and dangerous.

"Sugi?" he asked.

Her green eyes darted from her victim to him. They held no friendship. Slowly, very slowly, he drove his sword back into its scabbard.

"I'm a friend of your host," he said as he lowered himself and dropped the blade against the river bank. "See? I mean you no harm." Ren held his hands palms forward but received no reaction. "You are scaring me a little right now, and you are drinking Suzume's energy away, so I'm going to need you to let go of the spear and liberate her, all right?"

He gently took a step in her direction, left hand forward to grab the pole just behind its cross-blade. But a few inches from it, the girl stepped back and drew her arm, ready to strike. Ren read the bloodlust in her green eyes and swallowed hard.

"Shit," he said.

She kicked the ground and bolted at him, shouting. But before the spear could harm him, a great shape slammed into the girl and sent her rolling in the river. Her arm was knocked against a rock, and she lost her grip on the spear.

"Maki, stop!" Ren shouted, for the lion-dog was rushing after the inert body of Suzume to pursue the attack. She stopped on his command but growled threateningly.

After a moment of hesitation, Ren grabbed the spear and tossed it out of the water, then knelt to the girl's side and rolled her the other way. She was awake and immediately hid behind her hands, her body shaking with sobs.

"What have I done again?" she asked, voice trembling and tears pouring between her fingers.

"Again?" Ren asked.

CHAPTER 5
SPIRIT OF THE REDWOOD

It was a cold night, cold enough to freeze the lake over, cold enough to keep the dogs inside, and the hearth red. Yet it was the middle of it when the girl flung the door of her home open and braved the wind, dressed with nothing more than an untied kimono worn for too many years. Barefoot, hair unbound, she ran against the howling wind through the village, never looking back out of fear. Her eyes prickled with tears, yet she ran. The lake, she hoped, would mean salvation, as it so often had in the past few years.

Snowflakes flashed in front of her, carried too young to the ground by an unrelenting wind, a curtain that nearly prevented the girl from spotting the path. She knew it so well that she could have found it with her eyes closed, but her panic made her doubt the very air she breathed.

The path stretched from the lake's pier to the small island in the middle of the lake, where stood the mightiest redwood tree to be found on Shikoku. Thousands, tens of thousands, of people had trampled on the path over the generations, leaving nothing more than a smooth line of earth so narrow that one had to walk with one foot in front of the other to stay on it.

"Suzume!" a man's voice boomed above the wind. An angry voice. A sake-filled voice.

The girl looked above her shoulder but saw no one through the white curtain. Her father had braved the wind and the cold, too, and would be a few seconds behind. She stepped on the path. Her bottom lip shivered with fear, and she mumbled a prayer for her mother to help. The path was slippery, but her feet carried her through.

Her father, in his current state, would not manage, even though the path was no more than fifty steps long and even though the lake reached no higher than his shoulders at most. His drunken mind would not let him cross. It had stopped him before; it would again.

She scurried under the red torii marking the entrance of the island, out of breath, feet numb from the cold. Snow powdered less intently here; their path shielded by the sacred redwood tree's branches. Her mother used to say the tree watched over the people of Sugimoto, even when afar. She used to come here with Suzume, for as long as the girl remembered, to offer tangerines to the kami.

In front of the tree, the folks of Sugimoto had built a small shrine, no bigger than a shed, where they placed the treasure of the clan as a shintai for the kami. Suzume pictured the kami as a beautiful, strong, and brave woman, like her mother, and called her Sugi. Sugi-chan, the spirit of the redwood.

"Sugi-chan," Suzume said after she bowed and clapped her hands twice. "Please, keep him away. Please—"

"Suzume!" her father yelled from across the lake.

"Please, don't let him take me." She bowed once more, but nothing happened. Nothing ever did.

"Suzu—" her father called, slipping halfway through her name.

Suzume held her breath, hoping that his fall would snuff the last of his motivation. But when the wind dropped for the time of a heartbeat, freezing the flakes in the air, she saw him getting back up. The frozen lake had kept him from the water, and her father kept coming.

"No," she whispered.

"*Suzume, come back! Come back, damn it! I'm your father, and you will obey!*"

"No," she whispered again.

She had thought to find refuge on the island but was now trapped. There was nowhere to run. Desperation pushed her back against the small shrine. The doors parted from each other a little. It wasn't locked. It was always locked, but not tonight. Before she could think about it, she slipped inside. Disturbing a kami was blasphemy, but what would the kami do that could be worse than her father?

She could barely move inside the shrine, let alone stand. The hollowed walls kept the snow away but not the sound, so she made herself quiet. Feeling with her hands, she recognized a small table, an altar, she understood. A pole stood upright in front of it, thick as a broom but taller.

"Come here, you brat!" her father barked. She guessed he was now on the island and closed her eyes.

He had once been a good man. Her mother promised he had once been good before the war. Sometimes, the girl remembered the man who used to carry her with pride in the village, and those faint memories gave her courage through the bad nights. But something had broken in her on that windy, snowy night, and she could no longer take it.

"Suzume!" he called before tripping against the doors of the shrine.

She gasped with horror when his silhouette blocked her sight and covered her mouth with her hands, but too late. He put his face against the squared holes and searched through the darkness of the hall for her. She felt his eye dropping on her and whimpered. The doors flew open, and she screamed.

"There you are," he said, victory in his voice. He grabbed her by the ankle and pulled. She screamed harder. She kicked, cried, and kicked again, but her father was so strong. He yanked on her leg with his dirty fingers, and she grabbed the first thing she could to stay away from him. A pole, no thicker than a broom, firmly set in the shrine.

"Sugi-chan!" she yelled in despair.

The light went from her sight, the noise, too. It was peaceful and warm, like her mother's chest when she cradled her to sleep.

When she opened her eyes again, the snow was gone, the night too. It was a new dawn stirring Sugimoto from sleep. Already, folks were gathering in front of the lake. Suzume wondered why so many stood in one place and why they were all looking in her direction.

Her father was by her side, too. Some of him, at least. His hand was still wrapped around her ankle, but the arm was no longer attached to the body, and his blood covered the ground from the shrine to the torii.

Suzume screamed for help.

血

Ren gave Suzume enough time to gather herself or for a chance to say more, though he guessed nothing else needed to be said. The quiet flame of the fire he'd built swayed between them, its light giving life to her otherwise unmoving body. She kept her eyes down, a knee up, gathered against her chest by her arms. The spear lay on the ground by her side. She had refused to carry it, but Ren sensed she wanted it close to her, nonetheless.

They had made little progress after the hunt. Ren had originally hoped to reach the city of Nabari and spend the night in Sekita Shrine, but he guessed they had done a little less than half of the journey. If time hadn't been an issue, he would have hunted the rest of the kappa, but as it was, Ren could only pray they had been scared from the region for good.

Maki had not left the girl from her eyes as they journeyed through hills and meadows, and even now, she wouldn't let Ren part far from her paws. Suzume, however, refused Ren's food as well as his ointment to soothe the bruise on her arm from Maki's rescue. And after she told her story, Ren understood why.

"I'm sorry any of this happened to you," he said. Not knowing what to do with himself, Ren picked up a twig and poked the fire, sending sparks to die in the night air. "And I'm sorry I made you hunt."

"It's not your fault," she said, though her voice was muffled by her arms. "It's all mine."

Ren pretended not to see the tears. Maki, lying with her head on her legs, whimpered, so Ren patted her head. She seemed to sympathize with the girl.

"If Osamu had told me—"

"I asked him not to," she said.

"Why?" he gently asked. "I would have treated you differently. I... I... I would have taken it slower."

"Exactly," Suzume replied. "You would have looked at me the way you are doing now, but I wanted to forget. That's all I want." Her sob shook her body despite her best efforts to resist them.

Ren shared a sorry look with Maki. The lion-dog wanted to comfort the girl; Ren could feel it, and it was unfair that she couldn't, for surely it would help more than anything he could do, and that too was unfair. What on earth was Osamu thinking, trusting the girl to him?

"Listen," Ren said, "it's maybe not what you want to hear, but I got to tell you, Sugi is a powerful kami. And she obviously cares about you. I would say that as long as you stay with her, you have nothing to fear from anyone."

Suzume sniffed some snot back, using the back of her sleeve to wipe the rest, behaving as if she hadn't heard the hunter. Maki twisted her head in a confused way when Ren looked at her.

"All I'm saying is that with proper training, the two of you will make a formidable team."

"Maybe," Suzume replied faintly.

"And with some help, you might even learn to control Sugi's... temper," Ren said. All day long, he had pondered on the best way to help Suzume with her training. He'd reached the conclusion that no matter what, he wasn't the man for this task, and now that he knew her secret, he was even more certain of it.

"What do you mean?" she asked, finally raising her head.

The flames gleamed in those two gentle eyes, and Ren almost changed his mind. Then he remembered how they had glowed green and the vicious smirk. "I'm taking you to a friend in Nara," he said. "She will know how to help you. And she'll keep you safe while you train."

New tears pearled in Suzume's eyes, but she wiped them as soon as they bloomed. "Is Shirakawa-sama going to be all right with this?" she asked.

"Don't worry about him. Once I complete my mission, he'll be fine with anything." Ren had tried to sound joyful, but it landed flat, and the girl looked away.

"I understand," she said before lying down and rolling over, using her bag as a pillow and the small fire as her blanket.

Ren guessed she would not sleep anytime soon but needed to be by herself. He let himself slide to a lying position, too. Maki joined him right away and dropped her head on his chest. She still looked sorry.

"Don't worry," he whispered. "Hotaru-san will know what to do. She always knows what to do." The lion-dog yawned on those words, which prompted Ren to do the same. Silence fell on their makeshift camp, and Ren felt the weight of the lion-dog vanish from his chest as he fell asleep.

CHAPTER 6
DEER AND FIREFLIES

They pushed through a hard day of walking the wilderness and reached the forest protecting the eastern side of the old capital of Nara late in the afternoon. They didn't speak much during the journey, and the only thing resembling a conversation happened when Suzume inquired about the destination and if it was a detour for Ren's mission. The hunter told her it wasn't, though it wasn't the path he had meant to follow. He would have preferred to travel through the less populated Iga, a province that also provided better hunting, though he didn't tell her the latter part.

The road through Nara was just as good, he had explained, and in this, he was honest, though, at this time of the year, it tended to be busy. Which was why they never entered the city and melted into the forest as soon as possible.

They'd barely stepped into it, with the sun vanishing on their left, when a small herd of deer stepped closer. For once, Ren was glad for Maki's absence. This could have turned ugly. Suzume beamed with joy when the youngest of them left its mother's underbelly to lick her fingers. It tightened Ren's heart when she looked up at him with those warm eyes she had lost after the kappa incident. He would miss her.

"Nara's deer are sacred," he said when he returned a bow from the buck of the herd. At this time of the year, they had yet to grow antlers and would not harm them by mistake. "No one hunts them, so they're not afraid of us."

"My mother told me about them," Suzume said between two giggles. "I've always wanted to see the *shika* of Nara." This was good, Ren told himself. She wouldn't mind staying here. This place looked like her. Maybe it was part of the kami's plan.

Fondling through his bag, Ren picked up the two antlers he had acquired at the citadel. Kappa were afraid of deer antlers, and the hunter had thought to use them for the girl's training. He didn't need them anymore.

"*Oh, guardians of the forest. I return this blessing to you with my gratitude.*" With care, he dropped them on the ground at the buck's feet. The deer smelled them, then bowed again, thus accepting the gift. Suzume was still smiling at him when he patted the buck's head.

"That was kotodama?' she asked. "The power of words?"

"My poor attempt at it," he replied.

"It was beautiful," she said. The fawn bowed to get her attention and succeeded. *If I let them*, Ren thought, *this could go on all night.*

"We need to go. But you can see them again tomorrow."

It was getting darker, but just like in Ise Jingū, the forest harbored no ill will in Nara, and with a light heart, they walked through it. Farther west, a temple glowed brighter with sudden flames. Suzume gasped, but Ren told her this was a part of the Omizutori festival held in the secondary hall of Tōdai-ji, the great Buddhist temple of Nara.

For two weeks, every evening, the monks would purify and bless the visitors with the embers of great, burning torches. Everything in Nara was about its temples, especially during Omizutori. So much so that people often forgot the shrine within the forest, Kasuga Taisha, the place from where kami protected the ancient capital.

Suzume could not decide where to look as they climbed the stairs leading to Kasuga. Ren had behaved as such on his first visit. Groups of deer gathered on the sides of the stairs, accompanying the two hunters with bows and big, dark eyes reflecting the moon. Hundreds of stone lanterns gathered moss, some of them flickering with a feeble, reassuring light. The bells from the Buddhist temples announced the end of the fire ceremony, and soon, Ren spotted the entrance of Kasuga.

By day, it would appear bright red, green, and white. A single structure, low and long, unique in its architecture, both more ostentatious and yet more humble than Ise Jingū. The wisteria tree welcoming the visitors would soon bloom, and Ren thought Suzume would find it amazing. She was admiring the vault of branches illuminated by the bronze lanterns of the shrine when a voice hailed them.

"Ren Fudō. Why do you always arrive with the moon?" the woman asked, standing on top of the five stairs leading to the shrine proper. Her face glowed with the light of the tobacco burning at the end of a long pipe, revealing a wise, tired face.

"My apologies, Hotaru-san," Ren replied, bowing with a respect he showed to few people, if any at all, besides the old woman. Though old was not the most fitting description for the priestess of Kasuga Taisha.

She could not have been over sixty, and her graceful posture belonged more to a young woman than an elder. Dark bags hung under her eyes, and strands of gray hair accompanied the more stubborn black ones, but her wrinkles were few, and her eyes strong and willful. She was a hard woman but a kind soul, and

Ren esteemed her. "We need your help and could not push our visit to the morrow."

"We?" she asked, taking the first step down. "And who are you?"

Suzume recoiled as the priestess approached and kept her head low. They wore the same clothes, but could not look more different. Suzume wore them as a girl wearing her mother's garments, not that it didn't suit her, but Hotaru looked like the style had been created for her.

"My name is Suzume, from Sugimoto. I am a... traveling companion of Ren."

"A Hand, are you not?" Hotaru asked as she breathed out a cloud of tobacco that made Suzume cough.

"Yes," she replied, taking another bow.

"Told you she was good," Ren whispered to the girl.

"Another of Osamu's lost puppies," the woman said. "I swear, if he keeps sending me his lost causes, I'll start billing him." She tapped the back of the pipe and dropped the ball of tobacco, which she pressed on with the sole of her foot.

"Be my guest," Ren replied. "And then some more for me."

"Good boy," Hotaru said with a smirk before caressing his cheek with long, nimble fingers.

"But this time, we don't come from him," Ren said. "We were supposed to head straight to Kyōto."

"Of course, you come from him, sweetheart," she said, patting the cheek the way she would a child. "You just didn't know. What with his famed *eyes* and everything, believe me, he knew." She was right, and it hit him right in the stomach not to have thought so himself.

"Son of a—"

"Hey," Hotaru interrupted, snapping her fingers. "No swearing in my shrine. Not even to curse that old fart."

Suzume snorted a laugh. "So sorry," she said, and even through the dim light, Ren saw her blush.

Hotaru's smirk grew to a grin. "Come on then, Suzume from Sugimoto. Let's see what your kami has to say." She did not wait for a response and headed back upstairs while Ren and Suzume picked up their bags.

"How did she know?" The girl asked in a whisper.

"She's *really* good," the hunter replied.

Ren was fascinated by Kasuga Taisha. In many regards, it was one of the five most important shrines in Japan, yet it could all be visited in twenty minutes. Hotaru liked to pretend none harbored as many treasures, both sacred and secular, as Kasuga, but for the main part, it was one building hosting four kami, and that was it.

Within a few seconds, they reached the second gate. Then they stepped into a worshipping hall where the priestess had prepared tea, incense, and branches of *sakaki* to prepare the offerings for the next day. She had not been expecting anyone and sat back on the tatami behind the low table, where she invited the two hunters to sit on either side of it.

"Usually, no one is allowed here with blades," she said as her fingers worked strips of white paper into the branch of the *tamagushi* offering, "but I guess you need to keep yours for what's about to happen." She looked up to Suzume, who seemed indeed confused about her spear. "You, on the other hand," she told Ren, who was about to sit, "will give me the pleasure of leaving your cursed sword outside."

The young man sighed and walked to the door, against which he dropped his wakizashi. By the time he sat across Suzume, the girl was already pouring tea in three cups taken from a tray tucked under the table.

"Go ahead, tell me," Hotaru said, keeping the cold pipe between her teeth and working on another branch. This time, she tied bands of straw to it.

"Well, yesterday—"

"Not you," Hotaru snapped. "That's her kami. She speaks. Go on, then, we don't have all night."

Suzume looked at Ren like a beacon calling for help, but the hunter had nothing more to offer than an encouraging head tilt. "The redwood spirit of my village lives in this spear," Suzume said. "And has chosen me as her... host."

"*Humph,* chosen..." Hotaru said to herself, chuckling. "You called for her, didn't you?

"Well, yes, but—"

"Sorry, sweetheart, go ahead. What's wrong with her?"

"She is... violent."

"You don't say?" Hotaru asked. So far, she had yet to look at the girl and kept working frantically on her offerings. "A violent kami. What's next? A feathery bird? What a mysterious story so far. She kills a little fast, I assume, and without trying to separate foes from friends?"

"Tried to kill me," Ren commented.

"Who could blame her?" Hotaru asked.

"I don't want to hurt anyone," Suzume said, tears threatening to return.

"It wasn't you," Ren said defensively as Suzume hid her shame with the cup, from which she drank a long sip of tea.

"What on earth are you talking about, boy?" Hotaru said, slapping the hand he had put on the table, which also prevented him from picking up his cup. "It is absolutely her. Don't look at me like this; she has issues to resolve. Listen, sweetheart," she said, turning to Suzume. "I don't know what kind of idiocy this fool has taught you, but you are more than just a vessel. You're a catalyst. Do you understand the difference?"

Suzume shook her head. Ren was glad the question had not been asked to him and made himself discreet despite the insult.

"It means the kami adapts to you. Kami are not made for

human bodies. They tend to be overwhelmed by their host's emotions."

"But I don't want to harm Ren," Suzume said defensively, looking from the priestess to the hunter.

"Somehow you do, though," Hotaru replied. "Maybe not him directly, but would you have any reason to hate men in general or simply ugly ones, maybe?"

"Hey," Ren snapped. "Let's keep it civil."

"Look, sweetheart. I can see you're a good kid," Hotaru went on, "but your guardian kami doesn't know up from down and black from white when she steps in. You either need to learn to communicate with her, or you need to resolve your inner conflicts. Ideally both. Until then, you and her will be a danger to anyone around you."

"Can you help me?" Suzume asked, lips shivering.

"I don't know, my little sparrow," Hotaru replied, putting her other hand on the girl's wrist. "But we'll soon find out."

Suzume tilted her head in confusion, then frowned. Ren noticed small beads of sweat pearling on her forehead, and her chest began heaving with short breaths. She held the side of the table with both hands to avoid falling and looked at Ren with the same horror as when facing the wounded kappa.

"What did you do?" Ren asked the priestess, who was quietly resuming the assembly of her unfinished offering.

"I gave her some of my tea, that is all," Hotaru replied.

Suzume struggled to breathe. She meant to stand but could not find the energy to move her legs.

"Suzume, listen to me," the priestess went on. "You have nothing to worry about. You drank some tea spiked with mushrooms. Your heartbeat is rising, your mind is tunneling, but you are fine. Your body thinks it's in danger and will send a signal to your kami. Just breathe a little and grab your spear. I'll talk to the redwood kami."

"Hotaru-san, what are you doing?" Ren asked, lifting one knee.

"Sit back down," Hotaru snapped. "If the kami sees you as a threat, she'll kill us both. Sit, stay quiet, and maybe we'll manage not to ruin my hall with your blood."

Suzume, taken by hiccup-looking spasms, looked up at Ren, and the hunter almost stood to help her. This is not the kind of help he had wanted her to receive. She would never trust him again.

The priestess seemed to understand the source of his angst, of both their angst. "Suzume, look at me," she said. "I cannot force you to calm down, not even with my kotodama. It needs to come from you; it needs to be sincere. But I will use all my powers to protect Ren while we speak with your kami; you have my word."

Ren realized he was the reason for Suzume's resistance. Reacting as he had made her nervous. So he pushed all his anxiety down, as he had been trained to, and sat back in perfect *seiza* position. He pictured roots tying him from the waist down to the earth under the hall and letting the distress travel through the roots to vanish into the ground.

Empty of worries, he smiled at Suzume and told her in his heart that everything would be fine. She seemed to tremble less violently, nodded back, and closed her eyes. Her hand moved to the pole of her spear, and when she found it, the whole room suddenly felt heavier.

Ren tried to prevent his angst from resurfacing, but the green eyes looking back at him destroyed his faint chance, and he soon wished his blade was by his side.

Sugi lifted her knee while staring at the young man, hatred turning her face into a snarl. She was about to attack.

"Sit," Hotaru commanded.

The order had been given to the kami, who seemed to fight it, but Hotaru's kotodama was so strong that even Ren obeyed. Sugi growled at the old woman, powerless for a moment. Her hand lifted the spear with pain, as if it weighed more than usual, and readied to strike the priestess down. Hotaru's face turned strong as steel; she was about to use all her power.

"You will sit and listen," she said. Sugi's arm dropped. She growled in frustration. Ren was holding his breath.

The priestess then held the branch of sakaki on which she had tied the white strips of paper, turned it upside down, and offered it to the furious kami. She bowed her head, the power of her words faded away, and her voice came in a graceful tone. "*I humbly approach the kami in prayer and present this offering with a sincere heart.*"

Her words came with an impeccable rhythm, molded by decades of praying to the spirits. But Hotaru was taking great risks. Should she fail to keep the honesty of her words pure, the prayer would fail, and the kami would reject the offering. What would happen next, Ren preferred not to think about.

"*I beseech the kami to accept this offering and offer my gratitude for the kami's teaching.*"

Sugi seemed to hesitate and once again looked over the table at Ren, murder in her eyes. She then snatched the branch with an air of regret and sat back.

Ren feared a trap, but Hotaru was committed. She drew a leg backward, then the other, and kowtowed until her forehead touched her hands flat on the tatami. "Psst," she hissed, looking at Ren from the corner of her left eye.

Ren understood he was to imitate her, and while his mind screamed not to do it, he lowered his head and offered his skull for the taking. But nothing happened, and after a few seconds that felt like hours, Hotaru thanked the kami and sat back.

"What now?" Ren asked in a whisper.

"Kami-sama," Hotaru said, hands on her thighs, just above the knees, "may we speak?"

Sugi opened her mouth, but no word came out. At least none

that Ren could hear. Judging from her nodding, Hotaru could, but contrary to him, she had mastered the hogami. The kami seemed agitated and stabbed a finger toward Ren, then stopped speaking.

"What did she say?" Ren asked.

"That we can speak. As long as you do not. So shut up and let me do the talking. Kami-sama," Hotaru said, "why did you attack this young man?"

Sugi spoke again. And again, Ren could not distinguish a word. There was a faint ringing, like the whistle tuned for the ears of dogs alone. It was disturbing, yet Hotaru did not seem alarmed by the sharp gestures of the kami nor by her silent words.

"She says, 'Men are Suzume's enemies, yōkai are Suzume's enemies, big lion-dog is Suzume's enemy.' That's going to be difficult. Now she says that you tried to touch her. Really, Ren? I thought better of you."

Not like that! Ren thought and meant through his frown.

"Kami-sama," the priestess said, "does Suzume think of Ren as an enemy?"

Sugi did not answer right away. She seemed to search through her memory and shook her head.

" 'Ren is a friend,' " Hotaru voiced, " 'but also a man. We do not trust him.' Sorry, my boy, that must hurt. 'Ren wanted Suzume to hurt... a kappa? But Suzume hates hurting others. If Ren makes Suzume suffer again, we will cut his—' I'm not voicing that. Kami-sama, does Suzume want to help Ren, or would she prefer to stay here?"

Sugi returned her attention to the young man. Suzume might think of him as a friend, Ren told himself, but the kami clearly didn't. She spoke but kept looking at him with vehemence.

" 'She wants to help,' " Hotaru said. " 'But Ren is taking her toward danger. I refuse. He said she would die.' Ren, how dumb are you?"

"Kami-sama," Ren said.

Hotaru's tongue clicked her mouth, and Sugi hammered her fist on the table, which broke under the impact.

"Ren," Hotaru called. "Shut up."

But Ren shook his head. "Sugi," he said. "I cannot take back what I said. But I can promise I will do everything in my power to protect Suzume." His eyes went up as he spoke, following the face of the kami who stood up. He remained sitting and dropped his gaze when she lowered the tip of the spear toward his head.

"*I humbly speak to the kami of Sugimoto's redwood,*" he said, finding the quiet place in his mind, "*and offer my prayer with a sincere heart. May the kami strike me down if she perceives my words to be false.*" He wished he had given more time to the mastery of his kotodama, but it was too late for regret. Honesty alone could save him. "*I vow to protect Suzume with my life and to never lay a finger on her with ill purpose. I beseech the kami to hear my words and judge my honesty in them.*"

He waited for a long time, at least long to him. The tip of the spear pressed on the top of his skull, then Sugi let it slide down his forehead and along the bridge of his nose. It stopped by his lower lip, and Ren closed his eyes. He thought of his mother. Then the tension vanished, and he heard a thump. Suzume was lying flat across the broken table, spear out of her hand.

"Suzume," he called, getting to his feet.

"Calm down," Hotaru said. She checked the girl's pulse. "She's out. The kami took all her energy but left before it was too late. I'm too old for that crap," the priestess went on, patting the lower part of her back.

The hunter knelt at the girl's side and almost rolled her on her back, then remembered Suzume's story and instead took the spear. He went to drop it next to his sword, far from the girl. Hotaru was filling her pipe when Ren sat back by the broken table.

"That was good what you said," she said, twisting her hips so

90

that she could light up the tip of her pipe on the flame of a lamp from the altar. "Though, with a promise like this, you'll never get a chance to get into those pants."

"Hotaru-san," Ren barked. "That wasn't my intention." He had sounded more defensive than intended, and the priestess chuckled.

"No? Too bad for you," she said, pulling the first breath of tobacco. "She's cute. Not that you'd get a chance, of course."

She was cute, Ren agreed to himself, but this was not the reason why he wanted to help her. Or so he told himself. Suzume was just pure and undeserving of her fate, just as he had been, though in very different ways. He wanted to protect her from the ugliness of the world, and maybe he understood Sugi a little. This shrine, he thought, would serve such a purpose.

"You will take her then?" he asked.

"Me?" the priestess asked. "You heard the kami; Suzume wants to help you. You take her."

"I can't take her," Ren replied, hand on his chest. "She'll be in danger with me, and this lunatic kami will resurface. She needs a quiet place."

"Ren," Hotaru said after another puff. "You don't get to speak for her. She said she wanted to stay with you. I reject your request for asylum."

Ren sighed and was about to curse. He bit the inside of his cheek instead.

"It will be dangerous for both of you, though, I grant you that," the priestess went on, looking at the sleeping girl with sorry eyes. "So much anger in her."

"Right? Even for a kami."

"Not the kami, you fool, the girl."

"Suzume?" he asked. He knew she was in pain and that her heart must be full of sadness. But anger, he had seen none.

"Of course she's angry. She hides it behind a smile, but she's resentful, bitter. If she died now, she'd turn into a *yūrei*, a vengeful ghost. She would hurt, and because she's a sweet girl, she would hate herself for it. Her hate would make her stronger, and she'd kill again, and so on until the Yaseki took care of her spirit."

"And you want me to take her. I'm on a mission for Amaterasu, for heaven's sake. Who knows what I'm going to face?"

"That's why she needs to heal fast, and you will help her," Hotaru replied.

"How?" he all but shouted.

"Honestly, I don't know. This is a human problem before it is a spiritual one." Hotaru searched around her for a place to drop the used ball of tobacco but found none. She shrugged and tapped on her pipe so the tobacco fell at the center of the broken table. "But if someone can, it's you."

"What on earth are you saying, Hotaru-san?" the hunter replied, shaking his head. "I'm no Heart. I'm not even good enough with kotodama to keep her from harming me."

"Your kotodama isn't that weak," Hotaru said, "you will find the words. And you are no Heart, but you have a good one. The girl doesn't need your pity, and she certainly doesn't need prayers. She needs an honest, sincere friend. A straight arrow to pierce the darkness and rekindle her faith in people. And I know no straighter arrow than you, my dear boy." She patted his cheek as she had before, and Ren suddenly felt powerless. "In fact," she went on, removing her hand, "I'm betting this is why Osamu entrusted her to you. And for once, I can only agree with the old goat. How is he, by the way?"

"Who? Osamu?" Ren asked, taken aback by the change in the conversation. "Same as usual, I guess. Still talks of dark times to come while slapping my face with his damn scepter."

"How does he look?" she then asked. "Got a little fatter? Is he seeing someone?"

"Heaven and earth, I don't know," Ren answered, frowning. "Go check on him if you're so curious."

"I bet he got fatter," she mumbled to herself. "Now, for the girl. I have some ideas that might help you both. Call it a training regimen. It won't solve her problems, but she should be able to learn how to cohabit with her kami a little better. She'll need a lot of practice, though. If she faints out like this after just a few seconds, she'll be of no use to you."

"Thank you, Hotaru-san," Ren said, finally feeling like this was going somewhere. The priestess made it sound like a small matter, but he knew her; those ideas would make a difference.

"And stay away from the main road," she went on matter-of-factly. "I hear there is some agitation near Kyōto."

"I will keep your words in mind," Ren said.

"And, Ren," Hotaru said in a voice full of motherly love. "Be kind. To her *and* to yourself. That you are the best person for this situation isn't fair. We know you will do your best, and I trust you, just like that old goat trusts you. But, sometimes, our best isn't enough. I will pray every day that your best is, but if it isn't, be kind to yourself."

"I thank you for your prayer," Ren replied through the knot in his throat. "And for your wise counsel."

"Wise?" Hotaru asked, sounding hurt. "You make me sound so old. Really, my boy, you need to learn to talk to women." And on those words, Hotaru went back to her offering weaving as if nothing special had happened this evening.

CHAPTER 7
PON-PON

"Are you sure?" Ren asked for what must have been the tenth time since the sun woke them up.

"If it is fine with you," Suzume replied.

She had first refused to meet his eyes, and it took all of Hotaru's experience to reassure the girl regarding the events of the evening. Ren had discarded the pieces of the table and found a replacement so Suzume would not notice. It was as if the three of them had simply sipped tea until it was time for the kami to leave them in peace.

"Of course, it is fine with me," Ren replied, wincing from the pinch of Hotaru's fingers on his lower back.

"I don't mean to be disrespectful, Hotaru-san," the girl told the priestess. "I would have loved to stay here with you. But—"

"But you have a world to discover and an eye to keep on this rascal," Hotaru replied with a nod. Suzume giggled. It was a sweet sound. Ren was glad for it. "I understand. And I wouldn't want you to stay. You're too pretty. The believers would not look at me anymore."

"It would be their loss," Ren replied impishly.

"Don't try your charm on me, child," the priestess chided him. "But give it another five years, and I'll welcome the attempt." She winked and pushed him by the elbow to descend the stairs at the shrine's entrance. The voices of the first visitors could be heard approaching from the side of the courtyard. It was time to let the priestess resume her sacred task, and them their journey. "And don't forget to tell the old fart that he owes me for what I gave you and for the advice."

"I will," Ren replied.

Suzume waved every few steps until Hotaru vanished inside Kasuga Taisha. Ren guessed it would take a few ri before the awkwardness disappeared between them, but it was important it did. Thankfully, Suzume spoke first.

"What is it between Hotaru-san and Shirakawa-sama?" she asked.

"What do you mean?"

"I don't know," the girl said. "It's like she can't stand him, yet she keeps bringing him up in the conversation. Are they rivals or something?"

"You mean that you didn't get it?" Ren asked, amused.

"Get what?"

"They're married," Ren replied, taking great joy from the ensuing gasp. "Her name is Shirakawa, too. Technically, that's *her* name. He took it because he grew up a nobody."

"They're married?" she asked, astonished.

"It's a little complicated, but yes, they are husband and wife. And if you value your life, never, ever mention to him that you know. He's a little shy about it, but I think they love each other deeply."

"That's—"

"Amazing?" Ren guessed.

"I was going to say *weird*," she replied. "But I guess it makes sense now that you mention it."

A group of five travelers bowed to the girl because she was wearing the miko uniform, and, not knowing what she was supposed to do, she simply bowed back at them. The forest was slowly waking up, and deer emerged from behind trees as if to salute the duo. Suzume waved at them.

"You won't get to learn about them after all," Ren said.

"I will come back," she replied. "*We* will come back."

It was a sweet *we*, and Ren told her he would like that. But first, he explained, they had training to begin and, before that, some *sake* to buy.

"Sake?" she asked, seemingly confused.

"A gift," Ren explained.

"For a friend?"

"By the kami, no. But you'll like him." She tilted her head to ask for more. "A *good* spirit," Ren explained. "More or less."

Ren considered the time used at Kasuga Taisha a necessity, but it was time lost nonetheless, so he ordered balls of rice from the shop next to the brewery to be eaten on the road. The round-shaped bottle of spirit made his bag twice heavier, but it would soon be gifted. The rice balls were eaten as soon as they departed the old capital and cut toward the hills from the ruins of the ancient imperial palace.

And when the city no longer stood at their backs, Ren went through his bag to retrieve some of Hotaru's gifts. He randomly peeled two thin red ribbons from the stack offered by the priestess.

"Can I see your right hand?" he asked.

"What is it?" Suzume asked, though she held her hand out without resistance.

The hunter checked her eyes as he grabbed her wrist gently and, once reassured that they didn't turn green, proceeded to tie one around it. "These are mizuhiki strings, just like the one you tie your hair with, but a bit special."

"How so?" She asked.

"They have soaked in some of my blood last night. Don't worry, just a few drops," Ren said when he noticed her worried look. He then knotted the second one on the other wrist. "They will help us train you."

"Is it Hotaru-san's idea?"

"Yes. And, to be honest, I have no clue if it's going to work. But it's worth a shot." Ren had superstitiously decided to use the sunny side of a hill to begin the training, and, as far as he could see, no one lived nearby. "As Hotaru explained to you this morning, you need to get used to Sugi. In time, you will learn to invoke her at will and even control her while she controls you. You also need to get used to each other so she doesn't waste your energy too fast."

"All of that with ribbons?" the girl asked, understandably doubtful.

"At first, but the point is that you don't need them soon," Ren replied. "First, we need to get you to *feel* the moment Sugi comes to you so you retain some consciousness through the trance." The hunter repeated the words spoken by Hotaru, hoping that his lack of practical understanding did not show in his voice.

"How?" she asked.

"Like this," he said, just before snapping the fingers of his left hand.

The girl yelped and winced at the feeling of tiny needles-like shocks around her left wrist, where the ribbon suddenly turned white. When her eyes opened, they were green.

Ren stopped breathing; his heart beat like a taiko. Sugi did not attack. She seemed confused. There was no threat. Then she checked her left wrist, where a faint mark of burned skin had appeared. Her eyes shot back at Ren, full of violence and promising blood.

She growled and leaped; spear ready to strike. The hunter snapped the fingers of his other hand, and the same weak pain as before shocked Suzume's right wrist. The shock forced her fingers to open and release the spear, putting an end to the trance.

Suzume fell on her knees, her shoulders rising up and down with heavy breathing.

"Suzume?" Ren asked, kneeling to her level. It might all be too much, after all.

"That. Was. Amazing!" the girl shouted. "Ren, I felt her. I can still feel her."

"Good," Ren replied with glee. "Do you remember what happened this time?"

"No," she answered as she stood up. "Just a feeling. But I wasn't worried."

"Good," he said again. This would work. It would take a lot of tries and a long time, but this would work. "Let's wait a bit, and we'll try again."

"No," Suzume said right away. "Let's do it again, now."

And so they did. Again and again, for the next few hours, until the couple hundred ribbons halved.

The first ten tries happened exactly like the first, and for a time, Ren thought that Suzume needed a longer rest between each attempt. But her enthusiasm overpowered him, and he accepted to go on. Then it got worse.

Sugi, when she next took over, did not attack right away. She had understood the mechanism of the ribbons and snatched the right one before Ren could use it. The hunter had rarely feared for his life more than in the next moment.

The kami attacked with a savage roar, but just as he thought he was about to die, the spear stopped an inch from his throat. Sugi was struggling against an invisible force. Ren did not waste time and hurriedly tied another ribbon on her wrist, which he used right away.

Suzume rushed to him in panic, apologizing for what she had done. Ren told her he was fine and realized that she remembered. Risks to herself were not enough, he understood. *He* had to be in danger, too. Thus started one of the longest afternoons of Ren's life. They went on with only one ribbon to wake the kami, but Ren held a second at the ready, which saved his life on more than one occasion.

Suzume progressed slowly and sometimes regressed. For each couple of steps forward, she took one back. It would be fine if the said back step did not threaten his life every time. He resisted the temptation to call Maki, thinking that adding another threatening presence by his side would make it harder for Suzume to control her guardian. Still, he kept the idea in mind for a later time.

Sometimes, the girl managed to prevent a single step from Sugi, but this angered the kami so much that with the next attempt, she would strike before Suzume could control her. And Ren was left to fend off a pissed warrior spirit with nothing more than his words.

By the time he called an end to the day's training, Ren believed the greatest progress they'd made was with his kotodama. Sugi had scoffed when he first ordered her to stay where she stood, but a few hours later, he could stop her long enough to tie yet another ribbon.

Nevertheless, he had suffered the brunt of the training, and the early evening was spent applying ointment on a battered, bruised, and cut body. A sorry Suzume applied it, and, again, looking at him proved difficult for her.

"Hey," Ren said as she spread the lotion on a cut at the base of his neck. He dropped his head to try catching her eyes and succeeded, for a heartbeat. "It's not your fault. You're doing great."

"You wouldn't be bleeding so much if I was," she replied.

"I'm a Blood; that's what I do," he said, trying to sound boastful. "And I would be dead if you weren't doing great. Suzume, look at me."

He resisted the impulse to grab her wrist, which must have been more painful than anything on his body right now. They had wrapped them with talismans gently tucked over a thick layer of ointment, but even then, they would hurt. Instead, he cupped her elbow. She did not resist nor seem to notice but stopped working on his wound.

"I think I'm getting better," she said hesitantly.

"That's good."

"I remember all of it now, and I can tell her to stop sometimes."

"That's great," Ren replied, exaggerating a relieved eye roll that made her laugh. "Let's keep working on that. But not tomorrow. You need to recover. We both do."

"Are we going to meet your good spirit friend?" she asked, sitting back.

"Again, not a friend," Ren said. "And don't get your hopes too high. He's only good in the sense that he is not evil. And he might have moved. We should meet with him and his family tomorrow around noon and maybe spend some time with those little buggers. Then we'll head north and catch the main road to regain some time."

"Didn't Hotaru say we should avoid the road?" Suzume asked.

"Well, yes, but she doesn't answer to Osamu, I do. I'd rather take some risk if it means completing this mission on time."

"Fair enough," Suzume vaguely replied as she peeled the talisman from her left wrist with a hiss of pain. She put it back almost right away. It would take days for the skin to grow back completely, and by then, they would make it worse again.

Ren told himself the next part of the training should be to call the kami without relying on a physical sense of danger.

"What's his name?"

"Sorry?" Ren asked.

"Your spirit... acquaintance?"

"His name is Pon-Pon."

Ren woke before Suzume. She was exhausted, but they needed to go as early as possible if they hoped to catch Pon-Pon before lunch. Meeting Pon-Pon and his family, Ren believed, was exactly what she needed. The hunter could not express the reason behind his hunch. He knew firsthand Pon-Pon could be an ass, but he was wise, not only beyond his years but also beyond his nature. And he was, as Hotaru had said, straight as an arrow.

So they left the cold ash of their camp shortly before sunrise and walked all morning through fields and meadows until they reached the edge of yet another forest. A road lined the tree line. An old road mostly reclaimed by nature, though traces of wheels proved that people still used it. After a few days of journeying through the wild, Ren enjoyed the feeling of solid ground under his straw sandals.

He pointed at a statue bordering the road. A Jizō statue, peacefully accumulating moss with a warm smile. The red cap and bib given to the statue were new. Ren stood in front of the small statue at the feet of which passersby had dropped a few grains of rice and small stones. He then pressed his hands flat against each other in prayer.

"We have them, too, where I live," Suzume said as she copied him. "They always break my heart."

Ren knew what she meant. He found them sad, too, those smiling *bodhisattva*. His mother, a devout Buddhist, had told him of those saints who refused to become Buddha despite having reached enlightenment in order to help the souls of dead children and unborn babies.

Ren, still a child then, had cried, thinking that he too might be taken from her someday and that it was unfair. But his mother said they should be grateful for the Jizō who protected those infants until their mothers came to guide them across the river separating life and death. A new set of red clothes for the statue meant a mourning mother.

"But they are beautiful," Suzume said, echoing Ren's thought. Their hands parted, and they reopened their eyes to a quiet forest. A faint drizzle was threatening to turn into a downpour, but Ren felt like they would avoid the worst of it thanks to the eastern wind. "Are we meeting your friend here?"

"We'll soon find out," he answered, swinging his bag in front.

The bottle came out, and the hunter uncorked it. He had acquired a small, flat cup with the bottle and filled half of it with sake, which he gently dropped at the feet of the statue's pedestal. Ren shoved his bag back but kept the bottle in his left hand. He then took a deep breath that bloated his belly.

"Pon-Pon!" Ren bellowed, striking his belly with each part of the name. It echoed through the forest a couple of times and then vanished. But nothing happened. "Come on," he told Suzume, "help me out here."

She made big eyes full of surprise. "I have to do the same?"

"Yes," he replied just before inflating his belly again. "Ready?" he asked when she did the same. She nodded.

"Pon-Pon!" they both called, slapping their bellies twice.

"What are we doing?" the girl asked.

Ren lifted his finger over his lips to ask her to remain silent. Just then, they heard something shuffle in the closest bushes. The leaves trembled in front of them, and a pointy muzzle suddenly burst out. It sniffed the air for a couple of seconds, then the head popped out, and the rest of the tanuki raccoon followed. It looked up at Ren, then Suzume, who brought her hands over her mouth in excitement, and ignored both of them to scurry to the cup of sake. The animal sniffed the contents of the cup and lapped two sips.

"That's Pon-Pon," Ren said.

"He's so cute," Suzume said in something resembling a screech.

The tanuki stood on his hind legs, picked the cup with his left hand, and gulped its contents straight. "You're not bad on the eyes yourself, sister," the tanuki said in a low, sultry voice.

Suzume gasped in a stupor. "He speaks," she said.

"Oh, he talks all right," Ren commented. "Rarely stops even."

"Not only can I talk," the raccoon said, dropping his elbow against the pedestal to take a pose. "But I talk of love." The last word stretched in a seductive way that left Ren shaking his head. "And I also complain from time to time. For example, what is this cheap swine sweat you brought me here, Ren? Couldn't get a decent sake and had to make do with rinsing a mop into a bottle?"

"Fine," Ren said, pushing the bottle back into his bag. "I'll keep the rest then."

"Wait, wait," Pon-Pon yelped, losing his genial voice for a second and hurrying to Ren's legs. "No need to rush. I'll take that bottle."

"You grant us access to your forest?" Ren asked.

"I welcome you, brother," the raccoon replied. "And who's the honeycomb?" he asked, crossing the distance to Suzume in a few rapid steps.

"I'm Suzume," she answered, looking first at Ren to know if it was fine to reply.

"She's a friend. And not to be touched," Ren said.

"I see," Pon-Pon replied, playing with one of his whiskers. "Suzume, if I may?" he asked, taking a knee and holding his hand in her direction.

"He wants to sniff your hand," Ren explained when the girl looked at him incomprehensibly. "That's how they salute each other."

Suzume offered her hand, crouching to make it easier for the animal. Pon-Pon touched the tip of her fingers, sniffed them, bristled from nose to tail, and sighed with pleasure.

"Suzume," he then said in his most seductive voice. "Thank you for making my humble forest more beautiful with your presence."

"All right, enough of that, you pervy badger," Ren intervened, pushing himself between the girl and the raccoon. "Do you want that bottle or what?"

"Yes," the raccoon replied greedily, opening his arms to receive the sake.

"And are you going to invite us for lunch?" the hunter asked upon releasing the bottle.

"Yes, of course, of course," Pon-Pon answered as already his paws worked on the cork.

"Thank you," Ren replied sarcastically. "How is your wife, by the way?"

"Pon-Pon is fine," the raccoon replied, though the words were hard to make as he used his mouth to bite the cork too stubbornly inserted for his arms.

"I thought you were Pon-Pon?" Suzume asked. She crouched to help the raccoon with his problem.

"No," he replied. "I'm Pon-Pon. My wife's Pon-Pon."

Suzume looked from the tanuki to Ren, not understanding the difference.

"It's a tone thing," Ren said.

"Yes, a tone thing," Pon-Pon echoed.

"So, you're Pon-Pon," she said, getting a nod. "And your wife is Pon-Pon."

Ren sighed, and the raccoon shook his finger while gulping a full swing of sake.

"That would be my mother's uncle," he said after smacking his lips. "Don't worry, you'll get it. Shall we?" Pon-Pon did not wait for a reply and walked back toward the bush on his two feet, carrying the bottle against his furry chest.

"He speaks," Suzume said again in astonishment when Ren invited her to follow their host.

The forest indeed welcomed them with the sound of animals chirping and gnawing. They behaved unbothered by the two humans, knowing they were guests of its guardian. Few humans ever experienced the true life of a forest, and Suzume's mouth hung open at the sounds. The tanuki was walking a little ahead, sipping some wine every few steps before skipping on one leg or leaping in a pirouette. Soon, he started humming a song. He was happy.

"He is a yōkai?" the girl asked.

"I heard that," the raccoon said, interrupting the rhythm of his song.

"Not exactly," Ren replied. "He is a tanuki, just like any other, but he's lived long enough that he's developed a new level of consciousness. Some animals are capable of doing so, cats and foxes mostly. But while those two tend to become dangerous when they evolve, tanuki are more... mischievous than anything. They'll steal your food, your sake, your money too if they can, though only the kami know what they do with it. They're a little pervy as well. And," Ren said, holding his forefinger up, "they are insanely proud of their balls."

"Their balls?" Suzume asked, wondering if she had heard well.

"Listen," the hunter said, and just then, the humming turned to lyrics.

Tan-Tan-Tanuki's bollocks,
Even without wind,

They swing, swing, swing.

"Heavens," Suzume chuckled as Ren's head shook in horror.

"They like to pretend they can shapeshift," Ren explained as the forest grew denser. "But whenever I ask him to do it, he finds an excuse, so really, they're just good at hiding."

"Of course we can shapeshift," Pon-Pon proudly said, interrupting his walk until they caught up with him.

"Go ahead then, do it," Ren taunted him.

"Hum, you should have asked before I started drinking. We only shapeshift sober."

"See?" Ren told Suzume.

The tanuki resumed his song and gulped a few more sips of sake.

"What about the names?" she then asked the hunter.

"Ah, it's confusing. In the human tongue, all of them are either Pon, Pom, or Poko. It has something to do with the sound they make when striking their bellies, which is apparently unique for each of them. You just need to remember the tones, and you'll be fine."

"Pon-Pon!" the tanuki called, slapping his belly twice.

"Pon-Pon!" another voice, a female one, replied. She hit her belly, too, and three more sets of drums followed, smaller and higher pitched.

"I bring guests!" the tanuki went on. "Ren and a friend of his, uh..."

"Suzume," the girl said.

"Suzume!" the raccoon shouted.

"Come on then," the female voice replied. "Make yourself at home."

Pon-Pon waved them in and climbed over a sprouting root. On the other side, a fallen tree had torn a hole in the ground. The hole rested between three great oaks, was covered in dead leaves, and stretched wide enough for a person to lie down without being bothered.

Female Pon-Pon stepped out from under the tree facing them, rubbing some flour from her hands. From human eyes, she looked like the replica of her husband, a dog-sized animal between a badger and a fox, with fluffy light-brown fur and eyes circled in black. She smiled at Ren and Suzume when they climbed down the hole.

"Ren," she lovingly called, opening her arms for an embrace, which Ren happily returned. "And who is your lovely friend? A girlfriend, perhaps?"

"As if he could pull such a lovely sister," Pon-Pon scoffed. He reached the root from which his wife had emerged and used it for support as he lowered his head to look inside.

"My name is Suzume," the girl said with a bow. "Nice to meet you, Pon-Pon."

The female raccoon tilted her head toward Ren, probably wondering if Suzume knew she had mispronounced the name. "And I you," Pon-Pon replied, deciding that the girl had not noticed. "You came for lunch?"

"If that's not too much to ask," Ren replied.

"Never," the female raccoon said with a wink. "Sit down, make yourself comfortable, and I'll prepare bowls for you."

Bowls? Suzume mouthed to Ren.

"Uh-huh," Ren confirmed.

Female Pon-Pon disappeared under the roots, where Pon-Pon still stood.

"Boys!" he shouted. "Come say hello to—" Pon-Pon rocked backward under the assault of three miniature versions of himself. His children climbed all over him, moving from his belly to his back and between his legs despite his request for calm. The three heads then popped up as one and looked at the two humans without fear, just curiosity.

Ren knelt and offered his hand. The three children then scurried to him and together sniffed his fingers. Their tails suddenly started swaying, and they squeaked happily.

"Good," Ren said, "you remember me. Who wants a ride?" he then asked, opening his hand, palm up.

The three of them climbed along his arm and reached for his face, which one licked and the two others lightly scratched. Ren was taken by a bout of laughter when their little claws found his neck, and he soon had to bend over, thus opening the collar of his shirt into which the smaller one weaseled.

"Oh, no, no, no," Ren said, laughing even more and twisting on himself. "Wait, no, not there."

"Poko!" their mom called, stepping out again.

Immediately, the small tanuki emerged from the collar and climbed down from the hunter. His two brothers had already stopped playing with Ren and now stood motionless in front of the crouching girl.

"Hello," she said with a warm smile, slowly stretching her arm. The bravest of the two used her fingers to stand and sniffed them. He found the smell acceptable and pressed his head in her palm, eyes closed. "Ren," the girl said, sounding like a squeaking animal. "They are so cute."

"I know," Ren agreed. "Until they learn how to speak and talk like drunk lumberjacks on their way to a brothel."

"Guilty." Pon-Pon chuckled. "Talking of which," he went on, sitting like a human right next to where Ren now sat. He leaned closer to the hunter and held his hand out to shelter his voice from his wife's direction. "Did you visit the place I told you about in Nagano?"

"Oh yes," Ren replied with a wink before he spotted the glare from Suzume and coughed in his hand. "I mean, I don't know what you're talking about."

"Brother, that fox-lady," Pon-Pon said, scratching his inner legs, "she's something, isn't she?"

"What are you two talking about?" Female Pon-Pon asked when she stepped out of the roots, arms full with two bowls much too big for her.

"The weather," Ren replied.

"The sake," the tanuki replied at the same time, shaking the bottle. "The weather being the reason for this poor sake," he then went on as if it would explain everything.

Female Pon-Pon eyed them both as she dropped the first bowl into Suzume's hands, suspicious but not able to accuse them of anything. Ren swallowed a ball of saliva, and Pon-Pon offered his wife a toothy smile. She sighed and handed the second bowl to Ren, then headed back to what Ren assumed was their kitchen. Pon-Pon puffed with relief and shook his hand as if to say it was close.

The bowl had belonged to a human being, of course, but had long become the property of the raccoon family. Scars ran across its surface, mended by leaves and twigs, and yet somehow keeping the soup in.

Pon-Pon had served Ren the exact same dish on his last visit. A light broth, barely more than hot water, with uneven, thick udon noodles, *tenkasu* bits of fried flour batter, and a few rounds of green onions to accompany a pair of frog legs. They, being tanuki, did not use chopsticks, and Ren wondered if they had any.

Suzume, sitting a little on the side, made a face when she lifted a frog leg from her bowl. Ren pulled one between his teeth to show her how to eat them. It tasted rather good, he admitted, but not as good as the udon.

One of the little ones climbed on Ren's knee and stretched his neck until he could almost reach the bowl. The hunter helped him by pulling the soup closer, and soon, a noodle slurped from the bowl to the child's belly. One of his brothers behaved the same with the girl, who giggled when the little paws kneaded against her thigh.

"So," Pon-Pon said after his wife shoved a bowl between his legs. She remained by his side to share the contents of the bowl with him. "What brings you here, brother?"

"We're going north, to Kyōto," Ren answered after slurping a noodle.

"Oooh, bad idea," Pon-Pon commented. "Bad idea, I tell you."

"Why is that?" Ren asked.

"There is trouble brewing north. I can feel it in my balls," the tanuki replied. "You should stay here for a few days with us. Wait for it to pass."

Female Pon-Pon agreed with a heartfelt nod, a noodle stuck between her lips.

"And get drunk like last time, no thank you," Ren replied. "What kind of trouble?"

"Oh, I don't know. Human troubles. Humans fighting humans."

"We're too far to hear anything specific," his wife said, "but there are rumors of fire and war. Some cousins who had been living in the capital for years came back to the old forest recently. You should really stay here, and no need to get drunk." The last she said through her teeth while looking at her husband, who recoiled.

"Did you know," Pon-Pon said to change the subject, looking at Suzume, "that humans are the only species who kill their own?"

"Are we?" Suzume asked, a piece of frog flesh resisting between her teeth and the bone.

"Well," Pon-Pon answered, wiping his lips with the back of his hand. "We all fight with our own from time to time. Before I evolved, I had to defend my territory and my claim over the old chain and ball here a few times, but I never had to kill any of my brethren. Now, foxes, yes, I bled a few," he said proudly, though

Ren could hardly imagine a tanuki getting the better of a clever fox, "but never another tanuki. Yōkai rarely fight each other, especially if they belong to the same kind, and kami can be harsh to one another, but it rarely ends with a death. But humans... humans are ruthless."

"I didn't know that," Suzume admitted.

Ren remained silent. This conversation was for the girl's benefit. They came for it.

"Do you know why?" Pon-Pon asked. "Do you know why animals respect life more than humans do?"

Suzume shook her head. Ren noticed how difficult it was for her to swallow the meat in her mouth.

"Because you don't enjoy it," the tanuki replied. "You've lost yourselves as you got smarter."

"We got smarter?" she asked.

"Of course," Pon-Pon replied. "Just like us. You used to be barely more than monkeys. But you've evolved. Not one individual at a time, but the whole species."

"Not that again," Ren commented. "Don't listen to him, Suzume. No one believes his wild theory."

"But it's true," Pon-Pon went on, pushing the bowl aside. "You used to be like us, living one day at a time, treating the sun going up and down as the only thing that mattered. But you got smarter, and you invented, and you gathered, and because you gathered, you had things to steal and things to protect, so you fought, entire groups at a time. You started warring for what was yours yesterday, or to get more for tomorrow. And you forgot the simplest truth. Today, right now, is everything. Those around you as you breathe are everything."

Ren made a conscious effort to drink the soup without making a sound. He had heard all this before and yet hung on every word, just as the girl did. Female Pon-Pon caressed her husband's back with love, and the smallest of their kids came to his side for a hug.

"Do you think anyone on those islands has anything I would want more than any of this?" Pon-Pon went on, opening his arms to show the entirety of the hole he called home. "Sure, I don't mind a bottle of sake from time to time, and if I get to steal a fish from the humans down the road, I won't miss the chance. But none of it is necessary. My folks who moved to the cities seemed to have forgotten this simple truth too, so I can't say it's a uniquely human trait, but you've mastered it."

"So you think we should all go live in forests and on the hills?" Ren asked.

"Too late for that," Pon-Pon replied, waving the argument down. "Plus, who would brew my sake? No, it was before you fell down that path that you should have thought about it. Before you started creating yōkai all over the place."

"*We* created yōkai?" Suzume asked, baffled.

"Who else?" the raccoon replied. "Yōkai are born from lingering negativity, from the horror accompanying ambition. Those are human traits. Sure, now yōkai spread it, too, but they didn't start the whole process. You created your own monsters."

"But," Suzume said, "maybe the first yōkai came after some catastrophe? Earthquakes, tsunami, storms, they bring distress to the people too, no?"

"Aye, they do," Pon-Pon agreed. "It hurts when something stronger than us takes our loved ones or our homes. But suffering is part of life, as your Buddhist monks would say, but all we can do is to let it pass. It's hard, especially for you people with your frustration and anxiety. You cling to your suffering with something like love and let it define you when it would be so much healthier to... breathe, feel the sun over your skin, love, and sing a song about your bollocks. Well, not you, obviously," Pon-Pon said, waving toward Suzume's inner legs.

"It's not easy," Female Pon-Pon intervened, looking at the girl with understanding eyes. "It doesn't happen at once, but all suffering ends. Whenever life takes one of my young ones from me, a part of me goes with them. But then I pray to the Jizō and remember that everything passes, even pain. So why not let it pass by itself?"

There had been five puppy raccoons on Ren's last visit, but the hunter refrained from asking about the other two. If humans had once been animals, too, he thought, it was no wonder they had wanted to leave the forest.

"How do I do that?" Suzume asked, her voice shaking.

"Oh, sweetie," the raccoon mother replied, taking a few steps toward the girl and holding her hands with her paws. The compassion in her gaze and the warmth in her voice infected Ren, and he knew Suzume would not resist it either. "No one can tell you that. Pain is unique to each of us, as are the solutions to it. But there is a solution; be sure of that. There is always a solution."

"But it hurts," Suzume said. Her eyes swelled as fat tears blossomed, and she produced a crisped, tight smile.

"I can see, sweet sparrow, I can see," the mother replied, patting Suzume's hand.

One of the puppies quietly left his father's side, but Pon-Pon grabbed his tail and pulled him back.

"I can't tell you how to deal with your pain, but me, when it grips my heart, I don't try to smother it; I let it flow through me. I feel every drop of sadness reaching the tip of my claws and the end of my tail. I experience it all, and it weakens. As for you," she went on, reaching for Suzume's face, "maybe you can start by not fighting the tears with that brave smile of yours."

Suzume's face resisted for the time of a breath, and then Ren saw the words traveling to the girl's heart, and her face started shifting. The barrier holding the tears broke, and there was no stopping them.

The girl cried, first quietly. Then she bellowed like a wounded animal. The raccoon held her in her little arms, and Suzume held her back, wetting her furry back with tears that had waited to be freed for far too long. Ren fought his tears, too, and if not for Pon-Pon handing him a full cup of sake, he knew they would have joined the forest ground.

The puppies joined their mother and climbed over the girl, searching for a part of her to comfort with their childlike love. She accepted all of them, and the image of the miko covered in raccoons as the sun pierced through clouds and branches to bathe the scene with golden light carved itself in Ren's mind.

Pon-Pon was right, though; the sake was awful.

沺

"You're still going north?" Pon-Pon asked Ren a couple of hours later by the Jizō.

"We are," Ren confirmed.

"Suit yourself," the raccoon replied, waving his hand down. "But don't say I didn't warn you."

"Human affairs are not our problem," the hunter said. "We're just going to the shrine, do whatever Amaterasu is expecting us to do, and head back to Ise Jingū."

"Stop by here on the way back," Female Pon-Pon said. She held Suzume's hand in both hers, which forced the girl to bend to the side.

"I would love that," Suzume replied. Her eyes were puffy and red, but her new smile appeared genuine, and she looked exhausted.

"Bring some better hooch then," Pon-Pon said, scratching his now swollen belly. "Not that cat piss you brought today."

"You didn't seem to mind after a couple of sips," Ren scoffed.

"I'll feel it on the way down, though. Suzume, remind him for me. Some good stuff next time. And you, my delicate little bird," he said, lifting the girl's hand from his wife's paws. "When things go dark, think of me and sing a song. Any song. You can even take mine."

"No one wants to sing about your bollocks, you filthy badger," Ren said.

"Real men do," Pon-Pon replied, a satisfied smirk revealing his white pointy teeth.

"You keep telling yourself that. Now, if you'll excuse us, we have a long road ahead."

It took another couple of minutes for the three child raccoons to accept to leave the girl, who did not make it easier with all her snuggles and kisses, but eventually, the five of them returned to their hole in the forest, though Suzume and Ren heard Pon-Pon's voice singing for a long time.

"Just to be clear," Ren said as they resumed their journey. "I meant for you to meet the wife, not the pervy husband."

"He was funny," she replied. "I like him."

"Me too," Ren replied. "Me too."

CHAPTER 8
SPINNING WHEELS

Suzume, Ren felt, walked with a lighter step and even hummed Pon-Pon's song. He thought of postponing any training for the next morning to let her enjoy the rest of this beautiful day, but she offered to try while the tanuki's words still echoed in her chest, so Ren accepted. It did not stop Sugi from looking feral, but she did not attack him. So Ren removed the ribbon he had tied on Suzume's right hand and took his time doing so. Sugi growled when she found his presence lingering, so he stepped back.

"Are you finally accepting me?" Ren asked the spirit warrior.

She spat and shook her head, then opened her mouth and spoke, though Ren heard nothing more than a ringing.

"I'm sorry," he said, pointing at his ears. "I can't hear kami's voices."

She sighed and changed tactics. Sugi pointed at herself.

"Sugi?" Ren asked, understanding that she was signing words.

Again, she shook her head and repeated the sign, then gathered her hands and flapped them like wings.

"Oh, Suzume," Ren said, thinking the sign looked more like a pigeon than a sparrow.

Sugi nodded. She pointed at her eyes, then traced what he assumed were tears.

"Suzume cried?" the hunter asked. "Well, yes, but—"

Sugi growled for him to let her finish. She repeated the wings, the tears, and held up her thumb.

"*Suzume cried. Good.* Suzume cried, and that was good?" he asked.

Sugi nodded. And then the most amazing thing happened, she bowed her head. Only a little, barely enough to be considered a bow, but a bow nonetheless.

"Wait," Ren said. "Are you thanking me?"

Sugi snarled but nodded once more.

"Shit," Ren said to himself with a smile. "Can Suzume speak to me while you're here?"

The kami shook her head, then held a finger up, which she then circled over her chest, and then once more lifted the finger before pointing at her heart.

"One body, one heart," Ren understood. "But you can hear her voice? Like with Hotaru-san. Can she hear me?" Another head shake. "So, she can remember what happened, but after the fact, and she can hear your voice, but not mine. And you can hear her voice, but not yours. That's very practical."

Sugi pointed at Ren, then at her ear, made a cross with her finger, and back at the ear.

"What?" he asked, not understanding. "Ears, not ears? I don't get it."

The kami repeated the same gestures, but Ren got nothing more of it, and when she gestured a third time, the hunter felt her frustration swelling and held his hands for her to keep calm.

This, however, only served to anger her more, and she shook her spear vehemently. Ren feared the next moment, but then Sugi dropped to her knees, panting. The green in her eyes vanished when she looked back up.

"Suzume?" Ren asked as he lowered to her level.

"She meant that you shouldn't try to use your ears," the girl explained through her ragged breath.

"Not my ears? What does it mean?"

"I don't know," Suzume acknowledged. "But she doesn't want to talk to you anymore. For now," she added urgently.

And so the training ended for the day, which suited Ren just fine.

Clouds charged with rain still hung over their heads, and Ren meant to move from their path before they unleashed their water. He assumed they could reach Fushimi Inari sometime the next afternoon, and knew of a welcoming temple along the road from Nara to Kyōto, not too far from them. So, as planned, Ren led them back toward the main road.

The sky turned gray and forced the light to retreat before sunset. Storms were rare so early in spring, but faint booms threatened to turn the landscape into a nightmare for the travelers, so they walked faster and reached the road within half an hour.

It was deserted. The absence of travelers and the eerie silence disturbed only by a rising wind made Ren frown. There always were people on the Nara-Kyōto road.

"What is it?" Suzume asked.

"I don't know," Ren replied. "But we'll soon find out." He pointed his chin farther along the road, where a column of black smoke signaled a fire. They progressed toward the fumes, but before they could see its origin, hidden behind a curve of the road, Ren tied another ribbon around Suzume's wrist to call the kami if need be.

Past the curve and the hill was a crossroad where three roads met, and on the other side, cutting the main path, a barrage. Six soldiers manned a fence made of crossed, sharpened poles, leaving only a narrow space to pass through. A cart had been toppled by the side of the road, just in front of the fence. The donkey pulling it was lying on its flank, dead. From the smell of the fire burning near the cart, Ren assumed the donkey had been pulling a cargo of oil, though whoever led the donkey was nowhere in sight.

"Who are they?" Suzume asked as they reached the center of the crossroad.

"No idea," Ren replied.

The six soldiers stood at perfect intervals from each other and looked straight ahead toward the two travelers. They wore black armor bound with red cords and thongs. Conical hats of metal shining black masked anything above the eyes, and they carried straight spears as well as katanas in their belts. The crest on their hats and on the flag hanging from the back of two soldiers was unknown to Ren. It looked like a crow in flight, but from a distance, he could not be sure. Crow or not, he had never seen this crest before.

One of the soldiers, the only one with a scowling mask covering the lower part of his face and a pair of swords marking him as a samurai, raised his hand to stop them. His gait was stiff, and he held his hand up until he, too, halted a couple of steps from Ren and Suzume. The first drops of rain fell then, light and few.

"By order of the General," the samurai said through his mask in a perfunctory tone, "no one is allowed on the road to Kyōto."

"Which general?" Ren asked.

"By order of the General," the samurai replied in the exact same tone. His eyes were alert but seemed to watch through Ren.

"May we know what your general's name is, please?" Suzume asked.

The samurai's head twisted toward her. The rainwater slid from his hat's edge, but that, too, he did not seem to notice.

"No one is allowed on the road to Kyōto," he said.

His five men were professional in their manner, straight as the spear poles in their hands, staring ahead, not even the presence of steam from their breath.

"I am sorry to insist," Ren said, shoving his hand in his shirt, from where he fished a purse jiggling with a few coins. "But we have to go to Kyōto for spiritual purposes. Surely you *can* understand that."

The hunter held the purse by the string, closing it, and dangled it by the samurai's belt. The man did not even pretend to see the bribe. In other circumstances, Ren would have commended him for his incorruptible behavior, but this time, it was just odd. He exchanged a confused look with Suzume.

"Can we please pass?" she asked the samurai.

"By order of the General, no one is allowed on the road to Kyōto," he repeated in the same manner as before. "Step back, now."

His five men jumped above the fence with incredible lightness for soldiers wearing armor and immediately lowered their spears toward the duo.

Ren recoiled and thought they might just walk around the barrage, then realized the cart owner had probably shared the same idea and met his doom in the attempt. The donkey's neck was oozing with drying blood. Hotaru and Pon-Pon had been right; trouble was brewing at the capital, but this was not just human troubles.

Those men were no humans, or no longer humans, no matter how they moved or dressed, yet Ren could not figure out what he was facing.

"Ren," Suzume called with a hint of fear, "let's go."

She meant to pass the spear from her right hand to her left as she turned back on the road, but the samurai locked his gaze on the weapon, probably thinking she had meant to use it, and grabbed her wrist with astonishing speed.

"Uh-oh," Ren said. He hesitated between snapping his fingers or unsheathing his blade, but this second of hesitation was all Sugi needed.

The spear flashed and ended its course in the samurai's belly, going as deep as the end of the leafy blade and splashing blood from his back. But the samurai ignored that, too. There should have been a scream, a curse, or at least a grimace, but the only reaction came from the five soldiers who darted with their spears, ready to ram Suzume and Ren.

Sugi pulled her blade from the samurai's abdomen, letting it topple lifelessly, while Ren unsheathed his sword. The two soldiers coming at him harbored no expression at all, not even a hint of anger for their officer's death, but their movements were fluid. He would have no time to call Maki, so he let his sword do the talking.

The two soldiers lunged at the same time, both aiming for his throat. Ren ducked at the last second. He twisted on his hips and cut to the left, across their bellies, then to the right. Their armor absorbed most of the attack, but the sword was so sharp it still drew blood with each strike. Again, there was no scream. He back-flipped to avoid their next coordinated lunge. They should not have been able to muster another attack with those wounds.

Ren darted to the fence and used an inclined pole to jump and flip above them. Midair and head down, he twisted his torso, using his blade as a sickle. In the blink of an eye, he found himself hanging between his two opponents. One of them lowered his head by chance, and his metallic hat deflected the sword. The second had no such luck, and the sharp sword cut his face across the nose.

When the hunter landed, he kicked the survivor in the chest with a roar. The soldier flew backward and stopped suddenly with a spiked pole jutting from his sternum. He seemed to notice the piece of wood with curiosity, then his head lolled down.

When Ren shifted his attention back to Sugi, she had two

more corpses by her feet and held the last one from behind, using the spear pole to compress his throat. The soldier tried to claw at her face, so she broke his neck then let him go. She looked unhurt, but her expression was savage. She had killed four of whatever those creatures were in a few seconds.

"Sugi?" Ren asked after shaking the blood from his sword.

The warrior kami turned her attention to him, green eyes crossed with red veins and a snarl so pronounced he could see all her teeth. He was out of her reach, so she crouched, ready to pounce.

"Sugi?" Ren asked as he pushed his blade back into its scabbard. "What are you doing? It's me, Ren. Don't—"

The kami burst toward the hunter, stabbing the spear in one swift motion. Ren weaved to his left, but the spear would not have hurt him, anyway. Her attack ended abruptly; her right arm extended as the continuation of the spear planted in the samurai's throat. The same samurai she had killed a few seconds before, whose katana was now held above his head, ready to strike Ren. She wrenched the spear out of his neck, inviting blood to gush out in a great, red splash. The samurai fell again, without a sound coming from his mouth.

Ren did not understand what he was seeing. The samurai's eyes remained open, and a blue light gleamed like a flame for a second before vanishing and letting them turn gray. Sugi came by his side and offered her hand. She pulled him up with ease.

"Thank you," he said.

Behind her, from the fatal wound of the second soldier she had killed appeared a blue, incandescent light. It formed into a burning, shimmering ball and rose above the wound, emitting no sound besides that of a crackling fire consuming wet wood.

"Impossible," Ren said. He was about to walk toward the ball of blue fire, but Sugi grabbed his wrist and nodded her chin toward the two soldiers he had fought.

The same flames extracted themselves from the bodies. Even the samurai birthed such a ball, though his looked slightly bigger. They crackled, all six floating at hip level, and suddenly fell back from where they came. Ren bent over to observe the biggest flame and saw it insert itself back through the wound. As soon as its tail entered the body, the cut from Sugi's spear started healing.

The samurai's eyes flashed blue once more and blinked.

"Sugi, let's go," Ren said, grabbing her arm and pulling her to follow him. She did not resist. They dashed between two soldiers, but the last one was already on his knees, so Ren slashed his sword mercilessly across his neck. They ran from the road and back to the land.

The soldiers did not seem to pursue, but Sugi soon faltered and nearly tripped.

"Sugi," Ren said as he helped her remain on her feet, "you need to let Suzume back. Keep her energy for later. I doubt this is the last we will see of them."

She clicked her tongue in frustration but nodded, and the next time she blinked, her eyes were brown.

"What was that?" Suzume asked in sudden panic.

"I think," Ren said as he fought to regain his breath. "I think they were *kosenjōbi*, battlefield's fires. The spirits of fallen warriors rising from a blood-soaked battleground." He gently pushed her to keep walking, checking over his shoulder for any sign of pursuit. "They roam the place of their death, looking for their bodies. But... but they're not supposed to be able to find them. They can't control bodies. They are just spirits without form. They can't—"

His voice broke upon the sound of a blowing horn coming from the crossroad. A seashell horn, Ren recognized. He was about to draw his blade again, but then came the sound of creaking wood and spinning wind. Even through the strengthening rain, Ren could discern them as cart wheels moving at breaking speed, and from above the hill behind them came the faint orange light of fire.

"No," he said, eyes growing with dread. "Move!"

The girl obeyed, and they ran. Checking once, Ren saw the moment three *wanyūdō* yōkai rolled atop the hill, using it to spring in the air.

"Ren!" Suzume called in a panic.

"I know!" Ren shouted back, already working on the tassel of his rosary.

They would never outrun wanyūdō. Each of those yōkai from hell was as big as the wheel of an ox-pulled cart. Raging flames surrounded their bodies with a fire that neither water nor wind would extinguish. Where the spokes met, each carried an ugly, bald, puckered hub-face.

Even as the wheel spun, those faces remained straight, and the faster the yōkai rolled, the louder his maniac laughter rang. And those three spun fast, revealing big mouths opened to near tooth-less gums, courtesy of their mad runs through the roads of hell and the human world, where they chased unfortunate souls to drag back to their realm at the speed of a war horse.

The three wheel-yōkai were devouring the distance, even with all their serpentine moves. They crossed each other's paths, cursing and laughing in turn and leaving a blackened trail in their wake.

"Suzume, on my back, quick!" Ren shouted.

The girl was about to ask something, but Ren was already on one knee, planting a bead in the wet earth between his legs. The girl shoved herself on his back and wrapped her left arm around his neck just as cracks formed under them. The wheels were a few seconds behind. Suzume screamed when the ground exploded, and she was lifted into the air, but she held on.

"Maki, go!" Ren ordered.

The lion-dog heard the urgency in her friend's voice and

bolted a blink before two wheels rushed past each other where they had been standing. Ren felt their raging heat on his back, even with Suzume clutching him tightly.

"What are those?" she asked, screaming more than speaking, eyes closed against the wind of Maki's run and the raindrops turned needles by their speed.

"Wanyūdō!" Ren replied. "Watch out!"

The closest of the wheels whooshed past Maki and veered right in front of the lion-dog, forcing her to change direction. Ren clutched her mane with his left hand but was pulled by Suzume's weight when the guardian spirit swerved left. The two other wheels rolled on both sides of Maki, laughing a thunderous, deranged laughter. The one on their left had absurdly thick lips and bloodshot crossed eyes, while the other had lost one and blinked its missing eye to a fleshy vision of horror.

"Ren!" the girl shouted.

The hunter tugged on his bag to pry it from the trap of Suzume's body and opened its mouth with his right hand and his teeth. Maki was running with wide steps, making her cargo bounce frantically whenever her front legs hit the ground again. The hunter felt the arm around his neck tense as he searched through his bag, and he looked up.

"Maki!" he called, just as the two firewheels cut the lion-dog's path.

She barked and leaped forward, a katana's blade length above them. She landed with little grace and whimpered when she resumed running with barely a stop. The wheels' flames would have caressed her underbelly or her knees, Ren assumed. The third wheel was rolling right behind them. It had white hair flailing around its bald spot and a cunning in the eye that was missing from the other two yōkai.

Ren fished two blank paper talismans from his bag and shoved them between the fingers of his hand clinging to the bright mane.

He then used the edge of Suzume's spear, bouncing near his thigh, to cut his right thumb.

"Ren?" the girl asked.

"Tell me if they come closer," he said.

Pressing on the first piece of paper with his bloody finger, Ren traced a series of five characters, then repeated the process with the second. By the end of the second talisman, the small cut had stopped bleeding already. He wished he had taken three, but two would have to do.

"Suzume," he called. "Listen. Me and Maki will stop them. You have to continue alone—"

"No," she said in a pleading tone.

"Just a little," he said, "but I will be right behind. If for some reason I can't follow right away, you keep running east. You don't stop until you reach Iga Ueno. Listen to me, Suzume!" he shouted, for the girl was shaking her head. "You go to Iga Ueno, and you ask for Snake, all right? She should be there. Say it!"

"Snake," she replied between two bounces, "at Iga Ueno."

"Good," Ren replied, giving his best attempt at a reassuring smile. "Now, get ready; it's about to shake a little. Maki! About-face, now!"

The wind stopped all of a sudden as Maki planted her front legs on the ground. She twisted on them, sending her backside in a wide circle. Suzume lost her grip midair, and Ren kept her from falling by grabbing the pole of her spear. For a heartbeat, the girl swung in the air, held by nothing more than Ren's grip. Then, just as the twisting motion stopped, he let her go, and she dropped to her feet, taking a few tiny backward steps to avoid the fall.

Maki head-butted the white-haired wheel in the face as it tried to swerve from the impact. Ren heard the bulbous nose crunch, and a curse, then the wheel landed flat on its back, where it would struggle to get back up.

Already, the two others came, rolling parallel to each other with enough distance to pass on both sides of the lion-dog.

"Maki, I take the one on the right," Ren said, tapping on the right flank of the guardian with his foot. She whoofed and burst forward to meet the attack.

The hunter passed his left leg above the lion-dog's head and stood against her ribs, gripping a tuft of fur with his left hand and biting the two talismans with gritted teeth. The wheel with the missing eye was spinning toward him, its flames gaining in size as it laughed like a lunatic.

"Keep going straight," he told Maki.

The wheel came in, bigger and bigger by the heartbeat. For a moment, Ren feared it would keep going and smash against the lion-dog, but at the last second, it veered outward a little, just enough for Ren to jump.

He caught the yōkai by its empty eye socket and kicked his foot in its mouth for support. The yōkai cursed him in his foul language, fury shooting from its last eye, which Ren punched eagerly. The wheel wobbled uncontrollably for a moment, during which Ren stuck a talisman on the bald skull. The face turned red as the yōkai's anger grew, and the flames gained in intensity. Ren winced from the sudden heat and pulled his face as far back as possible, which made the wheel sway dangerously.

The second yōkai whooshed close by. It inclined to get closer to the hunter, and soon Ren was hanging from the first while the second rolled parallel to it. It spun closer and closer, lips turned into a vicious, hungry grin. Maki was running after them, but she would never catch up.

Ren pushed his fear deep inside and focused on his Blood gate.

"*To-ko-ro-sho-bo,*" he said, eyes closed. The letters of the talisman stuck on the one-eyed yōkai started glowing red. "*No-sa-to!*"

Ren leaped from one wheel to the next as soon as the incantation was complete and landed right on the second wheel's hub-face, knee first. The first wheel seemed to lose synergy and stopped within a matter of rolls. Unable to keep its balance without speed, the yōkai landed flat on its back and cursed, its fire dying now that the wheel was inactive.

"Maki! It's yours!" Ren shouted. He received a bark in response, and two seconds later, the yōkai shrieked.

Big-lips saw his companion die under the claws of the lion-dog and started shaking to get rid of the hunter, but Ren was tugging on its ears and would not let go. The talisman flailed in between his fingers. Nature was streaming faster than ever around him, and if he did nothing, the wheel would crash with him against a tree or a rock.

The wanyūdō tried to bite the tip of Ren's feet, which rested on hub-face's chin for support, and almost had him. He lost his footing in avoiding the bite and found himself taken by the speed, legs flying behind him. He let go of the yōkai's left ear. This, in turn, freed his hand holding the talisman. Fighting the wind, Ren managed to slap the talisman on the second yōkai's forehead, and as soon as he was sure it would remain there, he closed his eyes again.

"*To-ko-ro-sho-bo-no-sa-to!*"

The wheel stopped in the next blink of an eye, propelling Ren forward. He rolled on his shoulder, then with all his body for a few steps. He climbed back on his feet as soon as he could make out the sky from the ground.

Only the creature's eyes and full lips moved when Ren ran back to it, and it used both to spit its fury at the hunter. Ren shoved his blade in the yōkai's mouth halfway through a curse and slashed across his long nose, cleaving the monstrous face in half from tongue to skull in a curtain of blood.

The hunter fell on his ass, groggy from all the action. When he looked back toward his guardian spirit, the lion-dog was still busy tearing her victim apart.

"Ren!"

The voice was faint. Peering at the horizon, Ren spotted Suzume running on the edge of a hill, the white-haired fire wheel right behind her. The girl was looking back, spear balancing at the end of her arm. Ren would never get to her on time. But he didn't need to.

He waited, waited for the yōkai to gain some ground, and raised his hand in their direction. Then, when the wanyūdō rolled a second from the girl, Ren snapped his fingers.

Sugi spun on her heels and cut through the flashing shape of the yōkai while crouching. The circular silhouette slowed and crashed into two neatly split halves. Ren let himself fall on his back and welcomed the rain on his face.

"Time for a harvest of magatama," he told himself as Maki and Suzume jogged in his direction.

CHAPTER 9

FIRE OVER THE MOUNTAIN

Ren observed the two magatama in the palm of his hand, trying to judge how many days he would get for them. They were made of bronze and, as such, quite valuable. Probably a week each, he thought. He assumed the white-haired yōkai would have been even more precious. Maybe not gold, but silver, at least.

Sugi's implacable kill did not leave him time to find out. Its soul had already vanished by the time Ren reached the two halves of the wanyūdō. They quickly put some distance and agreed half an hour later that no one followed them anymore. Maki walked by Ren's side, a slight limp from her burned knee slowing her down. She had rejected his offer to return home, and Ren felt better for her presence.

"Technically, you didn't kill those two," Ren said as he picked one of the two soul shells and held it, arm stretched toward the feeble sun. "But it was a team effort. So why don't you take one?"

"Thank you," she said as she received the shell, though it sounded like a question. "What do I do with it?"

"Just keep it until we return to Ise Jingū, then give it to the

Clerk to knock some days from your debt," Ren replied as if it was the most obvious thing in the world.

"My debt?" she asked.

"Yes, your debt. How long is it, by the way? Five years, I assume, unless Osamu gave you a rebate for being cute, that old perv."

Suzume looked at him uncomprehendingly as if he spoke another language.

"You do have a debt to the Yaseki, right?"

"A debt of gratitude, yes," Suzume replied, though she could see this was not what Ren had meant. "I waited for three days on the redwood island. No one dared approach me until a Yaseki priest came. I'd still be stuck there if not for him, so I'm truly grateful."

"You were invited?" Ren asked, nearly shouting the question.

"I didn't really have a choice, but yes, he invited me in," the girl replied. "I stayed within a small shrine on Shikoku for a couple of days, then they took me to Ise Jingū, where I met you." She smiled with her eyes as she said the latter part, but Ren cursed inside. Another point Osamu had omitted. "Is something wrong?"

"Two kinds of people join the Yaseki," Ren explained. "Those invited, like you, abandon their former lives and are welcomed in, but they can never leave the organization. I hope they told you this, at least."

"They did. But it's not like I have anywhere or anyone else to go to," she replied. "I assume you haven't been invited."

"I'm a saved one," Ren replied. "They saved me and my mother from a yōkai, which, in the eyes of the kami, puts us in the Yaseki's debt. If we try to leave the Yaseki before it's been reimbursed, we forfeit ourselves from the kami's fortune. It's like they don't see us anymore, and, believe me, a person forsaken by the kami doesn't live long. So, any magatama I bring back reduces our debt, and once I have reimbursed it, my mom and I will be free to resume our lives."

Suzume looked at the magatama in her hand. "Osamu told me about your mother," she said in a tone of apology.

"He told you about that but not about the gates?" Ren asked with a scoff. "Typical."

She handed him back the magatama, which he accepted with a grateful nod. She didn't need it. "What about the soldiers from before?" she asked to change the subject.

Ren sighed and scratched his head. He had yet to understand what had happened at the barrage. "They looked like konsejōbi," he said, "but those fire-souls are not capable of possessing a body. They can be a little scary, but unless you touch them, they really can't do any harm. I've never seen anything like that, though. Nor have I ever seen wanyūdō in groups. Those spinning bastards usually work alone and in cities, not in the middle of the country-side." Ren thought about the nue. Something strange and unique was happening. Maybe Osamu was right, and something truly dark was afoot.

"What do you think is happening?" Suzume asked.

"I don't know. But one thing is certain, whatever is happening in Kyōto is not just a human problem. Yōkai are involved, and they seem organized, and that too would be a first."

"So why do we go east then?"

"I fear that no matter where we try to get in, Kyōto will be well guarded," Ren answered. "And the closer we are, the stronger those things will get. I don't know who on earth this general is, but he is playing with fire if he has allied himself with yōkai."

"So we're not going to Kyōto?" Suzume asked.

"Oh, we are going to Kyōto," Ren replied. "But from a different route. One they won't be guarding. Iga will provide a safe passage to the capital, along with some information maybe, and some help."

"This Snake you mentioned?"

"Not just her," Ren replied with glee. "If possible, I'm taking the whole ninja clan with us. If I can get the full force of the Iga, I pity this general who thought he could mess with us."

Suzume giggled behind her hand in response to Ren's optimism. And east they went, toward White Phoenix Castle, where the powerful Iga clan ruled the shadows of the nation from their mountain.

血

Ren knew something was wrong long before the sun vanished at their backs, but the darkness only served to make the fires appear brighter over the mountain. Iga Ueno was burning. They had spotted the huge black clouds an hour before, stretching from many sources across the mountain, and had moved faster from then on. Maki was limping harder, and Suzume was completely out of breath, but they reached the foot of the mountain in the early minutes of the night, though the night was disturbed by the sounds of battle and screams of the wounded.

"What's going on?" Suzume asked from behind the rock they used as cover.

"Something bad," Ren replied unhelpfully.

Blades clashed in many places, and explosions echoed here and there. The three-storied white castle was vomiting great tongues of fire. Other buildings were burning, too, and those fires stretched the shadows of fighting men over the mountain like giants battling for its ownership. Not just men, Ren realized. Some shadows had wings, others snouts. Yōkai were attacking the Iga clan.

He heard footsteps coming from the path they would climb to reach the castle. When Ren peered around the rock, he noticed a hooded ninja running down toward them, straight blade in hand, eyes wild with terror. Ren was about to hail him when two spine-looking projectiles burst through the ninja's chest and propelled him onto the ground, face first. He no longer moved.

A creature leaped on his back and pierced his body once more with knife-like claws before nimbly jumping back into the bushes with astonishing speed. *Kama itachi*, Ren realized as he regained the cover of the rock.

Maki was growling threateningly. She had smelled it, and Ren remembered how much the lion-dog hated those weasel-yōkai. And that was before, when they did little more than prank mountain travelers. He'd never heard of a kama itachi killing, especially not trained ninja.

"Maki," Ren called in a whisper. "You stay here, and you protect Suzume."

"You're going alone?" the girl asked in a high-pitched whisper.

"I can't fight all the way up and watch my back at the same time," he replied.

"I can help you," Suzume said. "Maki, too."

The lion-dog made a low bark of agreement. Ren pondered his choices. Seeing the enemy's activity, Suzume would not be much safer here, especially with Maki's mane glowing like a beacon. They could run away, but men were dying here, and Snake would be around if she yet lived. Ren could not just leave the ninja clan to its fate.

"Do you think you can keep the trance?" he asked.

Suzume nodded, eyes strong and determined.

"Up to the castle?" he asked, nodding toward the burning building.

She gulped, her confidence quickly peeling off, but still said she could.

"Try not to let Sugi in until it becomes vital." Ren's sword was already unsheathed, but he removed the scabbard from his belt to parry with and stormed the path.

Suzume gasped when they ran past the dead ninja.

The Iga clan kept the trees short and the buildings separate from each other to make the mountain more difficult to storm. There were also secret traps and doors leading to tunnels connected to the castle. Ren knew none of their locations and preferred to keep to the usually safe path. With so much chaos around them, discretion was not a priority; speed was.

They progressed unopposed for a couple of minutes, though they encountered three bodies on the beaten path, one of which belonged to a badger-looking creature. Then, just as they changed direction with the path snaking along the mountain came the sound of swords being drawn. Seven warriors stood in their way, eyes livid and mouths hanging, their bodies draped in a ghostly blue steam. They wobbled on unsteady feet, each wielding a katana that seemed to dangle from weak hands.

"Wait," Ren said, stretching his arms.

"Hokenjōbi?" Suzume asked.

"No, those are *shinchinin misaki*," the hunter said. "They are not real; only their blades are. We can't kill them."

"We go another way?"

"Whoever controls them will send them after us," Ren said, eyes scanning their surroundings for a trace of the ghosts' master. An explosion shook the castle and a great part of the upper roof shattered from the structure. They had to hurry. "Maki, find their master."

The lion-dog whoofed and sniffed the air, then leaped toward the closest trees and ran along the slope. The seven ghosts turned toward the guardian spirit and were about to engage in pursuit, but Ren cut their path. His sword came down on the first warrior's arm and slashed through nothing but fume. The gaping mouth moaned as its arm fell off with the blade. It would need a few seconds to reattach the arm and grab the sword. Only Hearts and some rare Mouths could deal with ghosts. To Ren, fighting those poor creatures was akin to fighting a swarm of bees.

He ducked under the wide swing of a katana and rolled on his shoulder to avoid a lunge. His sword came in a horizontal arc, cutting through ghost legs, but this did little damage to those dead warriors. Ren parried a sword aimed at his neck, and this at least felt real. Sparks flew where the blades met, and when the rusty katana came again, Ren met it with greater force.

The ghost's blade flew with the strength of the parry and ended inside a tree trunk, toward which the ghost then floated helplessly. He could use this, Ren realized, but just then, three of those warriors lunged, and the tip of their blades appeared wide with their sudden proximity. They all shot upward with a loud clang and spun in the sky as Sugi took her spot by Ren's side.

"Good timing," Ren told the redwood spirit.

She did not gratify him with a response and pressed on the attack, slashing the cross-blade through steamy necks and limbs. The ghosts focused on her. Ren was about to tell her it was point-less. But his words remained in his mouth, for Sugi seemed to know what she was doing.

Her spear moved relentlessly, twirling left and right, then on her back, parrying a sword or severing a ghostly arm from its owner. She bent over, and yet the spear kept spinning on her back. Then she widened her grip and swept the polearm like the tail of a dragon. Sparks flew wherever her blade cut and the seven ghosts moaned in frustration.

A yelp echoed through the trees, and when Ren searched for its location, he saw Maki running after a grotesque shape. It looked like a person, if that person was made of pink lumps of flesh and covered in dozens of eyes blinking independently.

The lion-dog barked after the *hyakume* yōkai, both running on the path above Ren. For all its twisted appearance, the creature could run, and Maki was hard-pressed to catch up. A small projectile landed straight into the hyakume's chest, and one second later, the yōkai exploded in a splash of flesh and eyes. One of them bounced on Ren's shielding arm.

The seven warrior ghosts vanished almost instantly, their blades dropping harmlessly on the ground. Sugi straightened up, sweating but unhurt. Ren was about to ask how long she could stay in Suzume's body, but Maki barked for help, so Ren kept his question for later.

The lion-dog was crouching in a threatening pose. When Ren walked around her, he saw two ninja pointing their blades at the guardian spirit.

"Wait, wait!" he shouted, hands open toward them. "She's with us."

The two shinobi relaxed a little and lowered their blades. "Are you from the Yaseki?" the one on the left asked, his voice muffled by the fabric of the mask covering his mouth.

"Yes," Ren replied. "I'm here to see Snake. Is she alive? What's happening here?"

"We don't know," the second, a young female warrior, replied, though Ren wondered which of his questions she was answering. "They came out of nowhere. First within the castle, then from all over the mountain." Another explosion then tore a large piece of the castle's annex.

"Master Snake was fighting in the castle," the first one said.

"We could use your help," the kunoichi then said.

"Lead the way," Ren replied.

Someone screamed as they died up the path, and it was all the group needed as a signal to start running again. The two ninja were fast, too fast for the three others, but the kunoichi suddenly stopped and extended her arms while twisting on her left. A yōkai slammed into her from the cliff, and both vanished down the slope. The hunter could not be sure but thought it might have been the same weasel as before.

"Leave her!" the other ninja, who had not even slowed down, said when Ren approached the path's edge.

The path turned once more and then stretched right up to the empty yard facing the castle's gate. Dozens of shinobi were fighting an army of yōkai of every sort, though all the warriors appeared wounded one way or another. They fought with broken blades, bloody limbs, and despair.

In other circumstances, this would have made for an amazing spectacle. Ninja were leaping through the air, vaulting from an attack and gracefully landing on nimble feet before engaging new enemies. Yōkai relentlessly cut, stabbed, and clawed at every piece of flesh they could reach, and while many died on the ninja's blades, there were too many of the creatures for too few humans.

The castle still stood, but come the morrow, it would be nothing but ash and blackened stones. Corpses clad in fire were jumping from the building, the flames clothing them preventing Ren from discerning people from yōkai. One landed right by his feet. He had been an old man. Sugi pressed Ren's shoulder and nodded toward the battlefield. They had a job to do. Not waiting for him, she entered the melee, and her spear claimed yōkai lives from the first strike.

"Let's go, Maki!" Ren said.

He was no better fighter than most of the ninja, but at least he knew what he was fighting and how to kill them. The closest shinobi was wrestling a nue—the normal kind—and kept the beast at arm's length while it tried to bite the man's face off. Ren arched his blade upward in a wide swing to cut the snake-tail.

The creature shrieked and turned its attention toward him. The shinobi used this chance to stab the nue in the belly with a dagger and opened it from navel to throat in a swift motion. A nod later, the shadow warrior left to fight somewhere else.

Ren went after Sugi, though she didn't need the help. She was easy to follow. One just had to go after the trail of yōkai's corpses or listen to their screams.

A tall shinobi landed on his back right in front of Ren and raised his empty arm as a useless shield against its opponent. Ren did not even see the yōkai as it sliced through the air and tore the shinobi's arm off. It flew upward, the severed limb in its talon, big owl wings on its back. The shinobi screamed as blood spurted from the fresh wound.

"Maki!" Ren called as he knelt by the wounded ninja.

The lion-dog kicked dust when she reached her friend, and Ren lifted the bleeding arm to her mane, where it immediately hissed. The shinobi screamed even louder as the arm cauterized, but remained conscious.

"Watch out!" he said through his mask, looking where the winged yōkai was descending.

Ren twisted on his ankle, raised his sword, and lowered himself. The blade sliced through the creature's belly, which then fell in a bloody mess of bowels and flesh, its momentum taking it almost to the castle's feet.

Maki jumped upward, maw open, and caught another of those owl creatures between her fangs. When she landed, she growled and shook her head violently. The yōkai called for help, then something broke, and it became limp. Maki tossed her head one more time and threw the yōkai right through the burning doors of the castle. It disappeared inside in a great gush of flames.

The upper floor of the castle exploded a heartbeat later. Yōkai corpses, broken beams, and curved tiles blasted in all directions. Ren shielded the wounded shinobi from the debris and managed to get a glimpse of Sugi using her spear to keep a grown kappa at a distance. The hunter blinked, and the kappa's head popped from its body.

The fire blowing from the castle grew in size, but right from its source appeared a black, vaguely human shape. She jumped through the fire devouring the third floor and opened her arms to let the burning sheet she had wrapped herself with go, then landed with grace at the center of the yard.

Another explosion shook the castle's ground, and Ren understood she was at the origin of it. The flames behind her made Snake look even more fearsome than usual. She stood up, dressed in black from neck to toe, her obi belt floating in the night like a tail.

Ren didn't know if it was her entrance or the last explosion, but no sooner had Snake reached the battleground than the yōkai started fleeing it. There was no signal of any kind, or none he recognized, but the rout began everywhere at once.

"Rooster?" Snake asked, frowning with pleasure. "What are you doing here?"

"We thought you could use some help," Ren said as he stood to meet her, Maki on his trail.

"You and the dog?" she asked.

"And the girl," Ren said, pointing at Sugi, who was disemboweling a shrieking yōkai.

"A Warrior Hand? Sweet," Snake replied, flashing a charming smile contradicting the situation. She was about to say something, but a loud, piercing shriek rang from the castle. Snake turned around and picked up the two short sickles tucked on her lower back in the same motion.

The screaming yōkai shot upward from the castle a mere moment before the structure toppled on itself. It kept rising for yet a couple of seconds before opening its wings and hanging in the air, right at the center of the full moon. Its feathers were gray, its beak yellow, and its limbs thin and dark. The beast had no hands, so it kept its leafy fan inside its talons and observed the battlefield with quiet rage.

"A tengu?" Ren asked in a stupor.

"It's just a *konoha tengu*," Snake said, nose wrinkling with hatred. "But—"

"It's stronger than it should be?" Ren asked, though he already knew the answer.

"Aye," Snake replied. "It's coming!" she shouted when the yōkai suddenly swooped downward toward them. "Watch out for its—"

But before Snake could finish her sentence, the silhouette of Suzume rose on the tengu's path and stopped it brutally, embedding the spear in the yōkai's belly. Taken by her momentum, Sugi twisted above the creature, and when she seemed to stand on top, skewered it and kicked it hard in the chest. The tengu shot downward like a falling rock and slammed into the hard ground of the castle's yard.

"Never mind," Snake went on, standing straighter. "Ren, who's the girl?"

"A redwood spirit," the hunter replied as he passed by the shinobi to meet with Sugi.

They stood around the mortally wounded konoha tengu, who pitifully spat blood from its broken beak. Both its wings had broken on impact and now covered its chest. No matter what, it was dying. Ren nodded at Sugi in appreciation of her talents, wondering how long she could remain in Suzume after such a hard fight.

The yōkai coughed some more. Maki then came closer, illuminating the pool of blood spreading from the beast's back with her glowing mane. A tengu, Ren thought, finally a tengu. Not the one he was searching for, only a minor tengu, but a tengu nonetheless.

"Who sent you?" Snake asked, grabbing the yōkai by the neck.

"The General sends his regards," the tengu replied with a chuckle. It didn't fear death.

"What general?" Ren then asked.

Its dead black eyes switched from the shinobi to the hunter, and its beak seemed to smile, if such a thing were possible. "You won't need to know," the yōkai replied.

Its broken wing then slowly brushed open, revealing a shredded shirt of silk hiding some kind of device. The word *bomb* came to Ren's mind just as he noticed the rope the creature held in its talons. Snake's hands dropped on Ren's shoulders as the rope tensed.

There was a silvery flash, and the yōkai's leg suddenly twirled in the air, a piece of the rope still stuck between its talons. The tengu then shrieked with pain until Maki grabbed it by the head and tossed it into the burning ruins of the castle, where it exploded.

"Seriously, Ren," Snake asked as they straightened back up. "Who's the girl?"

CHAPTER 10
BREAKING THE WALL

In the light of a new day, Hakuho Castle and the Iga domain were even worse for wear. Nothing remained of the main building besides the stones previously supporting the structure. Whatever residence or storage had flanked the mountain would fume for days. Snake laughed it off. Buildings could be repaired, and the clan would find creditors in no time. The lost lives, though, were irreplaceable.

Not just the dead, who numbered close to a hundred and were presently being laid in the yard under white blankets, but the broken ones, too. A third of the surviving fighting force of the Iga clan would never pick up a blade again. Between those wounded in the flesh and those scarred in their hearts, Snake declared she would be lucky to lift the clan back to full strength in her lifetime.

Ren told her she exaggerated, but she looked at him with this sorry look any Blood would understand. Few lived to see their hair turn gray, and she was close to it already. Snake was not only the Snake Blood but also the heiress of the Iga clan. Or possibly its current leader since her father had yet to be found.

Neither position made life safe. Shinobi being what they were, the Yaseki was no secret for them, and the cooperation between the two organizations stretched back to the clan's foundation. Their heiress being one of the twelve Bloods only made the bond stronger.

"Things would have gotten worse without you and your friends. I guess we've been lucky," Snake said, nodding toward Suzume, sleeping on a patch of grass.

Suzume had dropped a few seconds after the konoha tengu exploded, but her breathing was steady, and she was miraculously unhurt. Maki and Ren spent most of the night scanning the mountain for possible yōkai stragglers, but they found more bodies than corrupted souls and not a single magatama between them. The hunter afforded himself a couple of hours of sleep, and only because he needed to get on the road as soon as possible, sadly, with no reinforcement.

"I'm just glad we arrived when we did," Ren replied. He thought he had gotten used to death, but in those numbers, it was hard to witness.

"Still," Snake said as a young shinobi brought her a list that could have contained many kinds of information. "If what you say is true, something terrible is taking place. Nue destroying torii, battlefield fires possessing bodies, wanyūdō working as a team..."

"Not forgetting an army of yōkai invading your mountain under the command of a konoha tengu," Ren added. "A smart, powerful one at that. Do you think you can send a message to Osamu?"

Snake sighed as she looked around them. Every pair of hands would be needed to rebuild the castle or care for those who could no longer help. Some of the youngest would ask to be sent on a revenge mission. However, until more was known regarding the situation at the capital, spreading their forces was a mistake, as she explained to the young hunter.

"Why did they attack here?" Ren asked.

The shinobi knelt to a young, wounded shadow warrior who had most likely just received his hood and would never wear it on a mission. She peeled it over his face. His wounds had been too severe. "I assume to thwart our rescue mission," she replied.

"A rescue mission?"

"We are the closest fighting force to Kyōto besides the imperial guard. If something were to happen at the capital, we would be the first to rescue the emperor." The words came with a hint of guilt, as if she should have seen it coming. "I will still assemble a team as soon as things are clear here and go with them to Kyōto. Until then, I'll have to count on you and the redwood spirit," Snake said, dropping her hand on the hunter's shoulder.

"And I'll send someone to Osamu. The man you saved from the owl yōkai. He can't do much here, but he'll be happy to return the favor. If you don't mind, though, I'll instruct him not to tell Osamu you saved him. I can't lose another man, not even to the Yaseki, not even a one-armed man."

Ren didn't mind and had not even considered how his actions might have impacted the man's life with a debt to the organization. He had reacted more than anything. "Thank you, Snake," Ren said, defeat on his face.

Nothing had warned them of this attack. Ren had spent the last three years hunting corrupted souls, and Snake had acted both as a hunter and a shinobi for three decades. Yet, both were unprepared for what was shaping to become a war.

"Don't make this face," Snake replied, smiling a twisted smile that made her many scars stretch. She could have been pretty if life had not been so rough from birth. "My warriors know what they risk and fought with honor. We suffered the first blow, but we'll deal the hardest one."

"I pity our enemy then," Ren said with a faint trace of optimism, though his heart wasn't in it.

Suzume woke with a yawn and stretched her arms upward. For

a moment, she smiled at Ren and waved, then she remembered and noticed the bodies around her. The smile vanished right away.

"A redwood spirit, huh?" Snake asked, smirking.

"From Shikoku," Ren said as Suzume got to her feet.

"I sure never met a land kami with that kind of warrior spirit," the shinobi replied, arms crossed over her chest.

"What are you implying?"

"No idea," Snake answered. "Maybe whatever makes the yōkai stronger affects other spirits. Or maybe she's not what she says she is. Or maybe she isn't *just* a redwood kami. I think you're safer with her than without, but I would still keep an eye on her."

"Noted," Ren said. Suzume was a good soul, he had no doubt about it, and Sugi was a pure kami, albeit a violent one, but Ren was a chick compared to a veteran like Snake. Her words of caution deserved to be heard.

"You'll be on your way then?" the shinobi asked when Suzume reached them.

"Yes, and if possible, I'd like to use your tunnel to Kyōto. Don't make this face; it's no secret you have one."

"No," Snaked replied, "that's not the problem. It's just that I'm not sure you can even get in the tunnel."

泗

Most yōkai had left and scattered to the wind, leaving only one of them behind.

"A *nurikabe*?" Ren asked as they stood in front of the yōkai. "That's just great," he said, throwing his arms in the air.

"Is it dangerous?" Suzume asked in a whisper. The hunter and the shinobi did not bother with discretion.

"It's not dangerous," Snake replied while Ren stretched the skin on his face with despairing hands. "But it sure is a bother."

146

"They're walls," Ren explained. "Just dumb yōkai walls. They don't talk, they don't seem to think, and, once invoked, cannot be moved for a month, then they just vanish. And this one has been invoked right in front of the tunnel's entrance."

"At least it explains how they snuck into the domain," Snake said. "I don't know how, but they knew about the tunnel and used it from Kyōto, then sealed it with a nurikabe."

"Damn it," Ren whispered. "I guess we're back on the road."

"Why?" Suzume asked. "We can't destroy it?"

"Nothing can destroy a nurikabe," Ren replied, waving toward the slab of uneven plaster blocking the entrance of what appeared like a cave at the foot of the mountain. Two waves of plaster toward the top looked almost like eyes, but nothing else spoke of a living being.

"We have a few explosives left," Snake said, scratching her head. "We could give it a try."

"Keep them," Ren replied. "Blockhead here wouldn't feel it."

"Hum," Suzume said. "Sugi says it's just a wall. She can destroy it."

"You can hear her voice even now?" Ren asked proudly. "That's good. But I wouldn't recommend trying. The spear would smash against it, and then we wouldn't be able to call Sugi."

"Maybe we can dig around it," Snake said.

"Is there another entrance?" Ren asked.

"Nah, just a couple of exits at the other end."

The young hunter's tongue clicked in his mouth. He had wasted another day coming here, it seemed.

"Sugi says we should let her try," Suzume timidly said.

"Maybe Maki can do it," Ren said, ignoring the girl.

"She just went back; let her rest," the shinobi replied. "And besides drooling all over the nurikabe, I don't think she could do much."

"Talismans then?"

147

"For what? Wishing it to find love and go away?" Snake scoffed.

"I was just thinking out loud; no need to be sarcastic."

"Well, think better, then, not louder."

A sudden gust of wind passed between the two Blood Hunters, making their hair sway, their clothing wave, and the wall explode in a myriad of plaster bits. Sugi stood amid the cloud of fading dust, straight as her spear, which had remained intact after all. She lifted her right hand and tossed its contents at Ren. Another bronze magatama. No one had ever discovered what material nurikabe magatama were.

Mouth hanging, Ren looked up at the smirking warrior kami. She blinked, and the smirk turned into a shy pout.

"She really insisted," Suzume said, looking sorry and pleased with herself at the same time. Ren's mouth had yet to close when Snake whistled, understandably impressed.

"Keep an eye on her, all right?" the shinobi told the young hunter.

"Uh-huh."

血

They'd walked in the tunnel for hours, and it would still go on for another four or five. Snake had spoken of a twelve-hour journey, but she had also promised that torches would be lining the wall, and none were to be found. The yōkai who had used the tunnel in great numbers, judging by all the footprints, scales, spines, and an impressive amount of slimy liquids, must have taken them. When the ones given to them by Snake lost their fire, Ren was forced to call Maki again and used her mane to illuminate the path. He was down by three beads out of twelve, and they still hadn't reached Fushimi Inari.

Yet, despite all those troubles, and despite the monotony of this stretch of the journey, Suzume was jubilant. She skipped as often as she walked and hummed Pon-Pon's song when she didn't sing it. One wouldn't think, looking at her so joyful, that she had just experienced a brutal battle ending in many people's death. Snake's words of caution came back to Ren, and he wondered if this journey affected Suzume more than he had previously thought.

"Someone is enjoying the underground," he said when she ended another round of the song.

"Sorry," she replied, adjusting her steps for a few seconds before skipping again. "I'm just full of energy this morning or this afternoon... Do you think it's the evening?"

"The evening can't be far," Ren replied. "Are you all right?" he then asked Maki.

The lion-dog had not seemed thrilled to be called back so soon at first. Her knee had yet to mend from the fight against the wanyūdō, and she was spent from a night chasing yōkai from Iga Ueno. But she, too, seemed to regain energy as they traveled through the tunnel. Snake had mentioned nothing about such a phenomenon.

"Do you want to take a break?"

"Oh no," Suzume answered gleefully. "I'm just looking forward to being in the capital."

"Well, don't forget that we're not going there to visit. The shrine to Inari lies south of the city, so we might not even get inside Kyōto. And that's if we can set foot outside of this tunnel in the first place. Who knows what awaits us on the other side of it."

"Don't be so gloomy," Suzume replied, with the support of Maki's echoing whoof. "No matter what, there's always light at the end of the tunnel."

Ren tilted his head in something resembling an agreement. They were still alive and mostly in good shape, after all. Suzume kept looking at him with this new delighted grin of hers, expecting some reaction.

"Wait," Ren said, raising an eyebrow. "Was that a joke?"

"Yes, yes, yes," she replied, proud of herself.

"Suzume, did a shinobi give you a weird-smelling potion or something?"

"Nope, nope, nope," she answered between skipping steps.

"I appreciate this enthusiasm, Suzume, but we'll need to be discreet in Kyōto. So, try to keep it under control, will you?"

"I will," she said, joining her hands as a child promising to be good, which would have been more convincing without the ironic pout or the spear jutting between her crossed fingers.

"So let's hope there's no nurikabe at the other side because breaking it would not help our exit remain unnoticed."

"We don't think there will be one," Suzume said.

"We?"

"Sugi and I," the girl replied. "She believes the enemy trusted the previous nurikabe and wouldn't waste anymore effort protecting the other side of the tunnel. And she says the lack of yōkai here, in the tunnel, proves it. And I agree. So, yes, *we*."

"You seem to communicate much better with your kami," Ren said.

"We are," she replied. "She's actually quite fun. If you could hear the things she says about—"

"Yes?" Ren asked.

"Nothing," Suzume replied innocently. "Nothing, nothing."

The hunter looked back at the lion-dog, who returned nothing better than a drool-filled smile.

"I was wondering," Suzume said. "Why didn't Snake call a guardian as well? She's a Blood, right? She must be able to invoke lion-dogs, too, no?"

"Not every Blood has shared an oath with guardians," Ren replied, rubbing the chin of the komainu. "Snake could call the guardians of a temple, but Iga Ueno mountain has no shrine. Maybe she had a partner spirit in the past, but I never heard about it."

"In the past?" Suzume asked, her joviality suddenly winding down. "Do you mean they can die?" She asked the last in a whisper so that Maki couldn't hear.

"Just like any spirit," Ren replied. "And then their essence reforms over a long period of time. If something happened to Maki, she wouldn't exist for many years, probably several decades. No matter what, I would never see her again." He dropped his forehead against the side of Maki's head as he spoke and patted her mane with more conviction when she whimpered. "In a way, she would be dead to me."

"That is so sad," Suzume said, her eyes tearing up. "Let's make sure it never happens then."

The lion-dog whoofed again, and the sound bounced along the tunnel for a long time. The bark died, and Suzume resumed her little song.

This should have been good, Ren thought, but somehow merriment did not fit this place, nor this time. Something was happening to Suzume, and it was getting stronger. The young hunter wondered if a good mood and a boost in energy could be dangerous, but it seemed like the lowest point on his list of problems.

CHAPTER II
FOX AND OX

Suzume's optimism and Sugi's logic were not wrong. Nothing and no one guarded the exit of the tunnel. It opened to a broken door at the back of a dark room used for storage under a bridge of the Kamo River. Empty or broken crates littered the room, but nothing else.

The exit opening to a quay and a peaceful river contained no door, and the frame had been enlarged to let the biggest yōkai through. It was night. A dark, cloudy night. But even then, the glowing embers of the capital offered enough light for Ren to see that Kyōto would never be the same.

Leaving Suzume and the lion-dog in the storage room after activating his amulet, the young hunter sneaked onto the quay and then trudged the rising bank until he could witness the situation better.

This was the south edge of the city, not too far from Fushimi Inari. The mountain on which the shrine had been built was similar in size to Iga Ueno. Stone lamps following the many paths snaking to the summit illuminated it. Fushimi Inari had weathered the storm, it seemed, but it was the only part of the capital that was neither burning nor fuming. Too many buildings stood between the hunter and the shrine to be sure of the place's safety, though. He had to get closer.

A unit of six soldiers marched over the bridge in perfect order. Ren flattened himself and let them pass a few steps from him. They bore the same crow crest as those on the road, and their eyes shimmered blue. They paid no attention to the izakaya shop crumbling on their right or the cat crossing the street behind them. All they seemed to exist for was reaching the shrine. Ren slid down the bank as soon as they disappeared from his line of sight.

"So?" Suzume asked when Ren entered the storage room. Her young, freckled face was glowing with the light of the lion-dog's mane.

"It's bad," he said, scratching his head. "Kyōto is... Well, Kyōto is no more. I don't know what happened, but it happened over the last few days." Ren felt bad for the relief this recognition gave him. Even if he had reached the capital in a more timely manner, things would have been the same. "The shrine seems fine, but if I'm right, the enemy is gathering there. Getting inside will be tricky."

"Can we get close?" Suzume asked.

"With this, maybe," Ren replied, showing the amulet he had attached to his belt. A dark blue pouch, no bigger than his palm, engraved with golden threaded characters for safe travel. "I just activated it, and it should keep the enemies' eyes from us as long as we are careful and on some road. We won't be invisible, but it will keep us fortunate for an hour or so."

"Unfortunately," he went on, looking at Maki, who immediately seemed to understand and whimpered as she dropped her head on her front legs. "I'm sorry, Maki. You're not the most discreet travel companion, especially at night. But you know what," Ren continued as he squatted in front of her and pinched her cheeks, "they have a few lion-dog statues in the shrine. As soon as I see one, I'll call you, all right?"

The guardian looked away, disappointed.

"Should we go then?" Suzume asked excitedly.

"There's a second problem," Ren replied in an embarrassed tone. "The amulet *can* work for two people. But there's a trick."

Hand in hand, Suzume and Ren left the cover of the storage room, then climbed the bank and tiptoed toward the closest line of damaged houses. Most remains did not reach higher than chest level, so the duo had to progress bent over but still holding hands. If the contact broke, Ren had explained, the yōkai might suddenly feel a difference and find her, so he had tied their hands with some of the ribbons given by Hotaru. Her hand was soft, Ren thought with a blush hidden by the night.

The mountain grew bigger with each step. The burning city gave it an ominous appearance. It illuminated the paths covered in hundreds of orange torii, forming corridors for the pilgrims with an eerie light. People were moving through the torii, too small from this distance to be recognized, but Ren thought some wore priests' garments. He prayed that Kiyoshi Kuroda, the head priest of the temple, still lived. If anyone could survive this attack on the capital and mount a defense, it was the old Ox.

Twice, they stopped and froze to let a patrol walk away, all of them marching toward the mountain. Things became noisier as they neared the shrine, and soon, the sounds of men marching, bows being made ready, and horses trampling covered their approach.

Ren pulled Suzume into a fairly intact house that must have been a tea shop. The south side of the establishment had crumbled on half its length, but the rest still stood, though most of the shop's furniture or items had been destroyed or looted. Ren hugged the eastern wall, the one facing the mountain, and carved a hole through a weak plank with the tip of his blade.

"So?" Suzume asked as soon as his eye found the hole.

"So, we're screwed," Ren answered almost immediately.

Hundreds of soldiers surrounded the shrine, and if the same line spread all around the mountain, there would be thousands of them. They formed blocks of sixty men, perfectly aligned, patiently waiting on their feet. Ren shuddered at the thought of so many battlefield fires gathered in one place. Each block seemed to be led by yōkai of another kind, smarter creatures capable of making decisions and understanding complicated orders.

"I can see at least three konoha tengu like the one you speared in Iga and several kappa."

"Ren," Suzume called, tugging on his hand, which she seemed to clasp harder.

"Wait," Ren replied. "A samurai is walking toward the entrance of the shrine."

The officer of the yōkai army took a few steps toward the great torii, but no sooner did he raise his sheathed sword as a request for a parley than a couple of arrows thumped into his chest. He fell on his back, holding the pose, and two soldiers dragged him back. The fire soul did not rise from the body until they plucked the arrows out.

"That must be Kiyoshi's work," Ren commented with pleasure.

"It's Kuroda-sama for you," a voice called behind him.

Ren felt his heart drop to his stomach as he twisted on his ankle to face the woman who had spoken. Suzume had called for him because she had seen her, but she, too, remained stunned by her presence. His hand moved to the hilt of his sword, and he almost let go of Suzume, but the woman's appearance alone prevented him from drawing. Never in his young life had Ren met such a beautiful creature.

Her face was painted white, except for a thin layer above the eyes that left her skin pink. Red, full, severe lips clashed with the white of her skin, and well-drawn eyes ended in black tips that made them look like black magatama. The upper left side of her head was covered by a fox mask that seemed to gaze upon the sky, and a golden phoenix pin fixed her hair in an upswept, wide bun.

The *oiran*—for a courtesan of the highest rank she must be—wore a three-layered kimono with a red underlayer the exact color of her lips, overlaid by a golden second layer adorning a pattern of black clouds. The upper kimono, an ample, dark blue, unbelted *uchikake* trailing behind her heels, was decorated with an intricate design of a maple tree losing its autumn leaves to the wind. The thick pang of the obi hung over her belly, revealing a fox howling at a golden moon.

White, lacquered *okobo* sandals made of one block of wood attracted the attention to gracious, naked feet with toes painted blood-red, as were the nails of her hands. She walked in, one slow step dragging the bottom of her sandal in front of the other foot.

Ren was entranced by the allure of her gait. He brutally woke up to the present when she butted the tip of her black and gold umbrella against the tea shop's ashen ground.

"People sell their children for a chance to look at my feet. So please avert your eyes," she said in a cold, bewitching voice, a sensuous smile contradicting her words.

Ren remembered to close his mouth, and to breathe, and who and where he was.

"Kiyoshi sent you?" Ren asked when she stood but a blade length from him. Suzume had yet to stand. Her eyes could not open wide enough.

"*Kuroda-sama* sent me," she replied, not feigning the irritation in her tone.

"How did you get here?" Suzume asked. Ren wondered if he had heard the vehemence in Suzume's voice or just imagined it.

"Same as you, it seems," the courtesan said, raising the amulet tucked under the front pang of her belt.

Even with the amulet, Ren could not believe such an ostentatious woman could sneak out of the mountain unnoticed. No charm was *that* powerful.

"We spotted you at the river. Kuroda-sama assumed you would use the tunnel. Two days ago."

The hunter did not care much for her accusation, but she turned around, and the scent of the cypress imbued in the fabric of her kimono made him forget her tone.

"We are short of time. Shall we?"

Ren nodded and was about to follow her but remained on his spot when Suzume tugged on his hand. She frowned, and for a moment, Ren wondered if she was mad at him; then, she nodded toward the woman's feet.

What a fool, Ren accused himself for having missed the most obvious part of this woman's nature. The white, furry tips of two tails balanced in rhythm from under her kimono, sweeping the floor behind her sandals.

"I didn't catch your name, *kitsune*-san," Ren said.

When the woman looked over her shoulder, she smiled from a white muzzle, red eyes full of cunning. Her voice remained the same when she answered.

"My name is Fuyuko. Pleased to make your acquaintance." She bowed ever so slightly and resumed her human mask upon straightening up.

"That's fine," Ren whispered to Suzume, who seemed to grab her spear tighter. "She's with Kiyoshi. Probably." The Blood Ox might favor fox spirits, but Ren had learned to distrust them, and he promised himself not to let her charm take root in his belly.

Fuyuko guided them through the ruins without ever slowing

157

down, though her cumbersome sandals kept her speed moderate. The yōkai army stood on the other side of the line of buildings, yet no one seemed to care about anything but the mountain. An assault was bound to happen, and Ren asked the fox spirit what they were waiting for.

"We built a *kekkai*," she whispered back.

"A kekkai?" Suzume asked.

"A spiritual barrier, raised by Mouths," Ren told her. "Hason-tama can't pass through it, but it takes an enormous amount of energy to keep it standing and an unbreakable focus. Does it go all around the mountain?"

"Uh-huh," the fox replied.

"How many Mouths are working on it?" the hunter asked. "It must be a good hundred."

"All of them," she replied. "But they've maintained it for three days. I'm afraid they won't keep it for long now."

"Three days," Ren whispered, shaking his head.

"If you hadn't shown up today, Kuroda-sama would have led a sortie tomorrow with what energy we still possess. But between the drained Mouths and our few living warriors, our chances were slim. Though I do not believe two children will make a great difference."

"Children?" Ren asked, vexed.

"What happened in Kyōto?" Suzume asked.

"Kuroda-sama will tell you everything," Fuyuko replied. Ren had not even realized she had stopped walking. "But first, we need to get you inside the shrine."

The courtesan invited them to peek behind the wall of yet another ruined structure. When they did, Ren spotted a large unit with dozens of soldiers in a squared formation led by an armored kappa. He alone paced over his unit, nervously testing the strength of the kekkai with the tip of his claws.

The invisible wall waved and shimmered like oiled water

under his touch. When he hammered it with the flat of his fist, it created a ripple reverberating a few times. On the other side of the barrier stood a medium-sized torii, then the beginning of a path leading up the forested shrine.

"What's the plan?" Ren asked when he stopped looking.

"The soldiers don't matter," Fuyuko replied. "They've been told to watch ahead, and unless ordered otherwise by what passes for an officer among them, they won't stop anyone from getting in. They'll reply to aggression, though."

"So we neutralize their officer?" Ren asked.

"Such violent words," the courtesan replied in a suave, appreciative voice. "Let me take care of the kappa. Just follow me and stay close."

"I thought you said no aggression," Suzume said.

"Don't worry, little bird, I know what I'm doing," Fuyuko replied. "Once he has lost his head for me, just run toward the torii."

"You meant that metaphorically, right?" Ren asked.

He received a mischievous smirk in reply, and she left the cover of the building to step into the alley leading to the soldiers. Ren tilted his head when Suzume frowned her lack of trust in this overly simple plan. Then they walked after the courtesan, moving toward the gap between two units of puppet soldiers.

Fuyuko's gait was regal, as if those broken streets belonged to her. Suzume's hand was turning wet when they reached the back line of the enemy formation, yet none of them even shifted their gaze upon the two hunters.

"Hey!" croaked the warrior kappa, webbed hand extended to order Fuyuko to stop. "No one approaches the shrine! By order of the—"

His voice died when Fuyuko walked by him unopposed. The kappa seemed petrified; his eyes still transfixed on the spot where the courtesan had stood a second before. Then, a red line appeared from the center of his throat and extended across it.

Fuyuko kept walking, and Ren heard the click of her sword sheathing back into the umbrella's shaft. He had not even noticed her drawing it or that it contained a sword at all. The head just slipped from its neck and showered the closest soldiers in brown blood. If Ren and Suzume had kept going, they would have been drenched in it, too.

"It wasn't metaphorical," Ren said.

"We should run," Suzume replied, taking the first step.

All the soldiers turned toward their beheaded officer when the body fell to its knees. The sound of sixty sets of armor twisting toward the two hunters gave Ren all the motivation he needed to accept Suzume's offer. Ren felt the moment the redwood spirit took over when the grip on his hand became painful.

Sugi thrust the spear toward the closest soldier as he raised his blade, and caught him in the mouth. Ren round kicked him in the chest to make sure the spear didn't get stuck and was pulled by the warrior kami before his foot touched the ground again.

Because his right hand was tied to Suzume's left, he could not pull his sword out. It was a disadvantage of tucking it on the back, hilt on the right side, but until that evening, he had never needed to fight left-handed. The spear pole slammed into the face of a soldier on their left and sent him tumbling against his comrade. Looking ahead, Ren saw Fuyuko hurrying under the torii gate, leaving them behind to fend for themselves. The two blocks of soldiers closed on them, trapping them from the shrine and the courtesan.

"Never trust a fox!" Ren spat before grabbing the wrist of a samurai to prevent him from drawing his katana. There was no expression on the possessed warrior, not even when a whistling arrow jutted through his face and toppled him like a dead tree.

Another arrow whistled from the shrine, followed by a dozen

of them. The closest soldiers all fell except the one Sugi rammed with the butt end of her spear. She dislodged her weapon from the soldier's eye in a vicious twist a second before passing the kekkai.

They reached safety, leaving a battleground teeming with clumsy bodies and blue fires rising out of their temporary broken vessels. Those touched by the arrows seemed to take longer to recover, Ren thought, though his eyes quickly set on Fuyuko again.

"A little warning would have been nice," he spat.

She chuckled behind her wide sleeve. "You managed," she replied.

"Only thanks to your archers," the hunter said, tugging on Sugi's hand because the warrior kami seemed very eager to let the she-fox know how she felt about her methods. Her remark would not have been generous in words.

"And I hope it was worth it," a priest commented, approaching from the water pavilion he had used as a cover while drawing his bow.

The wooden structure was peppered with feathered shafts, proof that the kekkai did not stop arrows. Seven or eight of his companions made themselves seen when the priest showed himself. His bow, Ren guessed, was the *shintai* of an archer kami, and this marked him as a Hand. He looked exhausted, and so did the women and men coming to his side.

"Those were the last of our *hamaya* arrows."

Ren pretended not to notice the man's raw fingers or the way they trembled.

"Those two are the guests Kuroda-sama was expecting," Fuyuko told the man, opening her hand toward Ren and Suzume, who was now in control of her body again.

"Why did you leave them behind then?" the archer asked in anger.

"Just to make sure they were worth the hassle."

泗

Maki growled for a long time after Ren called her from the first guardian statue he could find, and he wasn't about to stop her. Cats and weasels, she disliked, but foxes she hated, and judging by Fuyuko's snarl, the feeling was mutual. Even though the courtesan didn't need to pretend anymore, she chose to keep her human appearance as she guided them through a corridor of torii.

Maki didn't fit under the arches, so she had to climb the slope from the side. They quickly passed the cordon of chanting priests and monks who fueled the kekkai. Some did not belong to Fushimi Inari, but they prayed nonetheless, and all looked on the brink of collapsing. Suzume asked Ren if they still needed to walk hand in hand, and the confused hunter swiftly untied the ribbons. Fuyuko chuckled at the scene.

"What is she?" Suzume asked Ren, nodding toward the courtesan.

"She's a fox," Ren answered in the most obvious manner. "Just like Pon-Pon, she's lived long enough to evolve. Foxes' tails split when they do and then again when they reach a certain age. She's a two-tailed fox, so not nearly as experienced or powerful as she would have us believe." He let his voice rise to make sure the courtesan heard, but she did not bite the bait.

"I hope this Pon-Pon you just compared me to is a handsome brother of mine and not, as I suppose, a filthy tanuki," she said in her suave voice. Even after what she had done, Ren found it enthralling.

"Oh, he is a filthy tanuki, all right," Ren replied. "A filthy, pervy, drunk tanuki."

"And you should consider yourself lucky we used his name in the same sentence as yours," Suzume said. Her cheeks puffed when Fuyuko smiled at her little outburst. Ren didn't think Suzume had this kind of dislike in her. "Is she like Maki then?"

"Not exactly," Ren said. "Maki is a guardian, a messenger of the kami if you prefer. Fuyuko here is a proper living being. She can't be summoned or *sent away*." The fox giggled when she heard his voice rise. "I don't know if she belongs to Kiyoshi, and I prefer not to imagine how she and him are linked."

"You're too young to have this kind of imagination, believe me," Fuyuko replied. The corridor split in two. Fuyuko chose the left one. "And I don't belong *to* him. I belong *with* him."

"What kind of man is Kiyoshi—Kuroda-san?" Suzume asked. Even if the fox hadn't clicked her tongue, Suzume would not have been able to call someone she didn't know by his first name alone, but Ren appreciated the insulting effort.

"He is the most experienced Blood there is," Ren replied with respect. "And has been around for so long that he has shared oaths with pretty much every kind of guardian that exists, even frogs. I met Maki thanks to him."

The lion-dog barked, and Ren lost himself for a second in the painful yet beautiful memory of his oath with the komainu guardians.

"As far as I know, very few Bloods ever became head priests of a shrine as important as Fushimi Inari. But Kiyoshi has earned the respect of the Yaseki's elders and has efficiently protected the imperial capital for decades."

"Until a few days ago," Fuyuko said, her head low. She sounded defeated.

Along the path, Ren saw several groups of civilians gathered under makeshift tents or simply sitting on wooden stairs. They had found refuge in the shrine when the fires spread and were now trapped between a yōkai army and the last resisting forces of Kyōto.

"Iga Ueno has been attacked and nearly destroyed, too," Suzume said, reacting to the change in Fuyuko's tone.

"Yet you used the tunnel," the fox replied, looking at the girl with a hint of respect. "Does it mean you made a difference there?"

"We did, I think," the girl answered, squaring her shoulders.

"Let's hope you can replicate this... miracle here." The hint vanished, and so did Suzume's fresh pity.

The number of people increased steadily when the hill flattened to a plateau. They gasped at the sight of Maki, who could finally rejoin her friend when they emerged from the orange corridor, but not one of them panicked. They had seen a lot of odd creatures over the last few days.

Ren noticed the quality of their clothing was improving as the density thickened. By the time they reached the wooden floor of a worshipping hall's yard, he and Suzume were surrounded by fine-looking courtiers, noble ladies, and even some ministers. Armored samurai protected the yard, though most were white-haired and carried parade swords rather than proper fighting blades.

Kiyoshi Kuroda, the Ox Blood and most venerable hunter of his kind, stepped out of the hall and extended long sleeves to welcome Ren. Or so the young hunter believed until Fuyuko settled inside the open arms and closed her eyes, face pressed against the old man's chest. When she looked up at the priest, Ren guessed love in her eyes and in Kiyoshi's, too.

"Rooster," Kiyoshi said, greeting the young man with a nod.

He had aged, Ren thought. Last they had met, Kiyoshi Kuroda still stood straight, and his shoulders didn't slump. He had been a wrinkled man, but those wrinkles came from a life under the sun. Now, they belonged to a person who had suffered decades of hardship. Ren wondered how much of those wrinkles had been there until a few days ago.

"It's good to see you, Ox," Ren replied, returning the nod.

Fuyuko seemed angry with the use of the nickname, and she

had yet to let go of the priest. Gently, the old man pushed his lover from his arms and climbed down from the building.

"I am glad Osamu-kun sent you," the priest said as they clasped their four hands together. "And you, young miko," he went on, taking Suzume's hands in his. "And you too, Maki." His mask of wrinkles curled up with a heartfelt smile for the lion-dog, who barked once with pleasure. The fifty or so people gathered in the yard gasped when she did so.

"I'm sorry," Ren said. "We were delayed on the road, and—"

Kiyoshi raised his hand to quiet Ren. "The kami and Osamu-kun chose you and your path. It all happened for a reason, and there is no need to be sorry. Though, I'm afraid coming here was the easy part of your journey."

"How can we help?" Suzume asked.

"We have much to talk about," the priest replied. "But first, let me introduce you to your mission." The last he said while opening his body toward the hall, where a young girl, no older than seven or eight, appeared.

She rubbed her eyes, either waking up to the commotion or fighting sleep from taking over. Her pink kimono decorated with threaded petals of sakura flowers covered her feet and hands, though half a kemari ball jutted from the left sleeve. The girl's long, unbound hair reached her chest in a wave because she'd been lying down before all this commotion. The bells trapped in the ball jingled when she stretched her arms with a yawn, and she locked in this position when she noticed the glowing lion-dog in the yard.

"A komainu!" she shouted, running down the step without bothering with shoes.

"Wait!" Ren said when he understood the child meant to pat the giant-looking dog. But the priest grabbed his wrist and prevented him from touching the girl. Unwillingly, Ren closed his eyes and winced in anticipation of the pain she would feel when reaching his guardian. But nothing came except her laughter.

"She's so cute," the girl yelped.

Ren opened his eyes to see the child rubbing herself against Maki's muzzle, unhurt. And if this was not odd enough, he realized with awe that all the people in the yard were bowing deeply or kowtowing, including Maki, Fuyuko, and, perhaps even more surprisingly, Suzume.

"Kiyoshi," the girl petulantly called, "who is this dirty man who does not bow?" Her ball jingled again when she pointed it toward Ren's face.

He felt a pull on his belt and was about to curse, but the pull was strong, and he fell on his right knee. Suzume had been the one pulling, or more accurately, he realized when their eyes met, that Sugi had. Her face had tensed, and her green eyes seemed to gleam with awe. She was even shaking.

"His name is Ren Fudō, Princess Ayako," the priest replied with a slight bow of the head. "And he is, from now on, your protector."

"Shit," Ren whispered to himself.

CHAPTER 12
NO WAY OUT

"You see why I needed your help?" Kiyoshi asked when Ren lowered the spyglass.

Just as the Ox Blood had claimed, the imperial palace was nothing more than incandescent charcoal, and most temples had succumbed to the same fate hours or days ago. Streets were empty besides the few units of puppet soldiers patrolling them, though most now stood around the mountain.

The soldiers, at least, were obediently marching, nothing more. The other yōkai, on the other hand, had the time of their lives with the carcass of the city. Ren spotted two nue stripping flesh from a large man's rotting body and another running after a street dog. Even if things ever settled in the capital, it would soon be infested by vengeful ghosts.

"A quarter of their forces came from the main road, but the rest had already surrounded the city. When the guards went to oppose them, they fell to an ambush, and the rest, well, you can guess the rest. They rushed straight to the palace and killed anything that breathed, including the emperor and all his children. All but one."

Kiyoshi paused in his tale just long enough for Ren to swallow the news of the emperor's death. Peace was still fresh in Japan, and such a loss would invite another civil war like nothing else. This, however, was human business. The threat spreading around the mountain was theirs.

"Ayako had traveled here with all those people to celebrate her seventh birthday. We were attacked soon after the first fires bloomed over Kyōto but managed to repel them long enough to raise a kekkai. For a couple of hours after that, people flocked to the shrine for protection. Those were the lucky ones. Anyone who tried after that was met by an army of those monsters. I pray for their souls, but seeing how they met their ends, I'd say we're bound to see them again."

"I can see how Kyōto fell," Ren replied. "But not why I have to be the one taking her away."

"If being chosen by Amaterasu isn't enough," Kiyoshi replied in his venerable, peaceful voice, "then consider this. I am the head priest of Fushimi Inari. I cannot leave the mountain as long as a single soul is sheltering on it, even if the princess asks me, and believe me, she asks for a lot of things."

"Oh, I believe you," Ren replied.

Ayako was everything Ren pictured of the Imperial family. Petulant, snobby, self-important, and she was a child. When she realized her socks were dirty, she called for fresh ones. When those proved too big, she threw them on the floor, then asked to be carried on Maki's back, even after Ren insisted she ask the lion-dog first. His guardian acted like a good horse, and Sugi was the one who lifted the child on Maki's back.

"She's of imperial blood," Kiyoshi replied, guessing Ren's thoughts. "Guardians, kami of the land, they are bound to obey. Besides, she isn't just a princess."

"So you said," Ren replied.

The daughter of Amaterasu, the bridge between the realm of

men and the goddess of the sun. It was hard to believe, but at least it explained why Amaterasu had spoken to Osamu, why Maki and Suzume had been so perky on the last stretch of the journey, and why Ren had to be the one taking her to safety, if such a place existed.

"I just happened to reach Ise Jingū after Osamu received the oracle from the goddess," Ren whined. "That's all, just bad timing."

"Surely *you* don't believe this," Kiyoshi scoffed, patting the young man's back. "Nothing happens by luck, you know it. We all sway between crests of fortune and troughs of misfortune."

"I guess I am deep into it, then," Ren said.

"Ren," Kiyoshi replied with a sigh. "You are being given the most vital task that's befallen the Yaseki for decades, if not centuries. You are to protect and guide the daughter of Amaterasu to her shrine. Japan's future hangs in the balance."

"All the more reason *you* should do it," Ren barked. "You have your own army," he said, gesturing at the plethora of statues gathered behind them.

This place had been a cemetery for the souls of the past priests until Kiyoshi ordered every guardian statue to be brought here, where he could summon them at will. Foxes by the dozens, boars, monkeys, frogs, and a few komainu all waited to be summoned, though not even Kiyoshi Kuroda could call so many guardians at one time. He might have been the greatest summoner of the Yaseki, but Ren, who could call up to three guardians before fainting, knew it was an impossible task.

Only the guardians standing at the lowest points of the mountain had not been moved, and just because it would have exposed whoever carried them to arrows and spears.

"Call one of them, hop on its back with the princess, and leave. You don't have to—"

"And what of all the refugees?" Kiyoshi asked, hardening his voice.

"Let me handle the diversion," Ren begged. "Maki and I can attract their attention long enough."

"We don't need a diversion. We need a full attack. That's the only way to give people a chance to flee. That's the only way *you* will leave Kyōto with the princess. You, Ren Fudō, not an old man."

"But you're going to die!" Ren spat. Once again, he had spoken of death on a shrine's ground, but he couldn't care less about the omen in it. He wiped the tears from the corner of his eyes before they fell and looked away to hide his powerless rage.

"And I will then join my ancestors," Kiyoshi replied.

He was a tall man and bent over until his face stood at the same height as Ren's. It was a gentle face, one full of compassion. Kiyoshi wore the same uniform as Osamu Shirakawa, stood at a fairly similar height, and was a couple years older than the head priest of Ise Jingū, but the resemblance stopped there.

A lifetime of soul hunting had twisted a serious face with too many scars to count and hardened his eyes like steel, but the last decades of leading a great shrine had softened his soul. He was wise and quiet, patient and kind. Osamu, Hotaru, and Kiyoshi were known in the Yaseki as the Three Demons of the Eight Gates since their young years, though Ren couldn't understand what Ox had done to deserve such a nickname.

The Clerk had once told Ren that people used to compare Osamu to the fire element, Hotaru to the thunder, and Kiyoshi to the wood element. He had assumed they compared him so because of his patient nature and respectful stature, but the Clerk had scoffed and told him it was because the Ox Blood Hunter was as stubborn as a century-old Oak. Nevertheless, if there was one person within the organization Ren could imagine serving one day, it was Kiyoshi. Or, it would have been Kiyoshi.

"The priests, miko, and monks currently under my services will be free to join me as we oppose this army, and they, too, will join their ancestors. But you, my young friend, need to keep going. Do it for your mother if you don't want to do it for Ayako-hime."

"It's not fair," Ren replied, a finger under his nose to keep it from running.

"No, it's not, but that's how it is. I don't want to die either, you know. It took me sixty years to find love, and I would rather enjoy it a while longer. But for Japan, and for Fuyuko, I will give my life. In the end, that's all we can hope for, a good reason to die."

Kiyoshi Kuroda straightened up and walked toward a corner of the cemetery. He stepped over a quiet stream and invited Ren to follow. The young hunter did not remember this part of the shrine but bet it would be a most peaceful place in usual times.

"There," the priest said, pointing toward the once-rich garden of a mansion a few minutes' walk from the mountain. The mansion was gone, but the garden's space remained, though it now welcomed a square of command drawn by black and white curtains adorning the crow crest. "That's where he waits for the kekkai to drop. Their *General*."

Ren lifted the spyglass to find the enemies' leader.

The square of command was empty, save for one person. Clad in dark, lacquered armor, wearing a *kabuto* helmet supporting a golden crescent moon, and holding a *dansen uchiwa* war fan in his right hand, the General sat still on a simple foldable stool. He raised his head and looked straight toward Ren. The young man dropped the tip of the spyglass, his heart beating like a taiko at a matsuri.

"He looked at you too, huh?" Kiyoshi asked rhetorically.

"Impossible," Ren whispered.

"It is him then? The White Tengu."

Ren lifted the glass again. He had to be sure.

The General stood from the stool when he found him again

and opened the wings on his back as if taunting the hunter. Dark wings, huge wings, wings of a tengu. But even without them, the General's face would have sufficed. A scowling white face with a fire-red mustache, thick eyebrows of the same color, and a long, large nose.

"It's him," Ren replied, cold sweat running down his back.

"Do you still doubt that you were supposed to come here?"

"All the more reason for me to stay. If I kill him, then my mother will wake, and maybe the blue fires will go away." Ren sounded hopeful and crazed in equal measures; even he could hear it. His nemesis stood there, not even a ri from him. Freedom and forgiveness were there for the taking.

"How would you kill him, Ren? There's an army between us and him. And he's clever. Clever enough to conquer the capital in one day. For all we know, he knew you would come and is taunting you. Using your thirst for revenge to doom Japan. Doesn't it sound like something a yōkai would do?"

"Damn it," Ren spat. Kiyoshi was right; he could feel it in his guts. But the White Tengu was there, and listening to logic was not his priority.

"This is not the end, Ren," Kiyoshi said, inviting the young man to follow him back toward the hall-turned-imperial chamber. "Deliver the princess to Ise, gather a fighting force, and then claim your vengeance. And mine, while you are at it."

Musicians played their instruments near the hall, and people laughed. For a moment, the gloom of their situation did not weigh on the refugees' backs, and it wasn't a bad sound. Suzume was clapping her hands to follow the rhythm of a beating taiko, Maki was skipping on two legs at a time, and the princess laughed to her little heart's content. She was pulling on the lion-dog's ears. So hard indeed that Ren had to resist the impulse of scolding her. But the lion-dog was taking it with pride, and Kiyoshi gently grabbed his wrist again.

"I do not envy you," the head priest said shortly before they rejoined the small crowd. "She might be the daughter of the sun goddess, but she's a brat."

"And I just happened to love children," Ren replied in a voice dripping with sarcasm.

"Ren," Kiyoshi then said, sounding suddenly sad and serious. "I'm already putting so much on your shoulders, and it pains me to do so, but I have one last favor to ask."

皿

"Why can't any of our servants come?" the child asked from Maki's back.

"They would slow us down," Ren replied without warmth.

"How about our guards then?"

"They vowed to fight to the death to give your escape a chance, Your Highness," Suzume replied.

Sugi had remained in Suzume for more than an hour the previous night and only relented when Ren told her of the next day's plan. Her devotion seemed limitless, and Suzume showed enough respect for two, a good deal considering how little patience Ren held for the child.

"Well, let's hope they fight better than my father's guards then."

"Hey," Ren spat, "do you understand that men are going to die so that you can live? How about showing some respect for their sacrifice?"

The girl seemed stung by the hunter's tone. No one, he assumed, had ever spoken to her that way. She found the strength to scornfully stiffen and humphed. "We don't like how he speaks to us," she said, raising a regal finger toward Ren's face. "Fuyuko, take him away."

"I don't think so, Your Highness," the courtesan replied with a hint of contempt.

"Excuse me?" the child asked, a hand falling on her chest as if wounded.

"In a few minutes, princess, my dear Kuroda-sama will summon an army of guardians. As he has asked, I will stay with you until the kekkai falls to make sure you do not miss the obvious. Then, I will leave you to rejoin my love and share his fate. We will never see each other again, so I might as well be honest with you."

As she spoke, the courtesan recovered her white fox's face, but the child did not seem to care about it. Ren shared a glance with Suzume, who knew as well what was about to happen.

"You are a brat, young lady, and I find it extremely unfair that so many will perish today to give *you* the opportunity to live."

"Impudent!" Ayako spat. "You, you..." Not finding the words, she squeaked through her nose and looked straight ahead. "Well, we sure are glad not to stay another minute on this horrid mountain, surrounded by horrid people, or animals, we should say. You," she then said, waving at Suzume. "We forgot your name."

"Suzume, Your Highness," the miko replied with a clumsy bow.

"Suzume. Please stand between those ruffians and us. The sight of them offends our eyes."

"Hum..." Suzume said, shifting her gaze from the princess to Ren, who rolled his eyes and waved for her to stand between them. This suited him, too.

"I'm glad we agree on something," the hunter told the fox. She was wearing her human mask again.

"It was petty, but it felt good," Fuyuko replied. Ren was truly sorry for her and what was about to happen. She and Kiyoshi deserved a future together. "Will you remember the way?"

"Yes," Ren replied. "Straight south until the mausoleum of

Emperor Ninmyō, then southwest until we cross the Katsura River."

"We will draw as many of them as possible, and the civilians were told to flee to the north, but still be careful, boy, the enemy isn't stupid. They will know you try to take her to Ise. Don't stop until you reach the coast, and no matter what, do not head back to the tunnel. It's the first place they will think of."

Fuyuko cared, Ren realized. He had known her for less than a day, but he could tell this wasn't her strong suit. Maybe, he thought, nearing death made her want to end on a high note.

"You do not fear death?" he asked.

"Death?" she asked, frowning in surprise. "No. As long as I experience it with Kuroda-sama, it is a worthy experience."

"She will want to stay with me," Kiyoshi had told Ren. *"Even if I asked her to go with you, she would refuse and sneak back to me. She is a trickster, my winter fox. You need to take her by surprise."*

A bell rang up the mountain, and many more soon followed. From the cover of the forest, as close as possible to the kekkai, Ren saw the agitation shaking the enemy's ranks. Not the soldiers, who remained as impassible as ever, but their officers started pacing. They met each other to bark questions and orders. A concert of croaks, roars, and growls soon echoed all around Fushimi Inari.

Next, Kiyoshi would call his many guardians and gather them right at the main entrance of the shrine. Calling them would deplete the priest of his energy and take him close to death, but his last gift would not be wasted, Ren had promised. And he had promised more.

Fuyuko's head shot upward. She frowned and sniffed the air. "The guardians are being called," she said. "Get ready."

"Princess," Ren called, stepping from Suzume's shadow, "keep your head down and close your eyes."

"A princess never bows her head," the child replied, her tiny arms crossed over her chest.

"Keep your head down," Ren replied in a singing voice, "or I'll come smack you."

"Humph! Suzume, please resume—"

"Ayako-hime-sama," Suzume gently called. "We will keep you safe, but we humbly ask that you lower yourself on Maki's back while we leave the city. You would do us a great honor in helping us protect you."

The child read the miko's eyes and decided to accept her request. Finally, she put her head down and gripped two tufts of golden hair.

A konoha tengu croaked. Most of the soldiers facing them turned to their left and started jogging along the mountain's edge. One unit of sixty soldiers remained and spread thinly to replace their comrades.

Ren could not see their leader, but the konoha tengu flew away at the head of his men. The hunter searched for the remaining officer, thinking that they would have to incapacitate him first. That was when the kekkai vanished in front of his eyes like a bubble of soap slowly popping.

"Well, I guess you didn't miss that," Fuyuko said as she turned around and dragged her sandal across the forest's ground.

"Fuyuko," Ren gently called.

"What is it?" she asked, facing him again.

Ren embraced her with both arms, hugging her as close to him as possible despite the thickness of her attire. She smelled wonderful and did not bother returning the embrace.

"What do you think you are doing, boy?" Fuyuko asked with a chuckle. "I understand the urge, but—"

Ren's hands met behind her back, where he tied the ends of a straw rope adorned with lightning-shaped white strips of paper. Fuyuko had been so preoccupied with rejoining her lover that she hadn't noticed how he held it behind his back beforehand, nor did she smell the sake imbued in the rope or the blood pearling from his thumb. And finally, as her body weighed helplessly on Ren's shoulder, Fuyuko understood she'd been paralyzed.

"Ren?" she asked, her voice shaking from a mix of confusion and rage. "Ren!"

"I'm so sorry, Fuyuko," Ren said, grabbing the sword umbrella and tossing it to Sugi. "Maki, let's go!"

The lion-dog barked a great whoof that echoed throughout the forest, and the child screamed, and the fox yelled, and the wind brushed all those sounds by Ren's ears as they rushed down the forest and jumped from the shrine's edge.

Sugi was already there, dashing so fast that she seemed to glide. She leaped just before the slope ended and landed spear first in the chest of a thick-armed nue, then used his falling body to spin from a puppet samurai's lunge. Maki head-butted the samurai into his comrades, opening the path for Ren.

The hunter managed to unsheathe his blade despite the curses of the courtesan and her attempts at biting him, but his grip was weak and he decided to trail the lion-dog rather than cutting through the soldiers. They burst through the thin line of enemies and stormed the smoking street, and the noise drowned in the background, except for the screaming child and the raging fox.

"Ren, let me go, or I'll bleed you!" Fuyuko shouted. Gone was the suave voice and seductive tone. Her body remained lumped over his shoulder, and its weight quickly tired his left arm.

"I'm doing this for Kiyoshi!" Ren shouted back when she wriggled enough to drop her chin on his back. He felt her whisker on his neck; she had shifted to her fox shape. She bit his shoulder with her back teeth, not deep, but painfully. "Fuyuko, stop!" Her teeth clenched even harder, then Ren's back got wet with tears.

The mountain suddenly seemed to roar. Bestial screams rose as metal met flesh, and a sequence of explosions shook the earth in succession. Looking back, Ren saw the birth of black clouds of smoke near the shrine's entrance.

"Sugi, Maki, right!" Ren shouted, fighting the pain on his shoulder. He tapped the back of his sword against Maki's right leg to let her know which way to go, and the beast swerved and slipped for a few steps, during which the child screamed. At least she was keeping her head low.

The great shape of the lion-dog entered a narrow street, opening the view of the road they'd been using to Ren just as he heard the twang of bows releasing their missiles. The archers appeared farther down the main street, their arrows coming straight at him. He raised his arm in a futile defense. Sugi sprang back from the secondary street and slashed her spear while in the air, cutting any shaft that would have threatened Ren or Fuyuko.

"Leave them!" he shouted at the warrior spirit, who started running after the archers. Both ran after the lion-dog, but Ren thought they needed to find cover before arrows started raining on them again or before the archers called reinforcement.

His lungs were burning, his arm was killing him, and Fuyuko had yet to release the pressure of her canine jaws. And yet the mountain stood on their right, not far enough to call it safe by a long shot.

Sugi put herself on his left, running with ease, the blade of her spear slick with yōkai blood. She nodded to ask him what next.

"The mausoleum is near," he said. "Right there." He pointed across the block of broken houses with his sword. The streets to access it were little more than alleys; Maki would never pass through them. "Get the princess," he told Sugi, who jumped over the lion-dog and grabbed the little girl by the back of her belt.

She screamed even louder when her ass left the comfort of Maki's back. The lion-dog seemed to understand and broke her speed with her front paws. Sugi landed with the child tightly hugging her chest and vanished inside a narrow alley.

"Keep them busy for a few seconds," Ren told his guardian, who then whoofed and ran backward to take care of the archers coming in pursuit. Arrows, Ren hoped, wouldn't hurt her. By then, Fuyuko's bite had lessened to a pinch.

"Ren, please," she whimpered, "please."

The hunter followed Sugi and penetrated the back alley. The warrior spirit was nowhere to be seen, but the courtyard wall surrounding the mausoleum blocked the end of the path, and he assumed she had jumped over. With his load, he wouldn't be able to do as much.

Maki barked farther down the street, and Ren forced himself to wait before releasing her. He dropped the paralyzed courtesan on top of the tiled wall, pretending not to see her heartbreaking tears, and leaped over. Once on the other side, he lifted her again, sat both against the wall and prayed for the lion-dog to return home. Her presence vanished halfway through a violent roar.

Ren hugged the fox-lady close to him and scanned the ruined mausoleum for a sight of the princess and the warrior spirit. Fuyuko was no longer fighting him. She bit her lower lip with utter frustration. Her whimpers twisted his bowels.

Explosions were still echoing in the distance, and one of them made the little shape of Ayako tremble in the corner of the courtyard. Sugi was keeping her flat on the ground under a plank that must have been a door. She nodded at Ren, her free hand covering the child's mouth. The hunter heard the rhythmical thumping of soldiers' footsteps in the street on the other side of the wall and pulled Fuyuko closer.

"We need to be quiet," he told her in a whisper.

She cradled him and let her tears run down his throat. The footsteps went farther. After a couple of minutes, without daring to do more than breathe, Ren waved Sugi and Ayako from their cover.

"He's dead," Fuyuko said, her lips twisted in a grotesque shape along her white muzzle. "He's dead without me." A gut-wrenching whimper followed her last word. It reminded Ren of the string of a *biwa* lute slowly scratched by long fingernails.

"What is wrong with her?" Ayako asked, standing in front of the fox-lady as if nothing special had just happened. Ren hadn't noticed she still held the kemari ball.

"She lost someone precious," Ren replied.

"No, we meant with her body. Why isn't she moving?"

Ren's tongue clicked in his mouth. Did the child have to be that callous? he asked himself. "I used a *shimenawa* rope soaked in a priest's sake," Ren explained just as coldly. "It paralyzes shapeshifters. Kuroda-sama taught me the trick yesterday and provided the rope this morning." This he said for Fuyuko's benefit.

She stopped whining, and her eyes filled with a few more drops of anger.

"I will free you now," Ren told her. "But before I do, you need to understand none of this was my idea. I would have respected your choice. Do you understand?"

The courtesan nodded, though her eyes remained drawn in thin, furious lines.

The hunter passed his arms around her again and unknotted the rope belt. He sat back slowly and breathed when Fuyuko massaged blood back into her hands.

The quiet mask she had managed to veil over her face cracked in the blink of an eye, and, eyes popping with furious red veins, she jumped at him. Her clawed hands wrapped around Ren's neck when she drove him on his back. She foamed at the corner of her lips and pressed on him with all her strength. Ren thought his windpipe was about to get crushed.

"You let him die without me," she roared through her fangs. "You shouldn't have come, you miserable fool!" Spittle flew from her bristling muzzle to his face, but this was the last thing Ren cared about.

The girl screamed again, then Ren heard more than he saw the flat of Sugi's spear thumping into the side of Fuyuko's head, and the fox fell on the side, finally letting go of the hunter's throat.

"Thank you," he said in a hoarse voice.

The warrior spirit helped him back on his feet. Sugi spoke in her kami language, nodding at the quiet body of the fox.

"She says she did it to keep her quiet, not to help you," Ayako said.

"You can hear her voice?" Ren asked, wincing through the pain of words traveling up his throat.

"Yes, we can," the girl regally replied.

"Good," Ren said. He rolled the courtesan on her back and shoved the umbrella sword Sugi was handing him into Fuyuko's belt. "Maybe you won't be entirely useless after all."

CHAPTER 13

SEA, SHELLS, AND SUN

The group chose stealth over patience and moved from the mausoleum a few minutes after they found refuge in it. Suzume had offered to stay there until the soldiers disbanded, but Ren worried that they might search the whole city when they found out the girl had left the mountain. There was no doubt in Ren's mind, the whole attack on the capital was due to the princess's existence.

As the daughter of Amaterasu, she was a threat to the yōkai and whatever they planned. And should those soldiers disband from Kyōto without finding them, they would thicken the cordon around the city and make it impossible to rejoin Ise. No, Ren told Suzume, they had to leave while the sounds of battle still shook the mountain.

He dropped Fuyuko on his other shoulder, and the princess found Suzume's back, using the spear as a saddle. It wouldn't be comfortable, but the girl agreed not to whine about it until they were out of the capital. She stiffened when Suzume used those last words, and Ren wondered if she'd ever gone out of Kyōto.

They progressed slowly at first and followed the Katsura River south for a while before finding a bridge that wasn't guarded. Then the explosions stopped, and since they hadn't met a yōkai for long minutes, they moved faster. The slum part of the city offered more cover and eased their exit, and by the time dusk veiled the capital, their feet trampled grass.

Fuyuko had woken up, though she refused to look at any of them or even speak, and Ayako slept on Suzume's back. The Hand Hunter refused Ren's offer to take over, claiming that Sugi did not want him to approach the princess. They disappeared in the night over a hill, and Ren gave a last look at Kyōto, where his friend had valiantly died, along with so many brothers and sisters of the Yaseki. Somewhere in Inari Taisha, the White Tengu was flipping bodies in search of the little girl and would soon throw his forces after them.

皿

The direction to follow was set, but the path was difficult. So close to the capital, many villages and hamlets were to be avoided, and many roads to cross hurriedly for fear of barrages or patrols. Ren did not let the group rest the next day but relented when the usually quiet Suzume complained of fatigue. It was night again. They found a clearing at the center of a thicket. The trees did not grow dense enough to allow them a fire, which, of course, meant a flow of grievances from the princess. She was cold, famished, tired, and displeased by her company. Ren tried hard to ignore her, but something in her nasal, whiny voice made it impossible for him to endure.

"Lower your voice," he warned her with an unfriendly stare, "or you'll find out that a yōkai's belly is a much warmer place."

"Why are you always so mean?" the princess asked, arms akimbo.

"Because you are always so insufferable," he replied, imitating her voice and tone. He thought he had done a good job of it, but Suzume's head shake made him regret his attitude. He sighed. "If I dig a hole and build a small fire," he told the child, "will you try not to speak up?"

The princess acknowledged his request with a prideful nod, and so Ren dug with his bare hands. He received no help from Fuyuko, who stubbornly kept to the side of the group in her fox shape, nor from Suzume, who could not step away from the girl without being called back with a pretentious harrumph.

Using a flame talisman, he birthed a fire on a bale of twigs. He added the rope of straw to the young fire, and it glowed warmer. The hole was so deep that Ayako had to extend her hands to receive its warmth.

"Fuyuko," Suzume called, "come closer. You must be cold, too."

"I will never feel warm again," the courtesan replied, though she accepted the offer and sat around the hole at an equal distance from both hunters.

Ren hadn't thought she would accompany them so far. Kiyoshi made him promise to take her away from Kyōto, but a sullen fox made for a poor traveling companion. If she wanted to leave them, it was fine with him. He had fulfilled his promise, after all. And she had yet to apologize for trying to strangle him.

They had left Fushimi Inari light in provision, and Ren now emptied his bag of its last three balls of rice. He and Suzume split one. She noticed he had left the sheet of seaweed on her half and thanked him with a nod.

"Why does it taste so bad?" the princess asked with a rice-filled pout.

"That's because they were at the bottom of my bag," the hunter replied, "under my dirty underwear."

The princess blanched and remained dumbfounded for a few seconds.

"He is joking," Suzume told the girl, her lips pinched in a repressed smile.

Ren wondered if Suzume knew he had been honest. Fuyuko snapped a few more twigs and tossed them in the fire while the rest munched on their rice. It was bound to be a long, sullen journey, Ren told himself.

"Where are we?" the princess asked once done with her meal. At least her appetite was limited.

"Somewhere west of Kyōto," Ren replied. "Probably not far from Hyōgo Province."

"Hyōgo?" Ayako asked. "Are you not taking us to Ise? We should be on the road south, not west."

"The enemy will have the south guarded," Suzume replied. "We have to use a detour. Wouldn't you agree, Your Highness?"

"Yes, we would," the princess replied. "So, which daimyo are we going to visit?"

"Daimyo?" Ren asked, frowning. "None."

"None?" she asked. "But surely the Hayashi clan of Himeji, or Lord Shimazu of Ōsaka, would grant us assistance. They could provide us with an army to reclaim the Chrysanthemum Throne."

"That's exactly why we don't go to them," Ren replied.

"Are you mad?" the princess asked, forgetting her promise to keep her voice low. "Is he mad?" she then asked Suzume, pointing a finger at Ren. The miko once again found herself trapped between the princess and the hunter and looked to him for assistance.

"Why do you think they would help you?" Ren asked the girl.

"Because it is their duty," she petulantly replied, showing him the side of her face.

"Because it's an opportunity," the hunter said. "Whoever helps the imperial princess back on the throne becomes her protector and thus the most powerful man in Japan. You would be married to their son in a matter of days and forgotten within a month."

"But—"

"And that's if they manage to defeat this yōkai army. A big *if*, if you ask me, considering that their soldiers don't die."

"I see," the girl replied, looking suddenly all smug. "You're trying to remain my only protector, aren't you? You want that power for yourself, Ren Fudō."

He was actually impressed that she remembered his name. "Don't flatter yourself," Ren replied when he bit into the last of his rice. "Kiyoshi said I was your protector, but I only see myself as the carrier of the most annoying package ever."

"Package?" she spat, reacting as if the term had wounded her deep in the chest.

"And believe me, the second we arrive in Ise—the very second —I'll deliver you to Osamu and won't think of you ever again," Ren said, brushing his hands.

"Peasant!" the girl pouted as she sat back down, making her untied kimono sway after her.

"Where are we going, though?" Fuyuko asked.

Ren was surprised the question came from her but hid it under a cough. "We're traveling to the coast and will cross the Seto near Akashi if we can find a fisherman willing to sail us to Awaji Island. I think there's a shrine to Izanagi at the center of the island with a few priests of the Yaseki."

"You *think*?" Fuyuko asked, her left eyebrow shooting up.

"I've never been there, so, yes, I think. And I hope they can arrange another boat for us to sail around Mie and drop us right next to Ise Jingū. It's gonna be a long detour, but it's as safe a road as I can think of."

"Safe," Fuyuko replied with a scoff. "I admire your optimism, boy."

"Stop it with the *boy* already," he replied despite himself. "You might wear the mask of a woman in her mid-thirties, but you can't be over twenty."

186

"Nineteen," she replied. "And I chose the human physique Kuroda-sama enjoyed the most, so show it some respect."

"I wasn't—" Ren replied as the fox stood and left the small circle around the fire to pout in the woods. He waved his hand at her back, then checked the little girl, who looked away pettishly.

"What?" he asked Suzume, who tilted her head reproachfully.

"I just think in our current company you would do well to be less... boorish," the miko replied.

"Boorish?" he asked, coughing the word. "Me, boorish?"

"No more than usual," she replied right away to reassure him, which, of course, failed. "But you will find the journey a lot more agreeable if *you* make an effort. Also..."

"Yes?" Ren asked, inviting her to speak her thoughts with a frown born from a growing migraine.

"I know I'm just a recent addition to the Yaseki, but I wish you'd asked for my opinion on the route we're taking. We are heading toward my home province, after all."

Ren sighed and slumped. Suzume was right; he should have asked her, if only because she was his only ally here.

"Five months," he whispered to himself. He suddenly felt cheated.

"Absolutely not," Ren said, arms crossed in a determined position of authority.

"And I say yes," the child replied, adopting the same position, standing in front of the hunter as if she wasn't half his size.

"You don't give orders here," he said.

"Yes, we do. And I say we join this group and take part in the festivities."

"Less than twelve hours ago, I told you we needed to avoid

villages and be discreet, and now you want to go to a matsuri. Are you even listening, oh noble daughter of the sun? Come on, Suzume, back me up here."

"Actually..." Suzume said, wincing in a sorry way.

"You too?" Ren asked, his shoulders slumping with the weight of this treason.

"We might learn some information," she offered, sounding unsure of herself. "Maybe someone spotted the enemy? And we could buy some food. Plus... it's a matsuri, Ren. People will barely notice us."

"Oh, you think?" he asked sarcastically. "Because we are so inconspicuous, aren't we? An imperial princess, a spear-holding miko, and a fox-lady. I cannot believe I'm the least remarkable-looking person in this group!"

"I can change back to my human form," Fuyuko replied.

"As if it would make you less noticeable," Ren said. "And whose side are you on?"

"Theirs, obviously," the fox replied, nodding toward the two girls, who then beamed and clapped hands.

"Why?" Ren asked.

"Because you're not. And they are bound to have sake there. Maybe not enough to drown my sorrow, but I'll take it anyway,"

Ren sighed behind his open hands. He should have known following the sound of music wasn't a good idea, but all attempts at caution flew to the wind when the four of them spotted the procession carrying an altar to the site of the festival. Ayako was the one who guessed it must be a matsuri dedicated to Ebisu, the kami worshipped by fishermen. Seeing how close they had gotten to the coast, Ren was inclined to believe her, and as she showed by reciting the deity's many names, the princess knew her kami.

"Don't you think it's a bit weird that just a few days after the capital fell, people celebrate a festival as usual?" Ren asked. "Am I the only one sensing a trap here?"

"It can't always be yōkai," Suzume replied. "And I doubt people here have heard about Kyōto already. It's quite far and remote."

"And if they did, maybe they decided that pleasing their kami would make them safer," Fuyuko said. She had already veiled her human face as if the conversation was over.

"Ren-san," Ayako said, grabbing him by the sleeve and offering him pleading eyes. "Please." The shock was so intense that for a second, he could not speak.

"You know this word?"

"Suzume said that if I used it and made this face, you would obey," the girl replied.

Ren looked up at his friend, who grinned with embarrassment.

"I didn't say *obey*," she explained in apology.

Ren sighed, and the girl pulled on his sleeve again.

"Please, Ren-san," she said again. She even managed to bring tears into her big, child eyes.

"Damn it, fine!" he barked, utterly defeated.

The two girls giggled and embraced, so proud of their victories that Ayako started tossing her kemari ball in the air. Ren caught it before it landed on her foot.

"But the second it goes to shit—and it will—get ready for the most loathsome *I told you so* of your lives."

"We are trembling," Fuyuko replied.

"And let's get our story straight," Ren went on, ignoring the sarcasm. "You are not the princess of Japan. From now on, your name is—"

"Maki!" the girl shouted.

"Fine, your name is Maki. You are my little sister, so is Suzume, and Fuyuko is—"

"Be very careful about your next words," the courtesan replied menacingly.

"Our aunt," Ren finished, receiving a nod from the fox-lady.

"We come from Izumo on a pilgrimage to Nara. Everyone will remember?"

"Yes, big brother," Ayako replied with a big grin spanning from ear to ear.

Ren looked up at the sky, a mouth full of prayers for the day to end.

四

They reached the back of the procession a few minutes before the sea opened to them. Ayako's eyes could not open wide enough as she was swept into the chanting, hopping, and dancing small crowd. Men, by twelves, were carrying a mighty altar in which the spirit of Ebisu was enshrined for the day. An old fisherman with more gaps than teeth grabbed Ren by the shoulder and forced him to take his place, which did nothing to his suspicious mind. Every mask hid a Hasontama, every child would shift to a pranking yōkai, and every instrument banging or blowing was the signal for an ambush.

Ren focused on the sword at his lower back, feeling its presence whenever his cautious mind warned him to pay attention. He lost sight of the child for a second and meant to let go of the altar, but the press of people would not let him. Then he spotted her on Suzume's shoulders, and farther down the crowd, Fuyuko was accepting a sip of sake from the bottle of a red-faced man. The poor man was then dragged away from the courtesan by his wife, who pulled on his ear so strongly that Ren heard his yelp.

The group of sixty and some people then arrived at the end of a plateau overlooking the quiet sea and dropped the altar close to the bonfire that would soon burn for the rest of the day and far into the night. Ren's shoulder was killing him, but each slap on his back was accompanied by waves of alcohol-smelling laughter, and soon, the hunter managed to quiet his inner sense of constant danger and laughed with those good folks.

No one asked him any questions about his identity or the reason for his presence. Nor did he hear any mention of Kyōto, a large army, or the emperor's death. It was a day of festivity and a day of gratitude to the kami watching over them and their boats. Come the morrow, they would resume their lives and face the dangers of the sea for a pittance, and surely all that was wrong in the world would weigh down on their backs again. But for now, they were dancing, singing, and drinking, and maybe, Ren acknowledged, it was exactly what the four of them needed.

The bonfire was lit during the afternoon and needed constant refueling. When the sun set along the coast, its warmth was barely needed, for most people's faces had turned red with sake. Ren lost the count of cups shared with him by friendly men he'd never met before, and their generosity to him paled in comparison to how they treated Fuyuko. She never spent more than a minute alone, and her laughter warmed his heart.

Women and children danced around the bonfire in a slow-moving circle, their steps and gestures dictated by the rhythm of a large taiko. Ren first refused to join them, but when a tipsy Suzume held her hand for him to follow her, he relented. She laughed whenever she looked above her shoulder, and while Ren found it slightly vexing, he soon laughed with her. The song ended, and Suzume darted toward the taiko. She all but plucked the sticks from the previous player, removed her left arm from its sleeve, and, looking suddenly very serious, started pounding the drum.

The energetic rhythm of her song pulled many people to their feet and into the circle. Smaller taiko and a couple of flutes joined the song, and the dancers seemed to agree on a series of gestures that matched the rhythm. His face hurting from all the laughter, Ren left the dance and sat in the outer circle, where men, mostly, more quietly drank and shared roasted fish. He had drunk enough, his belly was full, and Ren lost himself at the sight of his friend beating the drum with zeal.

"Didn't know she could do that, did you?" Fuyuko asked, wobbling toward him. She was carrying her clumsy okobo sandals at the tip of two fingers and walked on bare feet, then dropped right next to him.

"No, I didn't," Ren acknowledged. The courtesan put her shoulder against his for support, then let her head fall on it.

"So?" she asked, "no, *I told you so?*"

"I'm fresh out of them," the hunter replied with a smirk.

"You looked like you were having fun," she said. "And Suzume is having fun, and the kid is having fun," Fuyuko went on, nodding toward the princess who was laughing to her heart's content with other children, the kemari ball bouncing from each other's feet.

"And did you have enough sake?" Ren asked.

"No," she replied with a snort. "There will never be enough sake. And it will never taste as sweet as it used to." Her arms wrapped around Ren's, and the young man suddenly realized she was sobbing. "I miss him so much," she said in a whimper, hiding her tears in his sleeve.

"I *am* truly sorry, Fuyuko," Ren said.

"—so much," she repeated as she fell asleep.

He lay her head onto his lap when she could no longer support herself, then rearranged the bottom of her kimono to cover the two sprouting tails. No sooner did he do so that a man sat on his left.

"Your aunt is a rare beauty," the man said as he offered yet another flat cup of sake to the hunter. Ren recognized him as the chief of those people's village. He was a broad-chested fisherman with experience pouring from his dry, calloused skin and a thick, dark beard squaring an already squared jaw. He also looked more sober than most of his neighbors.

"She is," Ren replied with a hiss when both emptied their cups. "But she is mourning, so I wouldn't try anything with her tonight."

"Far from me, the idea," the man replied with a peal of genial laughter, hands opened in a sign of honesty. "I'm married. Just for getting close to your aunt, I will get scolded. I might be the chief of those people, but at home, we all know who leads. I guess you know what I'm talking about," the man then said, nodding toward Suzume, who was just finishing her song and received a chorus of applause.

Ren took a second to understand the meaning of those words, then blushed. "Suzume? Not at all, she's my—"

"—sister?" the man asked with a raised eyebrow. He was onto him, but Ren felt no malice, only a certain sense of curiosity. "Your family comes from Izumo, I heard?"

"We do," the hunter answered.

"I guess you have traveled a lot," the man said just as Suzume resumed playing the taiko with another rhythm. "Which is why your sister is playing airs from Shikoku."

"Is she?" Ren asked. "Then you could say those songs traveled a lot."

The chief chuckled and refilled both their cups. "Earlier, I overheard the child refer to herself as *we,* and your aunt didn't seem to know a single tale from Izumo, though she knew some from Kyōto," the man said. He smacked his lips after a sip and smiled back at an old lady who waved in his direction. "Look—Ren, is it? Look, Ren, I can see you are not bad people, but I can spot liars when I see them. All I want to know is if your presence puts my folks in danger?"

"Ren!" Ayako called as she stomped from the group of children to him. She planted her feet in front of him and dropped her fist on her hips. "That boy there refuses to give us—me my ball back. Go get it back for me."

"That's not a very nice way to ask something of your big brother," Ren said through his teeth with a slight nod toward the village's chief.

"Please, big brother," she said after a sigh punctuated by an eye roll.

"Maybe you can give them the ball," Ren said, just as Fuyuko suddenly snorted.

"Our ball?" she asked, seemingly baffled. "This was a gift from our esteemed father."

"And those nice folks gave us food and drink without asking anything in return," Ren replied. "Wouldn't it feel good to offer them a small gesture of gratitude? That's what people do, you know. And maybe you'll realize that giving feels better than receiving sometimes."

She pondered his words, twisted on her ankles, was about to say something, and finally nodded to say she understood and agreed. She returned to her new friends in all her regal attitude.

"She seems nice," the chief said with an ironic smirk.

"She's a piece of work, yes," Ren replied. From afar, Ren saw how Ayako gestured at her new friends that they could keep the ball, which was met with a loud cheer. A boy her age embraced her with naked arms and lifted her from the ground in a bear hug, and the princess looked as if he was made of mud.

"We are leaving tomorrow morning for Awaji Island," Ren said seriously. "You won't be in any danger. And if by any chance, black armored soldiers come to your village and ask about us, just tell them the truth. Do not try to fool them."

A long hum rattled the chief's throat as he drank Ren's words. "We've heard rumors about the capital," he said.

"It's probably all true," Ren replied. Fuyuko whimpered in her sleep, but when Ren put his hand on her back, she seemed to relax. "And if I were you, I would enjoy this matsuri. It might be the last one for some time."

"That is some good advice," the chief replied before he stood up. "And you, my young friend from Izumo, should try to get some sleep. One of us will sail you to Awaji tomorrow at sunrise, but if my intuition is correct, Awaji isn't your last stop, and the sea tends to be cruel to travelers."

"I think I will heed your advice," Ren said, but by then, the man was already moving toward the bonfire, where he soon picked up a child and tossed him in the air.

Halfway through the night, Ren felt Suzume lying next to him and heard Ayako joining them almost right away. No one had spoken of yōkai for hours. Ren told himself as Suzume grabbed his arm that once his debt to the Yaseki was paid off, and once the storm had weathered, he would come back to this place to enjoy its hospitality. Some bonfire, a taiko, and folks to dance with, if not for the White Tengu and his cursed blood, life would have been spent as simply as that.

CHAPTER 14

FROM THE BONFIRE TO THE POT

The sake had been good enough to remain in Ren's stomach when he stood, but his head, however, refused to stop spinning. Suzume rushed to the cliff to free herself of the previous day's food, and Fuyuko could do no more than grumble. She even set the fox mask over her face, either to mask the bold light of the sun or to cover a potential loss of her human features.

Ayako woke fresh as the dew, her piping voice ringing like a hammer on Ren's anvil of a skull. Her big eyes were shining with a new light, and despite his desire to toss her from the cliff, Ren found her changed. It was in the way her kimono hung looser, the red on her face from the bonfire, and the dirt under her fingernails, which she did not complain about. She even went by herself to pat Suzume's back as the miko fed the crustacean living down the cliff.

"I am so sorry," Suzume kept saying as if any of it was her fault.

"Well, you all wanted to join the matsuri," Ren chided her. "Maybe some roasted fish would make you feel better?" he asked mercilessly. Suzume's face turned from pale to green at the thought, and she heaved once more. "Maybe just some rice, then."

Many of the villagers did not bother to wake up, not even when the others started cleaning. The ashes of the fire were gathered, and whatever had not burned was given to the wind. Ren did not envy those who would have to carry the altar back, but he had promised to leave in the morning, and as far as he was concerned, they had tested their luck enough. He hoped Ebisu was pleased by the princess's presence and Suzume's taiko performance and would thus protect their crossing. The sea looked quiet enough, but a fresh wind was rising.

"This man and his brother are going to sail you to the island," the chief told Ren, holding a hungover fisherman by the shoulder. The poor man was massaging the sides of his head with both hands. "Don't worry," the chief said when he noticed the doubt in Ren's eyes, "he could sail the strait through a storm with his eyes closed."

"Aye, but if you ask me, I would rather do it tomorrow," the fisherman said.

"And miss this company?" the chief asked as Fuyuko joined them, her face unmasked and stunning again.

"Fine, fine," the fisherman replied. "But you tell my wife you made me, or I'll never hear the end of it."

Ren then remembered he had been the first to offer sake to the courtesan the day before and had been ear-plucked back in line by his wife.

"You have all our gratitude," Fuyuko told the man in her most alluring voice.

Ren could see the hairs on the man's arms stand and sensed him sobering up in the next second.

"Pleasure is mine," he replied, sounding and looking genuine. "Was going there soon, anyway. You can just wait for us down on the beach. I'll be there in a couple of hours."

And nearly two hours it took for Suzume to fill her belly with some rice soaked in hot water, find the strength to stand, and half walk, half be carried down to the beach, where the chief left them to wait for the boat. She melted down on the sand while waiting, shivering against the sea wind and regretting her evening's behavior, though Ren assured her she had pleased both the people and the kami with her music.

"And you made my Lord Kami proud, too," Fuyuko said.

"Inari?" Suzume asked, one eye closed to fight the light.

"He loves sake and those who enjoy it, and you sure looked like you did," the courtesan replied. Her words could have been taken as a mockery, but then she peeled off the upper of her three kimono to cover Suzume's back, and the girl thanked her.

"Will we be safe once over there?" Suzume asked. She tugged the kimono closer, leaving her head alone to sprout from it. "There" was the island that could be guessed on the horizon, across a blue and gray sea.

"We'll be safer," Ren said. "I haven't seen anything in that army that could cross the sea. Kappa might, but they usually stay away from salted water."

"After everything we've seen of them, I think we shouldn't consider them as usual yōkai," Fuyuko replied. "But I also doubt this army was made to sail."

"We know so little about their purpose," Ren said. The three of them seemed lost in their appraisal of the horizon. "Besides who they are after." The hunter then realized he hadn't heard Ayako's voice for a while, and a sense of panic gripped his bowels.

She was standing a little farther down the beach, and she wasn't alone. A woman dressed in rags, hair disheveled, was about to reach for the girl with thin, unsleeved arms. Ayako was handing her a skewer of white dango, a gift from the child who had received the kemari ball. Ren did not remember the woman from the festival, and his intuition, kept silent for the night, woke at the speed of a snapping bowstring.

"Ayako!" he shouted as the blade on his back left its scabbard.

Twenty steps farther, the girl turned to look at him and thus missed the moment the woman's face appeared from her frame of hair, incredibly white except for her yellow serpentine eyes and red forked tongue. She opened her fanged mouth to such an angle that the girl's head would fit in it with ease.

Ren would never make it in time. He felt a ball of power surge behind him and heard a thunder-like crack a heartbeat before a green beam flashed by his side. Sugi burst through the woman yōkai, cleaving her in half at the abdomen. The shock of her attack sent the princess on her ass. Ayako screamed when the upper half of the creature twirled in the air, bloodless, and hissed malevolently. Its arms stretched open when the creature found its balance, and its hideous face once again made ready to bite the little girl. It landed on the sand and crawled for a couple of steps before using its arms and the strength of its snake-like torso to jump toward Ayako's fear-struck face.

Ren stepped over the girl and offered his back to the creature rather than risk a wild cut. He screamed when the fangs dug into his left bicep, but the girl screamed higher still. The yōkai shook her head to bite deeper and locked her thin arms around his. She seemed to pour lava into his muscle, and the hot liquid pumped fast toward his hand and shoulder.

Sugi appeared behind the girl, remaining just long enough to secure a hold of her before they vanished. Ren used the girl's absence to swing his blade, but the creature guessed the thrust and forced his arm back.

"Damn it!" Ren shouted. The pain in his left arm was subduing, and any sensation with it.

"Down!" Fuyuko said just as she kicked him in the chest to pin him against the sand. Her clog-heavy foot then pressed on his shoulder, and the other squashed his left hand, though he barely felt it. Standing on him and trapping the creature under his arm, the courtesan aimed her thin blade and struck right between the yellow eyes. The yōkai shrieked when the sword came out of its face, so Fuyuko punched another three holes in the blink of an eye, and only then did its arms relax.

"What an ugly lady," the courtesan said as she used her sword to pry the fangs from Ren's arm.

"A *nure-onna*," Ren replied through his teeth. He felt the moment the monstrous fangs unsheathed from his flesh but not the pain that should have come with it. He wasn't bleeding, either. This could not be good, he thought. "Thank you, Fuyuko."

"Don't mention it. I can't stand ugliness."

"Ren!" Ayako called. The girl, shadowed by the warrior kami, rushed back to her savior, face smeared in snot and tears. "I'm so sorry, Ren. She looked hungry, and you said it feels good to give, and—"

"So now it's my fault?" he asked half-seriously.

Sugi did not look bothered by his state, but when she blinked back to Suzume, the miko dropped to her knees and apologized too, first for failing to kill the beast, second for leaving him to fend it off himself.

"Not your fault," Ren replied, sitting up with difficulty. "Sugi sure knows how to prioritize the mission. And that was a nure-onna," he went on as he knelt above the yōkai's carcass. "The snake part of her body isn't important. They can discard it at will, and it will grow back. You need to strike the head."

"Repeatedly," Fuyuko said just as her blade, now rubbed clean with the yōkai's rags, found its umbrella scabbard.

"Ayako, don't look," Ren said as he dropped the edge of his sword between the creature's lips. He did not check if the girl obeyed and drew a large smile across the nure-onna's face. The hunter then enlarged the gap by pulling it upward and downward until something sounding like ligaments snapped, then he shoved his hand in the cavity up to the wrist. "The good thing with them," he said as he shuffled through the brain matter, "is that their magatama isn't hard to find."

He knew what he would find, yet it never disappointed. A white and pink shell gleaming like the inside of a conch shell, smaller than most magatama but sometimes worth over a week. He chuckled when the shell landed at the bottom of his bag and wondered if he should feel so elated by what had just happened.

"Here you go," Suzume said as she tucked the end of the knot.

Ren had not even realized she had bound his wound with what appeared to be her towel. The arm fell limp against his body. When he felt it again, he told himself, it would hurt like hell.

"And I guess that's our ship," Fuyuko said, nodding toward the approaching boat, a sleek vessel mounted with a triangular white sail. It appeared at the edge of the bay, a few minutes from the group with this wind. Ren started digging with his one good hand.

"Let's not scare them with a torn yōkai body," he said when Fuyuko asked what on earth he was doing.

Suzume was the first to help him dig, then came Ayako. Fuyuko claimed it would look odd if the four of them suddenly crouched to play with the sand and did what she did best, attract attention by being herself.

"At least it seemed to have sobered you up," Ren gibed at Suzume, who had not even noticed. "Might be the most useful trick of the Hands if you ask me."

"I don't intend to need it again, ever," she replied as they shuffled sand on top of the corpse.

"So young and naive," Fuyuko said, receiving a chuckle of agreement from Ren.

The fishing boat turned to offer its stern to the four travelers. The captain waved for his brother to toss the anchor as soon as the sail went down and himself tied the rudder so that he could leave the ship. He jumped into the water, reaching halfway up his chest, and waded through the surf. His intentions went unsurprisingly toward Fuyuko, who graciously accepted his back.

Suzume and Ren shared an amused smile when the courtesan feigned shyness as she dropped her arms around the fisherman's neck. If only the man knew he was passing up the chance to carry an imperial princess for a fox courtesan, Ren thought with glee. Ayako did not seem to mind. From Suzume's back, she kept looking toward the pile of sand under which rested the remains of the yōkai.

"Don't overthink it," Ren told her when the sea reached up to his knees. "Nure-onna thrive on nice people willing to feed them. You were just being a good girl."

"But it almost killed me and you," Ayako replied, biting her bottom lip.

"Nothing will kill you," Suzume said right away. Ren barely recognized her voice. "And Ren is right; don't let what just happened bother you. Feeding the hungry is generous of you, Princess."

"Princess," the child repeated absently.

Ren read in her eyes that she started to understand her place in the world was changing. No matter their destination or the success of their journey, Ayako was no longer a princess. For the first time, the hunter felt sorry for her. "Your parents would be proud of you," he said without thinking.

"I don't know," she replied before lowering her head against Suzume's back.

The water was soaking the child up to the belt now, and Ren was struggling almost to the nipples. The sea was cold, but his left arm felt warm. The fisherman expertly climbed back on his ship, still carrying the courtesan, who yelped and giggled when both landed on the deck. Ren prayed no one else saw the two wet tails jutting from the kimono.

"Well, Sugi and I are proud of you," Suzume said when she

helped the child move in front so she could raise her onto the boat. The fisherman's brother, who must have been a good ten years younger, offered a towel to the child and even started wringing the bottom of her once-exquisite kimono without asking her.

"Up you go," Ren told Suzume, offering the flat of his right hand for support.

"Ren, your left arm," she replied, worry drawing her features.

"It's just numb, don't worry," he replied, tugging a little more on his sleeve to cover the purplish skin. "They're bound to have some Hearts at the Izanagi shrine. By this time tomorrow—" he said, stretching the last word as he helped Suzume up. "—I'll be as good as new."

The fisherman pulled Ren by the belt when he struggled to do more than climb up to his stomach, but he received neither dry towels nor a gentle wringing of his clothes. The vessel had been cleaned recently, probably in preparation for the matsuri, and only a faint smell of raw fish lingered. Nets and lines were still tucked inside straw baskets, proof that the brothers had not intended to go out to sea on that day. The fisherman invited them to sit toward the prow, for he and his brother would use the back of the boat.

"The wind isn't too mean today, but keep your heads low." Just as he spoke, the sail bloated with a gust of wind and almost slapped the fisherman in the face. He ducked under the wave of white hemp and walked back toward the rudder. "Should be there in about three hours. Close your eyes if it doesn't make you want to throw up." He had to shout the last part and seemed amused by his warning. Suzume did not find it funny. The rolling was still gentle, but, as she told the others, her previous crossing of the Seto Sea was far from her favorite memory.

Ayako flattened against the prow and welcomed each trough with loud enthusiasm. An enthusiasm shared by no one else in her group. Fuyuko wore a smile to warm the fishermen's future dreams, but the way her fingers tightened on her kimono told Ren she enjoyed the crossing a lot less than the child. Suzume had adopted a meditative state involving short breaths accompanied by a wince every time the princess cheered for the coming dive. Ren usually liked sailing, though he knew nothing of the skills involved, but after long minutes of this crossing, he had to admit that maybe his arm wasn't just numb.

"Boy," Fuyuko called, stirring him from the mumbling of a prayer to Sukunabikona, the kami of healing, "you're sweating."

He reached for his forehead with the back of his hand and realized he was not only sweating; he was burning. The confidence protecting him shredded then, and it felt as if the poison suddenly rushed through his veins. His head spun, his belly felt heavy, and his legs light.

"You should close your eyes," the courtesan said. "Regain some strength before we land. I guess we'll still need to walk for a while before we reach your shrine."

"No idea," he replied, "but I'll accept your offer."

Ren lay down, using his bag as a pillow and covering his face from the stream of waves hitting the prow with the lid of a basket. He shivered for a few breaths, during which Ayako welcomed more waves, and he thought he heard Suzume retch once more, and then his mind went dark.

He could not hang on to any dream, for the boat's movement and the various sounds of gulls and cheers pulled him from sleep. The fever soon twisted his sense of reality, and he shivered between minute-long naps and difficult bouts of coughing. Fuyuko's long fingers felt smooth and cold on his forehead. She asked Suzume if he could call Maki in this state, arguing that *she* would not carry him all the way to the shrine, but the miko said she did not believe so. Ren mumbled that even if he managed to call the lion-dog, the second he blacked out, she would vanish, and just as he said so, his mind retreated on itself again.

Next time he woke, it was to the sound of the boat creaking and lurching as if it hit a rock. The two sailors gasped just as his three companions did, and Ren blinked, his heart pounding with a new wave of panic.

"Did you drop the anchor?" the fisherman asked in anger.

"Why on earth would I do that?" the brother replied.

"What happened?" Ren asked through his confused mind.

"The boat just stopped," Fuyuko answered. She was getting on one knee, and Ren felt Suzume tense as she dragged the child back toward the deck. The heavy steps of the fisherman shook under Ren's ass as the man stomped to the prow, his frown as dark as his scruffy beard. He bent over to check what had so rudely stopped his ship but seemed to see nothing special and scratched his head.

"Maybe it was just—" His voice died suddenly when his body rocked backward, taken by the strength of a cudgel thrust from the sea.

The fisherman crashed into the mast and left a red mark on the white sail as he slumped like a bag of grain. Then, all around the boat appeared arms, legs, pinchers, and claws. Sugi cut the cudgel in half as its owner meant to climb the boat, and Ren understood from the flow of brown blood that it had been no weapon but the extension of a yōkai's arm. It looked like a mantis wearing the colors of a shrimp, and it shrieked until the spear struck its long head through the mouth.

Sugi stood above the screaming child and butted the back of her spear into another sea creature about to board. The crustacean yōkai rejoined the depth with a fractured skull, but already two more gripped the gunwale to take its place. Fuyuko slashed their fingers off as she ran toward the stern, where the fisherman's brother cursed against an eight-legged yōkai climbing on board. Ren had never seen its like.

The spider-like legs carried a heavy, furry body on which bellowed the head of a bull mounted by six unevenly spread eyes. One of its horns stabbed through the man's lower abdomen just as Fuyuko reached him, but all she could do was watch him being tossed into a coming wave. The spider-bull then rammed the courtesan and sent her back toward the prow, where she crashed against Sugi. Ren unsteadily unsheathed his sword and parried a heavy pincher about to hammer Sugi on top of her skull, but the shock shook his arm hard, and he could do nothing when the pincher came back toward his chest with a vengeance. His back smacked against the mast, stealing the air from his lungs with a cough of blood, and Ren landed right next to the unconscious, most likely dead fisherman. His vision darkened just as he noticed the back of the poor man's skull oozing blood. He fell on his belly, his useless left arm dangling next to him.

"Suzume," he called, his voice pitifully weak. The miko was hanging from a pair of pinchers, arms stretched and screaming as a crustacean yōkai kicked the spear farther from her grasp.

"Ren!" she shouted. She was in pain, Ayako was blanching with terror, and Fuyuko's eyes remained closed.

Ren dragged himself on his right arm and slashed as hard as he could against a skeletal shrimp leg appearing on the side. The blade cut through but then got stuck into the gunwale, and the last thing Ren saw before he lost consciousness was one of the eight legs of the spider-bull driving hard toward the side of his face.

CHAPTER 15

NAMU AMIDA BUTSU

Ren woke under the blinding light of the sun, lying on a donkey-pulled cart, his fever gone but his head feeling like a tree assaulted by a woodpecker. Someone was reciting sutra next to him, and he breathed out with relief, thinking this had been a nightmare and his mother was still by his side to chant his fever away. But as his senses came back, he realized the voice did not belong to her. He sat up and saw a woman—a nun, judging by her clothing—eyes bound by some kind of blindfold, pushing prayer beads between her fingers as she prayed. And she wasn't praying for him but for the other person in the cart.

"Mom!" the boy shouted in a coarse voice he hardly recognized. The nun did not even react, and neither did his mother move. She lay still, a coat-turned pillow under her head and a familiar blanket covering her body. "Mom!" the boy called again, grabbing her hand.

"Oy! Cut it out, will you, boy?"

The man who had spoken walked behind the cart and, despite his rude words, offered a warm, generous smile to the boy. His head was lost in a bushy beard that hadn't seen a shaving blade in decades, if ever, and his skin was marked by the passage of an old pox. A heavy naginata polearm balanced on his shoulders with his wide steps. Something about him felt reassuring.

"Who are you, and what's wrong with my mom?"

"Takeo's the name," the bearded man replied, pointing a thumb at his nose. "But you can call me Boar. This blind bat here is Kino," he said, nodding at the nun, who was indeed old, "and driving the cart is Yumi, but we call her Rat."

Rat wore a wide sandogasa flat bamboo hat that masked the upper half of her head but did nothing to cover her missing right ear. Ren could not guess her age, but the many scars marking her face spoke of a woman of hardship.

"You and your mother were attacked by yōkai," Takeo went on. "We drove them away, but you couldn't stay home, I'm sorry."

"You saved us?" Ren asked, eyes filling with tears.

Takeo the Boar shot a glance at Rat that contained more questions than answers. "Aye, we scattered them away," Takeo replied. "But one of them seems to have done something to your mother, and even Kino can't call her back."

"It was the White Tengu," Ren replied, looking at his mother's livid face.

"A white tengu?" Rat asked, speaking at last. "You saw a white tengu?"

"It was horrible," Ren replied, gathering his knees. "Why did he attack us? We're just tanners. My dad! Have you seen my dad?"

"We saw no one," Takeo replied hesitantly.

"There was no human blood," Rat said. "If your dad had been killed or hurt, we would have found traces. He was probably gone to get some help. I assume you had a raging fever?"

"How do you know?" Ren asked the scarred woman.

"Young man," Takeo replied for her. "This won't be a sweet story to hear, but the yōkai attacked you yesterday because your blood is special. They felt it waking up, and so did we; that's how we found you. We went through the fever, too, when we turned twelve, except that we were being watched over and protected when it happened. Why you, on the other hand, weren't registered at birth is a mystery. If we'd known you existed, we'd have been there days ago."

"You mean it's my fault they hurt my mother?" Ren asked, his voice trembling with the terrible realization.

"Yes and no," Takeo answered.

"Boar!" Rat barked. "You didn't choose any of it," she told the boy, her words somehow perfectly matching the rhythm of the clopping donkey.

"But the tengu came because of me," Ren went on.

"We're sorry this happened to you," Rat replied as Ren started sobbing. The sutra, the clopping, and the creaking of the wheels covered his whimpering for a few seconds, during which the boy despaired for himself.

"Look, boy," Takeo the Boar said. "We're taking you to Ise Jingū. Ever heard of it? Good. Someone will tell you everything about what you are there, and if you want to, we'll help you hunt this White Tengu you think you saw. They'll take good care of your mom, too. And, look, here is an early welcome present, or a birthday one, I guess."

The bearded man pulled a naked blade from his belt, and Ren recognized it immediately, the White Tengu's straight sword. Under the sunlight, the blade appeared almost bronze-like. The hilt was made of dark wood, laced with a dark blue cord, and the flame-shaped guard looked as if forged in the depths of hell. It was a marvelous yet fear-inspiring piece of craft. Neither Takeo nor Rat knew why the Tengu had left it behind, but Boar claimed the blade was just there, waiting at the center of a yōkai blood puddle. Takeo said they would have a scabbard made for it, and Rat promised to teach the boy its use, though some other Bloods had greater skill than her with swords, she claimed.

"Bloods?" Ren asked.

"That's what we and you are, little brother," Takeo replied with a *beaming smile. "The twelve Bloods of the Eight Gates. And just for you to know, you are our Rooster."*

"I am Rooster?" Ren asked.

血

"Rooster," Ren mumbled in his sleep.

"What a splendid idea," an unfamiliar voice said over the sound of a bubbling liquid. "Rooster, yes. It has been ages. Not some mean old hen or yet another rancid fish, no, rooster. A splendid idea."

Ren's head still spun and swayed, and he had yet to shake the blur from his eyes, though the feeble light wouldn't help much, anyway. There was a glow he attributed to a fire covered by a pot and tiny specks of glimmers along the natural walls of a cave, judging by the distorted echo of the small room.

The hunter winced against the pain in his skull and closed his eyes to force it to stop moving. Then he understood it wasn't just his mind that rocked; it was his whole body, except for his feet, roped together and hooked to the ceiling. His panic woke his senses when he realized he was hanging upside down. Everything else came faster. The humming of a song, the appetizing smell of a broth, and the drops plopping from the tip of his hair to the rocky ground covered in puddles of seawater.

"Now that I think about it, though," the voice said again, sounding disappointed. "I doubt we have anything but fish to add to this soup and, of course, you people."

"What?" Ren asked, using his painful neck to take an upside-down look at his captor. The movement made the rope tense and rub, and when he spotted the yōkai, Ren stopped moving. A crab, it was a crab, tall as a man, wearing the conical hat of a wandering monk and their black and saffron garments too. In his left pincher, the crab monk even held a *shakujō* staff mounted with six metal rings, which he swung to the rhythm of his humming.

"The broth," the yōkai replied, using his other pincer to lift a ladle from the large pot in which stewed a meal. "It needs some bones, some carcass, some brain maybe." Foam accumulated through the crab's mouthparts and made his words difficult to understand, but Ren guessed their meaning easily enough.

"I'd rather you didn't use mine for that," Ren replied.

"Well, not for this soup, that's for sure," the monk yōkai replied. "This one's already flavored. See?" He lifted the ladle from the pot and dropped it low enough for Ren to see the hand jutting out from it. A man's boiled fingers were curled around a piece of ear, while at the bottom of the ladle rested a dark mess of nori algae. Ren wondered if it belonged to the fisherman or his brother.

"Why am I here if not to join this soup?" Ren asked.

"Because my followers are always hungry. Another meal will be needed before nightfall, and I am a dedicated leader to all those poor souls." The crab sounded proud of himself and waved his pinchers with verve. "And when the Buddha provides us with such quality meat, I am bound to observe it, smell its sweat, and thus find the perfect combination of spice for the broth. Of course, in your case, I first had to suck the poison out."

"Thank you, I'm honored." Ren ironically replied, preferring not to think of how the poison had been sucked out and earning himself a crustacean chuckle.

"If it makes you feel any better, it was a tough choice. Not this one. No, this one won't taste better than my feet would, but he was already dead, and I'm not one to waste. But you," the crab said, pointing the ladle at the hunter, "and your friends, you all got me foaming at the mouth. Eighty years I've infested these waters; I have never gathered such a bounty."

"Look," Ren interrupted. "I can see you're the kind that likes to talk, and it's all fine with me, but could you please hang me the other way around? I won't last until dinner at this rate."

"Happy to oblige," the crab replied. The yōkai crept sideways, crawling on its six legs to Ren, and lifted him from the hook in the ceiling.

The young man fell like a bag of grain and immediately got picked up again, then hooked through the rope binding his wrists. This crab was strong and nimble enough with his clumsy-looking pinchers. Ren had hoped to catch an opportunity, but everything had gone so fast that he still reeled from all the movement when the priest resumed his joyful singing. The room was small and opened to a corridor shining blue from small fires bouncing on oddly carved walls.

"*Namu Amida Butsu. Na~mu Amida Butsu~,*" the yōkai sang.

"I assume my companions are still alive, too," Ren said.

"Oh yes, very much so," the crab replied as he chose a bottle of clay containing some oil, which he emptied into the pot. Ren could spot chunks of the fisherman whenever the crab stirred the broth. "I'm still hesitating between the fox and the miko for tomorrow. What do you think?"

"Why not the girl?" Ren asked.

"No, not the girl, no," the yōkai replied. "The General is looking for her; she's precious to us."

"So you work for him, huh?"

"For him?" the monk spat, tilting its head angrily. "Me? Working for that lowly turd? I am the King of the Coast! From south Wakayama all the way to Himeji and all around Awaji Island, there's not a yōkai who doesn't bow to the great Kanibōzu!" The ladle swayed as the yōkai-monk shouted, spraying broth all over the soaked floor of the kitchen. "Me?" he scoffed. "Once I deliver the child, the General will work for me, boy."

"Oh?" Ren asked, "You mean that there's someone above the General?"

"What? You thought *he* was our lord? Ridiculous. The General is nothing," the crab said, waving his pincher down and almost hitting the rim of the pot.

"I don't know," Ren replied, playing along. "He won a great victory in Kyōto. Humans pretty much lost the war. But I've never heard of you, and believe me, I've hunted yōkai far and wide."

The yōkai cleared its throat in a disgusting sound of phlegm and crunching sand, then walked sideways to the hunter. He lifted the biggest of his two pinchers all the way to Ren's chin.

"If you were as experienced as you claim, you'd know this was no war. This was just a mere... first wave. A message, a... a... poke, nothing more. War—" Another throat clearing. "When war begins, there won't be a living soul to mention it. The General is a scout, at best. He was there to sow chaos and to test you people. Aye, he won a victory, but with surprise on your side, victory requires no special skill."

"But you'd want him to work for you?"

"Why not?" the crab asked, going back to his bubbling broth. "That would be a nice spit in the eyes to all those *noble* yōkai who call themselves our betters because they never got their feet wet. If I get some of their officers for myself, they'll have to consider me as their equal."

"And then what?" Ren asked. "You'd stopped at being their equals?" He needed to keep the crab talking and learn more about the real threat behind the massacre of Kyōto.

"One needs to be humble," the crab replied absently. "An important lesson for the followers of the Buddha."

"You know, followers of the Buddha don't eat meat," Ren said.

"If my stomach digested anything else, I would close my eyes to flesh," the crab replied. "Good try, though. And stop trying to make me talk. I've got nothing for you, and you won't ever leave my kingdom."

"Can't fault a man for trying," Ren replied. His shoulder blades started hurting, and his wet clothes were freezing on his skin. "If I'm going to die, why shouldn't you talk to me?"

"Because *she* is always listening," the yōkai replied, lifting its scepter toward the ceiling. "And *she* doesn't like when we say things we shouldn't to the enemy."

"*She*?" Ren asked. "A bosatsu or something?"

"No," the crab replied, chuckling. "Not a bosatsu, no."

The hunter was about to press the point when the sound of scurrying legs rushed toward the kitchen's entrance. The spider-bull appeared, its six eyes blinking frantically, and it squeaked a series of sounds aimed at its leader. The crab slammed the ladle into the pot and butted the end of its shakujō staff on the ground. Something was not to his liking.

"You!" the crab spat, pointing his massive pincher at the hunter. "Who's after you? How did you signal them?" As he spoke, the yōkai scurried to Ren sideways until the tip of the blood-smelling pincher rested under his chin.

"You know who's after us!" Ren replied. "We were just talking about your General and—"

"Not yōkai!" the crab spat, sputtering foam. "Humans! Why are humans here? There's never been a human here that we didn't bring."

"How would I know?" Ren asked, going from anger to fear as the pincher opened and slowly closed around his throat. "You took me here unconscious." The crab hesitated, its tiny eyes moving between Ren's as if he could read his thoughts. The spider-bull got agitated and moaned to get his superior's attention.

"I will take care of them," the yōkai replied, squinting threateningly. "And if I find out you've signaled them somehow, I will come back and chop your fingers and toes one by one into this soup."

Ren found nothing witty to reply and contented himself in swallowing a hard ball of saliva. The crab monk broke contact, grabbed a kitchen knife and his staff, and hurried out of the kitchen, making skeletal noises with each of its many steps. The spider-bull followed suit, leaving Ren alone with the boiling pieces of the fisherman.

It felt suddenly quiet, though Ren could hear crustacean footsteps in the corridors running around the kitchen. He had to act fast. Whoever had the monk so rattled wouldn't last long against an army of yōkai. A quick check of the room let him know his options were more than limited. The only piece of furniture in the room was the table on which the crab had lined dozens of small jars and bottles, plus a cutting board, a bowl of algae, and a container full of clams and sea snails. There had been two knives by the cutting board, but the monk had taken the bigger one, leaving a gutting knife just big enough to crack oysters open. Everything was too far from him to be of use, anyway. Ren needed to get down from the hook first.

He tried to wriggle his wrists from the rope, but whoever had knotted them knew what they were doing; they wouldn't budge. Then he checked the hook better and despaired. It bent almost all the way up to the ceiling, making it impossible for the hunter to simply swing out of it. He needed to find support if he meant to pull his hands up from the hook, but his feet hung a blade length from the floor, and nothing in front of him was close enough to help.

But behind, he thought, and not one second later, Ren started arching and swinging to feel how far the wall stood on his back. His heels knocked it easily enough. It was a sharp, rocky wall, dug by time and water, as was most of this underground structure. Not able to see it clearly, he kept swinging and threw his feet backward in an attempt to find a natural spike or shard to use as a support.

Three times, he cut the soles of his feet in his search, and his abdomen was starting to hurt, too, with all those back-and-forth motions. The hunter stopped to regain his breath after another failed attempt when an explosion suddenly rocked the room, showering it with a layer of drops.

"A cannon," he whispered. Those humans came prepared, he thought. Cannons could kill yōkai, but those were well-led, and the reloading time would be all they needed to kill every last soldier. And, if by some miracle they somehow prevailed, Ren had to take the princess away before the battle ended. Ayako falling into the hands of a daimyo would be as damaging to his mission as staying here.

He swung once more and, by sheer luck, managed to get the rope between his ankles tangled into a piece of pointy wall. His back arched so much that he seemed to hang in the air with his belly down. Another explosion and another shower from the ceiling. There was only one cannon, Ren understood. He checked the hook once more. Then, after taking a long breath in, he pushed on his feet to propel himself forward and shook his arms upward. His wrists passed over the tip of the hook, leaving him free, and Ren fell face and belly first.

"Hurts," he spat after a long *argh* of pain. He had cut his lower lip in the landing and was almost certain a rib had cracked, but he was no longer roped to the ceiling. His fall had been less than discreet, and already, he could hear tiny footsteps in the hallway accompanied by nervous clicking sounds.

Licking his lip, Ren got on his knees, scrapping them against the pointy bits of the floor, and used the corner of the table for support. He grabbed the small knife, reversed its blade, and cut through the rope in one swift motion. The steps were almost there; no time to free his feet.

The hunter grabbed the container with all the clams and threw it toward the entrance, where it crashed against the appearance of a shrimp-looking yōkai. The creature squealed and clicked in surprise when the jar broke on the side of its head, but Ren gave it no time to recover. He rolled over the table and slammed his bound feet into the creature's face, just where its long antenna connected with the chin. He fell with the yōkai but managed to recover faster and, crawling more than anything, pulled on the creature's left eye and tore it free with a wide cut of the small knife. Regular blades could not harm yōkai, but even *they* had their weak spots, and the eyes were almost always one. The creature squealed harder and threatened through its mad thrashing to kick Ren from its back, so the hunter grabbed the remaining eye and squeezed.

"Hey!" he shouted. "Stop it, or I take this one too!" The tip of the small knife found the center of the eye and pressed just strong enough to give weight to the threat. The creature breathed hard but otherwise no longer moved. "Do you speak?" The yōkai emitted a series of clicks that Ren took for a *no*. "Too bad, then you'll just listen. I was taken here with three people. We had a few bags and some blades. You'll take me to the blades first, then the people, and if you don't do anything stupid, I'll let you go with one eye still attached to your brain. Understood?"

The shrimp yōkai nodded—or did something that looked like a nod—and Ren let it go long enough to cut the rope at his feet. Then, grabbing it by a panel of the exoskeleton on its back, pushed the creature forward.

The structure of corridors and random rooms was much bigger than Ren had assumed, and he was glad for the guidance. Underground rivers had dug this place, but surely those yōkai had worked for decades to enlarge it. Phosphorescent algae and clams illuminated the hallway in a timid blue light, and every time Ren stepped into a larger puddle, the same light waved through the water from the impact. It could have been a beautiful place had it not smelled like a month-old dead fish and felt as cold as a winter's fog.

The shrimp nodded toward a room appearing a little farther on the right. There were no doors in this place, so Ren noticed from the moving shadows stretching out of the room that it wasn't empty.

"Hey," he whispered to his guide, shaking it to stop. "If it's a trap, you'll—"

The threat lost itself under a sudden shriek. A blast of green light flashed from the room, and a yōkai body burst into the hallway, crashing into the wall. The yōkai, a near exact copy of Ren's guide, slumped dead, its broken back smearing blood and flesh in its descent. From where it came calmly appeared Sugi, spear in hand.

"Sugi!" Fuyuko raged, "he was supposed to take us to—never mind," the courtesan said when she noticed the hunter in the hallway. She looked unhurt, naked blade in hand, and walking on her okobo clogs. She nodded at Ren, who found himself lost for words. Sugi pointed her spear at him and spoke words he could not hear.

"You absolutely did not know he was here. You just got lucky," Ayako said in her commanding, princessy tone. "Hello Ren. You made a new friend too?" she asked as she, too, stepped out of the room and dropped her arms by her hips. In one of them, she held his sword.

"Had I known you could handle yourselves," Ren replied as he forced the shrimp to its knees. "I would have waited for you in the kitchen." He suddenly felt all the tiny scrapes and bruises on his skin, but he also felt a ray of hope at seeing his three companions safe and sound.

"Handle ourselves?" Fuyuko asked with a scoff, handing him

his shoulder bag. "Please. We came here first. I'd say *we* were rescuing you."

"Well, then," Ren replied as he retrieved the sandals from the bag. "Thanks for the rescue. Now let's get out of here." Another explosion accompanied his words. This one sounded somewhat stronger. "Hey, shrimpy. This here is an explosive talisman," he said, fishing one of the few talismans still usable from his bag. "If you move within the next ten minutes, you will go boom. Understood?" Ren asked as he slapped the talisman at the base of the yōkai's neck.

The creature pitifully nodded and sunk lower on its knees, a couple of steps from the carcass of its companion. It seemed to sob, and Ayako gently patted his back. Before they left it, Ren asked how many exits the structure had and, through a few guesses, understood there was only one, exactly where the explosions came from. They left the shrimp and ran toward the sounds of battle.

"Will it really explode?" Ayako asked, looking back at the shivering yōkai.

"Explosive talismans? That would be neat," Ren replied. "That was a talisman to help one find love. I hope it works," he then joked.

Shortly after, Sugi relented the body back to Suzume, who immediately embraced Ren as tears of relief ran down her cheeks. He reminded her they had to move but assured her he was happy to see her as well.

After many twists and turns, the air suddenly changed, and the corridor opened to a large, dome-shaped room. The ceiling stood three times higher than in the hallway, and the room was sheltering more than thirty yōkai. The whole group, Ren assumed. He and Fuyuko stood on the right side of the corridor's exit while Suzume and Ayako hugged the left side.

The crab monk was waving his staff at his creatures,

commanding them to get ready for battle. The ground under the yōkai's feet was made of wet sand and slime. There was no opening whatsoever, but another of those shrimps suddenly waddled up from the slime and popped out of it. It waved its arms and clicked words at the monk.

"A hundred!" the monk repeated, waving its armed pinchers for everyone's attention. "A mere hundred human soldiers stand on the other side." On those words, he moved the staff toward the wall they all faced, and sure enough, the next explosion shook pieces of rock from it. Those soldiers were going to crack it open with their cannon. Ren could think of only one reason why they worked so hard to breach the wall; they knew who stood on the other side, an imperial princess. "What are a hundred people to us? Nothing! We will crush them! The Wise Kings are on our side!"

"Listen," Ren whispered. "The cannon will eventually tear this place open. Then, the battle will begin. That's when we escape. It will get messy and—"

"Shouldn't we fight?" Suzume asked. "They'll get slaughtered without us."

"This is not our mission," Ren replied. "They'll flee when they realize their blades don't work, and most will survive. But us, we need to keep moving."

"But," Ayako started saying, though she looked away because she knew how her words would be met.

"I know what you're thinking," Ren said, gently dropping his hand on her shoulder to catch her eyes. "But we can't trust anyone. Whoever is there came for you, and I doubt they'll let us go to Ise in peace, especially not you. Ayako, I need you to trust me."

The next cannonball thumped into the wall and pierced it enough for a large ray of light to burst through the room. Ren raised his hand to shield himself from the debris and did not notice the beam of light bouncing against his blade. The reflection hit the spider-bull yōkai in one of its many eyes, and the creature bellowed as if hurt.

"Uh-oh," Ayako said when all the yōkai turned their way.

"Take the girl!" the monk shouted, pointing his staff toward the group of four. "Kill the others, but take the girl!"

"Ren?" Suzume asked as the thirty yōkai charged.

"Fuyuko, stay with the princess," Ren answered, plucking his scabbard from his belt. "Suzume, help me get to that slime!" he said, praying that Maki could be called through the sand, something he'd never tried before.

Not waiting for an answer, Ren darted toward the closest yōkai, a long, slimy creature looking like a moray eel slithering with no other weapon than its pointy fangs and feral eyes. It gathered on itself a few steps from Ren and uncoiled like a spring. By luck more than reflex, Ren ducked and slashed his sword and caught the creature right under the mouth. The yōkai's speed did the rest, and it landed behind Ren in two spasming halves.

The hunter felt he'd killed his prey but could not check, for already another was on him. This one looked almost human, if humans could grow urchin-like hair, and had webbed hands. It shouted with a lunge of his spear that would have skewered Ren through the sternum if he hadn't moved in time. He grabbed the pole under his armpit and thrust his sword toward the urchin-man's eyes, but the yōkai lowered its head, and the blade bounced on its spine hairs.

As his arm shot up under the impact, Ren saw another yōkai crawling on the ceiling and about to drop on him with a huge, hammer-like pincher first. The hunter let himself fall on his ass, dragging the urchin-man who refused to let go of the spear with him. The creature on the ceiling slammed into the urchin-man with its pincher, and both shrieked, one with pain, the other with rage. The first had its back broken from the impact, and the other Ren killed with a thrust through the mouth.

He rolled backward to avoid the tip of some harpoon and cursed at how close to his belly it had gotten. "Sugi," he called, "a little help here."

But Sugi was nowhere in sight, and when Ren dared a look backward, he saw that she stood exactly where he had left her, though she now stood with her spear across the girl, immovable and ready to defend the princess until the end of times, even though Ayako was pulling on Sugi's hakama and pointing at Ren.

The hunter could not believe what he was seeing. His eyes then flicked to Fuyuko, and he tilted his head in a plea. She rolled her eyes, sighed, and mouthed something that looked like a long, unhappy "fine," then uncrossed her arms and vanished from his sight only to reappear in the air on top of him, where she cut through the clawed hand about to tear his face to bits. The yōkai, whom Ren had not noticed, screamed as its hand fell, but no sooner did Fuyuko land on her heavy clogs than its head dropped, and the scream ended.

"Well," she told Ren, nodding toward the patch of slime on which the crab monk still stood.

"Damn it," Ren grumbled as he stood up.

Ayako suddenly yelped. Ren glimpsed behind and saw that Sugi had the situation under control, her spear jutting from the backs of two shrimp-yōkai. She pushed the girl behind her and used the entrance of the corridor as a shield. Nothing would get past her. The cannon shook the room again, and the open space grew wider, letting more light in.

Ren shoved his scabbard back in his belt and went for his pocket, where he had stored one of his prayer beads. The yōkai were now coming in groups of two and three. Even with the help of the courtesan, this fight would not end well. They had to call for some backup.

A yōkai wielding a rusty sword tried to thrust at Fuyuko, but she opened her umbrella just before the impact and parried the sword upward. The yōkai yelped, the momentum of its parried attack lifting its arm, and the yelp turned to shriek when the tip of Fuyuko's blade reached its armpit. She then twisted it, took a step back, and the yōkai's arm tore free of its shoulder, whirling bloodily through the air. The courtesan slashed through its throat as she leaped toward her next target, whose nose she shattered with the sole of her clog. Using the broken face for support, she flipped once more to avoid a swing of a cudgel and hammered the yōkai with the back of her heel, thus breaking a second nose within a couple of seconds.

Ren kicked the same creature in the face when he sat up and heard something snap under his foot. He ducked under one of the spider-bull's legs, leaped over the next, and cut through a third. The creature bellowed and fell on its side, nearly crushing Ren's foot in the process. But the hunter paid it no more attention when he saw Fuyuko landing on its back, grabbing its left horn as she would the pommel of a saddle.

"I offer you my prayer and this blood," Ren said as he drew some blood from his thumb, which he then smeared on the bead. The ground under his foot was still wet and rocky. He needed to go a little farther, where the monk crab stood threateningly on its six legs, spear-headed staff and his kitchen knife in his pincers.

"Protect me, guardian spirit," Ren continued, focusing on keeping his emotions in check to make the prayer more potent. *"And help me cleanse the corruption from this land!"* He ducked under the head of the staff and was about to plant the bead when the knife came in a wide arc that forced him to jump back. The monk did not pursue him, and Ren wondered if he could possibly know his goal. It smiled at the hunter, and Ren almost cursed again.

The presence of the spider-bull suddenly chilled his spine, but the beast zagged past him on its seven legs, its direction dictated according to how the courtesan twisted her blade stuck in the creature's neck. She forced him to charge the monk, and the spider-bull, in its mad, painful rage, obeyed. The crab lowered its stance and jumped up, twisting on himself and slashing his kitchen knife through the mouth and throat of its subordinate. The spider-bull died without a sound and toppled on the side just as the crab landed gracefully.

"Ren!" Fuyuko called in a panic. The monk was wobbling to her as she tried to push the carcass of the spider-bull from her legs to no avail. The monk raised his staff, head down, aimed at the courtesan's wincing face.

"Hey!" Ren shouted, freezing the staff in the air.

The monk turned its ugly, hat-wearing head toward the hunter, and foam started accumulating around its mouth. What it saw was the young hunter, thumb against the slime, where the smooth shape of a bead barely peered from the ground. Ren took a step back, then another. All the yōkai had stopped moving and were observing in anticipation.

"Maki, I call you!" Ren then shouted, raising his free hand.

And in the air his hand hung for long seconds during which nothing happened. Sand, it seemed, was not an acceptable conduit to call a guardian.

"Shit," Ren said after swallowing a ball of saliva.

"Just kill them," the monk crab lazily said as he raised his staff a little higher again. He sounded disappointed, though not as much as Ren was.

The hunter leaped forward, but as the staff darted down and as Fuyuko started screaming, eyes closed, he knew he would be too late. Her scream was high-pitched and loud. So loud indeed that it covered the bark of the cannon.

The crab's head suddenly exploded. He still stood, frozen in his attack, the tip of the staff a mere hand away from Fuyuko's eyes. White and orange flesh then showered the courtesan, and the creature finally faltered, its knees giving up one by one. The void where its head had been appeared clearly in the light peering from the hole in the wall, which was now big enough for a man to pass through.

For once, Ren thought, his height had saved him, for the cannonball had brushed his scalp after it tore through the monk crab. He remembered to breathe just in time to witness the panic spreading through the ranks of yōkai, and when the first of them yelped and dove through the slime, all the others started scrambling around. Some fled through the sand, others disappeared through the corridor, avoiding Sugi's spear as best they could.

"Ren, would you mind?" Fuyuko asked through her teeth.

The hunter sheathed his sword and rushed to the courtesan, crouching next to the crab's carcass so he could pull the body of the spider-bull from his companion's legs. She pushed with her hands, and once her left leg slipped from under the massive yōkai, she used it too.

"One more time," Ren said when he had to let go of the creature. "*Sē, no!*"

Her right leg appeared from under the spider-bull, and just as Fuyuko breathed out with relief, a shadow emerged from the cannon-made hole, that of a man clad in golden and black armor, wearing a helmet decorated with long, straight beams spread like a sun, and carrying a masterfully crafted katana. He stepped over the unbroken piece of wall and took a regal fighting stance as he appraised the room. His gaze fell first upon Ren, who wore a face of regret in the middle of the mostly deserted room. The samurai sheathed his blade and crossed the space separating him from the hunter. More warriors started pouring in after the samurai, and even their professionalism did not prevent them from murmuring at the sight of the yōkai bodies.

The golden samurai then noticed Fuyuko and offered his hand. She looked awestruck at the sight of him, and no wonder, Ren thought, for he was dashing. He was neither young nor old but carried the martial air of a veteran, though his face offered neither scar nor the violence of a man who has seen too much blood. Most samurai wore masks to instill fear into their enemies' hearts, but this one did not. Maybe it had something to do with his striking handsomeness, a quality he seemed aware of, as he showed with a ridiculously charming smile when the courtesan got on her feet. She blinked and remembered to remove her hand from his.

"Besides the most elegant woman in Japan," the man said in a silk-smooth voice, his eyes remaining on Fuyuko's blushing face while his head moved toward the hunter, "you wouldn't happen to have its princess with you?"

CHAPTER 16

THE GOLDEN SUN OF OSAKA

The great town of Ōsaka was abuzz with the return of its daimyo, Shimazu Ryōma, the Golden Sun of Ōsaka, as he was known throughout Japan, or, more accurately, the town vibrated with the news of what their hero brought back in his gilded cart.

His first order when they stepped out of the sea-yōkai residence was for a group of messengers to run back to Ōsaka and spread the glorious news. Princess Ayako was alive and on her way to Lord Shimazu's castle.

Ren had loved Ōsaka from his first visit to the pearl of Settsu Province. Its people were rowdy, noisy, and easily triggered, but friendlier than most in Japan and they didn't mind the occasional good brawl. Sake and food overflowed in this city that seemed to never stop eating, and since it stood but a stone's throw from the sea, it didn't need to. Even in the short years since he had discovered Ōsaka, Ren had noticed how much life had improved here, and all of it followed the meteoric rise of its daimyo.

Shimazu Ryōma was one of those men who had not only survived the civil war but had ridden the wave from his childhood humid rice fields all the way to the *jomon* gate of his very own castle. Through a cunning mind, battle-tested charisma, and a face one trusted on sight, the Golden Sun of Ōsaka had become one of the most spoken names in the nation, and always with respect. And Ren, within five minutes of meeting the man, not only understood how he had climbed the ladder in a mere ten years but also started distrusting him.

While his men whistled and prodded the yōkai's carcasses, Ryōma gave them no more than a glimpse and focused all his attention on the princess. He rushed to her, nearly getting Sugi's spear in the eye for his daring, and kowtowed with reverence, not caring for the water under his knees and forehead. He spoke educated words of respect to the girl, using a level of politeness Ren had rarely witnessed and would be hard-pressed to copy. But at the same time, the self-made daimyo did not tremble as one would in the presence of an imperial daughter.

Sugi did not let the child approach the armored man, yet she did not attack him, not even when his guards came to his side. Ryōma gently ordered them to sheath their blades, and he removed his sun-shaped helmet, revealing a tight bun of dark hair. His well-oiled mustache contained a few gray hairs, and wise wrinkles appeared at the corner of his eyes when he smiled at Sugi.

"From the bottom of my heart," the samurai said, dropping his hand on his chest and bowing again. "I thank you for protecting the daughter of the sun, noble miko warrior."

Ren spotted hesitation on Sugi's face. She struggled against this man's gentle will and frowned. The hunter came close to the daimyo, ready to defend him in case the warrior kami decided he was a threat. But, to his surprise, Sugi stood straighter and bowed back before letting Suzume resume control of her body. The young woman blinked in surprise and looked at Ren with a thousand questions on her face. He shook his head to let her know nothing was to be done, and Ayako finally stepped out of Suzume's shadow.

"We thank you for rescuing us," she told the daimyo in the voice and tone Ren thought she had lost during their short time together. "You may rise."

"Thank you, Your Highness," the daimyo replied before he allowed himself to stand. Even then, his head remained low, and only after Ayako accepted an escort of five samurai warriors out of the structure did he lift his eyes to meet Ren's again. "You and I, I believe, have much to discuss." There was no animosity in his words, but Ren felt that their discussion would not be a pleasant one.

"I would prefer that you let us go," Ren replied, trying his best to sound more mature than his years to match the man's charisma. "All of us," he went on, nodding toward the princess who was stepping out into the sun.

"My apologies, young Yaseki warrior," the daimyo replied, "but the situation obliges me to insist on escorting all of you to my domain, where you will rest, heal, and where we will talk. But do not fear; I guarantee you we are all on the same side here."

Ren shivered. This man spoke all the right words and adapted his language to his audience perfectly, but more impressive, he knew about the Yaseki and had guessed Ren belonged to it. He was dangerous, and he was genial. Monk-crabs, nue, kappa, and other yōkai, the hunter knew how to handle, but Shimazu Ryōma was a threat of another kind, and for the first time on this journey, Ren felt lost.

"We would be delighted to accompany you," Fuyuko said in her alluring voice.

Ryōma replied with his most charming smile.

"Would you mind giving us five minutes here to take care of some Yaseki business?" Ren asked.

The daimyo did not reply but, with a clap of the hands, invited his soldiers to leave the room and gather outside. Neither Ren nor his two companions moved while the soldiers left, but the low hum in Fuyuko's throat spoke of her appreciation for the daimyo's presence.

"That is one fine man," she said, biting her bottom lip. Ren scoffed. "And a dangerous one," she went on.

"That he is," Ren agreed. "Don't let him fool you. He might say we're on the same side, but that man has only one side, his."

"What do we do?" Suzume asked.

"No choice," Ren replied. "We follow him. But don't get too comfortable. First chance we get, we take the girl and go."

"Something tells me it won't be that easy," Suzume replied. She was startled by a drop of water that fell on her neck, and Ren used this as a signal to start moving.

He first retrieved the monk crab's magatama, which turned out to be made of a pearl-like white. He'd never encountered such a shell but hoped it would fetch a high price. The crab had not been the most powerful of foes, but he was ancient, clever, and organized.

The spider-bull offered a seashell magatama, just like the snake woman on the beach. Ren could not believe this had been a few hours before. By the time he was done with those two, most of the others had lost their souls already, not that he would have gotten much out of them. The last thing Ren did before leaving this cursed place was pluck the unused bead from the slime and drop it into his pocket.

Fuyuko and Suzume were invited to join Ayako inside the horse-pulled carriage, though it took a bit of negotiation for the miko to relent her spear before climbing in. Sugi, Ren assumed, must have been furious. He was allowed to keep his sword for the moment and given a horse to ride at the daimyo's side.

Ren's riding skills were poor, but the daimyo made no show of noticing and even proved to be a gracious traveling companion when he handed the young man his own calabash of hot water. Neither the hunter nor his horse would enjoy this trip, but as Ren quickly realized, it would be a short one. Ōsaka stood but a couple of hours from the beach, and Ren cursed himself at never noticing this yōkai lair despite his several visits to the region.

The monk crab had chosen the place well. Before the cannon shredded a hole in the wall, nothing would have betrayed its presence. Those yōkai came in and out from the slime ground and maybe even popped out from the sea, making their passage invisible for years. And, so close to a great city, their actions would have been diluted by the mass of accidental deaths and catastrophes. No doubt the sea would claim fewer lives around here from then on, though Ren would need to come back to clean the coast of all those yōkai who had fled.

"You must wonder how I know about the Yaseki?" the daimyo asked halfway through the journey.

"Not really," Ren replied. He had not meant to sound so blunt, but controlling the beast under his ass took most of his focus. "We try to remain discreet, but some of us are better at it than others, and if anyone would know about us, it's bound to be powerful daimyo." He winced and sucked his breath in when the horse suddenly tugged the reins from his hands and skipped for a few steps. The daimyo retrieved the reins while Ren regained his balance. "Thank you. I'm more curious about how you knew where to find us."

"Where to rescue you, you mean," the daimyo replied with his signature smirk.

"We would have managed," Ren lied. "Though your timing was perfect, I must admit."

"The chief of a certain village a little north saw you under attack," Shimazu Ryōma explained. "Apparently, he had hosted you at a matsuri the night before and worried the crossing might prove too much for people unused to the sea. I guess he was right.

231

A very nice fellow. Brave enough to follow your boat as those creatures dragged it back to their lair, though he couldn't find its
entrance because they vanished from his sight as soon as they
reached the beach, and the boat was left to float away. Then he
came to me, and with the help of some local folks who shared
rumors of yōkai using the beach, we found the lair. The rest, you
know."

"You acted fast," Ren said.

"Well, when the village's chief claimed one of you was a child
wearing a dirty kimono of amazing quality and talked of herself as
we, I pieced it with what I've heard of the attack on Kyōto and took
a gamble. I would say it paid off," the man said, sounding proud of
himself, though not arrogantly. The shadow of Ōsaka's northern
gate passed over them, and in this brief moment, the daimyo's
teeth shined from a smirk to a grin, and Ren shivered again.

"I wouldn't count your chickens yet," Ren replied, trying his
best not to sound threatening. "I am grateful for the help, I truly
am, but Ōsaka is neither my destination nor Ayako's. There are
things you do not understand at work here, and—"

The daimyo raised his hand to ask for Ren's silence and then
raised it higher to wave at the two rows of people lining the street
of Ōsaka.

"We will have this conversation," the daimyo said. "But not
here."

This conversation, Ren understood, would happen deep
within the lord's domain, at the center of the double-moated
castle, surrounded by hundreds of obedient Shimazu spears.

Through his few visits, Ren had visited much of Ōsaka but had
never entered the castle grounds. It was a fairly recent ensemble of
buildings, all of them built under the care of Shimazu Ryōma after
the then officer of the shōgun received this land in thanks for his
services during the civil war. Through years of expensive, back-
breaking labor, a typical three-storied *tenshu* and its few accompa-

nying buildings had been turned into one of the three most impressive domains in Japan.

The castle's keep was now six stories high, lacquered in black, and covered in huge golden peonies. The two decorative *shachi-hoko* dragon-carps standing upside down on the edges of the rooftop were said to be made of solid gold. Two warriors were dedicated to guarding each of those statues, and seeing how big they stood, Ren understood why the daimyo would be so anxious to keep them from thieves.

And even with all its magnificence, the keep seemed lost within the palace grounds. The inner domain was large enough to accommodate some of the most luxuriant gardens Ren had ever seen, worshipping halls, turrets, the daimyo's residence, and still, the keep stood at the center of an intricate network of easily defensible corridors and *masugata* death boxes. Two bridges connected the inner domain to the outer one, and four jomon gates allowed one to cross the outer moat. Invading this castle would be a nightmare, and Shimazu Ryōma understandably looked proud of his domain. Ren, however, despaired, for exiting it unnoticed would prove just as troublesome as conquering it would be.

As guessed, he, Fuyuko, and Suzume were asked to disarm as they passed the southeast jomon gate, and there again, Ryōma proved his wisdom by asking Ren to leave his prayer beads with his sword.

They were allowed in the keep and given a tour by the daimyo himself, though he never walked in front of the princess. Ryōma, as most daimyo did, lived in another palace. His was to be found between the inner and outer moats, where his family enjoyed more intimacy. He was nonetheless the master of the keep and had spent without counting on turning it into a wonder of luxury.

The walls of the many rooms were adorned with golden paintings from the most prestigious artists of the land. While Ren knew nothing of them, he liked those paintings enough. Most represented prowling tigers, cranes landing in quiet rivers of gold, and dragons roaming through swirling clouds. There was power in those drawings, and the hunter wondered if maybe some Hands had fleshed them out. A few of them even displayed yōkai, and Ren laughed inside at the incongruity of their looks, so far from their true, savage nature.

Ayako was in her element here. She patiently acknowledged the details Ryōma pointed out and remarked on some others by herself. Not once did she complain about the difficulty of climbing those six stories or about the cold, for cold it was in this huge, mostly empty keep.

Servants had peeled the princess of her dirty, previously pink kimono and veiled her with a splendid golden one decorated with swimming, black and orange, white, and yellow koi carp. No one offered anything of the sort to the three others, but Ryōma used Ayako's inspection of a well-sculpted bosatsu wooden statue to inform Fuyuko she could expect new robes as soon as the tour ended.

By Ren's estimation, it took another hour before they sat in a frugal *chashitsu* tea room. There, too, Ayako impressed Ren with her quiet appreciation of the bitter tea served to them while he and Suzume emptied their bowls in one straight gulp without taking the time to admire their designs. Ren knew he was supposed to do more than pretend to enjoy the tea but didn't care much about the etiquette. This whole charade had already taken too much of their time for his taste. As for Suzume, she blushed when she noticed the embarrassed looks on Fuyuko and Ayako's faces.

"We thank you for your hospitality," Ayako said, though Ryōma was the one who bowed to her words.

"Receiving the daughter of the sun within these walls is the honor of my life," the daimyo replied, head pressed against the tatami. "And I thank your escort for their patience," he went on, nodding toward Ren, who sat across from him, proving again that he understood more than he said.

"Lord Shimazu," the hunter called, breaking etiquette once more, "may we now speak in all honesty, or should we waste more time on bitter tea and paintings?"

The woman who had prepared the tea and who was slowly packing her utensils gasped at his tone, and Ryōma waved his hand for her to leave. She left her things in the room and only took the time to bow once to the princess and once to the daimyo before she scurried out.

"Apologies for my friend's tone," Ayako said as she bit into a corner of the pink, sakura flower-shaped sweet she held at the tip of three fingers.

"None needed, Your Highness," the daimyo replied. Now that only the five of them sat together, he allowed himself to look at the princess. "As you may know, I was born a peasant and find your warrior's tone refreshing."

"That makes one of us," Fuyuko replied as she lifted the bowl of tea to her lips.

"Fudō-dono," the daimyo said, "I understand your frustration, but perhaps we could speak in private, you and I, while the imperial princess rests. Wouldn't you agree?"

"If *we* wanted Ayako to rest," Ren replied, making the daimyo stiffen a little at his use of the princess's name, "maybe *we* shouldn't have asked her to climb six floors for a bowl of tea."

"Ren," Fuyuko whispered accusingly.

The hunter sighed and held his hand out in apology. "I thank you for thinking of the princess's health," he said more politely. "But I prefer we speak in her presence, as well as that of my companions here. I am not their leader and do not speak in their names." He pretended not to see the smile on Suzume's lips nor to hear the chuckle passing through Fuyuko's and focused on keeping his eyes on Ryōma's hardening glare. This was a man unused to being contradicted, and discussing important matters with women was not to his taste. But as long as the princess sat nearby, he would not argue, Ren thought, and was quickly proven right.

"Very well," the daimyo replied. "But the princess is still young and in need of rest."

"The princess," Ren interrupted, "is capable of telling us if she wants to stay or take her leave. She has seen more in the last few days than most grown men in their lives, and—"

"Ren," Ayako gently called from the seat of honor where she sat alone. "I am actually very tired." Ren finally saw what the daimyo might have noticed long minutes before; her closing eyes, the way she leaned on a hand to keep her posture and the depth of her breath. She had done her best to act with dignity but was getting close to her limits, and the hunter felt suddenly ashamed for his lack of foresight.

"I trust you, all of you," she went on, taking a few seconds to look at the four people in the room. "To discuss amicably in my absence, and I know you will all have my best interests at the heart of this conversation. But I would very much like to bathe and sleep."

"Of course, Your Highness," the daimyo replied with a nod. On cue of an unseen sign, a servant slid the panel doors open and came to kowtow at the princess's feet, then asked if she would follow her. Ayako allowed her to raise her head, and both left the room.

Shimazu Ryōma waited until the door slid behind a kneeling servant and dropped his mask. His eyes and lips lowered to straight lines. He slouched a little and brought his fingers to the side of his head to massage a threatening migraine. "Are we going to have a problem here?" he asked in a harsher tone than before.

"Ah," Ren barked happily, slapping his thigh. "Finally, we're talking to the real Shimazu Ryōma. You got me worried for a second."

"What?" the daimyo asked, frowning. "I wasn't acting or anything. I just wanted to welcome you all properly, but you, young man, made it incredibly difficult. So let me ask again, are we going to have a problem?"

"If you let us go with the princess," Ren answered, lifting his forefinger to mark his point, "we won't have any."

"The three of you are free to go," the daimyo replied. "Though I would love for some of you to remain," he added, looking at Fuyuko. "But Princess Ayako is staying."

"May we ask why?" Suzume asked, dropping her hand on Ren's wrist to keep him from boiling over.

"You know better than anyone why," the daimyo answered. "The emperor has been killed, his wife, and their three sons with him. All that remains of the imperial family is this little girl. I will keep her safe, here, until she can be reinstated on the Chrysanthemum Throne."

"And, being the one to put her ass back on the damn thing is not a priority at all?" Ren asked sarcastically.

"First," Ryōma replied, pointing a violent finger at Ren, "you'd do well to speak of the princess with more respect. Second, you are right; it has to be me."

"Why you?" Ren asked.

"Because," the daimyo replied, straightening up and slipping back into character, "any other daimyo will use this chance to sit their power in Kyōto. *I*, on the other hand, only care for order and the safety of the princess."

"Touching," Ren said.

"Believe it or not—"

"Probably won't," Ren interrupted.

"Believe it or not," Ryōma repeated through gritted teeth. "But I was born a peasant and have risen far above my station. I do not dream of higher skies and would rather protect all I have gained than risk losing it."

"You love that line, don't you?" Ren asked with a smirk.

"What line?" the daimyo asked.

"That 'I was born a peasant' line," Ren replied, imitating the daimyo's tone and gestures so well that Suzume could not suppress a laughing snort.

"So sorry," she mumbled behind her hands.

"But the hands holding this beautiful bowl do not belong to a peasant, even one who abandoned the shovel and the hoe decades ago," Ren said, nodding toward the daimyo's hands. Shimazu Ryōma looked at his hands curiously as if noticing them for the first time. "At best, you were the son of a landowner; at worst, you never even set foot in a rice field except to trample it with your soldiers. Even if you were truly born a peasant, your rise speaks of ambition. And you just got handed the means to further your cause. An ambitious man would not simply protect Ayako; he would use her."

"No one *handed* me the princess," the daimyo replied. "I saved her from creatures of the dark. What were you doing then?" he asked, using the same sarcastic tone Ren had used before. "Oh, that's right, you're the one who got her in danger and in need of saving. No matter what you think of me, I promise you the princess will be safe with me. Safer, at least. I have moats, death box corridors, turrets, walls, cannons, and you've seen but a fraction of the men I can muster for the sole purpose of guarding Her Highness."

"They're not creatures of the dark," Suzume said, stirring the daimyo's attention from Ren. "Yōkai," she went on when Ryōma answered with a questioning gaze, "are corrupted souls, not creatures of the dark. If you look for them exclusively in the dark, you won't be able to keep her safe."

"My friend is right," Ren replied. "You don't know what you are facing. Moats? Turrets? Those won't help you against this yōkai general and his armies. They can lurk through the shadows, slip between the cracks of your walls, and fly over your turrets. And what will your men do when their blades break against a yōkai's bare back or when they see their comrades eviscerated by sharp claws? They'll run, and I wouldn't blame them for it."

"You think you can do better?" the daimyo asked, somewhat seriously. "You and your Yaseki?"

"Yes," Ren replied, matter of fact. "We know how to fight them, and we have the tools to destroy this army. Then you will be free to bring order back to the nation."

"If you're so sure of the Yaseki's power," Ryōma replied. "Why don't you ask your friends to join us here and protect Princess Ayako?"

"Why don't you escort us to Ise Jingū instead?" Ren asked.

The daimyo sighed again. "I will not risk her life on the road."

"And I won't risk her life here," Ren said.

"This is not your decision to make."

"I agree. Neither is it yours."

"Listen," Fuyuko said when the two men started a staring contest. "While I enjoy this manly battle of wills very much, maybe we should keep this conversation for tomorrow when the princess has rested and is able to give her opinion."

"The princess is still a child," the daimyo replied. "Surely you, sweet Fuyuko, understand that adults must sometimes choose on behalf of children, don't you?"

"Usually, I would agree with you," she said. "But Ayako is capable, and if she's to fulfill her destiny, she will need to make her own decisions. Besides," the courtesan went on, suddenly looking determined, "the man I love gave his life so we could take the princess to Ise. So, unless Ayako asks otherwise, this is where I will take her."

Ryōma looked weary, probably thinking he had lost his only

ally in this room. His attention shifted to Suzume, but here, too, he was to be disappointed.

"I also wish to ask Ayako first," she replied. "And I know someone who would rather take her to Ise Jingū as fast as possible. No, not him," she said when the daimyo's eyes flicked toward Ren. "It's complicated."

"So all of you oppose me?" the daimyo asked. He sounded tired and sorry.

"You have to understand that you put your people in danger by keeping the princess here," Suzume replied. "The General will stop at nothing to get her."

"And he's just the first of an army," Ren said.

Fuyuko frowned at his words, so he shook his head to let her know he would tell her more about that later. Ryōma's next sigh was long and deep. His lips shut tight, and he looked up pensively. He started playing with his empty bowl, rotating it on its base.

"With your help," he said after a few seconds of silence, "things would go smoother for all of us. But I assume you will remain deaf to my pleas?"

"We want different things," Ren answered.

"So it will come to Ayako to decide whose protection she wants," Suzume said with strength.

"Yes," the daimyo said. "Yes. You are right. The princess will have the last word in this conversation. Which is why I cannot let you speak with her again."

The bowl stopped brushing the tatami, and Ryōma suddenly tossed it across the room. When it landed, somewhere by Suzume's feet, all the panels behind them, plus those on their left and right, slid open, revealing three groups of six archers ready to release their arrows at the trio.

Ren lifted his foot, but Fuyuko kept his other knee on the tatami with her gentle touch. One more move, Ren understood when those archers drew the strings to their limits, and they would die. Sugi was nowhere nearby, and both Fuyuko and he were without weapons. They stood no chance.

"Not acting, huh?" Ren asked, fist tightening with growing rage.

"I was not," the daimyo replied. "But the war has taught me to be ready for any situation."

"You will come to regret this," the hunter said.

"No, I do not believe I will. But do not fear; I am a generous host. And you have my word that as soon as the princess sits on her throne and order is restored, you will be free to return to Ise Jingū or wherever you wish to go."

"Oh, we are going back to Ise," Ren replied as archers came closer and forced his hands behind his back. "But it won't be just the three of us. You have my word, too."

Shimazu Ryōma tired of this argument and waved his hand laconically to order his men to take them out. Their hands were bound with rope, and their mouths gagged. They stepped back into the staircase leading down the keep, surrounded by soldiers and incapable of fighting back. Ren checked around him, hoping to see the princess peering through open doors. Unfortunately, the daimyo had been efficient, and Ayako was nowhere to be seen. And, as they walked to the basement where a cold cell of earth and metal awaited them, Ren wondered if maybe he could have played all of this differently.

Suzume and Ren groaned as they leaned over the map dug into the ground, the hum from their throats the only sound disturbing in the room. That and Fuyuko's incessant voice as the courtesan spoke to whoever guarded their room. She was currently telling her new friend about the most popular entertainment establishments in Kyōto, omitting to let him know those places had been destroyed in the attack.

Ren clicked his tongue, finding her voice troublesome to his focus, but Suzume seemed not to share this issue. Her eyes flickered along the lines of their makeshift map.

"There," she said, pointing at an angle of the line representing the outer moat. "It was sharper, more like this," she went on, using the tip of her forefinger to reshape the angle of the line. "If we get down there and wait between the two walls at night, they will miss us, probably."

"How do we cross the moat, though?" Ren asked.

"Maybe we can find a plank or something that floats?" Suzume offered. "I can swim and push it with Ayako on it."

"A plank?" Ren asked, one eyebrow lifted.

"Or a door," she replied. "Anything big enough for the princess will do."

Ren went back to observing the map of the castle's domain, or rather the half-map. Suzume had traced most of it, surprising Ren with this previously unknown talent of hers. She remembered the location of every building they had passed, the direction of every path, the presence of every guard, and even the length of the bridges from sight.

The procession leading them to the castle had first followed the domain along its eastern side, from north to south, because no guest should enter the castle from the northeast. From the southeastern gate, they had traveled to the keep and, as such, had seen nearly half of the domain. Suzume remembered most of it, though she could not guess the depth of the water surrounding the castle in the two moats.

The path out was easy to choose with what little they knew,

and Ren, while he disliked the randomness of their plan, also had faith they could pull something out as far as the escape from the domain was concerned. The greatest issue, though, was first getting out of the cell and second finding and retrieving Ayako.

The cell was a square room of cold, hard earth, closed by a solid door guarded by two spearmen. Twice a day, they brought platters of food, usually containing a bowl of white rice, another of fuming miso soup, and some fish. Not a feast, but enough that hunger wasn't an issue. The servants carrying the platters handed them to the guards, who then delivered them through a latch that could be opened from their side alone.

Ryōma had ordered three mats of straw to be given to them, along with blankets, wooden cups, and as much hot water as they asked for. On the second day, each of them was taken alone to a neighboring cell to wash in a barrel of hot water. And their bucket was emptied once a day. It was altogether a better treatment than regular prisoners might expect, but this was what they were nonetheless.

Ren had first thought to summon Maki with the bead he had kept in his pocket to burst the door open. From then on, they would rush to Ayako and use her as a hostage to get their stuff back before leaving on the lion-dog's back if needed. But their hope was quickly squashed when it turned out the bead was now powerless. Ren assumed its power had vanished when he tried to call his friend in the yōkai's lair, though the attempt had failed because of the ground's nature. Now, it was nothing more than a regular bead, and Ren passed the time by tossing it against the wall. It was Suzume who suggested they plan an exit route, but Fuyuko found no interest in it and decided she'd rather befriend the guards.

Her laughter suddenly resounded in the room, accompanied by a chuckle from the guards. Anything louder than this, Ren assumed, and they might get punished. The latch suddenly closed, and Fuyuko took an involuntary step back.

"Shift change," she vaguely said as she regained her mat, where she recovered her fox face with a sigh of exhaustion. Ren had come to understand that she needed to do so once a day at least.

"Learned anything?" he asked the courtesan, who then turned her muzzle toward them.

"Nothing good for us," she replied. "It seems the dashing daimyo has called all his troops back to the castle. Saburō said the granaries are being emptied into bags, then loaded onto carts."

"Saburō?" Ren asked.

"One of the two guards from the morning shift," she replied with a lazy wave of the hand. "A gentle, young man. Very polite and caring. You'd do well to emulate him, Ren Fudō."

"The daimyo plans to march?" Suzume asked before the conversation drifted further.

"It seems so," Fuyuko replied.

"I don't think he will," Ren said, going back to his observation of the map.

"Why not?" Suzume asked.

"Because he's made such a ruckus about the princess being in his care, you can be sure this yōkai army is on the way to Ōsaka as we speak. Believe me, three days from now, four, at most, and dear Saburō will be gathering his bowels before some nue."

"Do you have to be so graphic?" Fuyuko asked, leaning on her elbow.

"So we have three days?" Suzume said.

"Two," Ren answered. "In three days, the White Tengu will be here. We need to be gone before that."

"Do you think this *kanibōzu* spoke the truth?" Fuyuko asked, sitting up and using the wall for support. "This army is just a first wave?"

"I don't see why he would have lied," Ren answered.

"You know," Suzume said, and something in her tone led Ren to believe he wasn't going to like her next words, "if we are truly about to face a greater yōkai army, the Yaseki might not be enough. I don't know how strong we are," she went on defensively, "but it seems we are already struggling against one of their... officers. So imagine if they can gather more."

"I agree," Ren replied. "What's your point?"

"Well," she said, hesitating on how to formulate her argument.

"She thinks we should make an ally of the daimyo," Fuyuko explained. Suzume looked embarrassed but nodded.

"His cannons can destroy them," she said. "And with some guidance and the proper tools, maybe regular soldiers can learn to fight yōkai, too."

"With the proper tools," Ren repeated, "an ambitious man like Shimazu Ryōma would do more than crush yōkai. If we taught him what we knew, he would use it to assert his power over Japan."

"I don't know," Suzume replied, looking down. "I know he's ambitious, but I don't believe he's a bad man. If you ask me, he's just a product of his time."

"Even if you're right," Ren said, "this is Osamu's decision to make, not ours. Our responsibility is to bring the daughter of the sun to her ancestor's shrine. Then, if the old man believes it's the path to follow, we'll make alliances with powerful men. Of course, if we can't get out of this cell, there won't be much for Osamu to decide, anyway."

"Oh, don't worry about getting out, sweetheart," Fuyuko teased, adorning her human face again.

"You have a plan?" Suzume asked.

"The plan is already in motion," the courtesan replied. "And by this time tomorrow, you will realize what a sweet, sweet boy my little Saburō is and what a bad, bad girl I am."

Ren swallowed hard, wondering what kind of mischief the courtesan had been up to while he believed she flirted with the guards for some information. Then he went back to his observation of the map, for he knew at this time the following day, much would depend on choosing the right path.

CHAPTER 17
THE GREAT ESCAPE

Another bath was drawn shortly after the first meal of the next day. Ren and Suzume frowned at the sound of those poor servants going to the next cell carrying bucket after bucket, but Fuyuko seemed unconcerned. Only four days in this prison, and Ryōma had granted them their second bath. This was more generous and considerate than Ren had expected. One of the servants emptied his bucket and sighed with relief.

"If you don't mind, I'll go first," Fuyuko claimed as she stood from her mat. A mere couple of seconds later, the door opened to a spearhead and to a stack of towels presented to the courtesan by a young, blushing soldier Ren assumed to be Saburō. Fuyuko brushed the soldier's fingers as she picked up the towels, and his face reddened to a dark crimson. "I won't be long," she told them and passed the door, which closed with a heavy thump.

"That bodes well," Ren said.

Fuyuko was gone longer than he had expected, but not nearly as long as he feared. Just getting out of her kimono and freeing her hair from the pin was bound to require some minutes.

Even focused on listening, nothing sounded out of the ordinary, and Ren was startled when he heard the other door creak open. Fuyuko giggled in the corridor, and another couple of seconds later, their door opened. She was still laughing as she entered the room. Something about her was different. She wore the same kimono, which had been cleaned on the first day, and walked on her heavy clogs. Her skin was still wet and glistening from the bath. The only thing different about her was her hair, now tied up in a simple bun from which ran a few strands of undulating hair.

Suzume gasped when Fuyuko entered the room, and when Ren followed her gaze, he realized she too was looking at the courtesan's hair, or rather at the item she had used to tie it. It was hard to notice, for its color was close to that of Fuyuko's hair, but once Ren saw it, he too gasped. His beads.

Fuyuko looked over her shoulder to grace the soldier with a last smile and the sound of her giggle, then the door closed, and she turned serious, victorious eyes to Ren. She uncoiled the beads from her hair, letting it fall on her shoulders, and twirled the string with a long, gracious finger.

"How?" Ren asked when he finally found his voice. He crossed the room until he stood an arm's length from the courtesan, who then let the beads slip along her finger and into his palm.

"A woman has her secrets," she playfully replied, teasing the hunter with a wink as he placed the necklace over his chest.

"Fuyuko, you worry me a little. What did you do?" Suzume asked.

"You children are no fun," the courtesan replied with a click of the tongue. "What do you think I did? Over the last few days, I merely chatted with dear Saburō—"

"You seduced him," Ren corrected her.

"—and suggested that I liked nothing more than to take my string of beads with me in the bath. My beads and nothing else," she said, stretching each syllable of the last sentence.

"That's it?" Ren asked.

"I may also have suggested that the cell with the bath was a little dark, and I wouldn't mind the light of an open latch to make sure I cleaned every inch of my skin properly," she replied.

"So, you let him watch?" Ren asked.

"Heavens," Suzume said, hiding herself behind her hands.

"He didn't see much," Fuyuko replied. "I know what I'm doing."

"Wait, what did you do with my beads?" the hunter then asked, looking at his beads with a new sense of curiosity.

"I can give them back if you're not happy," Fuyuko snapped back. She crossed her arms over her chest, and for a second, Ren thought she would resume her fox face.

"Thank you, Fuyuko," Suzume managed to reply as Ren pulled one bead out of the string.

"Yes," he said, "thank you for your... sacrifice."

"That's better," the courtesan replied as she plucked the pin stuck behind the front pang of her obi and placed it in her hair in a few expert gestures. "Now, unless one of you wants a bath, too, I suggest we move before they drag you to it."

"Agreed," Ren said.

He knelt by the door and dug the hard ground with his thumb until he could plant half of the bead under the door frame. "You both remember the original plan?" he asked, keeping his thumb on the bead. Suzume nodded, and Fuyuko moved by his side. "And remember," he went on, "we do not kill people."

"You're the one who should heed this advice," Fuyuko replied.

The hunter voided himself of emotions and focused his energy on producing a kotodama prayer. When his training had begun five years ago, he needed a quiet environment, long minutes of meditation, and the soothing presence of Blind Kino to reach the Mouth Gate. Now, even stuck in a cold cell of Ōsaka's keep, Ren could summon his guardian in a few seconds. He bit the forever scarred tip of his thumb and smeared a pearl of blood on the bead.

"*I offer you my prayer and this blood. Protect me, guardian spirit, and help me cleanse the corruption from this castle.*" Ren hesitated with the last words and wondered if it was even correct to summon a guardian to deal with a human situation. He would tuck the point somewhere at the back of his mind to meditate on later. But for now, he had a princess to free and a castle to escape. He nodded to Fuyuko, who knocked on the door.

"Saburō-kun," she called in a seducing voice. "Suzume is ready for her bath."

The latch opened to a pair of brown, lively eyes. Fuyuko waved at him, and the soldier failed to notice Ren kneeling in front of the door. The latch closed, and they heard the soldier fondling his keys.

"*I call you, Maki!*" Ren then shouted.

The ground shook, and cracks appeared from under the door. The second soldier cursed, Saburō yelped, Fuyuko and Ren took a few steps back, and the door burst through the corridor, along with dozens of carved stones from its frame.

The glow of Maki's mane shone through the dust, and her bark resonated throughout the basement and no doubt above.

"Maki!" Ren called. "No time to explain, move!"

The lion-dog skipped from the broken door frame and into the corridor, then turned on her heels to find her friend. Ren unsheathed the katana of the guard who sat unconscious against the opposite wall of their cell and pointed it toward the staircase.

"This way, girl," he said.

The second guard was still conscious, though his right arm was bending at an odd angle, and he seemed on the brink of soiling himself at the sight of the guardian spirit. Ren paid him no attention; he was Fuyuko and Suzume's problem.

"Saburō-kun," he heard Fuyuko say, "did you see my umbrella near the beads by any chance?"

Whatever the soldier replied was lost to the sound of Maki bursting through the trap door blocking the basement from the next floor. There, too, soldiers flew from her path, but one who had stood a little behind attempted to thrust his spear into her leg. The pole broke with the impact, and its head bent harmlessly. It still pissed off the lion-dog. Maki growled at the soldier, lowering her snarling head so that her fangs flashed right by his face. The soldier raised both his hands in a plaintive plea. He whimpered, petrified to his spot, and Ren appeared by Maki's side just as tears fell from his eyes.

"Run, you idiot!" Ren said, pointing his katana the other way. The soldier accepted the offer after another bark and scampered away. Maki then sat back and smiled with her big tongue lolling out of her lumpy lips.

"Good girl," Ren said, scratching her under the maw. "Now, let's go. We need to find Ayako. Can you find Ayako?"

The lion-dog raised her head, sniffed the air, and whoofed with strength. She then lowered her head in an invitation for Ren to climb on her back, meaning that Ayako wasn't just next door. He found his place behind Maki's neck and grabbed her glowing mane with his left hand. Suzume appeared from the bottom staircase, a soldier's spear in hand, and Ren saw poor Saburō being pushed forward by a fox-faced Fuyuko. The hunter nodded at them and kicked Maki's flank.

She darted through the second staircase and just as easily shattered the door to pieces. They reached the keep's first floor, where a unit of spearmen was now gathering. Maki gave them no time to organize, and charged.

Two soldiers managed to raise their spears in time, but the smart ones jumped from her path. She bit one of the two spears and shook it violently until the soldier relented his grip and flew through the open floor. Ren parried a thrust and cut the spear right behind its head in the same gesture, leaving the soldier who had tried to stab him with a useless staff. The hunter raised his sword as if about to strike, and the soldier fell to his knees.

More were flowing through the main gate. Some even carried bows and arrows.

"Maki, where?" Ren asked. The lion-dog lifted her head and locked her gaze upon the upper floors. "Up? Let's go!" An arrow fizzed just as Maki resumed her run. It had been a wide shot, but Ren still lowered himself.

The lion-dog first used the stairs to climb the keep, but a wall of spears awaited them on the next floor. She propelled herself through the closest wall and smashed the panels separating two tatami rooms. Curses and footsteps trailed them, and Ren hoped that most soldiers were coming after them, thus leaving Fuyuko and Suzume in peace. He winced when he understood Maki's plan, whose next step was to get outside.

She broke through the harder exterior wall, nearly slipped on a series of black, curved tiles, and regained her balance in time to avoid a spear thrown from inside the castle. Using the edged roof, she jumped to the next floor, then immediately to the next one. Hundreds of soldiers were rushing from the whole domain toward the castle, and many were pointing toward the roof, on which a giant, glowing dog ran with great strides.

Maki rushed around the squared roof, always sniffing, always snarling, and barked when she stopped by the first balcony they had faced so far. She smashed the wooden windows and their paper lining with a heavy paw and slowly stepped inside the one room on the fifth floor.

The light pouring from the broken window flooded a large, mostly empty room, the biggest in the keep. Ren had visited this place a few days ago, but in the glory of the morning sun, the beams and the wooden floor appeared warmer. Shimazu Ryōma had proudly claimed this to be the only *Noh* theater built inside a castle and on an upper floor. Not only that, the daimyo had said, but this was most likely the largest indoor theater in Japan.

The Golden Sun of Ōsaka was currently standing on the roofed, square stage set in the northeast corner of the room as if acting in his own play. The real actors, along with the musicians and chorus dressed in light blue and black outfits, were running along the bridge connecting the backstage to the performance area. However, at this precise moment, they used it to flee from the feral-looking guardian spirit.

Maki was snarling, growling, and prowling toward the stage, her mane glowing stronger than ever and waving with the wind passing through the balcony. Ren had rarely seen her so menacing, but he understood her anger.

"One more step!" the daimyo shouted, lifting his *tantō* knife closer to Ayako's throat.

"Ren!" the girl called in tears.

The hunter patted his friend's neck to ask her to stop and slid from her back without letting the daimyo's eyes from his sight. He lifted his katana and pointed it toward the stage, though twenty steps separated him from the daimyo. The heavy footsteps of the actors vanished just as those of the soldiers thumped on the stairs leading to the fifth floor.

Ryōma would have looked glorious in his elegant, golden and black *kamishimo* outfit, but as he was, standing low behind the princess, his face crisped with an unfeigned rage, and his gaze shifting from the lion-dog to the doors, Ren found him pitiful. Several doors slammed open, and soldiers poured in. Maki turned around and barked a great whoof that forced them to take a step back. They formed a semi-circle around the beast and the hunter, though none dared come close enough to test the lion-dog's reach.

"That's how you protect her?" Ren shouted.

"You left me no choice," Ryōma replied.

"Ren, please," Ayako said, her face gleaming with tears. For a second, the hunter wondered if she pleaded for him to leave or wanted his assistance, but her next words turned his nerves to steel. "Help me," she said before she started sobbing.

"We can still do this peacefully," Ren said as he nodded reassuringly to the girl. "Just let her go, and we'll be on our way."

"I don't think so," the daimyo replied, raising the knife a little closer to the skin in response to Ren taking a short step forward. The girl tensed, the hunter too, and Maki reacted by shifting her murderous, bloodshot gaze toward the daimyo again. "You will leave my castle immediately, you and your friends, or the princess's blood will be on your hands."

"If you harm her in any way, I will make sure that my friend here tears your head from your shoulders in the next second," Ren spat.

"Then it seems we've reached an impasse," the daimyo replied.

"No, we haven't," Fuyuko said as she appeared through the broken windows, unsheathing her umbrella sword with Ren's tucked in her obi. She showed herself as a fox, and many soldiers recoiled at the sight of her.

Sugi jumped after Fuyuko from the lower roof and landed with grace on the wooden floor of the Noh theater room. She appraised the situation in a heartbeat and crouched in a fighting stance, ready to dash to the daimyo.

Fuyuko blocked her path with her stretched arm. "You said the princess would decide who she wants to go with," the courtesan told Ryōma. "Why don't we ask her?"

"She's just a child!" the daimyo shouted back. "She doesn't know what's best for her. Stop crying!" he shouted, shaking the girl, who burst into tears. "None of you knows what has to be done!"

"And raising a blade to a child's throat is the way to go?" Ren asked, his patience reaching its limits.

"Let us go," the girl sobbed. "Please."

"Shut up," the daimyo said. "I'm doing this for you. I'm doing this for Japan!" he shouted toward Ren, Fuyuko, and his soldiers. Some had dared a few steps forward, but a growl from Maki was enough to keep them at bay. "You'd take her to a shrine. A shrine! The imperial princess, locked inside a forested shrine, while I have a castle, cannons, and soldiers to protect her. You would have her hide while Japan drowns in another civil war. Do you know how many hundreds of thousands of men died in the previous one? Do you know how many good men I've lost? How many orphans and widows will be made because every warlord of Japan will see the chaos as their chance to rise? Let me take the child back to Kyōto and claim my place at her side, and no sword will be drawn for generations. We'll have peace throughout the land. Do you really want to ruin this chance because of a few... creatures?" he asked, nodding at Maki with disgust.

"There won't be peace," Ren replied, "as long as the daughter of the sun isn't in Ise. We need her light to shine on Japan, but if you keep her in your shadow, there will be war, yōkai will burn the land, and people will kill each other for a bowl of rice. Listen to me; we need Ayako to preserve the kami's fortune over the nation."

Ren, a voice called inside the hunter's head, startling him. He looked over his shoulder and saw Sugi looking at him, her dark green eyes shining with resolve. *He won't listen*, she said. Her voice sounded like Suzume's, only with more edge, but it was a kind voice. *I can take him.*

Ren shook his head slowly. He wanted to do it himself.

"Ryōma!" he shouted just as the daimyo took a step back, hugging the princess close to him. "Let's fight for her. You and me. A duel like you samurai love so much." The daimyo frowned at the hunter's words and stopped moving. "If you win, my companions will leave Ōsaka right away without the princess. If I win, the princess decides who she goes with."

255

"Just swords!" The daimyo shouted back after a moment of hesitation. "No magic."

"No magic," Ren agreed. "Ayako, just get on the bridge and wait for me. It's going to be all right, I promise."

The princess nodded between two sobs, and the knife under her throat slowly lowered. When the daimyo released her, the girl rushed to the bridge at the back of the stage, where she knelt against a pole, a face drawn with worry. The daimyo tossed the knife to the closest soldier and tied his sleeves at the elbows with thin, white ropes.

Ren, Sugi called again.

Don't worry, I got him, Ren told her in his mind just as Fuyuko handed him his sword. He had no idea if she could hear him back. *But if I lose, rush to the girl and take her to Ise.*

Sugi nodded. Fuyuko brushed his elbow when he took the first step toward the stage, and Maki whimpered anxiously. Ren patted her front leg but paid her no more attention. All of it was for the daimyo, who now received the katana he had been wielding when they first met. Ren wondered if he should keep the katana but decided that fighting with his usual sword was safer, and the longer blade bounced on the ground just as Ren climbed on the stage.

Shimazu Ryōma unsheathed his katana and held it in a basic yet perfect *chūdan-gamae* stance with the pommel close to his navel and the tip of the blade aimed at the hunter's throat. He judged the distance and slid a step back to use his reach advantage over the young man.

Ren lowered his weight, putting as much as possible on his thighs. He grabbed the hilt of the blade tucked on his lower back with his right hand and the bottom of the sheath with his left, thus completely opening himself to an attack.

The daimyo appeared as tall and robust as a tree in front of the crouching hunter, his decades of experience showing in his breathing, the position of his feet, the stillness of his blade, and his unmoving, cold eyes. Many a man had fallen to this sword, Ren guessed, looking at the tip of the katana. Hundreds maybe. Some would have been masters of their fighting styles and veterans of many battles. Yet, Shimazu Ryōma had never known defeat, nor had he suffered any serious wounds.

Then again, Ren told himself, neither had he ever faced a trained Soul Hunter.

A pearl of sweat ran down the back of his skull and slid along his spine. His grip hardened on both the hilt and the sheath. He felt the tension of the room shrinking on him, the eyes of the soldiers weighing on his back, and the prayers of the little girl calling for his safety.

Ryōma's front foot twisted ever so slightly as he readjusted his stance by wiggling his toes. He did not smirk. For all his greatness and experience, the daimyo did not take the young man lightly. The distance shrunk slowly as both men pushed through an invisible wall of fear. Soon, Ren thought. Almost.

Now! Sugi shouted in his mind.

Ren moved on cue, a blink after the daimyo.

Ryōma pushed his sword in a sliding thrust aimed at the base of the hunter's throat. The velocity of the attack was terrifying, and if not for Sugi's warning, Ren would have been skewered through the neck. Instead, he lunged and crossed both his arms forward in as fast an attack as he'd ever done. The scabbard parried the katana to the right, though not strong enough to avoid it grazing his shoulder. And the hunter's sword sliced through the daimyo's left wrist.

The soldiers gasped, and Fuyuko yelped. From her position, she would only see the bloody tip of the daimyo's katana jutting above Ren's shoulder. Then, a curtain of blood splashed over Ren, and the daimyo's shriek echoed through the theater. He let go of his sword, fell to his knees, and grabbed his ruined wrist as if he could stop the bleeding with the sole strength of his grip.

"Maki!" Ren called as he accompanied the daimyo's fall. The wounded hand remained connected to the arm by a piece of skin and lumped from the severed wrist like the tip of a belt. "Don't move," he told the whimpering daimyo.

Ren held the hand straight and sliced through what remained of the skin, pulling another shriek from Ryōma. He then dropped the hand and forced the bleeding arm toward the lion-dog's mane. The daimyo's scream reached new heights as his arm hissed against the burning fur, and suddenly, he stopped screaming and toppled to the side, unconscious but no longer bleeding. That is when Ayako decided to approach Ren.

"You're bleeding," she said in a caring tone. The princess no longer cried, but her sleeves were wet with tears, and her face stained with their passage.

"It's nothing," Ren replied, checking the pulse of the daimyo.

"I'm so sorry, Ren," the girl said, her lips quivering as she tried to fight another sob.

"You don't need to be sorry," Ren replied, "but you could say thank you."

Ayako did not, in fact, thank Ren, for her words would not pass her next wave of uncontrollable sobbing. Instead, she threw herself against his chest and hugged him tightly. So tight indeed that she reminded him of the rib he had cracked when escaping the yōkai's kitchen. He placed his arm around her and stood up. She kept her head against his neck as he carried her to Maki's back. He hadn't noticed that Fuyuko and Sugi were now standing on the stage, their blades pointed at the soldiers surrounding it.

"I defeated your leader and saved his life," Ren told them. "As agreed, Princess Ayako will decide who she wants to stay with. If any of you stand in our way, they would thus betray their lord's promise and disobey an imperial order. And my friend here," he went on, patting Maki's head, "will take care of those double traitors. So, who wants to keep their blade pointed at us, and who wants to wish us a safe journey?"

"All of you, kneel!" Ayako commanded atop the lion-dog.

The hundreds of soldiers gathered in the room dropped to their knees, and the sound of blades finding their sheaths drowned the theater like a chorus of excited, chirping birds. The daimyo was regaining consciousness, whimpering in pain, and Ren decided it was time to go.

"Are you coming with us?" Ren asked Ayako when they stood by the balcony.

"No," the girl impishly replied. "You are coming with me."

On this, she kicked Maki with both her heels, and the guardian spirit leaped from the roof and headed eastward toward Ise Jingū at last.

CHAPTER 18
A LAST PRAYER

Running through the streets of Ōsaka with a horse-sized dog raised its fair share of gawking bystanders and screaming children, but discretion was no longer a matter of great importance. The story of the fight at the keep would echo throughout the province within days, and an army of yōkai was bound to march into the neighborhood soon. Speed, Ren told himself, was of the essence.

So they ran, shoved aside any who would slow their path, and made for the eastern road for long hours before, finally, the hunter offered to cut through the hills for a semblance of discretion. He had first thought to guide them to Nara, hoping to receive some help from Hotaru once again. But the destination was too obvious, and the road too direct. So Ren devised a route a little south of the ancient capital, along an ancient path some called the oldest road of Japan, a path lined with millennial shrines now mostly abandoned. The hunter had used this path once during his training years with Boar Takeo, Yumi the Rat, and Blind Kino and thought he remembered a specific shrine where they had stopped for the night.

By the time he finally recalled its exact location, the sun was but a memory. Suzume had long reached the limits of her running capabilities, Fuyuko complained about progressing barefoot to no end, and Ayako had slept on the lion-dog's back, so she was fresher than the others when Ren happily pointed at the path appearing through untamed wilderness.

They pushed through brambles, stepped over ground-breaking roots, and ducked under a stubborn torii gate. Two small lion-dog statues protected the path leading to a rotting shed-sized shrine. The stone guardian with a ball under its paw was covered with so much moss that it looked deformed.

"That's the shrine you wanted to use for shelter?" Fuyuko asked, unimpressed.

"What's wrong with it?" Ren asked with a smirk. "It's hidden, no one seems to know about it, and it has guardians. What else could we ask for?"

"A roof," the courtesan replied.

"Servants," Ayako said as well.

"What kami is enshrined here?" Suzume asked, her gaze scanning the molding shrine. "Sugi doesn't recognize it."

"I think it's a shrine to the kami of alcohol quitting," Ren answered, recalling Yumi's words. "Contrary to Sugi or Amaterasu, this kami was a man. A warrior of renown who sadly lost his greatest battle on account of being drunk. He found his lord's forgiveness by leading his men to victory in the next fight, though he lost his life during the battle. They say he bitterly regretted his love for sake and made a vow to help all those who sought to quit drinking. I don't know his name, though."

"A sad story," Fuyuko commented with a hint of irony.

"The funny thing is," Ren went on, "farther down the path, there's a great shrine dedicated to the kami of sake brewing."

"Maybe that's where we should go," the courtesan replied.

"No need. Its roof has collapsed, and it's just as abandoned," Ren said. "Besides, we didn't come here for this kami but for what can be found behind the shrine."

Fuyuko raised an inquisitive eyebrow, and Ren nodded toward the back of the shrine. Ayako clicked her tongue for Maki to move, and the courtesan followed the lion-dog around the decrepit building. Ren was about to move too, then he heard Suzume's hands clapping twice. She was praying to the kami's hall in a fervent prayer. He waited for her hands to part, and her eyes to open again.

"I don't think you need his help that much," the hunter said mockingly as Suzume took a step back. "I mean, you did drink a little too much at the matsuri, but that was just once."

"I wasn't praying for me," the miko warrior replied.

"Your father?" Ren guessed. She nodded. "You have the heart to pray for him? I don't think I could."

"He was such an awful man," she replied, looking at her feet. "But I killed him, Ren. I butchered him."

"You didn't kill him," Ren replied. He got close enough to drop a hand on Suzume's shoulder, and she wiped a tear with her thumb. "Sugi protected you, that's all."

"No, Ren," Suzume replied, lifting her watery eyes into his. For a heartbeat, the hunter thought they looked like Sugi's. "I now know it wasn't Sugi. I wanted to kill him, she just reacted to my will. It was me, Ren; I'm a killer. I killed my own father."

Ren guided her into his arms, but to his surprise, Suzume did not cry. She just put her face on his shoulder and wrapped her arms around his waist.

"He deserved it," Ren said. "Don't be mad at yourself. He might not have been a yōkai, but his soul was corrupted."

"Maybe," she replied. "But he had once loved my mother, and she had loved him too. War and sorrow changed him. That and alcohol. In a way, he was like Shimazu Ryōma, a product of his time. That's why I prayed for him right now. Not because I forgive him and not to apologize. Just to let him know that I understand it wasn't *just* his fault."

Ren felt her heart against his as neither broke the embrace. Or maybe it was his that beat so eagerly. Acting on an impulse, he kissed the side of her head, and she seemed to huddle closer to him.

"You're a beautiful soul, Suzume of Sugimoto," Ren said. "And I'm glad we're traveling together."

Suzume scoffed a giggle and wiped another tear. "Took you long enough to feel that way," she said. Their hands brushed when the embrace broke.

"Not really," Ren replied. "Now let's go, or we'll miss the show."

"Ren," Suzume called, pulling his sleeve before he could turn around.

"Yes?" he asked.

She was frowning, searching for the right way to ask her question. "You said when we die, our souls merge with that of our ancestors to rejoin the kami of our family."

"Yes," Ren replied, though it sounded like a question inviting her to go on.

"Does it have to?"

The hunter remained dumbfounded for a couple of seconds, understanding that Suzume struggled with the idea of joining her father in death. "I don't know if there's another way," Ren replied. "We will ask Hotaru-san or Osamu when we have a minute, but there must be a way to—"

Ayako's shout cut his words short. The princess had called his name with urgency, though they heard no danger in her tone.

There was the memory of a path stretching behind the small hall, nothing but trampled ground that had yet to give up its fight against weeds. Ren wondered if he had been the last person to use it before that day. It cut through tall grass for a few seconds before opening up to a clearing.

Bare cherry trees lined the clearing, their branches carrying timid buds that would soon bloom into pink or white petals. There was enough space between the trees for a dozen people to stand without crowding the place. When Suzume and Ren stepped through the clearing, Ayako, Fuyuko, and Maki were standing close to the farthest tree, the three of them bending over a branch.

"We saw something," Ayako excitedly said when the two others joined them in their inspection.

"What was it?" Ren playfully asked.

"A firefly," the girl said.

"So she says," Fuyuko added.

Maki was twisting her head with a frown as she tried to understand what everyone else was looking at. Judging the location of Ayako's gaze, Ren bent a little and blew some air over the branch. A glowing, lime-green light, no bigger than the nail of Ayako's forefinger, shined when Ren's breath caressed it. The firefly turned around and, for a second, stopped glowing. It then took off from the branch, turning luminous again, and another decided to follow it.

"Woah," Ayako said as the two fireflies gently flew above her head.

Suzume and Fuyuko giggled at the girl's reaction. The princess then burst forward and blew on another branch until her face turned red. A firefly reacted to it but refused to depart.

"Let me try," Fuyuko said in reaction to the little girl's disappointed pout.

The courtesan took a step back and pointed her umbrella toward the tree. She opened it with strength, and a gust of wind brushed against the sakura tree. A wave of green lights pulsed, and when Fuyuko repeated her action, the whole tree seemed to come alive, and a cloud of fireflies shimmered and flew away like sparks from a popping log.

Ayako laughed and jumped. She tried to catch one and ran after it until it stopped shining. Her happiness infected Maki, who leaped after those lights and snapped her jaws at them. Ren winced when he saw a light vanish inside the lion-dog's maw, but thankfully, Ayako had not seen it.

Maki kept on leaping and barking, then raised her head seriously as if she had an idea and leaped again. The guardian spirit rose high and straight and landed heavily, kicking the ground with her front paws. The shock rocked the ground, and every tree surrounding the clearing was suddenly illuminated with tiny green lights. Maki barked once, and all those fireflies took off in a swarm of slowly flying bugs.

Ayako could not find her breath between great peals of laughter. She clapped her hands around those lights, catching some and releasing them immediately. Maki acted with just as much joy, though the glow of her mane seemed to scare the bugs from her. They flew from tree to tree, and the princess found new ways to call their lights. She removed her kimono and waved it at the trees, then kicked the trunks, though she used this particular method only once because of the pain it inflicted on her. And, finally out of breath and maybe a little tired of it, the girl gave the bugs their peace back and joined the circle of her friends just as Ren tucked a fire talisman inside a bundle of twigs and leaves.

"You can't use Maki for that?" Suzume asked.

"Of course not," Ren replied. "Maki only burns living things. She'd start fires wherever she goes otherwise. I don't know why, though," Ren said pensively. "*Oh kami of fire, I give you this prayer and my blood. Grant us your light and your warmth on this cold night.*" The talisman flickered and caught fire, and soon, the flames reached high enough to warm them up. Ayako came to sit next to Suzume and just as soon leaned against the miko. Her eyes started closing by themselves.

"Am I going to get locked in Ise?" she suddenly asked.

"No, Princess," Ren gently replied, wondering why she had remembered the daimyo's words now.

"I don't like when you call us—me princess," she said. "Call me Ayako. Please."

"No, Ayako," Ren said. "You won't be locked inside. Osamu, the head priest of Ise Jingū, will teach you everything he knows about worshipping the kami, and it might not always be fun, but you won't be a prisoner there."

"But I will not be able to leave whenever I want," she sadly replied. "Just like home."

"I tell you what," the hunter said before tossing another twig in the fire, "if you're tired of the old grump and wish to get away from Ise for a few days, you've just got to let me know, and I'll sneak you out. We'll tour Japan together, and I'll show you all the best candy shops I know. Sound good?"

"Sounds good," the girl replied with a delighted giggle that found its match in Suzume.

Fuyuko harrumphed in her fist and looked at Ren as if to say he shouldn't make promises he might not be able to keep. The hunter sighed. She was right.

"Listen, Ayako," Ren went on. "Things will never be as easy as they were back in your palace. Ise Jingū is a beautiful place, but it is not Kyōto, and people will come to depend on you more and more each day. You will have to grow up faster than you should have to, but no matter what, the four of us are your friends and *that* you can count on."

Fuyuko nodded in agreement.

"Do you think Shimazu-san was right?" she asked. "There will be war because I'm not in the capital?"

"It wouldn't be your fault," Fuyuko replied. "Men always find excuses to fight."

"And it will be worse if you don't go to Ise Jingū," Ren said. "Without the princess sitting on her throne, things might get ugly for a little while, but they will eventually improve. But without the daughter of the sun in Ise, Japan might never recover at all."

"So I'll be stuck in Ise after all," Ayako said to no one.

"Not for long," Ren replied right away. "I'll find this General and kick his ass, then I'll find those above him and kick their asses. I'll kick the ass of anyone who prevents you from enjoying your life, I promise."

"That's a lot of ass-kicking," Ayako replied with a chuckle.

"Then I'll smack them, shake them, pull their ears, and twist their necks," Ren said, mimicking those actions comically under the rising laughter of the princess. "I'll steal their socks, pull their underwear over their heads, cut their hair in their sleep. I... I..."

"Stuff their pockets with honey," Suzume said.

"Yes!"

"Rub sand against their teeth!" Fuyuko added.

"Put some dog poop in their soup!" Ayako said, which got a bark of agreement from Maki.

"Maybe not that," Ren replied as Suzume bent over with laughter. "But I will fill their baths with Maki's drool."

The princess's pristine laughter rose to a guffaw, and even Fuyuko gave up her usual gracefulness and cackled.

The list of punishments went on and on until their imagination ran dry, and someone had to fetch more wood for the fire. Once in a while, some fireflies would fly from one tree to the next and rekindle the girl's interest, but soon, her resistance weakened, and she lay down with her head on Suzume's lap. The miko warrior brushed her hair and hummed a soft song that left no chance to the girl. Her rhythmic breathing marked the moment she fell asleep, but Suzume kept her song going.

Ren observed the courtesan as she made herself more comfortable on her bed of grass. She had unpinned her hair, untied her large obi, and now used it as a pillow. Her two tails gently brushed the grass, and she seemed lost in the fire. The flames swayed in her eyes, and she smiled at her thoughts. Or memories, perhaps, Ren thought. He was going to ask her what she planned to do once this journey ended but decided to leave her with those happy thoughts.

"Osamu will be pleased to know you opened the Ear Gate," Suzume said in a lower voice than usual.

"I'm not sure I did," Ren replied, remembering that after Ōsaka's keep, he could no longer hear Sugi's voice, something the kami had found so frustrating that she'd kicked him in the shin.

"Still," the miko said, "you said Osamu took twenty years to hear a kami's voice. That will impress him."

Ren scoffed and waved his hand down.

"He'll probably get all jealous and grumpy. Which is why I will tell him, of course."

"Can you believe we left a week ago?" Suzume asked as she rearranged the kimono-turned-blanket over the princess.

"I feel like we've been traveling for months," Ren replied. "And I can't believe I'm about to say this, but I can't wait to bathe in the Isuzu River. Don't feast your eyes on me this time," he went on in a playful tone.

Suzume blushed and looked away, just as she had on that not-so-far-away day when they met over the bridge leading to Ise Jingū.

"Suzume," Fuyuko teased. "I didn't think you were this kind of woman."

"No, I... that's not what... Ren, tell her I wasn't staring—"

"She could not peel her eyes away," Ren told Fuyuko.

"What a naughty girl," Fuyuko replied, playing along.

Suzume stiffened a shout and kicked Ren in the leg, just as the redwood kami had earlier, but this time, it only prompted laughter. At least until the princess wriggled and turned around. The courtesan shortly after decided to follow her lead and offered her back to the fire, while Maki came to lie behind Ren. He scratched her under the chin and wished her goodbye, then closed his eyes and let Suzume's song lull him to sleep.

CHAPTER 19

DEAD END

The last day of the journey started under beautiful circumstances. A few sakura buds had bloomed early under a pinkish sun, swallows swooped for waking bugs, and white cranes passed over on their journey to the northern islands. Ayako was in a singing mood that quickly infected Suzume, and soon, even Fuyuko accompanied their songs with a discreet humming. Whenever their voices rose, so did Maki's, who gratified their performance with a joyful howl.

Ren would have preferred a quieter journey but knew discretion was no longer as important. Not that he believed they had lost their enemies for good. He just assumed that, so close to Ise, their advance would never go unnoticed anyway. Already, he could imagine the great shrine over the next few hills, the smell of the incense burning from the various worshipping halls, and hear the plaintive shō pipes accompanying prayers.

Osamu would be scowling over the bridge but would show the utmost deference to the princess. And once those magatama had been weighed by the Clerk, Ren would run to his mother and maybe introduce her to the daughter of the sun, along with his new friends. The anticipation made him less careful and more impatient. He had called Maki the moment they resumed the road after a short night in the wild, for he would rather have her ready to fight right away. That was as much preparation as Ren was willing to make.

The last stretch would be the riskiest, for nothing but roads, meadows, and low hills stood between them and Ise Jingū. An easy land to watch with enough pairs of eyes.

As such, the plan for the five travelers was simple: head straight toward their destination, hope no army had sneaked around Ise, and rush forward if anything happened. Ayako was to remain on Maki's back and trust her three escorts to carve a path through the enemies' ranks if need be. Yet none of them behaved as if this situation might happen. It was too beautiful a morning, and the end of the road was just so close.

A few drops of rain then drizzled over the meadow, though there were no clouds. Ayako called this phenomenon a fox rain. Ren guessed the name came from the mischievous nature of foxes, who, just like this rain, liked to hide their nature behind a mask. Fuyuko chuckled at his theory and said it was most likely due to rain revealing the beauty of nature without masking the sun. It was a fine thought, with a hint of a tribute to the princess.

"Actually," Suzume said, "it comes from the story of a fox marrying a tiger."

Ren invited her to tell more, for he had never heard this story, and neither had the two others. A few days before, Suzume would have blushed and struggled to find her words, but she now straightened, changed her spear to the other hand, and cleared her throat as if to get the attention she already held.

"A male tiger and a female fox fell deeply in love and, despite their relatives' disagreement, decided to get married. But the fox was loved by a cloud that hovered over the mountain where she lived. On the day of the wedding, the cloud, some say out of happiness, others out of sadness, went to hide behind the sun to weep. Rain thus fell over the newlywed couple, but the cloud was nowhere to be seen."

"Such a pretty story," Ayako said.

"I don't know," Ren replied with a pout. "If you ask me, it's called fox rain because foxes are dubious."

Fuyuko stretched her tongue in reply but once again refrained from commenting. The rain fell so lightly that she did not even bother using her umbrella.

If Ren had not been so enthused by the prospect of the journey's end, maybe he would have read something into this omen. Maybe he would have suspected the departing cranes or the unrest of the swallows to mean something. But it was not until the war horn blew like a bellowing bear that Ren understood how misplaced his optimism had been.

They stopped moving, their heads twisting left and right, forward and backward, in search of the call echoing through the tall grass and wildflower-covered meadow. A series of hills stood a couple of minutes on their left, and the land slowly lowered on their right for a long stretch. Two hours of walking that way, they would meet the sea while the shrine waited less than an hour ahead. There were no trees, rocks, buildings, or anything that could hide soldiers or yōkai, so, just like the rain, they were left to wonder where the sound was coming from.

A shape suddenly rose through the air with great speed a hundred steps or so from them, and its wings spread when it reached the peak of its flight. A yōkai, Ren cursed, just like one of those they had fought at the ninja's castle of Iga. Except that this owl-looking creature had a twisted ram horn wrapped around its face and used it to call its allies. From the direction its head rotated, Ren guessed the enemy would appear above the hills on their left, and sure enough, another horn resounded somewhere in that direction. It was close. Too close for comfort. But at least the path forward was clear.

"Here we go!" Ren shouted, unsheathing his sword at the same time as Fuyuko.

Suzume had removed her spear's sheath a while back and found her place in front of Maki, as planned. The hunter was about to tell her to keep Sugi at bay for as long as possible, for if a fight began, it would be a long, hard-fought one. But when she looked over her shoulder, Ren noticed the green eyes. He could only pray the miko had enough energy by now to feed the warrior spirit for what was to come.

The owl flew higher still and let them pass. They ran like the wind. The shrine would soon be visible, Ren promised. Maki's strides were long and heavy, her great maw wide open so that she could engulf enough air. Ayako lowered herself to the point that she seemed to vanish inside the golden fur, and Sugi dictated an implacable pace.

Fuyuko had removed her clogs and abandoned them in the grass, then took her spot on Maki's right, just far enough to avoid burning herself on the lion-dog's fur. Ren protected the left flank. The horn blew again and was replied in kind, this time from even closer.

"Shit," Ren spat when the first shapes appeared over the hill. Soldier's conical hats, too many to count, gave the hills the appearance of a dragon's spiked back. They flooded over, wave after wave of black armored warriors, led by the occasional yōkai, each carrying a sword, a spear, or some other blade. The soldiers did not yell, but even if they had, the trampling of hundreds of feet would have drowned the shouts. One of every ten blue-flame soldiers carried the General's black crow crest on his back.

"Don't look!" Ren told Ayako, but his words were lost on the princess, whose lips quivered in fear. They were running fast enough to keep the distance, and Ren hoped against hope that maybe they could preserve their advance until the shrine, where Osamu would mount a resistance in no time.

"Maki," he said after a lung-wracking effort to catch up with the beast, "no matter what, you keep running. You go to Osamu, all right, girl?" The lion-dog pushed her head forward, showing that she had understood, and Ayako yelped at the sudden burst of speed.

"Ren," Fuyuko called from the other side of the lion-dog. "What would happen to Maki if you—well, you know."

The hunter's heart skipped a beat, and his bowels twisted on themselves. He hadn't even thought about it. If he died, as Fuyuko seemed reluctant to say, Maki would vanish, and the princess would find herself alone. Giving her time was not the only priority. He had to survive until the princess passed under the shrine's sacred gates.

The mass of soldiers kept flowing on their left while those who had failed to catch up ran at their backs. The distance did not seem to shrink, and Ren's mind screamed with doubts.

Ren, Sugi called, looking over her shoulder. *It's odd.*

"I know!" Ren shouted between two bursts of painful, bile-tasting breath.

Maybe blue-flame soldiers could run no faster, and maybe those soldiers' position had been unfortunate, but where were the nue, the flying yōkai, or the wanyūdō? Where were all those creatures who could outrun them in a matter of seconds? He thought of veering to the right but increasing the distance to the shrine seemed no better solution and would send them toward the sea, something he would rather avoid after their last swim.

"I hear something!" Fuyuko said, her ragged voice betraying a struggling breath. And then Ren heard it, too. Creaking wheels. A couple of them at first, then more and more until the meadow sounded like the field of a chariot race.

"Wanyūdō!" he shouted a mere second before those cursed

creatures came tumbling from the hill, roaring with crazed laughter and scorching long stretches of grass on their trails. And they were not alone.

Yōkai of many kinds ran between the wheels, leaping on four legs, howling, screeching, and bellowing their pleasure at finally being released for the kill. They had one target, and she whimpered at the sight of those dashing creatures gaining ground by the heartbeat. And Ren despaired, for even those behind seemed to get closer now. The snare was tightening.

The wheel-yōkai spun faster and soon inclined their bodies to turn. Sugi also increased her pace, for she, too, could guess their purpose, and she meant to cut some down before they could block their path. Yet even the warrior spirit could not move fast enough, and two dozen wanyūdō swerved a few seconds ahead of the group and started milling in an impenetrable barrier of flaming wheels. The other creatures formed a crude line between the wanyūdō and the rest of the army, now mostly spread at their backs and left side. And yet, more soldiers appeared from the hill. There must have been close to a thousand of them already, Ren thought as they were forced to slow down.

Two Yaseki warriors, a young fox spirit, the daughter of the sun, and a lion-dog against an army of yōkai. They needed help, Ren told himself, if only to get through the front line of wanyūdō. Ren removed the sordid string of beads that shifted against his neck and begged his exhausted legs to push harder. Using his arms as much as his thighs, he darted ahead of Maki, joined Sugi, clumsily cut the tip of his thumb, and smeared blood over the five remaining beads of power.

"*Great guardian spirits,*" he said through burning breaths, "*I offer you my prayer and this blood. Protect us, and help me cleanse the corruption from this land!*" Ren stopped, kicked the ground hard with the edge of his foot, and slammed the necklace into the fresh, shallow hole.

Ren, no! Sugi shouted, sounding more like Suzume than ever.

His energy was sucked from his chest to his arm, then to the hand holding the beads. His throat closed, neither air nor sound passed through it, and his mind buzzed so loudly that he thought his skull was about to explode. He gripped his heart with his bloody hand and resisted his fall for a heartbeat before his vision darkened and his head smashed against the ground. Hands grabbed him under the armpits and dragged him away just as the ground shook under his back. The explosion that followed was marvelous and accompanied by a concert of barks and growls.

Ren opened his eyes, feeling his strength come back in gushes, and saw Sugi bent over him, though her eyes were fixed on the wall of snarling guardian lion-dogs. Their thunderous barks sounded faint and distant to the hunter at first, then echoed closer and closer until something popped in his ears, and it was as if the whole world was nothing but angry whoofs and laughing wanyūdō. As Sugi helped him back to his feet, Ren, dazed and confused, realized his summoning had worked, but his plan had failed.

The five guardian spirits could probably tear through the wall of yōkai facing them, but not before those behind reached them. The soldiers followed their various officers and spread around the humans so that instead of a wall of wanyūdō, Ren and the others now welcomed a thick circle of possessed soldiers. The yōkai officers raised their arms and shouted commands, forcing their troops to a halt twenty steps from Maki and the princess.

"Ren Fudō," the sharp voice of a guardian spirit called as she and her children formed their own circle around the daughter of the sun. "You've called us to unfortunate events."

Her fur was so gray that she looked silver, and her centuries of existence also showed in the scars crossing her regal face. Her left ear had been chopped ages ago, and so had her bottom lip been cut in half, yet nothing could hide the tense strength of the lion-dog queen. They called her Ginkō, and she scared Ren shitless. Of her kind, she alone could speak, and she rarely had anything kind to say, especially not to him.

"I'm sorry, Queen Mother," Ren replied. By then, Sugi no longer needed to support him, and she adopted a fighting stance against the enemies coming from the hill. "I wouldn't have summoned more of you if things were not desperate."

"You're a real turd, you know that?" she said through her yellowish fangs. "But since you summoned us to protect Amaterasu's daughter, I will delay your punishment to a future date. Your Highness," she then said, bowing her head toward Ayako, who replied in kind.

The shadow of the biggest lion-dog veiled Ren for a second as the spirit moved to Maki's rear in his usual, uncaring gait. Chibi was his name. Twice as large and taller than Maki, or really than others of their kind, Chibi stood like a mountain in front of the row of yōkai. If those blue-flame soldiers showed no emotion to it, the weasel leading them recoiled and trembled. If Ginkō relentlessly proved to be a hard queen, Chibi showed nothing but kindness, at least in usual circumstances. On the field of battle, Ren hoped, he would be deadly. Just as his and Maki's big brother would be.

Takumashii took his place between Ren and Sugi, no taller than a regular dog and no louder either, though a hundred times as dangerous. He was a runt, but none of his brethren dared mock him, for he fought like a demon and reacted to the slightest provocation in the blink of an eye.

Ren did not know the two others who went to stand around Fuyuko, but if Ginkō and her two elder sons had come, he guessed they must be just as fearsome.

He was about to share his plan with the lion-dog queen—though it was not as much a plan as it was a desperate charge through the enemy—when a war horn blew again. It was a long, booming note that ended in complete silence. Even the wanyūdō became still.

The ranks facing Ren parted away, creating a corridor of black armored soldiers at the end of which stood the enemy leader. He wore the same armor as in Kyōto, the same golden crescent moon on a helmet framing his pale, white face, blood-red eyebrows, and mustache. He carried the same war fan in his left hand. His large, black wings opened when his closest soldiers stepped away, and the General unsheathed his katana. He pointed the blade at his feet and nodded at Ren to get there.

"Ren, don't," Ayako called with a trembling voice.

But Ren would. In another circumstance, he would have used this respite to change the pace and call for all of them to charge forward. But considering the identity of the enemy leader, he could no more refuse the invitation than he could fly over those yōkai.

"I won't be long," Ren promised.

Sugi grabbed his wrist and shook her head. She did not speak, but neither did she need to. This was a trap, she would have said, and Ren would have agreed, but his curiosity was too strong, and any second gained before they attacked was a chance. A chance for what, though? Ren couldn't say.

"Princess, I would advise you to pray for a miracle," he said as he sheathed his sword and moved toward the General.

"Don't die there," Ginkō told Ren. "We would vanish, and this would be a very stupid death."

The hunter let her comment slide, not only because she was right but also because he was stepping through the front rank of soldiers. They kept staring ahead, except for an armored kappa, who sneered at the Soul Hunter. Soldiers stood motionless on both sides, like a wall of metal and skin. The unnerving precision of the distance separating them created an odd tension in Ren's heart.

He focused on the General, who showed his commitment to talk by sheathing his katana. The wings closed a little, and the General took two steps forward. This was all the respect he would give the young hunter. Ren stopped just out of the General's reach. At this distance, he could see the yōkai clearly, and everything he had assumed after he last dreamed of his twelfth birthday was confirmed.

"I don't know who you are," Ren said, "but I know who you are not. So why don't you drop your mask now?"

The sides of the General's face widened behind the mask as he smiled. His hands moved to the back of his helmet, where he unknotted straps. The General then took the mask of the White Tengu from his face, revealing crow-like features. His beak was dark, though flatter than a crow's, and his whole face was covered in black feathers. Everything was black on this yōkai's face, except for dark yellow irises that filled most of his vicious little eyes.

It did not surprise Ren, but he should have guessed the enemy's nature. A *karasu* tengu, the most powerful type of tengu after the hanataka long-nosed one, and a great deal cleverer and more dangerous than konoha tengu like the one who had attacked the ninja castle. They walked on human-like legs, had arms and wings, and the last thing they needed to evolve toward their ultimate stage was to shed their feathers and grow a protuberant nose instead of a beak.

"How did you know?" the yōkai asked in a profound, edgy voice. If a beak could smirk, this is what it did.

"The White Tengu's wings are white," Ren replied, nodding toward the General's wings. "I can't believe I failed to remember that sooner."

"Well spotted, Ren Fudō," the General replied. "Yes, I know who you are," he went on when Ren frowned. "The Ivory King, the one you call the White Tengu, has had his eyes on you for a long time. He longs to be reunited with his blade," the General said, nodding toward the sword on Ren's back. "And to claim vengeance."

"Vengeance?" Ren asked. "For what? He's the one who attacked me when I was a child."

"It does not matter," the General replied, though his reaction came after a short silence that led Ren to believe the yōkai had said more than he was supposed to. "What matters is that my lord will be generous for your sword arm. The rest of you matters not, so you, Ren Fudō, will die today, and all your friends will die too. I will make sure that you live long enough to witness their death, especially the girl. I will rip her head from her shoulders myself and shower you with the blood dripping from her severed neck."

"Unless?" Ren asked, trying hard to mask the anger in his voice.

"Unless?" the General repeated in a confused tone.

"You didn't ask me here to make some threats. You wanted to negotiate. So, go ahead, negotiate."

The General cackled through his beak, and the way he seemed to amuse himself with this situation tested Ren's limits. Then, from the periphery of his vision, the hunter spotted something. A cloud of dust appeared behind the same hill the yōkai had flowed from. None of them were coming anymore; the whole yōkai army stood around them. This cloud was odd, but it was still far.

"Very well," the General agreed. "I care not for the woman and the fox nor for all your pets. If you give me the princess, your right arm, and the sword, I will let the others go. There, my offer for you."

Ren scratched his chin as if thinking about it and hummed hesitantly. He could not understand the General's will to negotiate. Maybe he had lost too many yōkai, and losing more would be a liability, or maybe he had already used more time than he had been given. Knowing the power of his bargaining would have been useful to Ren, but there was little he could do about it. He looked up, hummed so more, and when he guessed the end of the General's patience, shook his head.

"Counter offer," he said, raising his finger. "You go. That's it, that's my request. You go, and we don't kill you all." Some of the yōkai officers chuckled and cackled, but not the General.

"I was being serious," the crow yōkai said.

"So am I," Ren replied. "After my friends and I butcher you, I won't be able to seal all your souls, but I will make certain yours is the first, and I dare believe it will fetch a nice price. I heard you creatures fear purification more than anything. Is it true?"

"Ridiculous," the General said in a disappointed tone. "You choose death for your friends, then."

"I choose to fight, and I promise to kill you," Ren said with more confidence than he felt.

The karasu tengu spat at Ren's feet and was about to turn around, but the cloud of dust was getting closer, and the hunter's intuition told him to stall a little while longer.

"You never answered my question," he all but shouted. "Who are you?"

"I'm no one," the General replied. "But when I bring the girl's head to the First, she will raise me as high as him," he went on, lifting the mask of the White Tengu.

"The First?" Ren asked.

"You pathetic humans," the General said after a vicious chuckle. "You have no idea of what awaits you. Your ridiculous organization will soon crumble, as will Japan, and the blame will lie on your ignorance. The First will cleanse your world, Ren."

"Unless Ayako makes it to Ise Jingū," Ren replied. The cloud of dust was now settling, and since no yōkai had appeared over the hills, he assumed the newcomers were no such things.

"She won't live to see the sunset," the General replied. "Go tell her that."

On those words, he waved Ren back and crossed his arms over

his armored chest. The conversation was over, and the hunter left. Many yōkai cackled on his path. They licked their fangs and promised to share his flesh, but he couldn't care less.

So? Sugi asked with a nod.

"So we better hope whoever is behind the hill is on our side," Ren replied. The only people he could imagine coming to their help were the Yaseki, though this would be some amazing timing on their part. And if not them, then chances were high that their lives had reached a dead end. "Did you pray hard enough?" Ren asked the princess, who had kept her eyes closed and her hands clapped in prayer.

"As hard as I could," she said, keeping the pose.

"Good. Now keep your eyes closed and stay low," he replied. "And you, Maki, if you see a chance, you run to Ise. All right?" The guardian spirit whimpered and looked at her friend with sad eyes. He was about to lie to her that everything would be all right, but once again, the horn blew, and thousands of blades slashed through the air as their wielders took a fighting stance.

The sound stole one of his heartbeats. Ren responded by drawing his blade, too, and felt ridiculous. With the next blow of the horn, they moved, and the circle shrunk. The lion-dogs barked and roared and skipped nervously. Good, untouched nature vanished under the yōkai army's feet. Little Takumashii yapped and snarled, barely able to control himself. Good, Ren thought, let's keep their eyes on us.

Sugi lowered her stance and pointed her spear forward. She locked her gaze on the kappa who had sneered at Ren earlier, and the hunter knew which head would fall first.

Amaterasu's light was suddenly veiled by a cloud, one made of arrows jutting and whistling in the sky. The yōkai officers looked up as the giant bird-like shadow stilled. The missiles peaked, arched, and fizzed down like a squadron of fishing birds, and then came the first screams. Those belonged to wounded yōkai pinned down by unexpected arrows. They hit more soldiers than officers, but those went down without a sound. The first rank remained mostly intact, but gaps and holes appeared at their backs, and the kappa leader was sneering no longer.

The second wave of screams was one of victory and battle-lust, pouring from hundreds of human mouths as living soldiers charged over the hill and rammed into the back of the yōkai army. A small unit of cavalrymen tore great lumps of obedient blue-flame soldiers from their organized units and just as soon veered on both sides of the yōkai army.

For the time of a breath, Ren had been ready to curse. Those men wore a golden sun flashing on an otherwise black field as their crest, the mark of Shimazu Ryōma. But when the said daimyo appeared on foot, flanked by wide-chested samurai, one of whom carried a great banner waving the words "Ayako of Ise's army" in the winds, the hunter realized a former enemy had turned ally and had brought his full force with him.

This was as long as Takumashii could rein himself, and with a last yap, the ball of nerves darted forward, and Ren lost him as he blinked. He followed the lion-dog's progress with the line of soldiers falling as one, their chests carved by a kemari ball-sized hole.

The soldier on the kappa's right tumbled, chest fuming, but the officer had no sooner returned its attention to Ren than its head popped and rolled, a line of blood connecting it to Sugi's spearhead before it kissed the ground. Then the spear moved again. Sugi leaped from an expert lunge and lopped off a black soldier's head while she flipped through the air. Blades jutted after her, but none reached high enough, and the miko warrior landed at the center of a gap torn by arrows, where she slashed her spear through numerous legs. None of them screamed, but the soldiers toppled, and Ren lost Sugi as she pushed deeper into the enemy ranks.

He fought the urge to follow her and Takumashii, but his place was by the princess, as she reminded him with a fearful shriek. A weasel-yōkai was standing on Maki's back while the lion-dog shook the body of a nue between her fangs. The weasel raised a short sickle, ready to claim the princess's life with one swing of its thin arm. Ren acted faster and threw his blade at the would-be regicide.

It sunk into the beast's neck, and its eyes suddenly grew wide with surprise. Ren leaped over Maki, grabbed the hilt of his sword, and twisted it out as both fell to the right side of the guardian. The hunter looked up just as the two unknown guardian lion-dogs shredded a kappa in half by pulling it apart with their jaws.

The fight was not as desperate here, Ren realized. The two guardians were ruthlessly butchering a thin wall of soldiers and their leaders, and Fuyuko was already running toward the front, where Ginkō would be fighting the wanyūdō by herself. Ren then heard the twang of bows releasing their arrows.

"Down!" he shouted at Maki, who answered his call a heartbeat before arrows brushed her back. None touched the princess, but many ended their course in the backside of giant Chibi, who roared with pain. Arrows would not hurt the great lion-dog deeply, but it pissed him off, and he responded with a sway of his huge paw that sent a group of black soldiers flying into their comrades.

When Maki stood back up, Ren rolled under her belly to regain his side of the fight and slashed his sword just in time to cut the spear pole of a soldier who had nearly reached the princess. There was no surprise on the soldier's face, not even when Ren sliced it across the nose.

A unit of those undying soldiers detached itself from the core, somewhere between Chibi and the flashes of Takumashii's blitz, and came straight at the hunter. They came in a perfect line of two, five soldiers deep, each raising their sword, ready to attack.

Ren lowered his stance, breathed out, and met the attack.

He pounced at the closest soldiers, slashing his sword through their arms, though the blade bounced against the last armored glove. He shouldered the soldier it belonged to into its comrade behind and then lunged this blade into another's throat. Twisting the blade free, Ren luckily parried the next attack and took a step back from a thrust. He replied with an upward slash that cut through the soldier's chest, though not deep enough to slow it down.

They kept pressing on, walking over their momentarily disabled comrades, and Ren took a step back. Then another. More soldiers filtered between the lion-dogs and the miko warrior. No sooner had Ren dispatched one than two more took its place.

Chibi toppled suddenly, and between two wide cuts of his blade, Ren saw the great lion-dog getting swarmed by black soldiers. Sugi suddenly bolted through them in a beam of green flashing light, followed by shattering limbs and heads. The guardian spirit got back on its paws, thick blood pouring over his pelt from many holes.

Takumashii yapped in pain somewhere within the enemy ranks, and since only he still fought on Ren's side, the hunter felt alone against the pressing army.

He thrust his blade into a soldier's face, then used the strength needed to pull it out and cut through another's throat. Yet even then, Ren was forced back by a precise spear thrust, and this time his back hit Maki's flank. The guardian spirit could barely move within the slowly, relentlessly shrinking circle of enemies.

Then, just as Ren cursed and parried another thrust, came the roar of voices. Human voices, warriors' shouts, unrelenting *kiai* from sword-wielding professional soldiers. They were close and getting closer still, and Ren felt a new surge of energy from this ray of hope.

He cut and stabbed, screamed and parried, using his shoulder, his knee, his bleeding fingers, anything to keep those once-dead soldiers from getting any closer. Ginkō let a furious howl through her jaw. Her giant son responded in kind, and somewhere nearby, Fuyuko cursed something foul.

Takumashii rushed between Ren's legs on his way to help the twin guardians, knocking a bunch of soldiers in the process. When hope once more started drying from the hunter's heart, the tip of a katana suddenly jutted from his opponent's face. And when the black soldier fell, a golden one took its place.

Ren raised his sword by reflex, but the soldier, his masked face drenched in brown blood, moved to the side and blocked a spear that would have otherwise harmed the hunter. The golden warrior wasn't alone. Dozens of his comrades had managed to breach through the enemy lines and now formed a new circle around the princess.

Though their armor was as black as the enemy's, their golden uniforms flashed under the noon sun like the scales of the dragon-fish on their castle's rooftop. And none appeared more glorious than the one-handed samurai with the wide beaming sun stretching from his helmet.

Shimazu Ryōma strode toward Ren, emerging from his unit of guards, blade drenched in yōkai blood and face drenched in sweat like a smith in his forge. Though Ren feared the man's thirst for revenge, Ryōma knelt right in front of him. Or, more accurately, at the princess's mounted feet.

"I came to fight and die for my redemption," he shouted, still bowing. "Will you grant me this right, Your Highness?"

Ayako looked at Ren with a thousand questions on her face. "We grant it," she replied after Ren nodded reassuringly.

The battle was raging on, and their slight chance of survival rested on this man and his soldiers' shoulders. "Deliver us from this place, and you will be forgiven."

"Ten thousand thanks, Your Highness," Ryōma shouted as he

stood. His eyes met Ren's, and the golden sun grabbed his ruined arm with a wince of pain.

His fresh stump must be killing him, Ren thought, yet the man had fought like a tiger to get here.

Ryōma managed to tame his hatred and rage toward the hunter and shook the blood from his blade. "You and I are not done," he spat at Ren. "Protect the princess!" he then shouted, raising his blade high in the air to rally his men. They replied with a chorus of cheers.

"Ryōma," Ren called. "Those soldiers in black are yōkai. Don't let their appearance fool you; they can't die like regular people," he went on, pointing his blade toward a group of blue-flame soldiers standing back up despite their missing limbs and hollowed chests. "Tell your men to cut their arms, legs, necks, anything they can. That will slow them down."

The daimyo nodded at the closest samurai and sent them to pass this information along the line. He and Ren were startled by an explosion from the new frontline, though they quickly realized from the mass of torn corpses that it had shaken the enemy's side. Sugi, Ren thought, must have had something to do with it.

"How do we win this fight then?" the daimyo asked.

"We get Ayako to Ise," Ren replied. "Killing their General will work too. Look for a crow-yōkai with black wings."

"Got it," the daimyo replied. "Brothers! My weight in gold to whoever kills the enemy leader!" The crowd of soldiers cheered, and the next wave of strokes seemed louder. "Leave the fighting to us and focus on opening the way for the princess," Ryōma told the hunter.

Ren did not need to be told twice. A nod later, he shouldered his way toward the front, where soldiers were fewer on account of avoiding the mythic battle between Ginkō, Queen of the Komainu, Fuyuko, and whatever was left of the wanyūdō. The courtesan had lost her pin, and her hair was trailing each of her elegant movements as she stabbed her thin sword through the brains of yōkai after yōkai, using her umbrella sheath to keep her next victim at bay while she finished her current opponent. And while she collected a heap of corpses wherever she struck, Ginkō smashed yōkai-wheels into piles of shavings.

By the time Ren managed to slither through the press of human soldiers, the silver guardian spirit was shaking a frightened wanyūdō as she would a toy and slammed it against one of its brethren, shattering both. The others just as soon started rolling away from the mother lion-dog, leaving a few fear-struck creatures to face Ginkō and Fuyuko.

Blue flames rose from bodies, floating at chest level for a few seconds before plunging back into their vessels, and the resurrection of those defeated soldiers soured the cheers of the living to curses and despair. Ren pulled a golden soldier by the belt to protect him from a rusty sword's thrust. He had been hacking at a corpse with the energy of the lost and even then attacked Ren by reflex rather than thank him.

A burly samurai yelled at him to stop, and this seemed to snap the crazed soldier from his madness, but no sooner had his eyes filled with understanding than a spear stabbed through his hip, and the golden soldier fell with a shriek. The black warrior who had struck him down was crawling on one arm, his two legs having been severed at some point in the fight.

Ren thrust through his brain, and the blue flame just as soon appeared from the hole in the skull. By instinct, the hunter tried to cut the ball of glowing blue, and the flame was instantly snuffed. In its stead, a clay magatama fell on the ground in two halves. The broken body did not come back to life.

"Cut the flames!" the burly samurai from before yelled when he observed the result of Ren's stroke.

"Cut the flames!" Ren shouted, too, looking back toward where he assumed Ryōma would be. But Ren did not see the daimyo.

Instead, what he saw was an army on the brink of collapse. The thick circle of golden soldiers he had left a minute ago had shrunk, and while some of their comrades would still be fighting within the melee, too few of them remained to face a hardly reducing number of foes. He had to take Ayako away.

He looked over to the princess, safely sitting on the back of his friend, though Maki was stuck between the backs of so many warriors.

"Ren!" Ginkō shouted. She roared at her closest foes, who were now coming in packs, but whatever motivated them surpassed their fear of the silver guardian, for they kept approaching her. "Take the girl! I'll open the path!"

"You!" Ren called, looking at a samurai officer. "As soon as I'm with the princess, tell your men to step aside. And as soon as the princess is out, reform a wall behind her. Understood?"

The veteran frowned to show how little he liked receiving orders from an unknown, younger warrior but acknowledged it nonetheless. Ren turned around to join Ayako and Maki. The return trip through the golden soldiers did not take as long as the first time, and he stood at his friend's side before he could recover his breath.

He grabbed a tuft of her golden hair, ready to climb on her back, when he noticed the blood on his hands. Both were matted brown and red and were shaking. He felt no pain, nothing indicating that he had been wounded, yet he must surely have been cut in several places, too. Never had he been trained for a pitched battle. His field of battle was the quiet night, the dark corners of cities, and the eerie depth of forests. Standing shoulder to shoulder with fellow men and facing death after death wasn't his life, neither should it be anyone's. A part of him understood where Shimazu Ryōma had found the will to threaten the princess child.

"Ren!" Ayako shouted.

He looked up to the girl, who pointed ahead, and there, right in front of his very eyes, Ayako vanished.

"Ayako!" Ren called, following the remnant flash of gold from her kimono.

The princess flew above the battlefield, hanging from the talons of an owl-yōkai, tears flowing from her tightly shut eyes. Her weight seemed to bother the yōkai, unbalancing its flight and forcing it to fly higher rather than forward. Ren climbed on Maki's back and jumped over the closest soldiers.

Following the owl's flight, he cut left and right, uncaring for the blue flames that would eventually surface. A nue suddenly stood on its hind legs and stretched its long ape-like arms to bar his route, but Ren blinked, and the yōkai's head disappeared. It rolled away from its body, which then dropped to its knees. Sugi took its place, her beautiful, savage face drenched in blood and sweat. She even seemed to smile despite the tiny cuts scarring her cheeks and ears.

"Ayako!" Ren then said, pointing at the sky. The princess was now hanging a couple of spear lengths above Chibi's head. If the giant guardian had not been so busy pawing a unit of archers into the ground, he would have noticed her. But the din of the battle prevented the giant guardian from hearing Ren's call, and the girl's rescue fell on the two Yaseki warriors.

Go! Sugi said. She then drew her spear arm back, pointing her left hand forward and upward to lock her aim. Ren understood what she had in mind and sheathed his blade. He then grabbed the flaming hair on the back of Chibi's hind legs and climbed on his back. The lion-dog did not react, not even when Ren ran on his back and stepped between his ears.

"Ren!" Ayako called when she saw her friend coming for her. "Help me!" She tried to stretch her arm, but nothing besides her hand could move from those fearsome talons. The owl twisted its head backward and gave a strong flap of its wings, increasing the distance from the hunter, who then stopped himself from jumping, for he could no longer reach the girl.

"Sugi!" Ren shouted as the owl gained even more ground, flying upward and forward now.

The spear brushed his cheek, burst through the air in a bolt trailing green, then ended its course in the owl's back. The yōkai fell like a stone, and the girl, though no longer trapped, with it.

"Chibi, up!" Ren yelled.

The lion-dog, whether he understood or not, whipped his head up and thus tossed the hunter in the direction of the falling princess. Ren fought the sting of the wind in his eyes and kept them open while Ayako screamed. He grabbed her just at the height of his jump, and his momentum dragged them both forward. The ground came fast, and all Ren could think of was hugging the girl tightly and offering his back to the meadow.

He landed on his shoulder and let his body absorb the shock as best it could without resistance. They rolled and rolled until the tall grass slowed their tumble, and Ren opened his arms. His left shoulder was fire in his flesh, his ribs had cracked some more, and the girl had knocked her head so hard against his chin that one of his back teeth had loosened, but the girl breathed, and so did he.

"Ren," Ayako called in a sob. "Ren." She seemed incapable of saying anything else and tugged the hunter tighter, uncaring for everything that was broken in him.

"Ayako," he said, the taste of iron flooding his mouth. "We need to move."

They now stood at the back of the battle. By a miracle, no one had seen them; their chance lay in sneaking around the fight while men died for her. But as soon as Ren sat up, he realized sneaking away was not an option.

Ten steps ahead, arms crossed over his chest, wings spread wide, the General waited. He waited as if he'd always known fate would drop the girl and the hunter at his feet, and slowly, he unfolded his arms. The General tilted his head, and Ren felt like a worm under the eye of a crow before the bird pecked it out. The yōkai general held his war fan in his left hand, his katana in the right, and took a step toward his goal.

"You fought well," he croaked. "And will die well too."

The General was now within reach, but Ren could not move, not even when the karasu tengu raised his sword higher, ready to strike them both down. Ayako was crying and held the hunter tight. He held her even tighter. There was no mercy in the crow's face, only victory. Ren would have apologized to her if he had been given the time. He meant to close his eyes, but a shape appeared from the side, running so fast that he failed to recognize her.

"No!" Ren shouted just as Suzume put herself between the enemy leader and the hunter, facing the General with her arms wide open. The blade came down faster than Ren rose. The katana seemed to do nothing more than brush the miko. Ren heard no sound of impact, and for a second lasting a thousand, nothing happened. Then a curtain of blood gushed from Suzume's chest.

"Suzume!" Ayako shrieked.

The miko meant to turn around but fell on her back.

Ren's vision blurred, but through the spraying blood, he saw his enemy with his blade down, a wolfish smirk on its beak. The hunter stilled his broken heart and leaped over Suzume before any thought or emotion could slow him down.

The General reversed the grip on his katana to cut the hunter with a backstroke, but Ren kicked hard toward the enemy's wrists, using the sole of his foot to keep the katana down. The crow gasped in terror. Ren pulled his blade faster than ever before and sliced in the swiftest motion through the General's neck. They both fell with the hunter's momentum.

Gurgling sounds accompanied the moment Ren got on his

knees, and there he saw the crow-tengu looking at him in a mixture of surprise, confusion, and fear. Brown blood pooled out of the gash across his throat.

The General tried to say something, but no words passed his beak, nothing but bubbling blood. A surge of anger burned through Ren's chest. This was too fast. For the second time in his life, a woman he loved had stood between him and a tengu and paid the price with her life. Dying wasn't enough; the creature had to suffer.

Ren straddled the enemy leader and dropped his hands around the wound to keep the blood inside his body. "I'm not done with you!" he shouted with rage.

But the crow responded with a croaking laugh that died with a plopping bubble of blood, and so did he. His head lolled on the side, and the light vanished from his small, yellow eyes. And finally, Ren cried for his powerlessness.

"Suzume," Ayako sobbed, calling Ren back from his tears.

The princess was kneeling by the miko's side, not daring to touch her. Suzume still breathed and raised her arm to caress a tear from the princess's cheek. There was no sadness on the miko's face, just relief. Pain did not even seem to touch her anymore.

"You were right," she said in an unrecognizable, broken voice when Ren knelt on the other side of her. "We die bloody."

The hunter did not try to stop his tears. They blurred his sight, but even if they had turned him blind, Ren could never have found the strength to stop them. He took his friend's hand. It was cold.

"Suzume," he said through quivering lips. "Don't leave me. We make a great team. I was wrong—"

"Ren," Suzume interrupted. She did not look at him. Suzume already could no longer see. Her graying eyes stared at the pale blue sky, and two furrows of tears ran to nourish the meadow. "Don't let me go back to him," she said. "Please, I don't want to—"

Her mouth stopped moving halfway through her plea, and there, flanked by the daughter of the sun and her first true friend, Suzume died.

Ayako's sob turned to a heart-wrenching bellow. Ren grabbed his departed friend's hand tighter and held it against his wounded heart. And when he finally looked behind the girl for whom so many had died, he saw that he'd been wrong. Killing their general had not stopped the yōkai. They still fought and killed, and many more men died under their cursed blades and between their fangs.

Chibi lay motionless on his flank. Maki had joined her mother in the carnage, but she, too, would fall. All of them would, Ren thought. The golden sun banners had fallen one by one until only a few yet stood over the field of battle. Fuyuko would be there, ruining her beauty on the enemies' blades. She would soon rejoin the man she loved. And Shimazu Ryōma, if he yet lived, would deserve his imperial pardon.

Ren wanted to get on his feet and use their sacrifice to take the girl away, but his strength had deserted him. He was spent, deaf to his mission, and even the thought of his mother did not move him.

Then, through the din of battle and the horrendous cries of the girl, the hunter heard something. Faint, almost muted, but gaining in strength, the plaintive notes of a shō pipe. Not just one, he realized, and not just wind instruments. The shō was soon joined by percussions banging in rhythm. Not a martial rhythm, but a slow, meditative one. Voices then joined the instruments, and the sounds of battle subdued. All the yōkai and all the humans that yet lived, as if agreeing to a truce, stopped fighting and turned their heads in the direction of the music. It came from the opposite side of the battleground, from Ise Jingū.

A yōkai screeched, and its fear spread toward its comrades. Hundreds of them woke from their torpor and fled from the field, throwing their blades and stripping themselves of their armor in retreat. The black soldiers, now leaderless, remained on their feet, motionless. The surviving golden warriors started hacking them down. Some Shimazu soldiers, their bravery rekindled by the enemy's retreat, ran after the fleeing creatures to cut them down. The whole army seemed to disband and expand.

A group of three yōkai spotted Ren and the girl and decided to finish what they had started. They changed their course and came running, swordless but still dangerous. Ren's legs shook as he tried to stand but gave up halfway through.

"Ayako," he said, his mouth parched and weak. "Can you run, please?"

She shook her head, even after she saw those three yōkai.

But through their run, they stopped, petrified on their spot as if frozen in a heartbeat. The battlefield opened behind them, and through the carnage stepped the full force of the Yaseki. Priests, monks, nuns, miko, and novices walked peacefully. They chanted prayers and mantras under the rhythm of the pipes, the drums, and the bells, and their voices overflowing with power purified the cursed souls where they stood.

Blue flames rose from unbroken bodies and swayed in the winds before vanishing. Yōkai screamed as their souls were torn from their bodies by the sole will of those hundreds of Yaseki members working as one. And the three yōkai who had thought their fame could yet be made flattened on the ground, powerless against the kotodama of Ise's head priest.

Osamu moved with his hands joined in prayer and passed by the trio without a glance for them, for they had already fallen to his will. Then he opened his eyes and moved with greater urgency. The few steps separating the old man from the hunter were enough for him to appraise the situation. Osamu's eyes drooped with sorrow when he knelt by the princess's side.

"Ren, I am sorry, my boy," the head priest said. His compassion was all Ren needed for another pulse of tears to fall.

"Why?" he asked, fuming anger blooming in his chest. "Why did you make her come with me? Didn't I tell you she would die? Huh, old man?" Ren was shouting, and Osamu took it with his head down. "Why did you make me care?" This question was meant for both the priest and the miko, who now looked at peace and yet sad. "She didn't want to join her family," he went on, speaking to no one but himself. "That's all she ever asked for."

"Princess Ayako," Osamu said, kowtowing to the girl who barely reacted. "We heard your prayer and came as fast as possible."

"My prayer?" Ayako asked. She no longer sobbed, and her voice was dry.

"Through Amaterasu," Osamu answered. "The goddess of the sun told us to come here and to bring you this."

From behind the priest came a miko holding a metallic disk. She was a couple of years older than Suzume and just as shy as the girl had been. The disk was a bronze mirror, Ren realized when she handed the item to the priest. An old, stained bronze mirror that would reflect nothing but their failure at keeping it clean. Ren would not even have called it beautiful. Yet, he knew this must be Yata no Kagami, the most sacred of the three treasures of Japan, for this was Amaterasu's receptacle in the human realm.

"For me?" Ayako asked as she wiped her snotty nose with the back of her kimono. Osamu handed her the mirror, extending both arms and keeping his head low. Ayako accepted the gift.

A wave of power surged through the ground, pulsing from the mirror to the girl, then expanding in a wide ripple that shook the meadow far and wide. The stains on the mirror fumed, and the metal started shining, reflecting the sun in a powerful, golden light. Ren squinted against the blinding light. The wave of power returned toward the mirror, pulling Ren on his hands.

"Raise your head, Ren Fudō," Ayako said, though her voice did not entirely belong to her. Half of it was that of the little girl he had met in Kyōto, but the other, strong and caring, belonged to a grown woman.

"Amaterasu Ōmikami-sama," Osamu said, dropping his forehead on the grass.

"Thank you for protecting my daughter," the goddess said, ignoring the shaking priest's bow or that of anyone else. Now that Ren could see through his tears, he realized that every living soul had come closer and dropped to their knees. Even the lion-dogs bowed their heads. Fuyuko, Ren noticed, was being supported by Shimazu Ryōma as both struggled to lower themselves. Unless she was the one carrying him.

"Amaterasu-sama," Ren, who alone did not bow, called. "My friend—" Her gentle beauty, even in death, blocked the words in his mouth for a moment. "She asked not to rejoin her family's kami. Can you do it? She fought bravely for Ayako and for you, and..."

"She did not fight for me," the goddess replied, using Ayako's lips to smirk a gentle, mature smile. "And not just for Ayako, though she did fight for her too."

"Can you do it, please?" Ren asked, a surge of hope bursting through his chest.

"No," Amaterasu replied, "but with your help, I can bring her back."

Ren gasped, lost for words. The few drops of hope became a stream, and Ren's lips quivered.

"We need to be quick. She's almost gone," the kami of the sun went on, brushing a strand of Suzume's blood-matted hair behind her ear.

"How?" Ren asked clumsily.

"Lady Fuyuko," Amaterasu called without looking at the courtesan. Her voice had been soft, yet the fox-lady heard it and rushed toward the princess on bare feet. "Will you fetch the spear of the redwood spirit, please?"

Fuyuko, fox-faced again, ran toward the owl-yōkai's carcass.

"Ren," the goddess said in her double voice while looking at the paling miko, "take her magatama."

"Amaterasu-sama!" Osamu protested. There was nothing more strongly prohibited than taking a human magatama from its body.

"It is fine," she simply said, nodding reassuringly at Ren.

The hunter closed his eyes and passed his hand over Suzume's chest, searching for the heat marking the presence of her soul shell. He could not feel it, and panic seized him. Her soul was already gone; he had failed her. Pushing his guilt down, Ren focused more deeply. Amaterasu thanked Fuyuko for the spear. Ren could feel the courtesan's growing apprehension.

"Ren," Amaterasu called as she put her little hand on top of his, "don't try to feel it. You need to call her."

"*Suzume*," Ren called from his heart. He summoned the image of the freckled young woman he had come to think of as his friend, remembered her voice singing Pon-Pon's song, the rhythm of her taiko drumming at the matsuri, and the warmth of her chest as they hugged near the firefly shrine. "*Suzume*," he called again.

A pulse responded to the call. A faint pulse, weak and tired, but a pulse nonetheless, right behind the navel. His fingers prodded through the lethal wound, then through the drying blood. He shoved the feeling of disgust from his mind as he searched flesh and bowels.

"*Suzume*," he called again, and just then, at the tip of his fingers, he felt the hard, smooth surface of her soul shell. Gently, indeed more gently than ever before, Ren plucked the shell out of its body. Blood slid off it and revealed a light-green jade magatama. Ren had never seen such a shell. It was a thing of beauty, but it felt light and mostly cold. She was almost gone.

"On the mirror," Amaterasu called, holding the mirror flat.

The shell clinked on the mirror, then Amaterasu nodded for

Fuyuko to come closer. She placed the spear next to Suzume as if uniting a couple in death. The possessed princess put her free hand on the flat of the spearhead and closed her eyes.

"*Dear redwood kami,*" she said in the purest of voices. "*I command you to abandon your shintai and present yourself in your most vulnerable form.*"

She slid her fingers along the spearhead, their tips glowing with a golden light, and when she reached the end of the blade, she held in her palm another shell, one made of solid, warm-colored wood. Amaterasu then put this second shell on the mirror, right next to Suzume's, so that they formed a perfect circle pierced with two holes.

"*Dear redwood kami,*" she called again, "*brave miko warrior, I offer you my blessing.*"

The golden light glowed stronger and warmer, to the point that Ren, Osamu, and anyone standing nearby had to shield their eyes from the sacred light. When it retreated on itself, the light revealed the two united shells, now forged as one. Half remained of jade and the other of wood. Ren knew without knowing that Sugi and Suzume had become one.

"Ren, if you please," the kami said.

Hands shaking, the hunter picked up the new shell from the mirror and sealed it with his blood. The shell suddenly felt heavier, as if trying to regain its body, and Ren placed it with care on top of Suzume's belly.

"What now?" he asked.

"Now," the goddess said, "you may pray for them to accept my blessing."

Ren closed his eyes and clapped his hands twice. His prayer was answered with hundreds of more claps. For the time of prayer, it felt as if the whole of Japan united their thoughts for Suzume.

CHAPTER 20

A NEW ERA

A dozen carp flapping at the surface of the pond disturbed the water in their usual wrestling, fighting for tiny pieces of fruit tossed from the hand of the daughter of the sun and former princess of Japan. The child laughed and laughed as she dared approach the voracious mouths of the colorful fish, ultimately pulling her fingers back at the last moment in a great wave of glee. She waved at Ren before picking up another handful of cherry bits, and Ren, from the opposite side of the pond where he sat on a bench of stone, happily waved back.

"Who would have thought that Ren Fudō was so naturally loved by children?" Osamu, who sat by his side, teased.

"It didn't start that way, believe me," Ren replied after a scoff. "I guess we grew on each other." Osamu hummed deep into his throat, and Ren knew before the old man spoke what his next words would be.

"Do you now see why it had to be you?"

"Still no clue," the hunter replied right away. He was going to lean on his elbow, but the pain in his left shoulder was still burning, so he simply twisted on his hips to chase the pain of sitting.

Ren truly could not comprehend why Amaterasu had chosen him unless the goddess had seen all that was about to happen. And if she had, why not send him sooner, before the imperial house collapsed and so many good people with it?

"The kami cannot do everything for us," Osamu replied when Ren said so. "They cannot fight our battles; that would make us weak. Or weaker, I should say. She sent you to protect her daughter, knowing what a tough, stubborn, caring animal you are." Ren scoffed again, though out of pleasure this time. "She knew you'd not only connect with the girl but would also gather worthy allies on the way."

"Allies?" Ren asked in a baffled tone. He wished Osamu sat on his left, for looking in that direction would not hurt as much. "I made no such thing during the journey. *You* dropped Suzume on my back, just as Kiyoshi did with Fuyuko, and both of you with Ayako."

"Let's say you made friends then," the head priest replied, and that Ren could not deny. "And you did make an ally of Ōsaka's daimyo, without whom Japan would have been doomed."

"I doubt he would call me an ally," Ren said. "I'm pretty sure if I ever step foot in Ōsaka, it will be my funeral."

"Give him some time, and he'll welcome you as an honored guest," Osamu replied, though Ren could not see it happening.

Ryōma had survived the battle with a new collection of scars. One ran so close to his eye that without the intervention of some skilled Hearts, he would have lost it. Yet the daimyo wore them with pride, for he not only had saved the daughter of the sun but also became the first man to ever set foot within the Yaseki headquarters without being part of it.

A third of his men would fight again someday, though few would have the stomach for it after such a battle. The others were either dead, wounded, or terror-struck. Osamu had extended an invitation for them to remain in Ise Jingū and join the Yaseki, but few accepted.

So the tale of the battle would spread throughout Japan like wildfire, and with it would die the secret life of the Yaseki. Some might keep their oath to never reveal the existence of the organization or that of the yōkai they had fought, but most would blabber at the first drinking hall or as soon as they returned to their family.

Japan would never be the same, but, as Ren so rightfully commented when he introduced the Golden Sun of Ōsaka to the head priest of Ise, good men would be needed for the coming war. The Yaseki would never be enough.

Ryōma left within a couple of days with a promise to gather more men and answer the call of the Yaseki whenever they needed it. Besides his pardon and the organization's gratitude, the daimyo had gained little for his intervention. Still, he was beaming like the crest on his back as he rode off.

"Do you think he will truly work to maintain the peace?" Ren asked, resurfacing from his reveries.

"He knows better now," Osamu answered. "The idea of fighting people for his ambition has soured in his heart. And if he plays his chess pieces right, he might still come out of this as the most powerful man in the nation."

"Even without her?" Ren asked, nodding to the girl who had removed her socks and tiptoed into the pond's cold water. She splashed some over the legs of her powerless servant, who awkwardly giggled with the former princess.

"They'll find someone else," Osamu said, meaning the daimyo and warlord of Japan. "A cousin, an uncle, maybe some secret brother. This is not our problem. Ayako was never going to rule; no empress has for hundreds of years. Her fate was always to become the priestess of Ise Jingū." There was a sudden sadness in Osamu's voice, and his eyes lost themselves on the reflection of the sun over the pond's surface.

Head priestess of Ise Jingū. The title carried so much weight for a little girl and meant a heavy responsibility for the old man. But more, Ren knew, it foretold Osamu's coming death, for there could only be one head priest of the most sacred shrine.

"Don't turn so gloomy," Ren cheered, dropping his right hand on the priest's shoulder and squeezing it hard. "It's going to take forever before she's ready."

"The teaching will take at least twelve years," Osamu confirmed.

"Right?" Ren said. "Twelve years, that's plenty of time. And it's not like you were going to live forever." Osamu tried to slap the hand off with the flat of his short scepter, but Ren removed it in time and laughed at the attempt.

"I'm not worried about me, you brat," the old man barked. "I just fear that I won't be able to teach her. I mastered the Mouth Gate, the Ear Gate, and have only cracked the Eye one open. Everything I know is within the Four Teachings, but Ayako... Well, you saw what she could do."

"She's the daughter of the sun. What did you expect?" Ren asked, though he, too, had been voiceless at the girl's powers.

She was, of course, born with the Blood, just as Ren, though Osamu had declared she could not be one of the twelve Bloods, for none had died seven years ago. And since Kyōto, she had proven capable with the other gates, too.

"She could hear Sugi, the redwood kami, from the beginning," Ren said.

"Thus proving she has naturally opened the Ear Gate," Osamu said, continuing Ren's thought. "And she also showed her capacity to use the Mouth Gate when she prayed and called me for help, though her prayer came through Amaterasu. Ren, I had never heard her voice so clearly; it was awe-inspiring."

"So you said," Ren replied, for the head priest had pestered him repeatedly with the story of Amaterasu ordering him to the field of battle with the full force of the Yaseki and a command to bring the sacred mirror with him.

"You sure she never used the Eye Gate?" the head priest asked.

"For the hundredth time, no," Ren replied. He had truly searched through his memory when Osamu first asked the same question, but nothing indicated Ayako could see the future or even call something resembling intuition. "But it doesn't mean she can't, especially with some guidance."

The priest sighed, probably thinking that he, too, would deserve some teaching on that point. "And she's also a Hand," he said, sending Ren back to the moment when Amaterasu possessed Ayako and spoke through her. The memory made him shiver with awe.

"And a Heart," Ren said as he went back to observing the future head priestess of Ise, who presently behaved as any child should and bothered her miko servant with splashes of cold, pristine water.

Deciding to fight back, Suzume kicked water over the girl too, but she had used too much strength, and Ayako found herself pitifully soaking wet, petrified with her heavy sleeves hanging from stretched arms. Suzume lowered her head apologetically as she twisted the water from the fabric of Ayako's kimono. Both Osamu and Ren giggled at the scene.

"A good Heart," Ren went on. One good enough to heal the dead, he thought.

The disk magatama had vanished into Suzume's cold skin, and the little girl, still possessed by her goddess ancestor, healed the wound that had killed the miko warrior. The scar remained, but life came back into Suzume with a loud breath.

Gasping and in need of words, Ren had helped his friend sit up and gently held her against him at the same time, incapable of doing anything but rocking her in his shaky arms as she regained her breath. Ayako fell unconscious right as Ren pulled Suzume from his embrace, and did not wake for two days.

"What she did with the two magatama," Ren asked, "what is the power of the Secret Gate?"

"I don't know what's the Secret Gate," Osamu replied with a frown.

"Come on, old man, you *must* know the nature of the Secret Gate."

"It's called the Secret Gate for a reason, you brat. Of course, I don't know. No one does. Maybe it was, maybe it wasn't."

"Thanks for clarifying it," Ren said.

"But when she pulled the magatama out of the spear, that was the Ki Gate," Osamu replied.

"That was the Ki Gate?" Ren asked, clearly disappointed.

"Don't make this face; it is an amazing power," Osamu replied as if he'd been insulted. "Forcing a kami out of its shrine, making it vulnerable, and then compelling it into another... Can you imagine what could go wrong if such a power fell into the wrong hands?"

"I'd rather not," Ren said honestly. At least now he knew why the old man worried so much about Ayako. As far as the hunter was concerned, she was safe here, and if not here, then nowhere. "But at least we know what *she* is."

"More or less," Osamu replied, though his gaze shifted to Suzume.

The sheer joy of seeing her alive and breathing was soon over-powered. She had meant to call his name, but no word came out. Not even the most expert Ears could hear her voice. Suzume wasn't speaking with a kami's voice; she was just mute, and no one understood why.

Suzume was healthy; her throat had received no damage, neither did her mouth, and her lungs had been healed by the sun goddess. But words failed her. And since Suzume could not write, expressing herself proved a chore for everyone, including her.

If it had only been her voice, things could have settled for the miko, but much had changed when she came back to life, starting with her eyes. The right one was still the hazelnut, warm, caring eye as the one Ren had known since they'd met. But the left one now shined dark green. And while she most of the time behaved as Suzume always did, foolishly and lovingly, Sugi was never far, ready to crack like the thunder. The desk of the chief Heart of Ise had shattered from a hard blow from the flat of her fist when the poor nun asked Suzume to recite the first five characters of the alphabet for the fifth time in a row. Suzume had been the most surprised of them at her reaction.

She cried as often as she smiled and seemed content the most when in the presence of Ayako or Ren.

"She's fine," Osamu said out of the blue, making Ren realize he had been staring at her for long seconds. "We don't know what she is, but she's fine. She'll recover and learn to control her strength, and at least now, as the bodyguard of the daughter of the sun, she can stay in Ise."

Ren moved his left arm in a wider gesture than advised by the nun who had healed him and winced when he felt a new surge of pain. He recovered by the day and longed to go back on the road, though he dreaded traveling without his friend. Suzume was better off staying with Ayako, away from sources of frustration while she discovered who she was.

"You take care of her, all right?" Ren asked. "Of both of them."

"Leaving soon?" Osamu asked as if he could hear the young man's thoughts.

"Tomorrow," Ren answered. He almost stood from the bench but granted himself a few more minutes of observing the two girls playing with the fish and the water, both safe and sound at the heart of the shrine.

"Where will you go?" Osamu asked.

"Everywhere," Ren answered. Everywhere yōkai gathered, everywhere odd rumors and accidents seemed to repeat themselves, and everywhere that harbored the murmur of a tengu's presence. "We know too little," he went on. "The Ivory King, the First, and whatever else conspires against us, they've caught us unprepared, and they're not done. Getting Ayako here was a setback for them, and I believe it bought us time, but we need to gather more information. Just as we need to gather more men. You take care of the latter; I take care of the former."

"Agreed," Osamu replied. "They've made fools of us, but we won't let it happen again." The head priest had taken the blow of all they had lost terribly, thinking that he, more than anyone, carried the blame. Yet, from the depth of a wounded heart, Osamu had snatched a new source of strength and walked with more verve than Ren had seen in years. Yes, it was time to fight back, and Ren knew where to begin.

"There's an old rumor," he said, though Osamu asked nothing. "A long-nose tengu is rumored to be prowling a mountain just east of Fuji-san. This is where I'll start."

"Taking a hanataka tengu by yourself... I don't like the idea," Osamu replied.

"By myself? I won't be alone."

"Oh?" Osamu asked, arching an eyebrow.

"Fuyuko is coming with me."

Ren had believed the fox courtesan would leave with Shimazu Ryōma, whom she had supported on their march back to Ise Jingū and who she obviously fancied. But as soon as the daimyo left, the courtesan went to find the headquarters cemetery and wept by the freshly carved stone carrying the name of her lover.

For three days, she ate little and slept even less. On the fourth, she stepped out of the lamenting ground and went to bathe. Clothed in plain robes, her hair unbound, and wearing simple straw sandals, she went to find Ren and begged him to take her away from this drab place and to the nearest town with a shopping district. He agreed on the condition that she stayed with him a little while after that.

"That's one I would rather have kept around," Osamu said with a playful air of regret.

"One more reason for me to take her with me," Ren replied. "She's safer away from you, you... old, married perv."

Osamu chuckled, and it was not a bad sound. Ren almost forgot this feeling of discomfort he had felt since the battle. Between what he ignored and what he didn't want to say, the head priest answered fewer questions than he brought up. Ren knew him well enough to guess a certain unease growing in the old man's mind.

And then there was the croaking voice of the General telling Ren that the White Tengu, the one they called the Ivory King, was seeking vengeance on *him*, though for what reason, the hunter could not understand. As far as he was concerned, *he* should claim vengeance. There was something Ren did not know or hadn't been told.

"Ren!" Ayako called from the other side of the pond, waving for his attention. "Come look at this one! It's so fat!"

"That's because you feed it too much!" he replied.

"Come see!" And if not for Ayako's plea, Suzume's brown and green pleading eyes convinced him to lift his ass from the bench, and, pretending a sigh and making his knees crack, he stood.

"Apparently, I'm off fishing," he told the chuckling old man. "Then I'm off hunting."

EPILOGUE

The Ivory King's footsteps echoed between the sharp, spiked walls of the fortress like the thunder following the bolt, scaring all the pitiful creatures that lived here back into their crevasses and pools of fuming water. He crossed a bridge of dark metal suspended over a river of magma, then entered the courtyard where, for the First's sole pleasure, souls screamed under the torture of expert yōkai. He paid no attention to those floating souls and contented himself in shoving them out of his path with a lazy wave of the hand. The Ivory King would be the last to stand in front of the First, for he lived far, and his invitation had arrived late. The three others would have had enough time to eviscerate his reputation in front of their leader.

Let it be, he told himself when the two stone guardians of the throne room slowly rotated and moved their bodies from the entrance to let him in.

The room bathed in a pungent, gray fog that rose to his knees and licked the walls where it crashed like waves against the cliff. His three siblings stood with their backs to him, their wings extended so that none of them stood close enough to the others to allow physical contact.

His hatred surged, and he almost spat, but the eerie shape of the First drew across the room, sitting on her high, narrow throne without moving a muscle. Her head, as usual, was encased in a deep, round *taigen* basket hat that had been pierced with three lines of holes so that all one could see of the yōkai ruler were two ember-glowing eyes. When those eyes fell on him, the Ivory King pushed through the line of his brothers and knelt. The distance from the throne was still great, yet he felt the First's blood lust like a sharp sword threateningly falling on his neck.

"My apologies for being late," the Ivory King said without raising his head.

He trembled, feeling the long, thin, skeletal arms of his ruler stretching like venomous ivy from her rotten body to his face. The tip of her fingers caressed his mustache, and immediately the hairs hissed and curled, turning from their usual blood-red to an ashen-black.

One of his brothers cackled behind him, most likely Seigyoku, the Sapphire King. Ivory would have ripped his head off for laughing if, by doing so, his brother had not unwillingly saved him. The poisonous hand retreated toward the throne. The White Tengu stood up and stepped backward until he bumped into his brothers, who gave him just enough space to stand in line. Seigyoku was still grinning and chuckling, and Ivory's will was tested by that infuriating deep blue face that never quietened.

The First then gestured toward the younger of the four, the Onyx King, standing at the left end of the line. Onyx bowed deeply with his gloved hand over his chest. Ivory hated him just as much as Sapphire, though for the opposite reason. He was a dog, obediently observing each of the First's orders like a lackey and never straying from her burning gaze. They were Tengu Kings, the only four of their kind! Where was his pride? Ivory roared inside.

"The First would like to congratulate you on your victory," Onyx said in a suave, dripping voice.

"Victory?" Sapphire shouted in his shrill voice, his grin turning to a disgusted scowl in a heartbeat. "You call that a victory?"

"I call it nothing," the younger brother replied, his white, thin mustache barely flinching over a moonless night face. "The First does."

Sapphire gasped something sounding like a hiccup, realizing his reaction could be taken as an insult. He bowed to their leader and begged her forgiveness. The smart thing, Ivory thought, would have been to remain quiet, but Sapphire wasn't known for his brain. The First waved back at the Black Tengu, leaving Sapphire with his head low.

"As promised, Ivory's general has won a great battle in Kyōto and sowed chaos over Japan. Moreover, Fushimi Inari has been destroyed, and this, upon the First's request, deserves praise."

"My little crow only acted to make you proud," Ivory said, talking to the First while looking at her feet.

"However," Onyx went on, and enough threat transpired from this one word that Ivory started sweating. Him, one of the Four Tengu Kings, trembling at the voice of his pedantic little brother? The thought made him want to vomit. "The First would like to know why the child lives and now lives within the walls of Ise Jingū? Did you not promise her head as a gift when the First agreed to give you the first battle?"

"I did, but—"

"And did you not swear that losing your arm and your sword of command would not impede your capacity to judge and lead your army?"

"Yes, but—"

"And isn't the boy who you failed to kill five years ago responsible for your general's death? The First wonders if killing children has become such a burden that you, dear brother, failed twice at the task."

The White Tengu's teeth ground with a horrible sound made worse by the barely suppressed cackle of his blue brother. Damn that boy, Ivory thought, remembering the cursed brat responsible for the loss of both his arm and his sword. He would reclaim the blade and hack every limb from the boy with it.

"You answer?" Onyx asked him petulantly.

"Brother," Ivory said, red veins popping in his eyes. "You speak for the First, but interrupt me once more, and I will rip your head off and feed it to your ass!"

Sapphire's laughter boomed uncontrollably, and Onyx dropped his hand over his chest as if he'd been terribly wounded by those words.

The fog rose and hissed and twirled against the spiked walls. Ivory fought to keep his balance on a now-shaking ground and returned his gaze toward the First, whose forefinger had risen and started swaying left and right. He knelt again, as did Sapphire, finally silent, as well as their elder brother, Akasango, the Red Coral King.

"The First forgives you," Onyx, who, alone in the throne room, stood, said, "for everything went as She planned. The pawns are now in place, and our agent has gained access to the Yaseki head-quarters. The child surviving is unfortunate but ultimately changes nothing."

None of this meant anything to Ivory, who started shaking with rage at the idea that he'd been used by the First and Onyx to move their chess pieces. Worse, he thought, he had now lost his chance and would have to wait until his useless brothers covered themselves in ridicule before he would be allowed to act.

"And now, who next among you will accomplish Her will?" Onyx asked.

Obviously not you, Ivory thought. The White Tengu remained

on one knee, knowing that another insult on his part would mean his death. That his head yet stood on his shoulders was a miracle in itself. Keeping a low profile was the smart thing to do.

Sapphire and Akasango stood as one and waited without a word for the First's decision. Nothing happened for a long time. Sapphire started shaking, though Ivory wondered if he did so because remaining still for more than a minute was beyond him. Then, in a nonchalant, quiet gesture, the First's finger rose again and pointed at the Red Coral King.

"Big brother," Onyx said just as Sapphire's tongue clicked in his mouth. "Your move."

"With pleasure," Akasango replied in a voice as deep as the deepest hole of the Dark Lands.

AUTHOR NOTE

In the author's note of Undead Samurai, I mentioned that I wrote it as a love letter to Japan. And it was, but a love letter to one side of Japan. The warrior side. The side that lives in my daydreaming and historical fiction mind. There's another side I needed to write a letter to, the spiritual side, the side I have encountered daily for the past ten years. Thus came *Blood of the Kami* and the *Yaseki Monogatari* series.

I am a lucky man, and among my great bouts of luck, I can safely say that calling Japan and Tokyo my home is one of the greatest. There's hardly a day without a new discovery or a new story popping up in my mind, and most find their origin in the shrines, temples, events, customs, and traditions I come upon within a few meters from my doorstep. Spirits are everywhere in Japan. They live in the heart of its people as surely as in its mountains. You can hear them in the rivers, the laughter of the crows, and the hand clapping of the worshippers. People rarely gather here, but when they do, you know a kami is involved. And yet, if you ask Japanese people what kami are and what Shinto is, you'd be lucky to even get an answer, especially one that would satisfy your curiosity. Even more so if, like me, it sits on a western mindset.

Researching those topics was a rabbit hole. A lightless, confusing, and ultimately dead-ended hole. The best answer I could find about the nature of the kami is that "they are" and that's it, don't bother trying to understand them. There are many reasons for their mysterious nature. One of them is that they were born at different times in Japan's history and answered different needs, which made them confusing to a "modern" mind. Some are as old as the people of this land and cannot be described; others helped settle a form of authority and plant its roots. Then came other people with their religions and customs, and the kami had to adapt. The spirits (kami, yōkai, and otherwise) have morphed and filled our screens as adorable creatures who can shoot lightning bolts from their red cheeks or spirit a little girl away. They, in turn, filled our imagination and awoke our interest in their ancestral forms through manga, anime, and some novels like the one you just read.

Blood of the Kami is thus the beginning of a story claiming roots as old as Japan, fed from the daily life of a foreigner in this beautiful country.

This being said, I am no expert in things related to Shinto, Yōkai, and Japanese folklore, and if you are, you may have rolled your eyes a few times when reading this novel. I put what little I knew and the even smaller portion I understand of those topics in *Blood of the Kami*, hoping that it will paint a picture in your imagination and ignite your desire to know more about this culture (if it wasn't already burning hot).

It is just my opinion, and it isn't worth much, but kami are to me inexplicable in nature, yet so easy to feel. You know when you are in the presence of something kami in nature, even if you can't explain what makes you feel so. It just is. All I can hope and pray for is that my stories contain a hint of their presence and that you too might know without knowing.

This was all a little heavy on the spiritual side, so let's get back down a little.

Blood of the Kami came from a simple idea: a soul hunter partnered with a lion-dog guardian.

I adore komainu statues. They are so vivid in their stillness and look both gentle and able to inflict violence. They're basically good dogs, and who doesn't love a good dog in a book?

Ren is the expression of my favorite characters in novels/manga/TV shows and so on. At the same time, I cannot say that any specific character went behind his creation. He was just there, waiting to be summoned along with his guardian lion-dog spirit.

The rest of the cast came effortlessly and naturally, starting with Suzume, who might be the most manga-like character I ever created. Fuyuko was a surprise character who arrived late in the plotting process, while Pon-Pon had to be there, no matter how quirky his presence might have felt. (I'm stupidly proud of his chapter.)

But, more than the characters themselves, I wanted to write about relationships. Ren is surrounded by amazing people and has developed strong bonds with many of them, starting with Osamu and Hotaru. There were a fairly big number of characters introduced in this novel, but that's the majority of the cast for the next books.

Talking of which, *Yaseki Monogatari* will be five books long, and I hope to publish one a year. Now, you know.

If you look forward to the next one, the best thing you can do to help me publish it is to share your thoughts on *Blood of the Kami* on Goodreads and/or the website where you acquired it. I rely on you to keep the dream alive, as do all the writers whose books you've read and enjoyed. There is much in this world you can doubt about, but our gratitude for your time isn't one.

And no matter what, you have my thanks for giving this book and this writer a chance.

心から感謝します。

Acknowledgments

More than any of my books, *Blood of the Kami* was a team effort.

Not the writing. The writing was a solo effort. Very solo indeed. But what came next was a testament to the value of friendship within the reading and writing communities.

A dozen people offered to beta-read *Blood of the Kami*, and half could not finish it. I almost shelved it. Faith and a few good souls defending it pushed me to send it to another batch of readers, and the great majority loved it. I owe all of them, whether they liked it or not, a debt of gratitude for their kind and honest thoughts. I won't name everyone here, but know that if you've received *Blood of the Kami* and replied with your impressions (positive or not) I am grateful.

Still, I have to thank a few of you personally.

Thank you, Wayne, Joel, Kris, and Z.B.Steele. Your notes were wonderful and the conversation we had even more so.

Thank you a thousand times to Andrés. I cannot disclose the nature of the impact you had on *Blood of the Kami*, but your notes and ideas shaped some pretty significant parts of the next books, starting with the second volume's title.

My thanks to Lara Simpson, my brilliant editor, who, though I didn't know before we worked on this book, also lived in Japan. As usual, your friendly communication and professionalism turned editing into a pleasurable experience.

Another thousand thanks to Christian Benavides, the illustrator to whom I owe this fantastic cover. I have admired your work for years and am so excited to keep working with you. I also would like to extend some sincere apologies for my impatience. Great art takes time, but damn, I was looking forward to seeing this one!

And, as usual and forever, thank you my dear Leeloo for your support. This last year has been tough in so many ways, but I never had to worry about being loved, and that makes all the difference.

To be continued in

Voice of the Kami

ALSO BY BAPTISTE PINSON WU

The Three Kingdoms Chronicles

Yellow Sky Revolt

Heroes of Chaos

Dynasty Killers

Forest of Swords

Undead Samurai

The Army of One

Blood of Midgard

Beasts of Jötunheimr

Vengeance of Asgard

It is this writer's hope that Blood of the Kami offered you an enjoyable experience and that emotions bloomed from the page to land in your soul.

If that is the case, all the work I've put into this novel was worth it and I thank you dearly for giving me purpose.

Should you have the time and the will, please share your thoughts about Blood of the Kami on Goodreads or whichever platform you bought if from.

Ren and I thank you.

www.ingramcontent.com/pod-product-compliance
Ingram Content Group UK Ltd.
Pitfield, Milton Keynes, MK11 3LW, UK
UKHW042006240325
456676UK00012B/105/J